Trinity
Atom & Go

By
Zach Winderl

Thanks to Jordan for putting up with a dream

The man lay dying, not by Atom's hand, but instead ravaged by a disease carving his lungs with more pain and precision than the gunslinger had ever inflicted on a living soul. Far beyond the help of doctors or medocs, the man dozed in a comfortable wandering, drug-addled haze.

His eyes drifted into loose focus. "Lilly, be that you?" He squinted up at Atom.

"No, sir," Atom said, shifting in his bedside seat. "I was just hoping to have a word with Lilly. Is she around?"

The man's eyes sharpened. He tried to sit up, but the drugs and disease had wasted his body to nothing more than a skin-covered frame. Atom crossed his arms and gave a sympathetic smile. He surveyed the man's face, taking in the parchment-like flesh hanging beneath a pair of deep, dark eyes.

"What's your business with her?" The demand brought a fit of coughing to the dying man's lips. Blood dribbled down his chin.

Discretion directed Atom's gaze out the window. "I just have a message to pass along." He studied a stand of hemlocks on a hillock across the narrow, alpine valley. He searched the dusky paths beneath the towering boughs. "Nothing more, for the time …."

"Have you seen her recently?" Atom turned back to the man and fixed him with a sorrowed expression.

"It's been a few years. She left me here." The man's wan smile threatened to split the paper-thin skin at the corners of his mouth as he panted out his words. "She promised to come back. She said she needed money … money for treatment.

"The sisters keep me … on charity," the man coughed through his words. "They keep me alive. Probably hoping she'll be back with money."

The man drifted. For a long moment, Atom studied the living corpse, then rose to his feet and stole to the window. He glanced over his shoulder before sliding it open to allow a cool autumn breeze to sweep the cloying scent of death from the room.

He took in a lungful of the fresh air.

The abbey overlooked a deep river valley. The sisters had chosen the site well, centuries before. Trees of gold and red swept down the steep evergreen slopes like hearty veins along the back of strong, hard hands.

Only the copse of hemlocks afforded a more ominous color to the brilliant landscape.

"Da." Margo galloped into the room on an imaginary horse. "Watch Turtle, please."

"Who's Turtle?" Atom turned back from the window.

"My horse." Margo rolled her eyes in exasperation and bunched her hands on her hips.

From the midst of her stance, Atom snatched a glimpse of the girl's dead mother.

"Oh, Turtle. Bring her over." A sad smile crept to his eyes.

"Turtle's a boy, Da."

"Lilly?" The dying man lifted his head with feeble strain. His eyes fluttered like delicate butterflies.

"No, sir," Atom said as he returned to his seat, leading Turtle with subtle turns of his wrist. "That's just my daughter, Margo."

The man lolled his head to study the girl.

Atom nodded to Margo and motioned her closer.

"I had a daughter. Once upon a time." The wet cough doubled the man in his bed.

"She here?" Margo wandered over and leaned on the edge of the bed as the fit passed and the man collapsed back like a lifeless doll.

"No, little one," he gasped, trying to smile, but the effort seemed beyond his power. "She's not here anymore. How old are you?"

Margo held up two fingers.

"Go." Atom beckoned. "Let the man be. He needs his rest."

"It does me good to see children," the man grumped. "All I get are stuffy ... old sisters. They're good souls. They care for me. No complaints ... but they don't smile. They don't have energy like a little one.

"Your girl does more for me ... than all of them together." The invalid pressed a button and the bed groaned to a sitting position.

"I heard that, you old coot." A grey-frocked sister strode through the door with a bowl of soup on a tray. "If I told the others how you really felt, they might start acting like little girls to amuse you."

"No, you're fine," the dying man whispered.

"Excuse me, ma'am." Atom rose, swept Margo up in his arms, and wandered out the door.

Outside, Atom slipped Margo to the floor and led the way through the building's maze of stone corridors to the front of the abbey. As they passed the ornate carvings of the front doors, Margo pulled at Atom's hand and halted to study the flow of scenes that followed the journey of the Sisters of Reflection across the stars to found their secluded refuge on Dathan.

Atom tousled Margo's chin length hair and with a contented smile, wandered onto the broad porch that dominated the front of the abbey. The heavens crackled with lightning and a curtain of rain swept over the crest of the hill like the skirt of a woman's dress.

Off to the side, Daisy and Shi sat in a pair of rockers, their attention on a game board hovering in the air between them.

"She here?" Daisy looked up from the game to squint at the approaching rain.

Atom shook his head. While Margo wandered over and stood on tip-toe to watch the game, he stepped over to the edge of the porch. He leaned on the railing and stared out into the muddying yard. The rain pounded in waves, blurring the view of the valley's upper slope.

The pilot rose, stretching his back as he joined Atom at the rail. "So, what's our play here?" He crossed his thick arms and planted himself just beyond the rain's reach.

Atom's whip-thin frame seemed a wiry sapling beside Daisy's solid trunk. For a time, Atom leaned in silence. When he rose, his hands drifted to rest on his rail-pistol slung low on his hip. He continued to study the rain, plans dancing through his head.

"We wait," said Atom as he looked up at the stormy heavens.

Daisy crossed his arms as he weighed Atom's words.

"You reckin she's really comin' back to this place?" Shi slid a piece across the holo-board before rising, hitching up her gunbelt, and sauntering over to join the pair at the railing. "Way I sees it, she ain't bin 'round in two plus, so she ain't comin' back now.

"Why's this wendy so valuable anyhoo?" Shi grimaced out at the rain. "She's jist one bounty on the board."

"Information." Atom puffed out his cheeks, blowing a slow breath as he turned to sit on the railing. Most of the rain fell out of reach, but a fine mist drifted in, beaded on his jacket, and dripped down behind him.

"You know I don't flip a toss 'bout yer reasons, but seein' as we've time to burn here, you might as well spin the whole yarn fer us. Give us somethin' to chew on while we wait out this here drizzle."

Daisy remained silent, but his eyes danced between the two gunfighters as he followed the conversation.

"Not much of a story, as I know it," Atom said. "This Lilly married into the Genkohan. Jackall is the boke she married. He was some upper in the han. The Genko's are a pretty influential family. Their han pulls a lot of weight at the Imperial Court."

"The stiff in there is a heavy?" Shi asked.

"He's not dead yet."

"Close enough.

Atom frowned. "We'll all be there someday. Fact is, he was high enough to have access to han secrets, and when he and Lilly bound the cloth, those secrets were open to her. When they took to the Black, those secrets went with them."

"And they're worth killing fer?" Shi's hands settled on her pistols.

"I didn't ask, but I'd wager they're not too pretty.

"Damaging to the han, or bigger?" Daisy asked.

Atom shrugged. "Worth something to someone."

"Then why're we here?" Shi grumbled. "Shouldn't we be trackin' this Lilly?"

"She's a ghost. That's partly why the Genko's are so riled. She has no trail and not even Kozue has been able to track her prior to marrying Jackall. They put the bounty because they think she was a plant to steal han information. They suspect she's from a rival clan, perhaps hired from the Ghost Tribes, but they can't prove anything unless they have her.

"She might even have imp ties." Atom shook his head and rubbed at his face.

Shi whistled a low amazement as she strained to see past the rain veil. "That info must be fair heavy. I hope we're makin' more than our usual pinch on this haul."

"The usual." Atom shrugged. "The job shouldn't be too tough, even if she is a ghost."

"It's tough killing ghosts."

"You have experience?" Daisy cocked an eyebrow over Atom's head.

"Well, not so much, but I imagine it's tricky makin' a ghost bleed." She pulled her pistol and checked the action. "Ain't no killin' without some bleedin'."

"Not ghosts." Daisy scowled at the gun.

"Why here?" Shi ignored Daisy's look and glanced up at Atom. "Years out and somehow you thinkin' she'll be floatin' back through? If'n we can't track her and we lack a proper start point, shouldn't we be touchin' off some a yer old sources to stir up some info?"

"When she left Jackall here, she stayed for several weeks by his side. She may have been a ghost at one point, but she gave that up to take the black. She built something with that man in there, and I'm wagering she'll be back around. He's on the doorstep.

"She won't let him cross over without a final goodbye." Atom slipped down from the railing and wandered over to the hovering gameboard.

In the absence of Daisy and Shi, Margo had taken over. Using the holo-cubes she built a pyramid for her hands to climb like conquering behemoths battling for control of the mountain.

"So, we wait here?" Daisy followed Atom. "How long?"

"Until she shows." Atom dropped into a rocking chair just beyond the board, kicked out his long legs, and closed his eyes with a contented sigh. "In the meantime, we just stay out of the way and play nice with the sisters.

*   *   *

Evening drew near, and the gloaming mixed with the continued rain to create a mist-swirled soup. Atom opened his eyes. He had not slept through the afternoon, but Margo lay sprawled across his lap, trapping him beneath her toddler mass.

"Koze," he whispered to his ship's AI. "Are Daisy and Shi still back on the *Ticket*?"

Margo stirred despite his attempts to remain quiet.

"They are still here." The AI, imprinted with his dead wife's digital footprint, spoke in a soft voice, as if she might wake Margo.

"Any ships break atmo?"

"Not that I have detected, although someone crossed the abbey's perimeter. From my mass calculation, it is a female, and she did an exemplary job of evading the security.

"She didn't count on me, though," said Kozue and Atom envisioned a smug smile pulling at his dead wife's mouth.

"What else can you tell me?"

"She appears … moving in a …." The connection fluttered. "Atom, I'm detecting …."

"Kozue?" Atom glanced around, shifting up in his seat as his eyes searched the mist. "Koze, can you hear me?"

The com remained silent.

Atom leaned Margo to the side and craned his neck to scan the yard. The mist swirled, and phantasms of all shapes and sizes rose from the shadowed depths of dusk. Atom waited. Uncertain of what to expect, he prepared for the worst. Shifting his arms beneath Margo, he began to move just as a figure appeared from the gloaming. This figure remained steady and did not dance as the other vaporous illusions had.

Rolling Margo from his lap, Atom rose. He wandered to the top of the porch steps and leaned against the support. Parting his coat, he hooked his thumb in his gunbelt with casual threat.

He studied the figure ghosting through the mist. A heavy cloak kept out the drizzle and mist, but did little to hide the slight build of the woman beneath. Atom watched as she slid toward him without stirring the cloak.

Keeping his hands in the open, Atom remained still. He reached up and scratched his stubbly cheek as he studied the woman.

"Can I help you?" the voice, low and steady, wafted from within the shadowed cowl.

"You're a hard woman to find, Lilly," said Atom with a knowing nod.

"You must be mistaken," she replied with the slightest hitch to her words. "My name is Marian."

"What brings you here, Marian?"

The woman halted at the foot of the stone steps, half-a-dozen feet from Atom. "I came to see an old friend." She stayed just beyond the halo of the porch lamps. "His last message seemed like his time was drawing short."

Atom's gaze drifted past the woman to survey the yard. He held his tongue, but returned to studying her vague, cloak-muffled shape. As the silence grew between them, she idly shifted the hem of her cloak enough to slip a booted foot forth and draw a line in the damp soil along the edge of the light.

"Jackall?" he asked.

Her foot froze.

"Unless your friend is hiding among the sisters," Atom trailed off with a shrug, leaving dripping rain to punctuate the silence. "But I don't recall any other men, and none of the sisters are sick, to my knowledge."

"Stranger, I don't know what business you think you have with me, but I suggest you step aside and let me be. It's a fact that I aim to see Jackall a last time, but after that, I'll disappear into the Black. I don't aim to harm any beyond those that seek to harm me."

A warm smile brightened Atom's face, but he noted her hands shift beneath her cloak.

"I've no quarrel with you." Steel edged into the woman's voice.

"Genkohan pays well." Atom drew his hand along his belt, pulling back his stained and battered brown coat to reveal his rail-pistol. "They prefer you alive to dead. That suits me fine as I don't relish taking a life I don't need to."

"You're a bounty hunter?"

"As the job dictates." Atom's smile grew frosty. "Hitman, debt collector, merch, smuggler, you call it, I've probably floated it."

"And why'd you take this job?"

"It pays ... food on the board, fuel in the tanks."

"What if it pays in death?" The woman edged forward into the light.

Atom gave an easy laugh. "I'm at peace."

"And her?" The woman waved a hand to indicate Margo curled in the rocking chair at the rear of the porch.

"She's ready, too." The smile faded as his hand drifted closer to his rail-pistol. "People have tried, but it always costs them more in the end than if they would have just walked away."

"And you always finish a job? What if I paid you more?"

Atom shook his head. "I've never failed to complete what I started."

"Even if the cause isn't just?"

"I'm not paid to judge, just to complete a task."

"Then I'm sorry to break your streak." The woman mounted the steps.

Atom pulled his pistol, but before he could take aim, a vice gripped his forearm and a metallic hand caught him by the back of the neck, lifting him bodily into the air like a fish jerked from the water. His legs kicked like a panicking swimmer, even as his offhand reached in vain to loosen his assailant's grip.

With graceful poise, the woman glided up the steps.

Atom followed her with his eyes. His head, piniomed by unseen hands, refused to move. He tried to angle his pistol towards her, but she reached out and slipped it from his numbing fingers. Then, she laid a gentle hand on his as she returned the pistol to its holster.

"You won't be needing that right now." She lifted her head, barely revealing a flash of teeth in the shadows beneath her hood.

Before he could gurgle a reply, the hulking assailant launched him into the stone wall at the rear of the porch, dropping him into a stunned heap beside the door. Atom looked up through swimming eyes to make out the hulking form of an armored golem. Gasping for breath, Atom tried to wrap his head around the disembodied scene before him.

"Leave me in peace." Lilly crouched down and placed a metal cylinder in Atom's hand. "You've shown me a kindness in the past and I'm returning the favor. Next time I'll aim to permanently preserve myself."

The woman rose and swept through the door. Her silent golem melted into the shadows of the yard.

Atom lay still as his vision clouded.

* * *

A few weeks earlier, when the *One Way Ticket* had set down on Nahant, Atom had left the confining walls to wander. No work, no buyer for his cargo of vaccines, he found himself with nothing more than time and frustration on his hands.

He sauntered along a random portside street, a hand tucked in his coat pocket and the other tapping out a light rhythm on the handle of the battered suspensor-pram.

"I love ship time." He smiled down at Margo. "But I love fresh air, too."

The toddler craned her neck to look at her father, upside-down, and scrunched her face in a juvenile grin. "Yaya, ship time." She furrowed her eyebrows, mimicking her father.

"Koze, what time is it here?"

"Three forty-two," Kozue said in his ear. "Sunrise is just under five hours from now."

Atom sighed. "I wish we had synched up on the inbound."

"You wanted the earliest possible arrival."

"And I got what I asked for." A yawn split his face, more from the circadian-disrupting light of the planet's twin moons than from actual fatigue.

Devoid of traffic, the center of the street allowed Atom the smoothest path to meander.

Every city looked the same. The people made the difference. Atom dwelled on that thought as he swiveled his head back and forth to take in the low-rise buildings surrounding them. Nothing stood more than two or three stories, but the brick and metal structures gave the impression of a humanoid canyon.

People made the difference with fashion and custom and cuisine. They all appeared different, unique, from one planet to the next. And sometimes the smells varied, but oftentimes, Atom picked out familiar scents in each port of call.

"What do you think, Fiver?" Atom asked, bouncing the pram to pop the front up a touch. "Is this place like all the others?"

Margo wore a studious expression. "Same," she cooed and then laughed.

Atom shook his head, and as he made to reply, a soft whimper caught his attention. He stopped, his hand drifting to the rail-pistol at his hip.

"Easy, Go." He surveyed the street. "Something's touched."

He twitched his head from side to side, sniffing as he did so, like a hound scenting his quarry. With eyes alert and searching, Atom searched out the source of the sound.

Soft sobs wafted through the empty street.

Scanning the storefronts that lined both sides of the street, Atom scowled. Most ocular windows slumbered, but farther down the street, a few patrons clustered in the soft pool of street glow outside a dockside tavern, and across the street, light streamed forth from an all-hours convenience store.

The folks outside the tavern spoke, but distance muted their words, and Atom turned his attention from the group.

He pulled the pram closer. "Hush now, Go. We'll find the touch."

Sensing the tension in her father, Margo dropped down on her stomach, leaving just her eyes poking above the lip of the suspensor-pram.

The sob echoed again.

Atom spun.

Behind and to the left, an ajar door leaked a weak trickle of harsh light and revealed stairs beyond.

Drifting back along the road, Atom pulled the pram along until he could see past the entryway. From the glassed-in foyer, rough slate steps curved upward to what he assumed to be living quarters. Atom scanned the stairs, his eyes dancing between the light and shadows of widely spaced lamps.

Flipping his coat back, he slipped to the door while eyeing the street with suspicion.

"Ho there," he called out, easing the pram out of the direct line of the stairs. "Everything all right?"

The sobs cut short.

He nudged the door open with the toe of his boot.

Atom stared into the silence. Peering upward, he tried to see around the curve of the stair.

A foot scuffed the slate steps, drawing into one of the shadow pools.

"Go, hop to," Atom said in a low voice as he powered down the pram.

The girl slipped from the metal basket and like a monkey, clambered to Atom's back. With his eyes locked on the stairwell, he settled her into place and hooked her to a discreet harness stitched into his jacket.

Keeping his hand on his pistol, he drifted left, pausing at the foot of the stairs to glance back out the door into the darkness. Then, one cautious step at a time, he moved, maintaining his focus on the curve of the stairs that shielded the source of the sobbing from view. Atom strained to hear and thought he could just make out the low, ragged breaths of someone fighting to remain silent.

Another step and a leg slipped into view.

Atom stopped. For several heartbeats he studied the leg and foot: lean, curved, muscular, and youthful.

He calculated.

"Miss," he soothed. "Can I help you with anything?"

"Get gone," a sniffle punctuated the words. "Leave me be."

Atom heard defiance, but scented fear and pain lurking just beneath the surface. He flipped his coat over his pistol and stepped into full view with his hands out, palms up, peaceable.

"I'm not looking to cause trouble, miss," he said. "I just heard you crying and I don't like to leave innocent folks hurting if I can help."

The curled figure walked the line between woman and girl. She clutched a flowered sundress to her chest. The dress, torn at the neckline slipped off her shoulder with each shuddering sob.

With futile persistence she tried to keep the dress covering her.

"What do you want?" she demanded, glaring through tear-stained eyes. "You want what they left?"

Atom gazed into her sea-green eyes for a moment, then gave a slow shake of his head.

"Aiming for no disrespect, miss," Atom bobbed his head. He took in the split lip, bruised thighs, skinned knees and toes, the damaged sandals that threatened to fall apart on her feet as she curled into herself. "I was just looking to help.

"Just hold a second." He stepped back down a few steps and unhooked Margo, his eyes scanning for threat just the same.

The girl stared at Margo with haunting sadness, a longing for innocence returned.

Atom moved back up the stairs, slipping out of his coat as he did so and with a gentle flourish that still brought a flinch from the woman, he dropped it around her shoulders. Tucking away in pain, she clutched the jacket tight to cover her.

"Are you hurt?" Atom asked.

Margo climbed up close to the girl and leaned over to peer up into her face. "Don't cry." She placed a gentling hand on the girl's bruised knee.

A wan smile crept across the young woman's face. Tentative fingers reached up and plucked back her strawberry-blonde hair, revealing hollow, pale eyes rimmed red as she met Atom's gaze for a furtive moment.

Atom started at the flash of calculating hardness, but the look retreated beneath the damaged façade like an elusive fish.

"Do you live far from here?" Atom reached out and tousled Margo's hair. He measured the girl as he dropped to a seat a few steps below his daughter. Something tickled in the back of his mind like a pebble in a boot, but the pain she radiated overshadowed any inkling of a ruse.

"Upstairs," she whispered in a hollow voice.

"Is someone waiting for you?"

"No." She shook her head. "I've a flat with a couple girls, but they'll be sleeping.

"I'm not usually out this late." She dropped her eyes and a pair of crystalline tears darkened Atom's dusty brown coat. Like the tears, the words began to drip between fresh sobs. "Gims asked me to work late. We had a handful of late docked haulers. Hungry crews mean big tips. If I fly.

"Gims knew that." She lifted her doe eyes to Atom, haunting and frightened. "He weren't aiming to pop me in trouble. Just trying to help a girl out."

"I understand." Atom pulled Margo into his lap as he leaned against the wall.

"I didn't expect nothing. Didn't expect what happened," she sobbed.

"Nobody does."

"What do I do?"

Atom sat in silence for a moment, listening to the girl's ragged breaths. Then he rose to his feet and shifted Margo to his hip. "First off." He began to sway with a gentle rhythm ingrained in a father cradling his child. "You're going upstairs to take a shower. Wash this night off of you. Then you're sleeping. Take something to help if you need it."

"Don't know if I can."

"You will," Atom's fatherly tone calmed the girl. "And you're going to put tonight from your mind. You are bruised and beaten, both physically and mentally. Some will say you have to embrace the pain and others to bear it in silence.

"But I say," he dropped his voice, leaning in with intimate vengeance. "It's part of you, but it doesn't define you. You can't pity yourself, but you know it's a part of your life now. Grow stronger and move forward. If you dwell, it'll consume you."

"I don't know...."

"Live in the moment and be a new creation with each breath, girl," Atom commanded.

Despite her eyes remaining downcast, the girl seemed to gather resolve.

"I wouldn't wish your night on anyone." Atom turned and started back down the stairs with Margo smiling up at the young woman. "But, there are a couple things I need of you."

"Yeah." The girl fiddled with her broken sandal as she watched them depart from beneath her veil of shimmering hair.

"I want you to bring my coat back tomorrow. Look up the *One Way Ticket*. That's my ship."

"And the other?" The girl crawled to her feet and rubbed her nose with the back of her hand.

"In the pocket of my coat you'll find a plasma punch. I want you to keep it and if you ever find yourself in a situation that could lead down tonight's path, I want you to hide it in your palm. When they get close, you tuck it up against their knee and press the trigger.

"I guarantee they'll leave you be." He waved farewell without a backward glance.

"What if I see them again?" she called after him.

"Don't worry." Atom paused at the door and looked up to the girl huddled deep inside the folds of his coat. "They're freighters. I don't think you'll ever cross paths again."

"But what if …."

"You have your heart, it's strong enough to overcome." He flashed a lopsided grin. "And now you have a plasma punch to back up your heart."

Atom nodded a final time and left the girl standing alone, clutching the railing as she watched them disappear into the night. He swung Margo around with one arm and dropped her into the pram. Accustomed to the sway of the suspensor-pram, she reached out and steadied herself as Atom stalked down the street.

"What do you plan to do?" Kozue asked.

"You don't harm innocence." Atom's jaw clenched. "If they were my crew, I'd wait until we were aloft and walk them out the airlock without a wave goodbye."

"Well, they're not your crew. Plus, you don't know who they are."

"She's just a girl, Koze. Not much older than our daughter Aamu would have been today." Atom headed for the garish light of the nearby pub. "It's one thing if she were older and willing. Happens she doesn't fit either category."

Kozue refrained from further comment.

As Atom approached the port-side bar, he looked up at the name. Despite several darkened letters, he read After-Burn by the soft glow of the city lights. The dozen loitering men fell silent and parted as Atom guided the pram toward the open door.

"Ever feel like every planet's the same?" Kozue asked as Atom walked into the neon glare of the interior.

"How so?" He stopped, surveyed the scene, and then selected a corner table.

"Seedy bars, loose women, flat beer?"

"There are loose men too." Atom sensed the shrug from his AI. "And how do you know the beer's flat?"

"Atom," Kozue chided. "I'm a part of you."

A long-toothed waitress with too much lipstick bustled over, flashing a weary smile as she tucked a tray under her arm and pulled a touch-screen pad from her apron. "What'll it be, sweets?"

"This Gims' place?" Atom leaned back and laced his fingers behind his head.

The waitress glanced to the bar, a newfound wariness in her eye. "Who's asking?"

"I've no problem with Gims. I just ran into a mutual acquaintance." Atom stifled another yawn. "I just thought a quick word from Gims would settle a bet I have with my Eye.

"I'm not looking for any trouble, promise." Atom held a hand over his heart.

"That a fact?" The woman brushed purple dyed hair from her eyes and locked Atom with a conflicted glare.

"Well, if things turn the way I'm hoping, there might be some trouble for some folks, but not on you or your lovely establishment. I'm professional enough to see to that.

"So," Atom said as he leaned on the table. "I'd like that word and a mug of red chi."

"Hot or cold?"

"Hot, one drip."

"Hot with a drip of sweet. That'll be half ko."

Atom pulled a chit from his pocket, punched in the cost of the drink, plus a hefty tip, and slid it across the table.

The waitress plucked the chit from the table and turned to walk away. Her eyes widened as she registered the amount entered on the digital readout. Glancing back, she bobbed a thanks at the soft smiling Atom. "I'll see if Gims is still here," she called over her shoulder as she wove her way to another table sprouting five new freighters.

Atom sat for a few minutes before the waitress whirled back with a tray full of drinks. She chose Atom's heavy mug of chi from the forest of tall glasses and set it before him.

Without another word she disappeared into the neon aura of the bar.

After watching her bustle away, Atom spun the pram so Margo could look out over the bar. "See what you have to look forward to." Weariness began to set in as he picked up his mug and savored the bitter-sweet scent.

Margo pouted and leaned forward to rest her chin on the lip of the pram.

"Dregs." He shook his head. "Scum of the Black that give the rest of us a bad name."

The scattered patrons sat at three tables, two groups on the far side of the bar and a solitary drinker tucked in a booth to Atom's left. The two tables on the far side held the most disparate groups in Atom's mind. Tucked up beside the bar, three hard-looking spacers sat with a harder looking woman who the men obviously deferred to.

The other table drew Atom's attention.

Six men surrounded a small table laden with half empty glasses and three pitchers of an earthy blue brew. Unlike the other tables, theirs remained boisterous to the point of disturbing. They laughed and cursed and acted like they owned the bar.

As Atom sipped his chi, the men from outside the door returned and squeezed in around the table.

Atom scowled at the men, his mood foul.

Turning back, he rolled his shoulders and settled his mind. After closing his eyes for a moment, he opened them to Margo's stern glare. The look caught him by surprise and a chuckle eased more tension from his shoulders.

"Ease up, girl," he blew at the steaming mug.

Setting the drink down, he knuckled her jaw. As he leaned back in his seat, the waitress appeared at the end of the bar with an older man. Paunched and saggy, the man studied Atom before tossing a bar-rag over his shoulder and waded through the empty chairs like a swimmer through the shore-break.

"I heared you's looking for me," the man gruffed as he whipped the rag from his shoulder and polished the spotless table behind Atom.

"You Gims?"

"Aye," the man replied without looking up.

"You got a young girl that waits for you?"

"Aye, Genny."

"Anything odd happen on her shift tonight, or perhaps just after she got off?"

The man stopped cleaning the table and straightened up with a sigh. He stared hard at Atom's back. With an oblivious calm, Atom sipped his chi. He followed the man's movements in Margo's gaze. Without looking he nudged out the chair beside him.

The man drifted into the seat, a conspirator's look in his eye as he leaned forward. "What do you mean?" Concern framed his eyes and his jowls quivered.

"Did anything happen that stuck out in your mind?"

The man dropped his eyes to study the artificial grains of the table. His gaze darted along wooden paths as if searching through a series of images in his mind. Of its own accord, Gims' hand drifted to the table and he wiped at a ring left by Atom's mug.

"Genny," Margo tried the name out as she rocked back in her pram.

The soft voice jolted the man from his ponderings.

"What was it?" Atom set his mug down and leaned toward the old barkeep.

"Table with all them bokes." Gims gave a slight nod. "They're our usual type. Spacers fresh from the Black looking to blow steam. All handsy. Genny kept it pro-type, smiles and friendly, but nothin' more. They wanted more, but she'd keep busy. Tickly thing, when she floated off her shift, ever last one of them up and out for a puff of fresh air.

"Least I 'ssumed that's where they headed," Gims said with panic flooding his eyes. "Is Genny a'right? Those 'stards

20

did'n do nothing to my Genny. If they did a'swear I'll tear them …."

Atom laid a calming hand on the man's arm. "But that's them? All of them?"

Gims rose to his feet. His breath came in ragged bursts as he wrung his rag between his worn hands.

"Are any missing?"

Casting a glance over his shoulder, Gims leaned with a heavy hand on the back of his seat. "That's all," he sputtered.

Sipping his drink, Atom studied the boisterous crew.

"Go about your business, old man," Atom said as he set his mug on the table and rose to his feet. "Don't worry about those bokes, you won't be seeing them again, or me. Look to Genny. Love on her."

Rolling his shoulders, Atom grabbed the pram and maneuvered it from behind the table. Like a cautious driver, he hovered the pram down the narrow alleys left between the chairs and tables. Instead of heading for the door, he detoured near the rowdy table.

"Gentlekin," he called out over their raucous laughter. One by one they fell silent and turned their baleful attention on the interloper. "I don't suppose I could bother a couple of you to help me with my skiff outside. I'm having trouble raising my crew and need to get back to my ship. If you'd be so kind, I'd be happy to buy the next round."

Promise of payment shifted the mood and a pair of the men rose on unsteady feet. "Lead the way, guv," the taller of the two slurred as he tried to smile.

"Obliged," Atom murmured as he knuckled his forehead. With a meek bow he turned and shuffled his way through the maze of chairs to the front door.

The men followed.

On the street outside, the cool of the eve hid Atom with a refreshing wave of energy. He stepped aside to let the men exit the bar.

They looked about in confusion.

"Where's your skiff, gramps?"

Atom turned halfway back, addressing them without the dignity of looking on them. "What can you tell me about Genny?"

An unbidden smirk broke the tall man's face a moment before Atom's rail-pistol smashed into his cheekbone. Before the other man could react, Atom snapped the pistol sideways and punched a round through his chest.

"Bleedin' hell," the freighter's words whistled through his crushed face as he stumbled back toward the bar. "What's wrong with your bleedin' brainpan?"

Atom stood in silence, tracking the drunken merch each step of the way.

"Brovers," the broken man whimpered through the door as he steadied himself against the frame. "That there boke just ...." He turned to point at Atom just as a round slipped through his good eye.

A moment of silence followed before the crowd of unruly freighters poured from the bar, weapons raised and ready.

Atom stood in placid contemplation of his rail-pistol.

"What's your malfunction," the leader roared as he trained an auto-shotgun at Atom's chest. The other dozen men held a ragged arsenal of cobbled, merchant-ship weapons.

Atom stared them down.

As the freighters stood, shaking with drunken adrenaline, their eyes took in the blood of their companions pooling at their feet. They failed to register the pram drifting towards them.

"The name Genny mean anything to you?" Atom growled.

"Don't mean nothing to me," the leader muttered. "Anything to the rest of you?"

A scattered shaking of heads and grumbled negatives answered the query. Their weapons wavered as Atom glared through the men.

"Any of you remember a waitress that you followed out? Short, slight, light hair, she wore a white dress with gold flowers," Atom paused as recognition lit on several of the men's faces.

The leader, however, grew dark as Atom spoke. "What's a servy to us?" he demanded.

"Obviously, nothing." Atom spat in the dust of the empty street.

"You mean you killed two of my men over a bar-slut?" Rage bubbled to the surface as the spacer advanced. His shotgun drifted from Atom's chest to his face. "There are a billion willing wendys all over the Black and you decide to drop over this one?

"I'll kill you personal-like," the man said with a shower of spittle.

"It wasn't the doing, so much as how it was done. You didn't give her much choice."

"We didn't even do nothin' to this one. She was all flirty and smiles on the job, but when we tried for more she gets prim. So's I busted her gob, but she limps and that ain't no sport. We just chucked her in the alley so's she ain't out in the open," he growled, his shotgun wavering with passion. "Why's this one so big to you?"

"She reminded me of my oldest daughter, Aamu," Atom said with quiet malice.

The freighters took a moment to register how close the pram had drifted during the conversation. A look of universal surprise mirrored on every face as the pram began to spin like a top. Margo gripped the sides and held on for dear life. Before any of the spacers could react, energy blades hissed out from the suspensors and began carving through the lower extremities of the panicking men.

They dropped as the humming blades sheared shins and severed legs refused to support bodies.

Not a shot sounded from the merchantmen as they writhed on the ground, but Atom stalked among them, a grim-faced death affording the coup de grace even as the pram slowed in the midst of the bloody carnage.

As the pram resumed its previous hover, Margo looked up at Atom with a dizzy expression. Her hands clutched the pram's sides with white knuckled tension, but grim determination hardened her face.

Atom stood above the shift leader last. The man, in mild shock from the loss of his left leg, held up a feeble hand to shield himself from Atom's wrath.

"For innocence lost," Atom whispered as the single shot echoed along the empty street.

Atom stood over the dead man and holstered his pistol. Then, without a backward glance, he took hold of the pram and set out down the street. He laid a gentle hand atop Margo's head and she looked up to him with a sad, knowing smile.

"For Genny," he whispered to her as she reached up and patted his hand.

Just before rounding a distant corner, he looked back to catch Gims creeping from the tavern so survey the damage.

*   *   *

He awoke a short time later to Margo poking his shoulder. When he regained enough sense to sit up, he looked down at the object tucked in his hand.

His eyes widened in wonder.

Heaped against the abbey wall, Atom coughed. Novas exploded behind his eyes. He tried to gather his wits as they skated around his pan, twinkling fireflies on a hot summer's eve. Willing breath back into his body, he tried to shift, but darkness threatened to overwhelm him again.

His last image before slipping back beneath the surface superimposed a half-dozen grey frocked sisters clustering around him in concern.

*   *   *

"Dear captain, where are we floating?" Hither perched cross-legged in the navigator's seat, chin propped in her palm as her absent stare absorbed the lengthy fingers of the God's Hand Galaxy wisping across her consoles.

"Following a hunch." Atom frowned at the pilot's HUD.

"Lot of Black out there. How do you know we're headed true?"

Atom spun away from the full spectrum canopy. For a moment he studied his long-time friend, taking in the soft curve of her neck as she cupped her chin. Twirling her long auburn hair around a finger, she gazed through her console out into the Black. Her eyes caught the light of distant stars and twinkled, twin emeralds in an ivory sea.

Atom cracked his neck with a grimace. "Just a hunch," he said, expecting Hither to engage.

She only shrugged.

"Don't you want to hear the hunch?"

"I guess." She slipped her bare feet to the floor and blinked from her stupor. "I've always assumed if you had a hunch, it's a good follow.

"It's not like you've ever steered us into trouble," she said sarcastically as she rose and stretched her back with feline grace. "What is this master plan?"

24

"I didn't say it was a plan." Atom ignored the tone and turned back to the Black.

"So, this 'not plan,' what are we doing?"

"Heading to Gomori Alpha."

"The space station?" Hither yawned and stretched, studying Atom through slitted eyes as she covered her mouth with the back of her hand.

"It's the closest refueling point."

"You're gambling that Lilly didn't bother to top off before she got the drop on you?"

"Would you, if you were rushing to see me on my deathbed and didn't know how much time you had."

"I'd probably take the time to go for a full rejuve treatment." She locked Atom with a half-smile. "You know, I'd want to make sure I looked my best for your funeral. And who knows, maybe you'd drop dead when you saw me burst through your door all lovelified."

Atom spun and thrust himself up from the pilot's chair, ignoring Hither's banter. "And in my defense, it never crossed my mind that she might have a golem under her control. The last time I saw one of those was during the Bastet Insurrection when the emperor sent a death squad into battle to make a point."

He stepped closer to Hither and dropped his voice. "They terrified me, and they were on my side."

"What about this one?"

"I'm surprised I didn't void." Atom chirped a mirthless laugh. "I'll have to figure out how to take her without that thing tearing our arms off."

"Public setting?"

"That might be the best scenario. You don't think she would turn a golem loose on bystanders?"

"Doubtful." Hither padded up beside Atom with her arms crossed protectively and leaned her head on his shoulder as he stood looking out into the Black beyond the pilot's canopy. "I've been over everything we have on the girl and assembled the best profile I can. Spec says she avoids the eye at all costs. That golem is her last line of defense. She wouldn't show that card unless she had no other choice."

"Then she expected trouble at the abbey?"

"She expected something. Whether that something was us or maybe Gehkohan retainers, you'd have to ask the girl."

Atom slipped an arm around Hither's shoulder and snuggled her close.

For a time they stood in silence, admiring the depths of the Black, losing themselves in the eternal silence. Atom calculated. He ran contingencies in his mind and trusted that his gamble would pay in full. He hoped that love trumped common sense. If love proved true, the odds shifted to his side of the table.

"Kozue," he said, closing his eyes and leaning a cheek on Hither's soft hair. "Call a meet in the commons."

"Will do, Cap," she replied in a chipper tone.

Atom waited.

After another minute he let go of Hither and turned away from the Black. "Come on, girl. Let's go figure out our next step."

Hitching up his gunbelt, he strode from the bridge with Hither padding along behind.

"Looks like this job just took a turn for the interesting," he said as he crossed into the galley and took a seat at the table with a dapper smile.

The rest of the crew sat around in various poses of disinterest. Shi slurped at a bowl of noodles. Daisy skimmed a book on his pad. And at the far end of the table, amid a spread of random parts, Byron tinkered with a handheld explosion of wires and soldered bits.

"That a bomb?" Atom asked as Hither slipped into the booth.

"Combo alarm-disarm plasma cutter, jib," Byron said around the smoking soldering iron clenched between his teeth.

"As long as it won't blow a hole in the side of my ship."

"We meetin' 'bout blowin' holes in ships or how's about we chatter 'bout how you gotcher hind whooped by a lil' girl." Shi grinned and cocked her head with bird-like jerkiness as she slurped another mouthful of noodles from her bowl.

Atom frowned and rubbed at his temples.

Daisy's shoulders shook like an almost imperceptible earthquake. Byron looked up with a startled expression, the smoking iron wreathing his face.

"It's true," Atom's words crawled out as he rehashed the events from the previous day. "From what we know about Lilly Prizrakov Genko, or Genny as she was known on Soba 4, or

Marian on Dathan, is that we can't pin down what we actually know about her."

"Any chance that Ghost Tribes rumor has weight?" Daisy asked without looking up from his book.

"Or, is that what we have to expect?" Hither looked around the table. "If she's a ghost, then we know she's capable of almost anything, with resources we can't underestimate. I've never had any direct dealings with the Tribes, but I've come across some of their handiwork in my old job. The Tribes are masters of all things shadow – assassination, subterfuge, espionage, theft, to name a few."

"Don't forget their dedication." The hulking pilot swiped a new page with a thick finger. "Once they accept a job, only death can stop them."

"Soundin' like somekin we know." Shi finished her noodles and pushed the bowl away from her. "If'n I din know better, I'd say our mighty Cap, hisself, was from the Tribes. I see 'im bend every rule to comp a job."

"And what of it?" Atom grinned behind his fist.

"As long as I ain't yer contract, I'm square with it."

"He en't never changed 'ow he looks." Byron squinted at his project and waved away the smoke.

"Maybe that's my disguise," said Atom.

Byron raised his eyes to stare at Atom.

"So, a little girl beat me soundly," Atom said with a laugh, holding up his hands in resignation.

"Do we know for sure that she's from the Tribes?" Daisy set his pad on the table and turned his full attention to the conversation. "Was this knowledge given to us when we took the job? If not, I don't know that we need to continue down this path."

"I took their money."

"Can you return it?"

"On what grounds?"

"They violated our contract through non-disclosure." Daisy leaned back and frowned as he folded his arms across his belly. "We have the right to know what you're facing when you choose to take a contract from any client."

Atom pursed his lips in thought. "They mentioned suspicions of training, but no hard evidence. We could probably walk away, but at this point, my interest has been touched."

"Interest?"

"A girl whooped me."

"She's from the Tribes," Hither interjected.

"We don't know that for sure." Atom glanced at her.

"It's looking that way, Atom. You build me a scenario where a girl, somewhere between sixteen and twenty-five, infiltrates a large, mid-level han. Bypasses all the security checks. Disappears into the Black with damaging information. And then resurfaces to gently put you down with a golem she has imprinted on …."

"What's a golem?" Byron's eyes danced from person to person.

All heads at the table swiveled to Byron in amazement. For a moment they sat in shocked silence. Then, like a pendulum, the heads swung back to Atom.

"You've never heard of a golem?" the captain asked.

"Oi, I've 'eard jibbers and floaters from the Black of golems, but that don't rightly know what they are, or 'it' is." His voice rose as he spoke. "Last I knew, golems swept from the Black to snatch unruly kits."

Atom nodded and slipped into lecturer mode. "The golem is an unholy melding of man and machine. They considered it a deep fringe project, but that went out the hatch when the emp unveiled them at the Battle of Tokai.

"Essentially, they are soldiers who have died in battle and then been fused into their battle armor. If their brains survive the process, their neural signature and consciousness is tied to the armor. They are no longer limited by the human body. Instead, a golem is as close to synthetic life as we have come to producing."

Byron pinched his lips together, contorting them into elastic shapes as he digested the information.

The others waited in silence.

"They're basic bots wiff brains." He furrowed his brow. "Fourteen circs an' I'm still bein' learned new tids.

"I ain't seein' what makes these metal bokes somefin' tougher 'an imp marines or deaf drones." He picked up his soldering iron and turned his attention back to his project. "Shouldn't an EMP handle 'em tight?"

Atom turned to Hither for help.

"They run on bio-energy and have been modified so that all their internal parts are biosynthetic," she said. "They function like an organism, not a machine."

"That'd be a rough toss." Byron remained focused on the tiny board inside his project. "All the strength of armor wiff none'a the weakness.

"An' this wendy got 'er 'ands on one?" He paused, glancing up from his soldering.

Atom shrugged. "The bigger question is how she imprinted with the thing."

"If you say so," Shi chirped. "I say it all boils to how we're takin' her on without that beast catchin' us unawares."

"Truth," Atom sighed.

"What's our next jump?" Daisy asked.

"Headed out to Gomori Alpha." Leaning back in his chair, Atom laced his fingers behind his head. As he spoke Margo wandered into the galley. Atom waved her over and pulled her up into his lap. "I'm banking on Lilly making for the nearest refueling station.

"There's no record of her ship at either of the two ports near the abbey, which means she either topped off before dropping in, or she burned through to make the best time and dropped near the abbey, but off the grid. With no record, there's no fueling taking place, which points us towards Gomori Alpha as the nearest fueling depot."

"Don't ya'll think she'd anticipate us trackin' her there?" Shi drawled. "Seems only logical-like that she'd be better at coverin' her tracks when she knows good an' well that she tussled with you back at the abbey.

"She knows you're on 'er scent."

"Probably." Atom stared off into the thoughtful beyond as he strapped up one of Margo's little boots. "But do you have a better path to follow?"

Shi thought on it for a moment. "Naw, I reckin the straight shot is the most likely course. Even if she's pullin' a skipper an' toppin' just enough to jump to the next system, we've a headin' to follow."

"Against the Ghost Tribes, I'd imagine it's easy to overthink and overanalyze actions," Hither added.

"Agreed." Daisy grinned. "This is like a cosmic game of pawns. When there are too many strategies in play to predict the opponent's true intentions, it's best to resort to the simplest steps. We take the simplest, most conservative approach until we can determine our enemy and their true thoughts."

"So, Gomori?" Shi stared into her empty bowl, willing it to refill.

"We split when we arrive." Atom tapped his chin in thought. "She's seen me and Go, but she hasn't seen the rest of you. Pair off and we sweep the station.

"If you find her." Atom paused to look around the table. "Nearest group goes to assist, the other locks down her ship. The last thing I want is for her to panic and call in the golem on a space station."

"That would be a death sentence for the entire station," Hither agreed. "She most likely imprinted that golem like a hound. It'll stop at nothing to protect her."

"We have a day and a touch to Gomori. Shi, you're with Daisy. Hither, you'll float with Byron. You can concoct whatever cover story you want, but make sure it is solid between the two of you and there's enough to back it. We'll go light arms, nothing that would draw attention from the authorities or hans."

"You sure you're up for this?" Shi asked. "I mean, you dinged your pan."

"I'll be fine, the medoc cleared me." Atom set Margo down and rose to his feet with a grin. "Said I just needed some rest."

"Good to hear." Shi focused on picking at her thumbnail. "Then now's a good time."

"Good for what?" Atom asked with concern.

"Payback." She looked up with a wicked grin, just as Hither, who had risen in silence behind Atom, kicked him in the thigh with all her considerable power.

The blow dropped Atom to the deck to writhe in pain, clutching at his leg.

"What?" he managed to grunt between short gasping breaths. Fighting through the agony, he tried to rise to his feet. Only Daisy's stone grip saved him from collapsing again.

"She won't be as purdy as my shined eye, but I'd say we're square."

Centering himself, Atom watched as Shi rose and scooped a wide-eyed Margo from the deck. She hitched the girl on her hip and strolled with Hither from the galley, chatting and laughing about docking at Gomori Alpha. With a growl he shook his head and patted Daisy on the shoulder.

"Her shiner served a purpose." He looked to Daisy. "That was just vindictive."

Daisy shrugged. "Bruise for bruise ...."

"Makes the whole hand purple," Byron said with a laugh as he buttoned up his project and flipped a short plasma blade from the stock with a smug look of approval.

*   *   *

They approached the outer docking ring of the station, carving through the silent Black as Daisy reversed engines to slow their approach. Atom stood in the center of the small bridge and watched as the pilot tweaked docking vectors and eased back on the engine output.

"What are the specs on this station?" Atom asked Hither.

"Small," she replied from her seat at the navigator's console.

Atom cocked his head to give her a sidelong glance and she smiled back.

"She has a perm-pop of less than two-fifty." She skimmed through data scrolling across her hovering holo-screens. "Looks like she can handle around twenty-five hundred mouths at a time. She has twenty slips and handles up to medium class freighters."

"Current occupancy?" Atom leaned over Daisy's shoulder and squinted into the Black, trying to pick out the station from the gas giant she orbited and refined for fuel.

"Six. Two single passenger system hoppers, three mid-sized merchant ships, and the biggest ship is a modified Falcon-class marauder."

"Merc or kaizoku?"

Hither's fingers danced along the board and her face pinched in concentration. The *One Way Ticket* drew closer to the planet, and Atom located the station as it rounded the horizon and dropped into the golden-red backlighting of the giant.

"Seems legit merc," Hither said, sticking out her lower lip as she back-scrolled through the information. "Although, there are several blanks in their reported dockings."

Kozue chimed in. "These gaps correlate with attacks throughout the lower Fingers. Through deduction, I surmise this group maintains a legitimate appearance, but doesn't pass on opportunities to slip a few ko in their pockets. Their fuel docks are too widespread. Either they are docking in smuggler stations, or pirating fuel from targets of opportunity."

"Can you tell me about the attacks?" Atom asked.

"No survivors." Hither looked over from her screen. "There is nothing to actually tie that ship to the attacks except the gaps in her documentation and her travel vectors."

"Well, they're docked here." Atom straightened and stretched his back. "I'm assuming that puts them on the up and up for the moment. I say we proceed as planned, but keep ourselves light-footed around the merc crew. We all know how unpredictable mercs can be.

"What's our dock time?" He watched the station loom.

"We're looking at twenty-three tocks." The pilot glanced at his console.

"Keep us on track, Daisy." Atom turned from the Black. "The rest of us need to get ourselves ready. We move fast. As soon as Lilly marks us she'll drop back in the Black."

Hither slipped from her seat and followed as Atom ducked through the hatch, leaving Daisy in peace.

*　　　　*　　　　*

As they drew near the station, Atom returned to the bridge with Margo on his back and his rail-pistol at his hip. He unclipped Margo and set her down. With a giddy giggle she ran past Daisy to press her nose against the plasteel canopy framing the pilot's station.

Gomori Alpha loomed, like a two-hundred-kilometer silo, spinning on its side.

"It's been a while since I've been on a fueling station." Atom dropped into the empty seat at the com-station, across the narrow bridge from Hither's usual seat. He propped his feet up on the console. "Not much money to be made here, just money spent."

"It's what makes them fun," Daisy growled as he tapped the tiller to adjust vector.

"Although, I wonder if I could pick up a deal here?"

Daisy looked back, curiosity tickled. "Pass or parcel?"

"Depends on what needs delivering and where the drop is." Atom pulled his rail-pistol and checked the load. "I'll put you and Shi on that. Checking the boards will give you two a legitimate errand while you keep your ocs split for Lilly. We find something that fits and we might put a little bonus on top of this job."

Before Daisy could reply, Margo yelped in fright and leaped back just as an object thudded off the canopy.

"What was that?" Atom demanded as he shot to his feet.

"Looked like a body," Daisy stated, adjusting course again.

"A body?" Atom squeezed himself in beside Daisy and strained to see beyond the ship.

"It's gone, whatever it was." Daisy focused on the station. "We're still moving too fast for anything like that to stay with us. Plus, we probably sent it off on a tangent that'll make it tougher to track."

"Kozue," Atom called out as he gathered up Margo and stepped back behind Daisy. "Did you get a good look at that with the sensors?"

"Daisy was correct. I am impressed by his observational skills. IDing an object in space on the fly takes uncanny ability." Her voice lent a sense of surrealism to the moment. "The object that struck the ship was in fact a body. By my sensors, it was a male of approximately sixty-two kilograms."

"Was it a burial or a tossing?"

"He was not bound, so I would surmise he was forced into space alive."

Atom hesitated, weighing the situation. "Daisy, take us in easy. Last thing I want is to run into something worse than a body. I'll be down in the hold with the others. Meet up with us as soon as you've completed docking procedures."

Daisy grunted and kicked up the power to the reversed engines.

Casting one last glance at the growing space station, Atom turned and headed for the hold. At his hip, Margo hummed a soft lullaby Kozue had once sung to the children. She clutched his jacket in a firm grip as she scanned the familiar halls of the *One Way Ticket*.

Just as Atom reached the top of the hold steps, Kozue cut through the silence. "Atom, there is an incoming communication," she said with concern.

"From the station?" Atom pulled up, waiting with one hand resting on the railing.

"No, this communication is being relayed through the station, but I'm still trying to track the origins. Do you want me to patch it through or would you rather take it at the com station?"

"Just patch it."

"Atom Ulvan?" a voice asked after a brief pause.

"Speaking."

"This is Naomi Roberts Genko," the woman let the name sink in.

"What's the pleasure?"

"It has come to our attention that you failed in your attempt to apprehend the target. We consider this a breach of contract and as a result the contract is being terminated," the woman fell silent.

Atom traced a finger along the railing, his jaw clenched, but his voice remained steady. "Is there a reason I'm not being permitted to carry out this contract? I've never failed to fulfill a client's order."

"A representative of our han will find you to retrieve our deposit." The woman cut the communication without another word, leaving Atom in stunned silence.

Atom set Margo down. The girl instantly scampered down the open steps to join the others on the hold floor. As she left, Atom dropped his head and gripped the railing until his knuckles popped.

"What's ailin' you, boss?" Shi called from the front of the empty hold when Margo's approach alerted her to Atom's glooming presence.

Atom rubbed his scalp with agitated vigor and stalked down the steps after Margo. It took him long enough crossing the hold to compose himself. Shi, Hither, and Byron stood near the front lock, waiting for the docking sequence to complete.

"We lost the job," Atom growled as he approached the others.

They stared at him in amazement. They stood frozen, a tableau broken only by Margo tugging at Hither's hand, wanting to be picked up.

"We don't lose jobs," the redhead said as she scooped Margo into her arms. Concern laced her features as she rocked the pint-sized girl. "Is there more? Do we have legal repercussions to worry about?"

"I don't know. The Genkohan is sending a rep to collect the deposit."

"Couldn't they have requested that you send the money back through one of the banking guilds?"

"That would have been the easiest solution, terminate the contract electronically and give me a chance to send the funds back through the guild." Atom closed his eyes and rubbed at them for a moment before snapping. "But they're sending someone. In my gut I'm not seeing a single scenario where that's a good thing.

"Just means we have an extra helpin'a trouble on our tails." Shi crossed her arms beneath her rough poncho. "Ain't like that's nothin' new to us. We got the whole dim 'pire up our pipe. Jus' notch one more han on the list."

"What's this mean for the girl?" Hither's swaying lulled Margo and the girl's head drooped in slow bobs.

Atom shook his head. "I haven't folded that into my mind yet."

"Do we press the plan?" Byron spoke up for the first time.

"Yes," Atom said after some deliberation.

"What's the end-game?" Hither asked in a hushed tone.

"That I haven't figured out yet. I'm hoping to find my path by the time we find her."

"Is she even here?" Shi grumped and hitched her gunbelt.

"She's here." Atom lifted his eyes to meet the gunslinger's steely gaze. "And one more wrinkle, we've a merc ship in dock, so we change on the fly. I'll go first and if they're playing by civilized rules you all can come aboard. Lie low until I give the word."

Around the circle a series of unhappy, yet understanding responses met his words.

*   *   *

Atom pushed the pram across the docking umbilical that stretched out from the station like a searching proboscis. On either side of the delicate structure, windows looked down to the swirling maelstrom of the gas giant below. Blues and greens danced in an eons old hurricane that measured against man like a stone beside a blade of grass.

The umbilical, built to handle larger ships, stretched out from the docking ring and left the *One Way Ticket* tethered on semi-rigid struts, several hundred meters from the station.

"I've heard they have wonderful baths here." Margo spun her head to look up as Atom spoke. "It's a byproduct of the gas mining. There are supposed to be healthful minerals lacing the water. Hopefully, when we get this all pressed out, we'll have time for a relaxing soak. I'm pretty sure the crew could use the down time."

Before Margo could reply, a man burst through the far lock and sprinted down the gangway toward them. Atom slowed his pace, but continued moving forward. Instinct forced his hand to flip his coat back and expose the rail-pistol at his hip.

Atom furrowed his brow.

The man drew closer. Blood seeped down the front of his tunic. As Atom watched, the man staggered and left a long, bloody swath down the window as he reached to catch himself.

"Help me," he croaked and sank to his knees.

Atom eyed the man, both curious and cautious as he drifted the pram to the side, shielding Margo from the potential danger. As Atom closed on the man, his hand drifted from the pram to caress his pistol with absent-minded love.

The man, from his knees, stretched out a hand toward the pram.

Atom's fingers slipped around the pistol's familiar grip, but the man pitched forward with his arms flung wide and lay still. Without breaking stride, Atom kicked up the suspensors and floated the pram over the body with casual disdain.

He focused on the far hatch to the gangway.

As he approached, the portal hissed open to reveal a rough looking pair of mercenaries. Atom measured them as he drew near. Two men, tall and muscled in mismatched jumpsuits, they stood with arms crossed, barring the path into the space station. One wore a patch over his right eye and both desperately needed a shave.

"What brings you to this deck?" the patched man demanded.

Atom dropped his brown coat over his pistol and flashed a weary smile. "Fuel up and the pools." He nodded back to his ship. "We're running shy and I need a rest."

The men exchanged a glance.

"You sure picked a rot time to drop in, but who're we to deny your need for fuel." The patched man bowed and spread his arms wide in mock welcome. "Come on in and fill your needs."

As Atom moved to walk between the men, blasters appeared in ready palms, their muzzles pressed to Atom's temples with magical swiftness. "But don't hold us topped if you stay a touch longer than you'd planned," the man said with a grin as his finger brushed the well-oiled trigger with familiar tenderness. "Oli, see to his arms."

Grunting in assent, the wordless mercenary pulled Atom's pistol from its holster and flipped it to his company without his blaster wavering. Atom's eyes tracked the gun as it arced over Margo's head.

"Ideas?" the patch asked, noting Atom's attention.

Atom turned to the one-eyed man as the mercenary examined the pistol. Like his companion, he kept the muzzle of his blaster jammed against Atom's temple.

"No." Atom shook his head. "Family heirloom. It's worth more in my mind."

"That's a bold one." Patch grinned and slipped the rail-pistol into his belt. "This here's a top shelf rail-pistol, eight shot cylinder, with a belt clip auto-loader. Probably costs more than some of those ships docked out there.

"In heart-touching honesty, I've only seen this rail-pistol in vids." The man cocked his lonely eyebrow. "Only eight shots though. I'd prefer a blaster that'll get you through a fight without a recharge. Why do you go that route?"

Atom looked at the man, thoughtful. "Stopping power. That gun will punch through just about any armor and shields don't do a thing. It takes more skill than a pray and spray."

The other mercenary pulled Atom's second pistol from the back of his gunbelt.

"That's not near as expensive," Patch said with a shrug. "But it's still a fine piece. Oli, you can hold onto that one. I'd believe it was the family heirloom over the first one."

Oli grunted.

The patched man smiled a toothy grin and holstered his blaster. Oli followed suit. "Right this way, pops."

"Who are you bokes?" Atom asked with an innocent air.

"Us?" Patch laughed. "We're nobodies. We're ghosts.

"Follow us, though," he hitched up his sagging jumpsuit and headed for the interior of the station, waving for Atom to follow. Oli fell into step behind, like a specter, with his hand resting on the blaster thrust in his belt. "We'll show you to the best inn on this platform. There might even be a room left for the two of you."

"Koze, tell the others to stay put," Atom mumbled. "It's worse than I thought."

"You say something, pops?" Patch asked without turning.

"I was just telling my daughter that everything's going to be fine."

"It's not good to lie to your kids." A deep belly laugh shook the shoulders of the patched man and he led the way towards their unknown destination.

Atom strolled in stoic silence, following the path the mercenary carved through the space-station. Looking around them as they moved, Atom noted the destruction flowing through the streets and alleys of the station's shopping decks. Storefronts and restaurants stood smashed in and filled with debris.

What had once been a thriving space-station now seemed a smoldering grave, full of ghostly whispers and the hiss of air flow. Sparks and emergency lights augmented the few remaining overhead lamps.

Observing with muted concern, Atom wrapped his head around possible outcomes to their venture.

Margo squeaked as a young woman burst around a corner and dashed into their path.

"Help me," she pleaded, her hands on her knees.

Atom looked to the patched man, but he shook his head in warning and stepped to the side with his arms crossed. Oli loomed up behind Atom, waiting for an excuse. Calm reflected in Atom's eyes as he returned his gaze to the girl in silent apology.

Before Atom could open his mouth, a hulking brute rumbled around the corner and grinned as he caught sight of his quarry.

Crying out in terror, the woman sprinted past Atom and fled down the corridor.

"Evening, Igs," Patch called out. "What's the word tonight?"

"Fresh meat." The towering man leered after the fleeing woman as he lumbered after her. Drawing near the group he unlooped an electra-bola from his belt. "I aim to eat."

Twirling his wrist, Igs scowled and measured distance. Then, with a powerful flick, he sent the bola sailing after his prey. For a moment Atom thought the woman had a chance, but the glowing, whip-like weapon snapped true and snaked around her ankles faster than a viper's strike.

The young woman fell. With a thud that knocked the wind from her, she landed among the scattered debris and trash. She lay motionless, frozen with fear.

Igs laughed and trundled down the corridor to pounce on his hapless victim.

"Help ...." her cry cut short as Igs' massive hand closed around her throat and pinned her down.

Well-practiced routine guided the giant's motions as he unwound the electra-bola with one hand and looped it back onto his belt. Then, with a sadistic grin, he flicked out a razor-sharp knife and slipped the thin stiletto up the woman's pant leg. Looking into the woman's fear filled eyes, he slid the knife up, slicing the pant leg with exaggerated slowness.

Atom looked on with indifference. Turning his head to look down at Margo, he flipped a control on the pram and a hard shell flipped up to enclose the girl.

"A gentlekin," the patched man laughed. "This too much for you to stomach?"

"It's more than I wish for my two-year-old daughter to witness." Atom turned to his escort and noted a thin, older man creeping around the corner. Atom's eyes remained impassive.

Patch shrugged at Atom and turned to watch the show. Igs' knife reached the woman's knee when a ragged piece of metal struck the giant in the small of the back and bounced into the debris with a clatter.

With a jerk, Igs turned to find a skeletal man charging towards him.

While Atom and his escorts looked on, Igs dropped his electra-bola from his belt and whipped it at the approaching man with a flick of his thick wrist. The bola flew with more power than before and snapped taut around the man's neck. The electrically charged wires bit and charred through flesh, melting down to bone and then burning white hot as they slipped through the vertebrae.

Igs grinned at the patched man and turned back to his conquest, only to finder her neck snapped in his enthusiasm. The giant stared down at the smooth, doll-like countenance for a moment and then he closed her eyes with contrasting tenderness.

"No fun if there ain't no sport." He frowned with childish exaggeration as he rose to his feet and plodded back to join Atom and his escorts.

"You headed to The Crown?" Patch asked.

"Might as well," Igs replied. "Not much left to do around here anymore. Seems everyone has gone to ground."

As the caravan pressed through the ransacked space-station, a few stragglers fell in, hard mercenaries, men and women both, who gave Atom questioning looks as he pressed forward with stoic aplomb.

*   *   *

The Crown turned out to occupy the top three decks of the station. Atom squinted and tried to picture the inn without the scourge of mercenaries infesting the common room. Pressing through the sonic barrier at the door, Atom stepped into the waft of sound like wading into an oil scummed pond.

Conversation drifted as Atom surveyed the room. Seeing no immediate threats, he cracked open the pram and allowed Margo to look about.

The obvious leader held court from a faux-wooden booth at the back of the room. His presence helped maintain a modicum of order. Atom nodded in acknowledgement of the power. The man nodded back and ran a hand over his bald pate as he stared at Atom with a familiar intensity.

The patched man guided Atom and the pram through the crowded room to where his captain sat.

"This gentleman and his daughter dropped in for a top off and a trip to the springs." Dark humor slithered just beneath the surface of Patch's words. "I told him we'd try to be accommodating, but I don't know how much room we have left in the inn."

The patched man laughed, but the mercenary captain sat in silence and studied Atom.

"I know you," said the bald man.

Atom matched the studious stare for a moment before speaking. "I think I'd remember you." He glanced over his shoulder. "And your crew.

"The name's Adam Wolf." Atom looked back to the mercenary captain with a tentative smile. "Once an Imp Marine and now just a lonely merch trying to stay afloat in the Black. I've a quarter hold of haz-drone brains, so if you have some merch to move, I might be able to work a trade for it."

The man glowered.

"I checked his manifest," Patch chipped in. "He's true."

"Rolf, scram," the captain said, waving the patched man away without taking his eyes from Atom. "My mistake, friend, you look like a man I crossed vectors with a while back. I don't seem to remember him being a marine, but I suppose that could have been overlooked.

"Allow me to introduce myself." The man rose from his seat and gave a slight bow. "Julien Anders, captain of the Lithium Bear.

"Johansen and Nezumi." He indicated the two men flanking him at the table. "They're my lieutenants. If you have any problems with the crew you are welcome to speak with them. We've just come off a victory at Wyoh in the Armstrong System and my guns are blowing off some steam."

Anders settled back into his seat as Atom acknowledged the two other men at the table. Johansen sat silent, focused on his drink. Atom measured him in a glance, bearded and broad, he appeared ready to meet trouble with fist or the auto-shotgun strapped to his thigh.

The other man squirmed, a bundle of energy strapped in a slight, gaunt frame.

Nezumi squatted on his seat, perched and poised to explode as he peered up at Atom with feral intensity.

Without warning, Nezumi launched a cup at Atom's head. With minimal movement, Atom tipped his head to the side and avoided the incoming missile, only to have a high gauge blaster bolt rip past his other ear and sizzle a scorch mark along the ceiling.

Atom froze, his face a mask of indifference.

Nezumi cackled and bounced on his haunches.

"There's plenty more," he sang in a high-pitched voice. "If you like to play. Plenty to play. Play with you. Or with your kit. I like games."

Atom made note of the hidden blaster strapped to the inside of Nezumi's forearm.

Margo looked at the lieutenant with a puzzled expression and then up to Atom. "Him's bouncy, da."

"Johansen," Anders spoke as if Nezumi did not exist, but he mustered a warm smile for Margo. "Take this merch and his little one upstairs to the private dining room and see that he's comfortable.

Rising like a mountain from the ocean, Johansen departed without a word. Atom guided the pram after the man, wending his way through the thronging dining room. As they approached the lift, Atom glanced back and found Anders staring at him with a troubled expression. Nezumi crouched next to him like a twitchy stoat waiting to pounce.

Anders' expression gave him pause.

Once the doors closed, Atom's somber nature returned. Like removing a mask, Atom slipped from the sloppy-go-lucky merch to something more akin to a snow leopard. Just behind Johansen's line of sight, he measured the man, weighing his options. In the confined space he knew the man's bulk would play against him, but speed and surprise could swing an encounter in his favor.

From her seat in the pram, Margo began to sing.

Johansen turned with a relaxed smile to listen to the childish ditty.

Atom's mask returned. The love that beamed through his smile proved true. Johansen's smile widened as Margo noticed the attention and grinned up at him. The mercenary paid no notice to Atom as he reached out and patted Margo on the head.

The lift bumped to a halt and Johansen turned back as the doors opened. He stepped from the coffin confines into a wide lounge that hubbed a half-dozen radiating hallways.

"You can wait here," the lieutenant grumbled, gesturing to the lounge.

"What about a room?" Atom asked in dismay. "I planned on staying a couple days and taking a soak in the springs."

Johansen cast a suspicious, sidelong glance. "Ain't you seein' what's happenin' around here?" he demanded in a low voice. "Ain't no place for a lil miss. If I thought you had half a chance to skiddle, I'd float you on your way. Afraid there ain't no chance for that now, so I'll just recommend you lay low as the rest of these bokes." He gestured to the scattered denizens of the lounge.

"I'm not as addled as I may seem." Atom leaned in. "I knew I was in too deep as soon as I saw Rolf and Oli, but I figured I would see more danger if I turned my back to run. So, if I can just ride this out in a room, I'd be obliged."

"Talk to one of them." Johansen pointed to a uniformed trio huddled around a low table on the far side of the lounge. "They're staffers and should be able to scare somethin' for you. I'd carve wide of the main floor. Nothin' but trouble for the lil' miss down there.

"The lifts will take you up to the spas, but you'd have to talk to the staff," he grumbled on his way back onto the lift. "Our crew has avoided the waters. Nothin' much to take there."

Punching the doors shut, he left Atom to work the situation on his own.

"This place is gutted," Atom whispered to Kozue as he surveyed the despondent features of the ragged group of survivors. "Keep the crew informed. I'm working on angling us out of here."

"Have you spotted Lilly?" Kozue asked.

"I doubt she'd get swept up in this."

"Too smart?'

"Maybe." Atom maneuvered the pram over to settle beside a low table surrounded by empty couches. "The Tribes have a knack for avoiding situations they can't control …."

Atom trailed off, his mind jumping.

"What is it?" Kozue asked.

"She was on Soba." Atom spoke through the puzzle as he dropped onto one of the couches, lifted Margo out of the pram, and balanced her on his knees. "I assumed she'd been raped, but perhaps she just wanted me to think that. The Ghost Tribes control their situations, which means she could have avoided that. She was after something."

"Or perhaps she simply used you to tie up loose ends."

"That would mean she knew that I was tracking her and that she knew I was there …." Atom trailed off with his gaze lost in the thoughtful distance.

Pulling a blanket out of the pram, Margo slid down to sit on the couch beside Atom. Ignoring his words she snuggled in close to his side and closed her eyes.

"Theft?" Kozue computed.

"From those bokes?" Atom asked with an incredulous laugh. "I doubt it. They were just a shift on a hauler. I can't imagine they had anything she would need or want."

"Information?" Kozue fished.

"It's possible. Run a check to link those men to the Genkohan."

Atom shifted Margo's head to one of the couch cushions with a parent's stealth and rose to his feet. Looking over the room, he pulled the friendly smile back out. "Let's play a game." He thrust his hands in the pockets of his worn and battered brown coat. "Ten people in a room. Let's figure out who they are and what they do."

The handful of haggard inn patrons kept their eyes down and their words hushed as Atom looked them over. He turned to the inn employees first.

"Maid, cook, and …." He frowned and rocked back on his heels. "Clerk?"

"Close. The first two are correct. The last works in the spa."

"Good, that means we should be able to get some food and a bed to sleep in."

"And you should be able to visit the mineral springs you keep rambling about. They are fully automated and seem to be untouched by the merc crew. Perhaps the spa-man can arrange that for you."

Atom nodded. "Three down, six to go.

"Boke sitting by himself in the corner is military." Atom sidestepped the low table and wandered to an automated bar where he prepped a cup of black bitter. "I would guess he's a rear gear, otherwise he'd be doing something about the mercs."

"Correct, he's an appropriated passenger on a layover."

"And the three playing Solace are merch caps. The passenger must belong to one of them and whichever unlucky merch has the joy of carrying him to his destination is probably the same one losing all his money in that game." Atom plunked a spice cube in his bitter and wandered back to Margo. He blew a wisp of steam from the top of his mug as he turned his attention back to the merchant captains. "They're smart though. They know they're good enough with the mercs to ride this out. There was probably a payoff of some sort, but they don't seem to be sweating too much."

"They line up with the three merchant ships currently docked," Kozue said.

"I'm guessing their crews are still aboard their ships, because they aren't here."

"Safe assumption."

"That leaves two." Atom yawned and sat down, careful not to wake Margo. "Lass and lad. I'd say the lady's a wandering tumbler and the gentleman's syndicorp. He's too polished for this riff."

"That is possible," Kozue sounded puzzled. "It would appear that the ship registered in his name is a shell. It belongs to him, but there's a maze of files on how. I'm sure the name on the registry is false and I'm having trouble tracing its system of origin."

"He's *kuza*." Atom sipped from his mug. "And the tumbler? She's a little old for her trade. Does the last ship belong to her?"

"No."

Atom froze, his eyes drifting to the woman. "What do you mean?"

"It's not tied to her at all. That ship doesn't exist. It's a ghost."

"How did it dock?"

"Oh, there's a name and papers, but they run in more circles than the *kuza's*. They end nowhere, meaning the ship technically doesn't exist.

Atom sipped at his bitter and studied the woman over the lip of his mug. She sat on a low, backless couch and leaned against the wall with her eyes closed in weary resignation. She wore a crimson half-kimono, cut high in the front and long in the back. A black obi wrapped her midsection. Matching black and red heels sat on the coffee table as the woman stretched her legs out, crossed at the ankle.

Her eyes drifted open and she caught sight of Atom. An explosion of surprise flashed across her face to vanish behind her mask, leaving to Atom to wonder if he had seen it.

Atom caught his breath. "It's her," he whispered into his mug.

Before he could react, the lift whispered open and a blaster bolt sizzled through the air to burn a hole in the couch beside Atom's arm. Margo snapped upright, but remained silent. Atom froze, his eyes locked on the aging tumbler.

Her eyes slid shut, like an alligator before submerging.

Around the hub all conversation ceased. Then, as if the mercenary embodied a diseased animal, everyone fled as far away as possible without abandoning the room.

"Think you're better than I am?" Nezumi snarled. He took three steps and leaped to land in a crouch on the arm of the couch at the far end from Atom. Margo edged closer to her father, but remained silent and still. "Anders said you could have killed me downstairs and there's nothing I could have done about it.

"He's a liar." The skeletal man stalked to the floor and stood over Atom. Without warning he struck Atom just above the ear, like a soft-pawed cat toying with a mouse.

Atom froze, feigning fear, but in reality, sitting firm with stoic resolve.

Fury building, Nezumi shifted a step back and crouched on the low table before the couch. He perched there like a gargoyle. Leaning forward, he sprayed Atom's face with spittle as he screamed with unchecked rage. "He's a liar. I could have killed you without taking a breath."

The lift door opened once again and Captain Anders, with Johansen and Rolf flanking, stepped into the lounge. They remained silent, watching the interplay.

Atom's mask remained in place. With fear his stare remained on the dark-haired tumbler.

"Tell me he's lying." Nezumi slapped Atom again. This time across the face.

Atom remained silent.

Nezumi jammed his wrist-blaster beneath Atom's chin, forcing his head back.

"Tell me." Nezumi leaned in close. "Or I'll end the conversation right now. Nobody will stop me."

The merc stared hard into Atom's unwavering eyes.

"Tell me," he screamed, firing a shot wide that left a furrowed burn on Atom's neck. "If you won't tell me I'll ... I'll ash your kid." He hopped to his feet on the table, towering over Atom as he shifted his aim to Margo.

The girl met his wild eyes with indifference.

Nezumi's nostrils flared as his breath slipped out in animalistic pants.

"She don't mean nothin' to you?" he demanded.

"Ah, have a heart," the tumbler called out from the far side of the room. "Can't you see you've backed the poor boke into a peachy pinch? He's terrified. He opens his mouth and you kill him. Where's that leave his lass? He sits there like a dumb mutt, so you kill his girl. Then he follows.

"Either way, he's dead." She brushed back her dark hair and leaned forward to slip on her shoes.

Atom followed every movement with his eyes.

"Shut up, you dumb whore," Nezumi snarled. "When I want you, I'll toss a ko your way."

"Speaking of which." The woman rose to her feet with a whisper of silk, adjusting her obi in a seductive twist that revealed ample cleavage. "This man's already made a deposit. If you want to kill him, you'll have to wait for us to conclude our business transaction."

Nezumi's mouth fell open as the tumbler made her way to Atom with dainty steps that accentuated the curve of her hips. She sidestepped the mercenary and pulled Atom to his feet. "You stay put, darling," she spoke to Margo in a sweet, soft voice as she ignored Nezumi and escorted Atom from the lounge without a backward glance.

Atom followed like an obedient puppy as the woman led the way to her room.

"It's you again," Atom said after the door hissed shut. He perched on the edge of her bed as she kicked off her heels and took a seat at the small desk in the corner of the room. Without giving him much thought, she studied herself in the mirror mounted above the desk.

"It's me," she agreed after she finished adjusting her hair and turned to Atom. "How did you know?"

"Your eyes, when you looked at me there was a flash of familiar."

The woman spun back to the mirror and examined her eyes. "Interesting." She held her head at various angles to let the light play off her features. "Is that why you came here, to look at my eyes?"

Atom rose and stalked to the door. With his hand on the release, he stopped and turned back, his eyes traced patterns in the worn carpet as he spoke. "I was on my way to fulfill the contract on your head." He lifted his gaze to the handsome woman in time to catch her hand drifting toward her obi. "But the Genkohan has terminated that contract with me. It seems I owe you another debt, so I'll settle with information. The Genkos have hired someone to take my place.

"What name are you going by with this face?" Atom held his hands up in peace.

"Since you've seen through the mask, you can call me by my real name, Lilly," the woman said as she shifted to face Atom, folding her hands in her lap like a delicate flower. She looked up to study Atom. "Do you know who they're sending?"

Atom shook his head. "But it can't be good if they think this boke is better than me."

"Cocky?"

"Confident." Atom made to slap the door open, but paused when he caught the woman's amused expression. "What?" he demanded.

"Seems quick for a tumble."

"It's been a long time in the Black," he snapped and punched the button.

As he left the room, he adjusted his belt and slacked his face.

"If you're cutting her loose, what's your play?" Kozue asked as he returned to the couch and lifted Margo with practiced ease.

"Get out of here alive." He rubbed Margo's back as he kicked the auto-servos on the pram and set out to find a room.

*   *   *

The springs, a mineral rich byproduct of the station's gas mining process, occupied an entirely separate ring above the top deck of the inn. A hundred meters across, the spa spun on a gear independent of the main station gravity fields. An oasis of steamy pools and faux rocks tucked between the barren waste of the Black and the hubbub of the refueling docks, the spa provided a singular draw for spacers of all walks. The centrifugal force of the spin held the steaming mineral waters in the synthetic rocky channels wending through the space-bound paradise like a low-grav river.

Atom, clad in a fluffy robe, carried a naked Margo through the lock that linked the springs to the inn.

A squeal of delight escaped the girl's lips when she saw the swirling pools and the lavender scented steam rising from the mineral waters. After the lift dropped them to the floor of the ofuro ring, she squirmed until Atom set her down on the synth-stone pavers. Shameless in her innocence, she bolted for the nearest pool of mist-wreathed water like a little brown missile, only to stop at the very edge to squat down and poke a finger into the water.

Her face lit with delight and she plopped down on the edge to dangle her toes in the steaming water.

Atom, with more discretion, draped his robe across the back of a chair and slipped into the waters beneath Margo's perch. He drifted deeper into the waters with a contented sigh, allowing the heat to seep into his sore neck and leg. Closing his eyes, he leaned back against the rock and listened to the trickling water that fell in a spreading, three-hundred-and-sixty-degree waterfall from the spinning hub of the ofuro cylinder.

After her feet adjusted to the heat of the pool, Margo slipped in to stand beside Atom. She kept a small hand on his shoulder for stability.

"Hot, hot, hot," she chirped as she danced around with the water at her belly.

Atom smiled at the serenity of the moment.

"That's a lot of scars for a merch," a soft voice swirled out of the steam.

Atom lurched up, disturbing the tranquil waters. He scanned the surroundings and found nothing to further arouse suspicion. Allaying fears he turned to the voice.

"Who's there?" he called out, a hand beneath the surface drawing Margo close.

A figure swam from the mist with barely a ripple, a head floating towards them like weathered driftwood. Atom watched the head approach and relaxed as he recognized the face of the seasoned tumbler. Lilly. She swam closer, but settled on a rocky seat at a discreet distance.

The water lapped at her chin. Atom followed the pale flow of her hands gliding just beneath the surface, like flashes of koi dancing in a decorative pond.

"I needed to get away from the press." She closed her eyes and soaked. "Sometimes I just need quiet to talk to the voices in my head. My ship is my usual refuge, a quiet sanctuary, but I can't get there right now."

"I can relate." Atom settled back, keeping his eyes on the woman. "Except I don't care who sees me talking to myself."

Margo eluded Atom's distracted hand and wandered along the seating ledge towards the trickling waterfall. She crawled out of the pool with childish care as she padded on all fours like a bear to keep from slipping down the water-smoothed stone.

Atom watched, studying her movements.

Without warning, Margo turned, stood tall, and threw herself into the center of the pool.

Sitting still, Atom watched as she plunged beneath the surface. The waters closed over her head and settled. Atom remained motionless, a stern scowl on his face. Bubbles plopped to the surface.

Lilly leaned forward, but Atom held up a staying hand.

Surging water broke in a spray that wet the side of Atom's face. Margo thrashed with wild panic, then gasped a huge breath and settled enough to remain afloat with novice proficiency. Spluttering water from her mouth and nose, she beamed and doggy-paddled to the ledge near Atom.

Standing in the water up to her waist, she thrust her hands to her hips. "Look, da—I swimmed," she stated with proud emphasis.

Atom smiled and pulled her into a tight hug.

A squeal erupted from Margo as Atom tickled her ribs, then he turned her loose to paddle around the infinite pool. With water in her eyes, she ended up pulling herself onto the ledge where Lilly sat with an amused smile.

Fondness filled the woman's eyes as she studied the toddler. "She's beautiful," Lilly said as she reached out and turned Margo's face to study her features. "True beauty."

Margo pulled back from the touch, not in fear, but with mild distrust and anticipation. The child cocked her head and returned the studied stare. Lilly's hands slipped back beneath the surface like the retreating flukes of an orca, death and beauty wrapped into one silky being. Trusting herself, Margo stepped forward and with child-like intensity, touched Lilly's face.

"Wha's wrong wiss your face?" Margo kneaded the fine cheekbones and moved up to trace the outline of Lilly's eyes.

The woman laughed, a light, gentle tone that trilled across the waters like music.

"Your daughter has true-sight." Lilly took Margo's hands in her own and kissed them. "I have yet to find an adult who can match that."

"It's why I keep her around." Atom smiled at the interaction and drifted in the water.

"I was taught to trust what children see. They are more perceptive than we adults could ever hope to be."

"What does she see?"

"She saw in a moment what has taken you three meetings to begin to suspect." Lilly smoothed Margo's damp hair. "She knew the first time we met. This is just the first time she's been close enough to confirm her initial perceptions."

"Is it true?" Atom wiped steamy sweat from his face.

Lilly nodded.

"So, you're from the Ghost Tribes?"

Lilly rolled her eyes. "Why has it taken you so long to see what is so obvious."

"What family?"

"Baugs."

"Lilly Baugs?"

"Lilly Prizrakov Genko-Baugs, if you must know." Lilly held out her hands to Margo and the girl settled into the embrace on Lilly's lap. "Although, with my husband's death, I suppose it would be appropriate to drop the Genko."

"Baugs?" Atom searched the water as he dug through his memory for any mention of the name. "I don't remember hearing that one."

"Body augments." Lilly bounced Margo on her knee. "I have more body augments than I can count. They allow me to change shape and size to slide into any role I am assigned, or any character that will keep me alive."

"That's interesting."

"I can change my height and shape, bust size, hair and eye color. You call it, I can change it. I can even change the shape of my face and alter my age. The only thing I can't change is my total mass, but looks can deceive the eye. I can be the heaviest, tiny child or the lightest giantess, but you would never be able to tell from looking at me."

"In all my years, I've never heard of the tech for what you're telling me."

She held a finger to her lips as she shrugged a smile. "Tribe secrets."

"Why are you telling me?" Atom tensed. "Death information?"

"No." Lilly shook her head. "I'm already dead to the Tribes. We seem to have started a bad habit of sticking up for each other. I'm guessing this is the start of a relationship, not the end of one, and in my estimation you're outside the imp-law.

"Even if you started telling everyone I am a shape shifting monster, there's no proof," she laughed. "Plus, I know who you are. A word in the wrong ear and you are dead."

"Threats?"

"Hardly. We are dancing together all peaceably, but we are holding each other's privy bits at the same time. It's a little dangerous, a little exhilarating, a little helpful, and it assures we burn together.

"I guess, it would be akin to going into battle with an umbilical hooking our ships with the hatches open at either end."

"Doesn't sound like a solid place for either of us," said Atom.

"Well, if we are in the same orbit, it's best we know we are not aiming to kill each other."

Sitting in silence, Atom let the information wash over and through his mind. He nodded as his eyes drifted back and forth, allowing plans and formulations to float his mental tide. The trickle of the waterfall eased the flow of his thoughts.

"Two things need to be worked out and gravved for me to be comfortable with this." His eyes drew back into focus as he slipped off his rock to drift nearer to Lilly. His voice dropped as he drew close. "What do the Genko's have to do with all this and how does the baug work?

"I may have a thought that'll get us off this rig if it fits in your parameters." He kicked his feet out behind to float free.

"Neural integration." Lilly shifted Margo from her lap and floated out to meet Atom in the deep part of the pools. "Basically, I just focus my mind on what needs to be changed and my augments do the rest."

"Can you imitate someone?"

Lilly nodded. "The looks are the easy part." She swam lazy circles around Atom, forcing him to spin to keep facing her. "I can do that in a matter of minutes, fifteen if I am fitting into a completely new skin. I would actually have to talk to the person to match vocal patterns. Personality and mannerisms are a whole different beast.

"Usually it takes a couple hours for the perfect voice, but I can manage in a pinch if I know my target. And it takes at least a week tailing a person to fully mimic their persona. You buy me that time and I'll replace a person to their mother, minus some of their deeper memories."

"The deeper stuff doesn't matter. I would just need you to look enough like someone on this merc crew to get aboard their ship. Is that something you could pull off?"

"If I don't have to talk to anyone, I could pull it off in fifteen tocks."

"Good, pick someone out and get prepped. I'll talk to my crew back on the ship and bring this plan together."

"You know I could just get some boke to tumble me back aboard their ship." A smirk pulled at the corner of her mouth. "It would save me fifteen minutes of breaking myself to fit a new mold."

"But they might anticipate that. I know I would."

"Nothing I couldn't handle."

"My way makes for a better story." Atom laughed and backstroked to his rock. "If we can add to that story, it makes us both more marketable."

"The story of Atom Ulvan Meriwether?" Lilly stopped her spin, but continued to tread water, her movements slow and graceful as she locked eyes with Atom. "I'm from the Tribes. Even as an outcast I have connections and information avenues that others cannot even comprehend."

Atom resettled on his rock and returned the stare. "You already said that. What do you really know?"

"I know who you really are." She spun and rolled over onto her back to float with casual grace and poke her toes up from the depths like tiny round icebergs. "Not that you've done much to hide your identity. Dropping your han name is not exactly going to ground. And from what I can tell, you haven't done a single thing to alter your appearance. That means any face-cog is going to pick you up."

"I'm not exactly hiding." Atom watched her float with just her head and feet poking up from the water. "I'm wandering. If they find me, I'll kill any Walkerhan. If I find them, I'll kill the same Walkers."

As he spoke, Margo clambered back up to the rocks and sat in the steaming waterfall, kicking her legs and laughing, oblivious to the conversation below. Atom glanced to her and warmed at the innocent joy.

"The Tribes have no mark against you." Lilly swam to Atom, coming to a stop where she could stand on the stone bottom of the pool with her chin touching the water. "Even when you held the seat of Lord High Admiral they had more contact with you than you ever imagined. Several of your agents and a couple advisors had close ties to the Ghost Tribes."

"Did they send you to find me for some reason?" Atom asked. "Have the Walkers contracted you for my head?"

"No to both questions." A light laugh helped ease the tension of the moment. "I have my own contract that has nothing to do with you."

"Genkohan?"

Lilly inclined her head, but held her tongue.

Nodding in understanding, Atom rubbed his stubbled chin. "Are you still contracted?"

She shook her head. "Not anymore. I found what we were looking for and submitted the package to the clients ...."

"But?"

"I found a couple other things, information useful to the Tribes."

"And love?" Atom chuckled as she glanced away. "Never mix love and business."

Lilly remained silent and a sadness filled her eyes.

"I'm sorry," Atom softened his tone. "I've lost love too."

"I know." She looked up at him from beneath long, dark lashes.

"What else did you find?"

"Something worth killing for." Anger darkened her features. "Mix love and death together and you get a volatile cocktail."

"Leave it for now," he said with understanding. "Focus on what we need done to get out of here alive. I'll visit you in your room later."

"To talk or tumble?" She winked at him and with a coy smile drifted back through the mist to her rock, where she settled and closed her eyes. Margo slipped back down into the water and curled into her lap.

Without opening her eyes, Lilly began bouncing the girl on her knees.

*　　*　　*

Tucked against the wall of the circular lounge, Atom watched Margo run between scattered couches and tables, playing a game with herself. The girl twisted her jacket into a helmet, complete with a faceguard fashioned from the jacket's arms wrapped around her neck.

"Kozue," he said with a smile and a soft voice. "Patch me through to Shi."

Atom waited long enough to sip his rekan cocoa.

"Kips, boss," Shi's rough voice cut through the fusion of chatter and lounge music surrounding Atom. "Kozue said you've got words fer me?"

"I've worked a plan and I've need for you and By to suit up for a little walk."

"Oi, you want what now?" Byron cut in.

"Kozue, I said I wanted to talk to Shi," Atom mumbled in exasperation.

"It sounds like he is part of this plan." Saccharin sweetness dripped from the AI's voice. "I assumed this would efficiently save Shi the trouble of repeating your plan to him."

Atom's face pinched in annoyance as he hid behind his mug.

"I ain't steppin' foot out in no Black," Byron's voice drew up in a frantic pitch. "Last I suited up you near on left me on the float. If Shi hadn't been there I'd still be a frozen roid in the deep—"

"Micro asteroid," Shi interrupted with a laugh.

"Don't matter none, I'd still be there," Byron grumped. "No sense you even tryin' to suit me up."

"Shi." Atom set his mug on the low table and blew out a calming breath before continuing. "My plan is for you and Byron to slip aboard the merc ship and rig up something similar to what he did on that ship out in the Mary System, only a little smaller."

"That took me weeks, you boke," Byron screeched in Atom's ear.

"Kozue, cut him out of this conversation now," Atom snapped.

The com calmed as Byron's protests cut out.

"He's the wiz," Shi drawled. "Whatcha need me for?"

"He needs someone to calm him down. He trusts you, and I trust you to keep him on task and to protect him if the need arises."

"Righty, boss. So, we jaunt over, plant some det-line and a lil' bug. Then what?"

"Head back." Atom picked his legs up as Margo crawled under and took off again. He picked up his mug and sipped, relaxing back into the couch as the plan solidified in his mind. "I'll have a way in for you guys so you won't have to hack or cut. I'm working that angle from my end. The situation here is cluttered and I need to clear a space for us to slip out. This diversion will hopefully do the trick."

"Won't a boom like Mary take out the station and us?"

"We don't need anything near that big. We just need a small pop that will trip some sensors. I want something that will look like an accident and leave the mercs more worried about fixing up their ship than the need for revenge."

As he finalized the plans with Shi, a thin girl in her early teens wandered into the lounge from the elevator. She planted herself before the self-serve bar and perused the options. Long, deft fingers worried at a thick blue and purple braid that hung over one shoulder, contrasting with the shaved scalp on the other side of her head. The girl stuck the tip of the braid in her mouth and chewed for a moment before making a selection and taking the proffered juice. As she turned back to the room, she caught sight of Margo.

Bouncing on the arm of the couch in lieu of a horse, with her fingers cocked as blasters, Margo noticed the girl watching. Freezing, the toddler returned the studied stare. Then with a squeal of joy she pulled the jacket from her head and clambered down to hug the girl's legs.

Atom watched the interaction with interest.

"You ever find Lilly?" Shi asked.

"I did." Atom shook his head and waved the girl over to join him. "Just have By ready to suit and float on my word. I'm not sure of the exact timing yet."

"Aye, cap," she said and closed the com.

"Interesting get-up." Atom studied Lilly as she shed the upper half of her grungy coveralls and tied the arms around her waist.

Lilly set her juice on the table and scooped Margo into her arms. She flopped back into the empty couch beside Atom and with teenage disdain kicked her feet up on the table. "Interesting? More like uninteresting. I've found this age group is one of the easiest ways to avoid detection. Young teens are old enough to not warrant close supervision, and young enough to blend into the background most of the time.

"This girl's name is Tilt. I'm not sure why." Lilly retrieved her cup as she crossed her legs to create a comfortable cradle for Margo to sit in. Lifting her cup to Atom with a smile, she drained the contents. Then, like a true teen, she jammed the cup between the cushions of the couch. "But I'm guessing this will do exactly what we need."

"Did you kill her?" Atom asked in a low voice.

"Nope." Shaking her head, Lilly giggled and tickled Margo under the chin. "I shot her up with seds and tucked her away in my room.

"I'm guessing we'll be done with our bit by the time she even thinks about waking up. Speaking of which." The smile drifted from her face and a mature, business-like demeanor took hold. "What's the plan and what's my part in all this? I trusted you enough to go through the trouble of an ident-jump in the middle of what'll probably end in all our deaths."

"Just a little stroll …."

She raised her eyebrows, waiting for more.

"On their ship," Atom concluded.

Lilly stared at Atom, trying to work the angles out. "Am I a plant?" She played with her braid with nervous fingers, flipping the end around and popping it in her mouth to chew on.

"Not really." Atom glanced around the room. "No need for you to stay. I just need one thing … an open hatch.

"Do that, slip off, and we should each walk peaceably back to our own ships and burn for the Black on our own courses and never see each other again. We part on friendly terms, avoid a stand-up fight, and live."

"Think it'll work?"

"No idea." Atom chuckled. "But we're too outnumbered for anything else.

Lilly spit her braid out. "Yeah, I guess this seems the least suicidal path forward. At least this way there's a chance they don't toss us all out a lock.

"And your head is just too darn pretty for that." She pulled Margo close, rubbing noses with the girl, until she looked up with a start. "But what's to keep them from popping a torp up our pipes on our outward burn?"

"I'm hoping the other ships will follow suit so we're just part of a scattering burn." A weak smile pulled at Atom's face. "Otherwise we'd better hope they're too drunk to aim."

"Just one hatch, I can do that. What's the timing?"

"Sit on the aft airlock." Atom rose to his feet and collected Margo from Lilly. "I'll set everything in motion with the other caps. You just be ready for a knock on that door and then slip back up here before the dust up. I want to make sure we all head to our ships at the same time so the mercs don't get spooked by someone popping seal early."

Lilly looked up at Atom as she weighed her option. "And there's no way we just ride this out?"

"You've seen the station. They won't leave any survivors, if they have a say."

Understanding and resignation forced her smile away. "We were dead when our feet hit the deck of this station."

Atom nodded and strolled away.

*   *   *

The plan rolled into motion and like an experienced conductor, Atom orchestrated and adjusted as the players moved about. Only when the station's klaxons began screaming did he rise from his table, take a last sip of his reka, and load Margo into the pram. Then, as the other 'guests' in the lounge panicked and flew about like a gaggle of disrupted geese, Atom strolled to the lift. He waited only a few moments for the doors to admit them and then he closed out the cacophony of the lounge.

"How is the plan proceeding?" he asked Kozue as they descended.

"It seems to be proceeding as predicted. My scans show most of the mercenaries headed for their ship as we speak."

"Most?" The lift doors parted to a rapture-like scene. The dining room of the inn sat empty, tables overflowing with glasses and plates, chairs overturned, and soft music amplifying the stillness.

"There seem to be a dozen mercs doubling back to the inn."

"What, they didn't get the memo on the emergency procedures? A shipboard emergency means all-call and that means everyone," he growled, as he maneuvered through the jumbled mess of the dining room. "I was hoping to avoid any awkward farewell scenes."

Atom eased out the entrance, moving with cautious steps into the empty street beyond. "At least we visited the baths." He leaned down and tickled Margo's neck.

"Da, 'top it," she giggled, scrunching against his fingers.

"Did By and Shi get home safe?"

"Firm. The mercenaries appear …."

Captain Julien Anders rounded the far corner, hands thrust deep in his pockets as if out for a relaxing stroll. With his head cocked to the side, he stared up at the synth-sky that glowed a ruddy, evening skyscape from some far-off planet. Behind him his contingent of lieutenants and select muscle filled the street.

Atom pulled up short as the group halted a dozen paces away.

Anders pulled a capsule from his pocket, slipped it in his mouth, and cracked the casing with an audible pop. He inhaled sharply, held his breath for a moment, and then blew out a haze of heavy smoke. He spat the used plastic on the ground.

"Evening, gentlekin," Atom called out as if pleasantly surprised to see Anders.

Lifting his scowl, Anders popped another capsule in his mouth and wreathed his head in smoke. "Seems someone's been messing with my ship." He pulled a third capsule and held it in his palm a moment before tossing it back. "And here I showed nothing but hospitality and courtesy when I let you pass peaceable-like.

"Why'd you have to go and do a thing like that?" he sucked at his teeth and spit out another cartridge to bounce at his feet. "It upsets me something fierce."

Atom followed the motion, measuring the situation.

Instinct slipped his hand to his empty holster. Rolf caught the sleight of hand and grinned as he patted Atom's rail pistol tucked in the front of his belt.

Atom froze.

As one, his eyes, shoulders, and weathered brown coat drooped in surrender. His gaze fell to Margo as she sat in the suspensor pram, watching and waiting with defiant intensity.

"Tsk, tsk," Anders chided, taking a step towards Atom. "And now you aim to draw on me? What's the Black coming to? A man wanders in, looking for a room and a bed, then he has the gall to turn on them as offered the helping hand.

"Boys, go collect the other guests." He turned his back on Atom and waved his underlings away. They skirted Atom and the pram to enter the inn.

Johansen and Nezumi remained.

"I aim to leave peaceably." Atom straightened his coat and his shoulders. "No sense in causing a stir. You leave Fiver and me out of this and you can keep the rail-pistol. It's worth a pretty sum."

"Now you're bargaining?" Anders whipped back.

"Beats dying." Atom hooked a thumb in his belt.

The merc gave a slow nod of understanding.

"Problem is, I keep the pistol whether you live or die, so it don't count as much of a chip. Neither does your boat." Anders turned to Nezumi who trembled like a rabid tweaker. "Keep eyes on him. I told you earlier that he was dangerous and this quiet father act is worse than if he would just come out and fight.

"What's taking so long?" he yelled to Rolf, who stood in the inn door.

"They're coming now," the patched man replied.

As if on cue, a group of mercs, led by Oli, herded the guests out into the street. Like cowed sheep they gathered around Atom.

"Koze, can you control the pram?" Atom asked as a plan drifted about his mind.

"Firm, what do you have in mind?"

"We'll see," Atom scanned the guests clustering around him. "Just follow my lead."

"Where's the tumbler?" Anders demanded as Igs ducked through the inn doors carrying a motionless form in his arms. "And what in the void are you doing with Tilt?"

"She's not dead, is she?" Anders pressed forward, shoving the last stragglers out of the way to get to where Igs stood cradling the girl against his chest like a tiny kitten. He inspected the girl, feeling for both pulse and breath.

"Who did this?" he demanded in a dangerous tone as he spun to face down the small crowd pressed around Atom. "I'll kill every single one of you.

"I don't care if you had anything to do with this." His eyes flew wide with rage as he drew his blaster, aiming it with wild abandon into the flock of hapless bystanders. "Nobody lays a hand on my crew and expects to live. I was going to give each of you a chance to live." He stepped forward. "But not anymore."

Everyone crumpled to the ground, expecting blaster fire to rip into them. Only Atom remained standing. Around him a field of whimpering voices sprang up.

"Was it you?" a chill crept into Anders voice like frost across a windowpane.

Atom stared back with impassive defiance.

Reining in his anger, Anders advanced another step. The mercenary captain locked eyes with Atom, and he dropped his pistol to his side as he sized up the lanky captain.

A slight smile pulled at Atom's cheek. He raised his hand in a childish mockery of a pistol and aimed it at Anders' head. With exaggerated slowness he fired and slipped the pistol back into his empty holster. Atom repeated the process as if in a finger gunfight.

A shudder ran through Ander's frame as he tried to control the laughter welling up inside. For a moment he maintained his composure, then the laughter erupted into a gale-forced bellow. Wiping a tear from his eye, he doubled over and propped himself on his knees. Behind him the rest of his crew stood in uncertain silence.

"Can you believe this guy?" he laughed over his shoulder to the crew.

For a moment they remained silent, but then the infectious laughter rippled through their ranks.

"How about your life for my ship and safe passage out of here?" Atom asked.

Anders wiped another tear from his eye. His shoulders continued to convulse as he fought to regain his composure, but he rose to take in Atom's steely gaze. The gunslinger dropped his mock pistol to his side and returned the gun to the holster with an imaginary flourish.

"You're bargaining with my life now?" The laughter threatened to overtake Anders again. "You have nothing. Are you planning to throw the pram at me?"

"That won't be necessary." Atom drifted the pram closer to himself until it bumped against his hip like a ship moored against a pier. With a light caress he stroked the handle. "I have all I need right here. What do you say, Anders? I let you live and my daughter and I walk away from here and never look back."

Anders looked at Atom, as if trying to understand a foreign language.

"Follow my lead," Atom whispered and then he turned his attention and finger pistol back to Anders. "Last chance."

Anders shook his head.

Before he could open his mouth to reply Atom pulled the trigger on his finger pistol one final time. In the same moment the turbo-blaster dropped from the bottom of the pram and fired. The bolt caught Anders just below the eye, snapping his head back and knocking him from his feet to land in a heap before his crew.

Slapping the handle of the pram triggered a hidden compartment and Atom reached down just in time to catch a pistol as it dropped. The turbo laser fully spun into action even as Atom whipped the pistol up and fired. The mercenaries scattered.

Atom's first shot blew out Nezumi's knee as he turned to run. The skittish lieutenant dropped, all bravado gone as he clawed his way through the debris of the space station.

Behind Atom, Kozue guided the pram's targeting and laid down a barrage.

The narrow street erupted into a blazing firefight as the mercenaries began taking pot-shots from cover. In the pram, Margo ducked low and followed the fight with just her eyes peeking over the armored rim of the death machine.

Stalking forward, disregarding the scattered return shots, Atom made for the shattered storefront where Rolf had taken refuge. He ducked into the alcove of the next store and hugged the metal wall as he spun the cylinder on his pistol to check the load. Ducking and darting, he plunged through the empty window on Rolf's blind-side. Atom hit the patched man with a gut shot before he registered his presence. Rolf groaned as he sank to his knees. Cocking his head to take in Atom with his good eye, the mercenary's glare fused hatred and pain into a palpable force.

Gasping through the pain, the patched merc tried to lift his auto-pistol.

"I told you that was a family heirloom," Atom spoke without anger. "It would have been nice if we could have just walked away."

Rolf grunted a stream of blood. He squeezed his trigger, but only managed a wild shot that punched into the floor near Atom's feet. Atom shook his head. He gave the man a sad smile as he slipped the pram pistol into the holster at the back of his belt. Bending low, he pulled his rail-pistol from Rolf's belt and checked the condition.

He spun the cylinder on his palm, a quick check for dirt and grime. Then he pressed the muzzle to Rolf's forehead.

"I'm sorry it came to this." He nodded and pulled the trigger.

As the body collapsed, Atom noted the silence outside.

He stepped back out into the street. Like tumbleweed in Tombstone, the mercenaries had disappeared. Only Johansen remained. He stood motionless in the center of the street beside Anders' body with his thumbs hooked in his belt.

"Is it my time?" Johansen sounded bored. He stared at the body.

Surveying the street, Atom counted four dead beyond Anders. Nezumi curled in a whimpering ball against a wall, clutching his ruined knee.

"Depends on your intentions." Atom held his rail-pistol at his side as he wandered over to stand before Johansen. "It's been my aim to walk away. I've no direct quarrel with your people, you just happened to cross my path at a bad time. I still aim to leave. Whether you stand in my way or not is up to you."

Atom turned away. He walked to Oli's sprawled body and retrieved his backup pistol. He tucked it in the front of his belt.

He glared at Nezumi, who lay just beyond the dead merc. "You still itching to stick me?" he growled at the whimpering man. "I could have tossed a bullet in your pan, but figured this would send more of a message. Be careful who you aim to tussle with. And, by the void, listen to your captain when he tells you to steer clear."

Shaking like a chilled chihuahua, Nezumi curled tighter into himself.

Turning back, Atom holstered his rail-pistol and flipped down his brown coat. As he walked back to the pram he called out. "What's the word?"

"Something tells me it ain't safe for me aboard my ship." Johansen tracked Atom's movements, but folded his arms across his chest to keep them away from any semblance of hostility.

"You figured that?"

"Why else trip an alarm that sends an all-call?"

"It would have cleared a path to my own ship."

Johansen chuckled and shook his head. "We would have been on you before you cleared the system."

Atom shrugged and powered the pram towards the docks. The turbo-blaster tracked Johansen's immobile position. "What's your answer?"

"Peace," Johansen said without hesitation.

"Then check your system when you're aboard." Atom paused to turn back to Johansen as the blaster retreated into its hidden port in the pram's belly. "It wouldn't have killed you, but it would have compromised a hatch and forced you to address the problem instead of following us."

Johansen nodded. "Who are you? Anders respected you more than a true merch."

"The name's Atom Ulvan, Captain," he said and strolled down the spacer's boulevard.

"Wait," Johansen called after him. "What do you mean 'captain'?"

"I just removed several links from your chain of command." Atom continued strolling away. "That should put you next in line for the chair."

Just before turning the corner, Atom stopped and looked back. Johansen stood in the same position, but Igs, still cradling Tilt, had crept out to stand beside him like an oversized child. Atom scowled at the brooding giant.

Drawing his pistol, Atom drew a bead on the man's forehead. Confusion stared back. "Keep a tighter leash on that one." Atom narrowed his eyes as he studied the man. "He's liable to get into trouble if he's not watched. He might hurt someone that doesn't need hurting.

"As for you, Captain." He returned his rail-pistol to its holster with a smooth flourish. "See to your hatches. They can pop a seal without regular maintenance."

"Wait," Johansen called out as he ran to catch up with Atom.

Atom flipped back his coat, but eased as Johansen held up his palms in peace.

"I know why she was here," he said as he drew near. "The tumbler."

"You knew what she was?"

Johansen nodded.

A ripple of blaster fire ripped from a byway and caught the fresh captain in the side, tearing through his jacket and the light armor beneath.

Kozue's reaction time saved Atom from a similar fate as the pram's shield snapped up to collect the stray blaster bolts. Atom grabbed Johansen and dragged him behind the shield before popping up with both pistols drawn to send a return volley down the alley.

Johansen clutched at Atom, pulling him down. The stench of death and charred flesh filled Atom's nostrils as he leaned in close.

"Find the Shepherd," Johansen croaked. Words slipped and slurred into nothing as Atom sought to understand. "The tumbler will know," the merc panted as his eyes rolled back. "Find the Shepherd."

More blaster bolts slammed into the shield as Johansen drifted away, his captaincy short lived.

Scrambling with crab-like efficiency, Atom plunged down the road, leaving Johansen's body behind. Pulling the pram behind him shielded them from death as the blaster bolts continued to rain down. Kozue dropped the turbo-blaster and sent suppressing fire winging back towards their assailants, buying enough time for them to escape around a distant corner.

Daisy disengaged the couplers and drifted away from the station the moment he registered a positive seal on the docking hatch. Atom blew out a sigh of relief as he felt the reverberations of the couplers retracting into the hull, and the pulse of the engines flow through his feet.

Space meant freedom.

*   *   *

He lifted Margo from the pram and set her on the floor. As he turned away, Kozue kicked up the suspensors and sent the pram gliding across the almost empty hold to tuck under the fore-stairs. Margo skipped to the steps and began climbing, two feet to each metal stair. Atom watched her climb as he pulled his rail-pistol from its holster. When she clambered to the top and disappeared through the hatch, he looked over his gun, making sure Rolf had taken care of the valuable weapon.

He spun the eight-chambered cylinder on his arm again and listened to the soft clicking of the mechanism. Happy with the whispered music of death, he holstered the weapon and followed after Margo.

As he mounted the upper landing, Dairy chirped in his ear. "Atom, you'd better hop up to the bridge." The pilot sounded concerned.

Atom kicked into a jog, only to skid to a halt as he popped into the mess. Sitting at the table with an enraptured Byron, Tilt flashed a radiant, bewitching smile. Atom caught her mid-laugh. Without a hitch, she turned her eyes to the captain and quirked a questioning eyebrow. Then, as she twirled her braid with playful innocence, Tilt turned back to Byron.

"Leave him be," Atom snapped. "You're old enough to be his mother."

Byron turned his head to Atom in shock.

"Prove it, old man," Tilt sighed and leaned back with a childish pout.

"Why are you here? Wait, I don't have time for that right now. Something's up, but when I figure out where we float, you and I will have some words. In the meantime, don't toss any pans aboard this ship." Fixing Tilt with a business-like glare, Atom turned away and bolted through the far hatch.

"Shi," he called out as he ran. "Meet us on the bridge."

Atom burst through the hatch to find Daisy hunched at the pilot's console with both hands gripping the tiller. Sitting at the nav-console, Hither glanced over her shoulder as Atom skidded to a halt.

"What's happening?" Atom scanned the Black, searching for a threat.

"A new ship just jumped the gate and dropped in system." Hither's fingers flew over her board, pulling up an image on one of the holo-screens. "She's burning hot."

"Do we have an ID?"

"*IS Graff*," Hither sifted the data streaming across her screen. "Forty-gun frigate."

"Toks Marshall," Atom whispered. "Let's hope she's not on our trail."

"Why else would she be here?"

"Maybe someone slipped a distress call out from the station," said Daisy.

"Doubtful." Hither continued pulling information from her boards. "From what I gathered while you were aboard, the station habs have an understanding with the mercs. They turn a blind eye, go to ground while the mercs have the run of the place. The mercs don't kill any habs and the cap pays for any damages, plus a bonus when they leave. The only corpses are spacers who aren't in on the arrangement and the station scraps off the ships."

"Lucky we made it out." Atom turned away from the nav-console and squinted over Daisy's shoulder, into the Black. "Daisy, we're going to have to skip the jump gate. Get us out of here. Let's hope it was a distress call.

"Hither, follow Daisy's vector and get us some off-gate coords," Atom sighed. "Waste of fuel this way, but I'm not tangling with a frigate."

"Atom," Kozue sounded puzzled. "I've gone over the information from that secondary attack. I don't believe the assailants were mercenaries."

Daisy swung the ship in a graceful arc and burned for the system rim.

Atom glanced back to the nav-console and grimaced. "What do you mean?"

"I've isolated images. They appear to be Imperials."

"Advanced scouts? How did they slip in?"

"I have no relevant information on that," Kozue answered.

Shi trotted through the door.

"Nice of you to join us," Atom said and waved her to the com-station across the narrow bridge from Hither's seat.

Shi dropped into the seat, waving off Atom's snark. She powered up her consoles and squinted as information began flowing across her screens. "Cap, we've an inbound," she said, her demeanor all business.

"A second ship?" Atom asked.

"Torpedo."

"They think we're rabbits?" Hither asked, plotting evasion courses and flipping the potential trajectories to Daisy's floating display.

Pulling down the com-set from the ceiling, Atom called out. "Byron, get Tilt and Margo strapped and settled, we have incoming fire. Daisy should be able to keep us clear, but there may be some rattle in our bones."

He slapped the com-unit back onto its mount and braced himself against the overhead piping. "Time to impact?"

"Two-sixteen," Shi called out. "Cap, they're sending a com."

Atom hesitated. "Patch it through. Keep it audio only. I don't want to give her a visual, she might peg me."

A burst of static solidified into a hard female voice that filled the bridge. "This is Captain Marshall of the Imperial Navy. Identify yourself," she demanded in a voice accustomed to obedience. "I have been dispatched to investigate reports of unauthorized mercenary activity in the region."

"I'd slow for a chat, but you seem to have launched a torp before opening channels of communication," Atom said with a light air of indifference that he knew would needle Marshall.

"That is a simple shot across your bow to inform you that we are executing our orders with all gravity," Marshall snapped back. "Now identify yourself. If you continue to flee, we will be forced to assume your guilt."

Atom muted the com with a wry grin as his veins filled with iced adrenaline. "What's she really after?" he asked without tearing his eyes from Shi's screen.

Shi shrugged.

"It's never been protocol to shoot first unless war has been formalized, even with rogue mercs." He turned back to Hither's screen. "Koze, have they scoped us yet?"

"Negative. Their array is focused on the station. The merc ship is powering up and preparing to decouple. Also, I took the liberty of using a chimera to mask our transponder as soon as I detected their energy signature dropping into the system. They are currently reading us as The Terror out of New Haven, captained by Aubrey Droll."

"Although, if they had a scout ship in system earlier, they could have pinged our true code." Kozue seemed perplexed by the uncertainty.

Atom studied Hither's flowing charts. "Aubrey Droll?"

"Thirty to impact," Shi intoned.

"Daisy, can we punch any harder?" Atom asked.

"Ask By," Daisy said, gritting his teeth. "I just fly this crate.

"Byron," Atom called into the com. "You down in your hole?"

"Aye, cap," the mech replied. "I rabbited as soon as I 'eard 'em skies got tight. Buttoned up the lasses first, sir."

"Can you squeeze anything extra out of our core?"

"We'd risk burnin' aux drives and maybe poppin' our core."

"Give me a two on main and auxiliary drives, then prep for a hard burn for the ring."

"Are we outta the grav-well?" Byron asked, worry straining his voice.

"Ten seconds," Hither informed them.

"I hope we're close enough." Atom grinned and unmuted Marshall. "Looks like we've already established our travel vector. I don't have the time or money to throw away on the kind of burn it would take to slow us. It's been a pleasure, Toks. Perhaps we can sit down and chat next time and swap old stories over a cup of chi."

"Toks? Who is this? Identify …."

Atom slammed the com closed. "Hope I bought us enough time. By, go for burn."

The ship lurched to the side as Daisy rolled the *One Way Ticket*, stressing the grav-plates and forcing everyone aboard to brace. Byron eked every scrap of power from the main and auxiliary drives. The torpedo detonated in the space just vacated by the fleeing vessel, peppering the underside of the ship as Hither brought the nav-core online and ripped the ship from the system.

*   *   *

Atom swept into the galley to find Lilly sprawled in the booth, her feet dangling off the bench and bouncing to an intricate, internal rhythm. Still dressed in Tilt's prepubescent clothing, Lilly had grown to womanhood in the few minutes of their escape. Her light brown hair had returned and for the first time, Atom felt he could see Lilly in her true state.

Margo sat at Lilly's head, playing with her hair.

"Why are you here?" He slid into the opposite side of the booth.

"I didn't aim to be here." Lilly sat up and tucked her legs up beneath her. "I had hoped to slip off the merc ship and back to my own, but when I tripped the all-call, they locked down the hatches. The crew could get on, but nobody was getting off.

"I'm lucky Byron and Shi were still prepping for the jump back to your ship." She gave a tired smile and tucked a stray strand of hair behind Margo's ear. "I caught them just in time. They were suited and ready for the walk. I managed to squeeze into a suit and tag along.

"I'm kind of lost now," she said with a wan smile.

"What about your ship?"

"It's locked down for the moment." Lilly shrugged. "I have fail-safes to keep anyone stupid enough to poke around from getting in. I'll have to head back at some point or send a retrieval code."

"And your golem?"

She hesitated. "Ash is in stasis. He should be quiet until I pick up the ship."

"You don't think the imps will impound your ship?"

Lilly curled in on herself, with her arms resting on the table. "I hope they just overlook it. There's nothing to draw attention to The *Hellkite*. She's just an old system-skipper and her fees are paid up and linked to a deep account."

"You're probably right." Atom rose and wandered to the counter to pour a mug of black perk. "I don't know why the imps were there. I know the Genkohan terminated my contract on you, which squares us, but they said they'd be sending someone to retrieve their deposit.

"I don't remember the Genko's having that kind of pull with the imps." Atom leaned back against the counter and cradled the steaming mug, scenting the dark fluid. "You know anything?"

"A couple minor connections. Nothing that would bring an imp frigate. Unless …."

"Unless?" Atom left the word hanging.

"Unless the imps got wind of what I'd stumbled on in the Genko archives."

"And that would be?"

She hesitated, as if weighing Atom. "Do you remember the *Ave Maria*?"

Atom scowled in thought for a moment. "You mean that legendary treasure ship that disappeared when our great-grands were kids. I remember my da telling me bedtime stories when I wasn't much older than Margo.

"As I recall, she was lost with all hands. Fell in a hole during the Afkin War. The stories always said she carried a fortune in crystals, relics, bio-weapons, or whatever else can be sold from the Afkin homeworld. It was all just a legend, no hard evidence to anything of the sort." Atom scrunched his eyes closed, trying to recall the old stories.

"Wasn't she the last ship out of Afkin before it was destroyed?" Atom opened his eyes and looked to Lilly.

The Baug nodded. "That's the story. The *Ave Maria* fled the planet just before its destruction and was never seen again. She carried in her hold something more valuable than anything the stories mention."

"The *Ave Maria* is pure legend, just a bedtime story," Hither said as she stepped through the hatch and slipped into Atom's vacant seat and looked to Lilly. "That's what you're after?"

Lilly eyed Hither with unconcealed suspicion.

"It's ok." Atom watched Margo climb to her feet and amble around the loop of the booth to drop into Hither's lap. "My crew works most of my side jobs with me. We aim to fly legit as much as possible, but sometimes we have to work outside the establishment."

Lilly gave a slow nod of understanding. "I've never played well with others." She slipped from the booth and joined Atom at the counter where she dispensed her own mug of chilled blue chi. "My story summed up, I was hired by the imps to infiltrate the Genkohan on grounds of unauthorized corp merging. You know the stance."

"Too much power in one han is bad for the stability of the empire," Hither recited.

"Exactly." Lilly sipped her steaming mug. "My cover was getting a mark to fall in love with me. I executed my assignment to perfection. I was so convincing, I fell in love myself."

"You mean the Tribes aren't immune to human emotion?" Atom asked in mock shock.

Lilly rolled her eyes. "We're still human."

"Fair enough." Hither shot Atom a look. "Keep going. I want to see how your falling in love links to the *Ave Maria* and the Afkin War."

"Well, I fell in love and married Jackall Meiyo Genko. He is, was, a distant cousin to the han's leading family, but he was smart and held a good position in the han. I married him and worked my way into the family.

"It took two years to find the evidence I had been sent to collect on the han, but in the process I stumbled on something else." She paused to take another sip, despite the looks from Hither and Atom. "I found information about the *Ave Maria* indicating that the ship hadn't fallen into a black hole. Instead, if the han records are true, the ship crashed on an uninhabited planet somewhere on the galactic fringe.

"And the *Ave Maria* might not have been alone. Records are shaky, but it seems like the ship might have been part of a convoy or flotilla."

"Why would the Genkos have any of this?" Atom asked.

"The captain of the *Ave Maria* was a Genko."

Atom stepped away from the counter, frowning in thought. He dropped his eyes to the floor, brow furrowed. "How did the information get out and why hasn't the han gone after the treasure?"

He looked at Lilly.

She shrugged back. "From what I could tell the captain managed to fire out a relay drone that confirmed the survival of the ship, nothing more." Setting down her mug, Lilly drifted from the counter towards the rear hatch. "It contained a crew list and a message saying 'all hands lost' as a memorial. However, someone in the Genko's uncovered a single piece of information buried in the code of that limited message."

Pressing herself into the corner beside the hatch, she cocked her head, a snake scenting prey. Then, with a viper's speed she darted a hand through the door and like an expert noodler, dragged Byron into the room.

"Hands off, you cullion," he howled as she frog-hopped him by the collar.

"Easy." Atom held up a hand to halt her progress. "The lad's just a touch nosey. No need to rough him up."

"Sorry, habit." Lilly released the mech.

"Whadja do wiff Tilt?" he demanded, shirking his shoulders to settle his rumpled shirt.

Lilly looked to Atom.

"Well." He scratched at the back of his neck. "She hasn't gone far."

"I was playing at Tilt," Lilly said. "Using her likeness to get us aboard that merc ship. My real name is Lilly."

Byron drooped, then glared at her. "You're the wendy we've been after?"

"Yes," she said with a smile as she chucked Byron's chin. "That conversation you had with Tilt, it was really me. You've got a future. Don't worry."

She pushed him toward the booth with a gentle hand.

"Why haven't the Genko's gone after this wreck?" Atom led the way back to the table and brought the conversation back on track. "That war sailed so long ago, I'm not even sure what it was fought over. I don't remember anything more than a brief mention in school. Kozue, do you have any more information?"

"Sadly, no," the AI replied. "All I can gather is that it was a rebellion by the Afkin homeworld against the Empire. Strange, it's almost as if sections of the network have been scrubbed. I can find lists of Imperial ships and soldiers who served, but no real information about the battles themselves, other than the expunging of Afkin from the Empire. I'll keep digging. Perhaps I can find something deeper in the nets."

"History, wiped clean?" Atom looked troubled. "Fact is, I heard more about the *Ave Maria* in the bars and barracks than I ever did among fleet commanders. She was an old ghost ship."

"Ghost ship sounds about right," Lilly said as she retrieved her mug from the counter. "The information buried in the code referred to three. The other information was that list of the crew. I sat on that info for almost a year and all I could come up with is that three names on that list are important."

"Survivors?" Hither asked.

"That could mean the Genkohan thinks someone survived the disappearance?" Atom took a seat, shoving Byron deeper into the booth.

"There's no evidence they ever figured that out, or even pursued the matter." Lilly sipped her drink, made a face, and dumped the liquid into the sink. "I mean, there was no record of anyone looking into it in more than a couple generations."

"So, three names ...." Atom started.

"What do you have to do wiff this?" Byron interrupted.

Lilly looked to Atom and then back to Byron. "I completed my assignment. By the time the Genkos figured they'd been compromised, it was too late, but they were able to track down my file access. They know I've poked the *Ave Maria*, but I don't know if they were able to put the pieces together.

"Fact of the matter is, I torqued myself into a corner something fierce," she said with a sigh. "If I had followed protocol, I would have slipped out and the Genkos would have been left chasing a ghost ...."

"But you had Jackall," Atom filled in.

Lilly nodded.

"I thought I'd made it out intact, but taking Jackall compromised my anonymity. We ran and tried to disappear." Pain flashed across her face. "Evidently, nobody likes the way I left things. The Genkos want my head for exposing them and digging into the *Ave Maria*. And the Tribes don't let their people walk away."

"Sounds like you're in a tighter fix than I am." Atom shook his head in amazement.

Lilly shrugged.

"Question is," Atom continued. "How are the imps involved and what's the plan?"

"I'm guessing that imp commander is your replacement. The Genkos probably figure their chances are solidified with a bigger hammer.

"Genkos be damned." She grinned. "Jackall's passed on. I'm thinking, if I can find that treasure ship, I should have a good chance to buy my way back into the Tribe. At least I won't have to live the rest of my life five minutes from death."

"I thought you used the Tribe to figure out who I was," said Atom.

Lilly laughed. "I still have connections, even if I am a leaf on the wind."

"Fair enough." Atom paused and looked thoughtfully at Margo perched in Hither's lap. "The way things sit, we have evidence that the ship is out in the Black. Do you have a location?"

"Why would you think I'd give you that? No such thing as a free lunch."

"Seems I just saved your life," Atom said.

"And I spared yours, and you helped me out, and so on, and so on," said Lilly. "Seems we're twined."

"So, a location?" Atom asked with a half-smile.

"Not exactly …."

"I don't like the sound of that." Hither cast a sidelong glance at Lilly.

"There's clear evidence the ship didn't drop in a hole. I thought that's where the story would end, but I cross-referenced the only information I had . . . the ship crew list. Out of a crew of over twelve thousand, three names and their corresponding DNA codes resurfaced in the records in the years after the Afkin War.

"I tracked the whispers through some of my old Tribe connections. That's where I've been the past year." She wandered to the table and took the seat at the head. "I tracked down an old man who claimed to have been the grandson of one of those names. He claimed his granda had made it back from the deep Black aboard a lifeboat. Story he told me was that the captain sent three ensigns off into the Black just before the ship ducked into the gravity well of some no-name planet. Each sailor was given one piece of information: system, planet, and location."

"Why din' they share on the boat?" Byron stared at Lilly with wide-eyed enrapture.

"The son didn't say."

"Sounds like something I've no interest in chasing." Atom rose from the table. "I've no love for the Genkos and no bullets for the Tribes, but I don't want to get my people wrapped in something we have no stake in."

"You sure?" Lilly showed genuine surprise.

"I can drop you in a safe harbor," Atom said as he headed for the hatch. "In fact, light of our past crossings, I'll even leave you with some ko to hold you over until you can make it back to your ship. But I've learned that old rumors tend to be just that: rumors.

"And before you go offering to hire us." He turned back in anticipation. "We don't run on spec."

"I have something better."

"And that would be?"

"I know you talked to Johansen." Her words brought Atom to a halt. "He's the grandson of Moira Johansen, one of the sailors from that skiff.

"Was." Atom nodded and glanced to Byron and Hither. "Go get Daisy and Shi," he said to the mech as he returned to the table. "I think they need to hear this story and have a say in what happens next.

*   *   *

Everyone sat around the table in silence. Lilly had repeated the story. Now they digested and weighed action.

"Hither," Atom broke the silence. "Would you show our guest to one of the passenger bunks? Lilly, if you would stay there until dinner, that would give us a chance to discuss and vote on this.

"And," he continued as the women rose from the table. "Whatever is decided, we will do it on friendly terms. I might even have a job from time to time that could use your talent."

"What might that be?" she asked.

"Odd jobs here and there. Nothing outside your skill-set."

"I'll never say no to a job I haven't heard of yet." She smiled as she trailed after Hither.

"Thoughts?" Atom asked when Hither had returned and slipped into her seat.

The crew remained tight-lipped, exchanging glances as they gauged the temperature of the water. Atom watched their silent interaction.

"Who's first?" he broke the ice.

"I won't complain after a treasure hunt. It'll break our normal routine," Daisy said with a shrug. "It shouldn't be too dangerous. I mean, there shouldn't be anyone shooting at us. It's just a dead ship floating somewhere out in the Black.

"It would be nice to know what the payout is going to be." He leaned on the table.

Hither looked to Daisy and nodded in agreement. "I don't know what we'll be up against," she pondered out loud. "I'm not sure I agree that we're just burning for a dead ship. We don't even know where it is. Lilly said there were three pieces to this puzzle. As things stand, you have one, she has one, and there's one floating out there in the Black somewhere.

"My fear is wasting time and money on a ghost ship that may, or may not, exist." She stroked Margo's hair as the girl nuzzled into her shoulder. "There's no guarantee. I'm not sure I would burn on this possibility."

"Byron?" Atom shifted his attention around the table.

"Ko is the solid, cap, even on spec." The mech grinned at the others.

"Here." Daisy thumped a fist on the table.

Hither maintained a quiet indifference.

"Shi." Atom turned to the silent gunslinger. "You don't have a thought on this matter? I expected you would speak for the payout first."

"I don't trust 'er, cap." Shi chewed at her thumbnail. "Somethin's off."

"Elaborate."

"She's from the Ghost Tribes." Shi scowled as she gnawed on her cuticle. "It's just hard to trust a ghost.

"And I find it a might peculiar that she abandoned her golem so easy," she said, thrusting herself up from the table. "Grain a salt and I'm along fer the float. But I ain't sleepin' easy and I ain't strappin' down my girls."

Atom steepled his fingers in thought as the others rose from the table and left him in solitude.

*   *   *

"Kozue, I need you to hold the dinner bell a touch," Atom said as he sprawled in the booth with a hand propped behind his head. "I need to turn this and figure it before I can even think about food."

"What do you plan?" the AI asked.

"I need to talk to Lilly and figure out where the path could take us."

"The crew seems on board with the venture."

"And you?" Atom lifted his head from the table and looked over to where Margo played in the open space with Daisy's cat, Mae. The cheetah-spotted mouser hopped about playfully, but routinely purred against Margo's legs for a proper petting.

"I have reservations about the proposal, mainly based on lack of information. I would agree with Daisy that the probability of danger seems low, despite the wanted nature of both you and Lilly. However, the distance of time pushes any further danger from the picture. The job will be classified as deep salvage and so the statistical danger would be in the decayed state of the ship, if we find it."

"And that's a big if," Atom said as he steeled himself and slipped from the booth. "We don't even know if the wreck is actually out there."

"Or what the cargo might be, if it remains intact."

Atom could hear the hesitation in her voice.

"There's an off chance the ship was scavved long ago, but I imagine we would have heard about someone discovering a massive treasure ship." He whistled to catch Margo's attention and she snuck one last scratch to the cat's head before hopping over to fall in at Atom's side. "Unless it really is lost."

"That's the probable outcome to this venture."

Atom frowned. "Nothing gambled, nothing gained."

Before leaving the galley, Atom glanced through the opposite hatch and caught the silhouettes of Daisy and Hither up in the cockpit. Their quiet words and laughter drifted down the hallway, a peaceful reminder of their ship family.

He nodded to himself, reassuring himself that pressing forward presented no danger.

Passing through the crew quarters without a thought, he took the stairs with absent-minded speed. Only when he stood on the floor of the hold did he note Margo's struggle to keep up. She stopped on the fourth step and looked at him with a gleam of mischief in her eyes. Like a cat's tail wiggle, Margo's intentions became apparent.

With a wide grin, she hurled herself off the steps into Atom's waiting arms.

He spun her in a wide arc before settling her on his hip.

"Go see Lilly?" Margo played with the collar of Atom's old shirt.

"Yeah, that's the plan, Fiver." Atom wandered from the hold into the passenger passageway and paused outside the only closed door. "This whole notion hinges on what we can come up with in there."

He set Margo down and knocked on the door.

"Yeah," Lilly called out in a sleepy voice.

"Mind if we chat?"

The door cracked open a few moments later and Lilly blinked him into the room, rubbing sleep from her face as she slapped the light bank to a dim glow. She still wore Tilt's jumpsuit, which fit with snug comfort. Flopping barefoot on the bed, she tucked a hand behind her head and propped herself in a comfortable position.

"Come for a personal dinner invite?" Her warm smile relaxed Atom as he trailed Margo into the room.

"Not quite yet." He sat on the foot of the bed and lifted Margo into his lap.

"So, business then?"

"Right, we're floating right now, a slow burn up the Finger. I'd rather be heading somewhere than nowhere. Problem is, I don't have a heading to give Daisy and I'm not sure you do either."

The smile drifted from Lilly's face.

"Level with me," Atom continued. "Johansen talked to me, but I can't exactly make heads of what he told me. He gave me a name, but it doesn't match any planet or system in our nav-comp. I've had Kozue run the name against the available Imperial records from our target timeframe, and crossed them against the *Ave Maria*, and come up with an empty hold.

"How did you come up with your piece of the puzzle?" Atom watched as Margo climbed from his lap and crawled down the bed to sit cross-legged in front of Lilly.

Lilly smiled at the girl and reached out to chuck her chin.

"I told you straight, I found the three names and tracked the first one down. That's where I found the story about the lifeboat." Lilly rolled onto her back and laced her fingers behind her head as she stared at the ceiling. "No lies in that. I used the Tribe's archives to sift through and verify all three names. I've been tracking that second name for a couple months now, but that merc crew is hard to nail down."

"And that's what you were up to when we crossed paths at Soba?"

Lilly frowned up at the ceiling. "The captain of that freighter had some ties to the mercs. I sweet talked their next port of call out of them. They were planning a rendezvous with the merc ship, the *Lithium Bear*. Unfortunately, things didn't go exactly as I had planned."

"You sure about that?" Atom raised an eyebrow in doubt.

She shrugged.

"Well, it worked out the way it did and the way I see it all the loose ends are tied in a pretty little bow." She glanced down at Atom. "Moving on, this is the fairest way to figure stuff. You keep your name and I'll keep mine. We track down the third together and work from there. I have a name too, and like yours, it doesn't match to any system that I can find on the star-maps, but it does match too many planets, cities, and other random locations."

"That must mean the third piece is the system."

"That's the hope. Sound solid?"

"No cutting?" Atom stretched out a hand.

"We're balanced, so it wouldn't work anyway." She slapped his offered hand.

"Where are we headed?"

"A little frontier rock called Lassiter and we're looking for a grandpappy known as Blondie, Earnest Blonde."

"He was on the skiff?"

"No, but his father was," Lilly said. "At least I hope he was."

"It's a start." Energy surged through Atom as he hopped to his feet and swept from the room. "I'll give Daisy the heading.

"Dinner's in five," he called from down the hall.

*   *   *

Eight days later, they dropped into orbit above a small, icy moon.

"You think someone with that kind of secret would be richer." Daisy reached up and flipped a few switches on his overhead console.

"How do you know this Blondie isn't rich?" Hither spun her seat to peer at the small planetoid, spinning like a snowball beneath their keel. "What if this is the winter playground of the han heads?"

"Think they could have kept it a secret?"

"I guess not, but that doesn't mean Mr. Blonde's a bum."

Daisy chuffed a deep chuckle. "We're hanging onto this finger of the galaxy like a hangnail."

"Ever stop to think knowledge might not always be wealth?" Atom asked.

"True." Daisy pushed the yoke and dropped their approach vector. "By can disassemble the engine mid-flight and have it back together before we choke on our waste-air. But I don't see him living a life of luxury."

"He's more comfortable than I was at his age," Atom said.

"Sounds a tale for a pint or two," Daisy said over his shoulder.

"Ask Shi what it's like being an indent in the service."

"I thought you were from a decent han," said Hither.

"Not one big enough to avoid the annual indent."

"Seems like things burned for the uppers." Daisy nosed down into the atmosphere with a slight hiccup of turbulence as the *One Way Ticket* turned and burned to decelerate. "You went from a little han to running the empire for the emp himself."

"And look where that ended me," Atom grumbled as he pulled down the com and put on a chipper voice. "People, this is your captain speechifying your newest garble. We're on a vector that should drop us near the hab where Mr. Blonde resides. It should be a short walk to the front door, but it's downright frigid outside, so please, no open-toed shoes or silk shirts.

"We are looking at touching down within ten tocks. Dress warm. Arm light. See you in the hold." He clicked off and hung up the com.

"Aw, I was looking forward to seeing you in that beach getup again. In fact, I might pay good ko to watch you try to get that wrap to stay up. Just because things are local, doesn't mean you need to wear them, Atom," Hither said, forcing Daisy to work hard to control his laughter. Feeding on his laughter, she continued. "If you want to break your own rules, I think I have a parasol that would fit your personality perfectly."

"Does it come with a matching floral bonnet?" Daisy grinned down at his controls.

"Funny." Atom's sarcastic smirk brought a fresh round of laughter from the pair. "Just stay warm."

He swept from the bridge.

Passing through the galley, he found Lilly seated at the table in solitude. Curled in on herself, she stared into her thoughts.

"You'll need something warmer than that jumper." Atom stopped at the head of the table and looked down at the baug. "I'm sure we can scrounge something for you. Hither would probably be closer in size than Shi."

"Atom." Lilly looked at the captain like a teacher at a student who had just stated the obvious. "You give me a coat and I'll fit."

"Right." Atom retreated. "Think we'll face any trouble?"

Lilly shrugged. "They're frontier folk. Most times we walk in peaceable and they're happy for the business. But sometimes people are out here because they want to be left to their own."

"You are calling it right with light arms," she said with an approving nod as she slipped from the booth. "Nothing out of the ordinary with a sidearm out here in the Skin. Now, if you decided to walk with something heavier, my experience says we'd have trouble on our hands."

"Solid." Atom turned and continued on towards the crew quarters. "Let's see if we can't scrounge something for you."

*   *   *

"Do you really trust her?" Kozue asked as Atom stepped inside the berth he shared with Margo and pulled his ratty brown coat off the hook just inside his hatch.

"I'm not sure," he replied.

"Meaning?"

"I don't think she would ever try to kill me." Atom pulled his rail-pistol from a shelf and looked it over with his expert eye. "She's already had more than enough chances to put me down and she's passed each time."

"But what if she's kept you alive for the information in your head?"

"Death options predate that information."

"I don't trust her, Atom."

"I don't either, with the treasure." Atom holstered his pistol and flipped his coat down to cover the firearm. "I'm pretty sure she would take an opportunity to walk away with the entirety of the treasure, but not at the cost of my life."

"What do we do?"

"Float like a leaf on the wind." Atom smiled at the reference and picked Margo up from where she sat on the bed.

"One step ahead of the rain," Kozue continued the quote. "Statistically speaking, there's a 68% chance she betrays you."

"I hate it when you stop sounding like my wife." Atom scowled up at the ceiling as Margo played with his collar, trying in vain to tuck it under the edge of his coat. "Kozue never spouted numbers at me."

"No, but she studied them," Kozue's retort caught Atom off guard.

"And her tongue was quick," said Atom with a laugh.

"Quick like a mongoose." The AI shared his laughter. "I'll keep eyes on Lilly, but recall that you trust her somewhat."

"30%"

"32% for precision," Kozue snarked back.

*　　　*　　　*

Atom looked over his motley crew with a touch of pride as they circled up at the hold's side hatch. They had been fired in the crucible of his personal war and emerged stronger on the other side.

"How you see this goin'?" Shi drawled as she pulled the hood of her thermo-skin up over her head to cover all but her eyes and nose. She worked her jaw to settle the thin material. "Is there any intel on what we're moseyin' into?"

"We're just aiming to chat." Atom watched as she adjusted her familiar poncho. "Wouldn't it have been easier to just wear a jacket?"

"Sure, boss, but I fancy my poncho. This way I don't look all crammed up like y'all. Plus, my ladies are handier when I ain't a puffer." She flipped her poncho back to reveal the deadly vipers strapped at her hips.

Atom nodded as he turned and slapped open the hatch. Icy wind swept into the hold, swirling about their legs like sinuous ice cats. The crew hunched into the gale with uniform pain as they stepped out into the fresh morning air. Atom led the way, pushing the bubble-insulated pram before him like an ice breaker.

"Be careful with your ...." Atom started as Byron let out a yowl like a possessed beast. "Breath."

Atom grimaced in understanding. "The cold will freeze your snot."

A string of expletives lanced from Byron's mouth as the boy clutched at his face.

Hither wrapped an arm around the boy and pulled him close, even as she grinned behind her thermo-skin shield. Turning into the wind, Atom squinted and pressed forward.

Behind them the hatch snapped shut.

"Lock her down, Koze," said Atom. He shielded his eyes against the biting wind as he turned to Lilly. "You got a heading? I can't see anything through the ice glare.'

Lilly squinted as she unfolded her holo-pad and pulled up terrain mapping. As she rotated, the map re-oriented. "Looks

83

like the hab should be just over that ridge there." She waved at an ice rill rising off to their right.

Atom turned, and with head bowed against the wind, led the way up the incline. The others fell in step behind him, crunching through ice rime into the shin deep powder beneath. They walked in single file, their shadows casting long fingers along the colorless landscape.

The trek proved easy enough, but the bitter cold stole breath, and made the going slower than Atom would have liked.

"There she is." Lilly pointed to the low-slung habitation bubble that rose from the icy plain, a man-made blister on the face of the planet.

"Looks to be a single-family unit." Atom halted and the others stepped up to form a line on the crest of the ridge. "How far from town are we? I couldn't imagine living too far from other people on a planet like this."

"Up the valley, in that cleft." Lilly pointed to an ice ridge several miles across the open snow. "See that steam plume? That's their powerplant borehole, just beyond the dome of their little town."

"How'd we miss that coming in?" Daisy asked.

"It's down the hole, below the surface. It's easier to conserve heat down there out of the wind. And the town is under a bubble, kind of like this one."

"Speaking of, let's get out of this," Atom cut in. "Do they know we're coming?"

Hither replied, her voice muffled by a heavy scarf. "I sent a message to the coordinates Lilly gave me with an open introduction and greeting."

"Any response?"

"Not before we left the ship," Hither said and looked to Lilly. The baug glanced at her pad and shook her head.

"Well, I suppose we should just go knock on the door." Atom powered up the pram and set out down the low ridge. "I don't know about you, but I don't fancy dawdling in this breeze any longer than we have to."

The others watched Atom stride forward, the pram running before him compressing a path with its suspensors until they joined a well packed track arrowing to the front hatch. He followed with one hand on the pram and the other shielding his eyes from the ripping wind as the flaps of his coat whipped about his legs beneath the puffy tuck of his thermal jacket. With his head turned from the wind, Atom pressed toward the hatch to the hab.

He glanced back and spurred the others into motion without a word.

A few minutes more brought Atom to the entrance and into a short tunnel that protected him from most of the wind, if not the bitter cold. "I can't tell if I can feel my toes," he muttered to Kozue before the others joined him.

He reached out to hit the door chimes, but hesitated.

"Byron, take a look at that." He gestured to the wiring hanging from the bottom of the door controls.

Stepping to the side, he hiked up his thermal puff and drew his rail-pistol. Following suit, the others pressed themselves to the wall, their eyes alert even as the howling wind deadened their ears.

Only Byron remained unarmed as he scowled at the controls.

"Rough bypass," he yelled, playing with the wiring. "They ripped fer speed, not finesse."

"Who is they?" Atom asked.

Byron shrugged. "Guts splayed." He shifted his hood to scratch his head. "Could be anykin aimin' fer a quick in an' out. They din kill the controls, so that means they wanted this 'ere door to keep workin'."

"Get us inside," Atom snapped.

"On it." Byron twisted several wires together and the door slid open.

Atom ignored the wall of warmth that caressed his face as he slipped through the hatch. Just inside the door, he shed his puffy jacket and dropped it where he stood. The others unlimbered as well, and pressed to the walls as they edged forward.

Byron, last in, closed the doors with a whisper that locked out the howling of the wind. Silence settled over them.

A thud reverberated through the floor as the circulator cycled on to combat the heat loss at the hatch. It completed the cycle and fell silent.

Atom slapped the inner hatch open and maneuvered the pram over the threshold into a lush garden, fifty paces across.

Rising in tiers of hydroponic life, the garden housed enough foodstuff to feed a family of ten with left-overs.

"Blood." Shi scented the air like a hound.

They moved.

"Clear." Atom stalked through the orderly rows of plants to the far side of the hab as the others fanned out and combed through the gardens.

"It's empty," Hither called out from the left flank.

"Same," Daisy replied from the opposite side.

"Then we go down," Atom said as he approached a ramp descending into the soil along the curved wall of the hab.

Without waiting for the others, he pushed the pram down the ramp. He kept his pistol drawn in his hand. Dropping the insulating bubble on the pram, he instead flicked up the shields as he stole around the curve into the first level of habitation. The ramp opened into a broad living area comprised of an open kitchen, dining table, and recreation area. The outer wall stood lined with open doors that appeared to house the family storage.

The family sat around the table.

Atom drifted to a stop when he saw them. The others, flowing down the ramp, halted when they caught sight of Atom standing motionless.

"What's wrong?" Hither hissed.

Lilly stole down to Atom and shed a soft curse.

"They're all dead," Atom grunted and continued his downward spiral.

At the base of the ramp he positioned the pram to guard their escape route. Margo looked to him, then returned her attention to folding and unfolding her blanket. With his pistol ready, Atom made a quick circuit of the room, checking each of the storage lockers before spiraling his way in toward the table.

The rest of the crew stood around the dead family in silent reverence.

"Shi, Daisy, sweep the lower levels." Atom holstered his gun. "I don't want any surprises."

Without a word, the pair trotted away.

Atom circled the table, examining the scene with his expert eye.

"I'm guessing this is Mr. Blonde." He came to stand behind the seat at the head of the table where a grizzled man with long grey hair slumped. Blood wept from a gaping hole in place of the man's jaw.

Resting a hand on the back of the man's neck, Atom looked at Hither. "He still has some heat. This can't have happened too long ago."

"Then they could still be here?" Lilly asked.

"Doubtful." Atom looked around the corpse table. "I'm guessing they got what they came for."

"Or they didn't."

"Then why kill them all?" Hither asked.

"No witness, or maybe they were leverage." Lilly tapped at her temples and studied the scene. "Their temperature is on a scale."

"What?" Atom gave her a quizzical look.

"Ocular implants." She spread her fingers as if to display her eyes. "I can cycle through the full spectrum as well as thermal and a few other trickier visual aids. I can see that their temperatures run in a circle around the table. They are only a degree or two different, not enough to tell an individual story, but I can look at the whole picture. It would appear that whoever was looking for information moved through the family from oldest to youngest.

"They killed the little girl last, right before her father." Lilly blinked her eyes back to normal and dropped her head. "I don't think he gave them what they wanted."

"Why do you think that?" Atom asked.

"The kills were spaced out." Lilly took time to look over each of the victims. "It looks like he was given time to think things over.

"If he had given them the information, they would have executed the family in a shorter time span." Lilly scowled at the table and walked closer to Blonde. She bent over and studied the remnants of his face. "I don't think he knew anything. There's nothing in any of his files to indicate he could withstand torture. Especially for information that meant nothing to him.

"He was just a farmer caught up in something bigger than he knew," she said with a sigh.

Daisy and Shi returned.

"Empty," Daisy said with a shake of his head. "What are we finding up here?"

"Not a thing." Atom tapped his pistol against his thigh and then holstered the weapon. "It appears the boke didn't know anything. Maybe this is a clear sign we are in over our heads and should cut our losses."

"Maybe," Hither replied as he looked around at the downcast crew. "But the least we could do is clean things up and set the family presentable for the townsfolk."

Daisy nodded in agreement.

"Any chance this is the wrong Blonde?" Shi asked, pulling her hood back and roughing up her spiky blonde hair.

Atom cocked an eyebrow at her and then glanced to Lilly.

"I don't think so." Lilly frowned, her eyes moving as if tracing unseen pathways. "His was the highest probability, by far."

She dipped her fingers in the man's blood. Rubbing her fingers together, she stood for a silent moment, focused inward. "DNA matches perfectly. This is the man we were looking for. As to whether he is the man we needed, that's a touch less certain."

"But he didn't know anything?" Hither pondered.

Atom wandered to the family rec area and dropped onto a plush seat. He scratched his stubbled jaw, willing a solution to manifest itself.

Margo grew tired of her blanket and looked out over the scene.

"Dead, dada?" she asked as she monkeyed down from the pram.

"Yes, Margo." Atom flashed a sad smile that overrode his frustration.

The others sidled over and took seats in the rec area. They began speaking in hushed tones, firing through ideas and thoughts, both about the location and the attackers.

As they discoursed, Margo made her way to the table to wander in slow a circle. She took time to look up at each of the dead as if to memorize their faces. Stopping at the youngest daughter, she stole out a hand and caressed the dead hand with a heartbroken look of sorrow. As she turned to continue around the table, something caught her eye.

The sound of a scooting chair caught Atom's attention and with a quick jerk of his hand, the conversation fell. He turned and watched as Margo pushed aside the little girl's chair with all the care a two-year-old could muster. The dead child slipped, but Margo laid a gentle, steady hand on the body and settled the corpse.

"What are you doing, Margo?" Atom leaned forward, trying to match her height and see what had caught her eye.

"Picture, dada." Margo crouched down and crab-walked under the edge of the table.

"Where?"

"Bottom the table," she said, pointing up as she looked back at Atom with a proud smile.

Like a dart, Atom hopped over the back of his seat and covered the distance to the table in two long strides. Dropping to his knees besides Margo, he craned his neck to see the underside of the long table.

"What is it?" Lilly demanded as she led the others and followed him to the table.

"It's a ship's insignia," he said in wonderment. "We're definitely in the right place. This is the captain's table from the *Ave Maria*. Kozue just confirmed."

Daisy clasped his hands behind his head as he circled to the far side of the table. "I don't get it. If the ship's going down, why would you toss a table on the skiff? Just three people and a table?" He crouched down and tucked his head between two of the bodies to peer at the carving on the underside of the table. "Why not save as many people as possible?"

"Could be a trust issue. Or could be they didn't want to be saved. Or maybe they weren't in as much trouble as the stories would have us believe." Atom rose and gestured for Shi to lend a hand as he pulled one of the chairs out and grabbed the body under the arms. Together they carried a middling child and laid him with care on the open floor beside the ramp. "Whatever they were carrying aboard that ship was too valuable to let it fall into just anyone's hands. I'm guessing there was a kill order on the crew and they all knew it.

"The cap made a judgement call." He knelt and crossed the child's arms upon his chest. "They went down with the ship . . . unless the ship didn't go down," he said, pondering the possibilities.

"Either way, the ship is lost for the moment," Daisy said as he scooped the smallest child and held her against his chest. "But why the table? Was the cap planning some galactic-scale treasure hunt from the beginning? We going to find a treasure egg at the end of this trail? There has to be some overlaying plan to have all these scattered bits coming together." He laid the girl beside her brother with reverence.

"I don't know," Atom said, casting a glance to Lilly, who shrugged back.

The others followed suit and the dead soon lay in a long line, from oldest to youngest. Hither found blankets in a heavy wooden chest and draped them over the bodies.

Then, as if it weighed nothing, Daisy flipped the table, taking care not to damage any part of the heavy wooden puzzle piece.

Atom ran his hands over the lower surface. "It's smooth," he muttered as he leaned close to examine the curves of the insignia. "Nebulous hand, sword and gun wreathed by the thorny rose of the emperor.

"She wasn't Afkin ...." He looked up at the other, puzzled. "The *Ave Maria* was imperial?"

"Then the story is wrong?" Daisy looked to Lilly.

"Intentionally?" she countered.

"I don't know that it changes anything." Atom rapped at the table, listening for any unique sound. "This reinforces that the ship is out there. Whether it's imp or Afkin, we'll find out when we find it.

"Now, listen for any hollow spots." He bent his ear closer to the table.

Without hesitation, the others joined in. Even Margo followed suit.

After the crew had covered the table twice over, Kozue chipped in. "You look like a crew of fools," she laughed. "I'm detecting a slight irregularity in the insignia. Run your hand over the Hand, especially towards the Fingers."

The crew sat back with sheepish grins at their exuberance.

Closing his eyes, Atom brushed the surface with his fingertips. He traced back and forth over the painted lines of the God's Hand Galaxy.

"I said the hand, Atom," Kozue said with impatience.

Atom's eyes snapped open, but he followed the AI's guidance.

Running his fingers over the nebulous hand, he frowned as he traced the edge of the pinky finger. "There's a tiny dent just off the edge here." He looked up to the others. "Hither, take a feel."

Kneeling down beside Atom, Hither leaned in close to examine the table from several angles before running her hand over the surface.

"That's not an irregularity," she said as she laid her cheek on the wood and squinted. "It looks like someone used a punch. It's very slight, but it's there and it doesn't look like an accident. See how there's no drag to it and the dent is dead on?"

"That's a straight shot." She rose to her feet and looked around. "Do we think that's what we're looking for?"

"Koze, run that point against the astral map," Atom said as he hopped to his feet.

The AI hesitated. "It is in close proximity to a small system well beyond the outskirts of the Skins."

"Inhabited?"

"Firm. It appears to be under loose control of the O-Sue Han."

"Meaning?"

"They lay claim to it and have a han presence, but being so far outside the travel lanes, the Nemo System seems to be on its own. It appears the major system industry is scrapping. My estimation is that the remote location plays into the illegal salvage market."

"Well, we have a system to burn for." Atom turned to look over the bodies laid out in their neat row. "Now, what do we do with these people?"

"I say call it and burn," said Daisy as he stepped up beside Atom.

"That would peg us," Lilly replied. "They will have marked our arrival. They know we're here and when they find these bodies the local authorities will put these deaths on our heads, even though we found them this way."

"We could wait," Byron chipped in.

Margo wandered over and took Atom's hand, worming her way between the captain and the pilot.

Atom sighed. "Why do things always have to be so complicated?"

"Probably a good idea for us to actually take this to the authorities," said Hither as she wandered back over and took a seat on one of the fluffy chairs.

"How do we explain moving the bodies?"

"Protect Margo?" She shrugged. "We needed to be out of the cold and didn't want to leave them sitting where the poor girl would have to look at them. Or just being civilized and laid them out proper."

"They'll still be mad, but it should work," Atom scooped Margo and made for the ramp. "Daisy, Shi, flip that table back so it's not quite so obvious what we were looking at."

*   *   *

Atom strolled through the hatch to the *One Way Ticket*, rubbing the crusty snow from his face. "Let's get properly settled," he called out as the others started to wander away. "We don't know how long we'll be here, but I don't want the weather to kick anything loose."

He froze.

A grenade bounced. Metal tinked against metal as the small sphere hopped along a haphazard path across the hold floor like a fleeing kangaroo rat.

Atom felt the breath suck out of the room in a collective spasm as all eyes tracked the erratic journey of the fast-moving grenade. In an instant too brief for reaction, he tried to anticipate the detonation point and figure an escape route for any of the crew.

Wide eyes.

Bouncing metal sounded almost like tinkling glass.

As the rudimentary AI guided the grenade to the point of maximum damage, Atom leaned in front of Margo. He scowled at the artificial, sporadic hopping that made bouncers so deadly.

The grenade slowed.

The crew tensed.

Leaning back from the center of the room, they held their breaths as the grenade paused, mid-hop, to scan the hold. These grenades tracked movement, keying in on the panic its metallic clinking tended to inspire. The crew, however, remained frozen. As if seated at a Russian roulette table, they hung on a razor's edge, waiting for the next bounce. Or not....

The grenade dropped, bouncing with greater force against the plasteel matting of the floor and leaped chest-high in the air.

Atom slapped Margo to the ground, just as the shockwave slammed into him.

*   *   *

"Margo," Kozue whispered.

A few months shy of her third birthday, Margo perked at the familiar sound of her mother's voice. Crouched with her hands over her ears, she cracked open her eyes and looked around.

"Margo, I need your help," Kozue spoke with hushed urgency. "I need you to listen to my instructions and follow them carefully."

Instinct and her father's shielding body had driven Margo into a little ball behind one of the few crates stacked near the hold wall. Pressed low, she shifted to lift her head and peeped around the corner of the crate.

"Behind you is a vent," said Kozue.

Margo pulled back and turned to the wall.

"I'm going to open the vent," as she spoke the vent hissed open. "I need you to crawl inside. Go now."

On all fours, the girl monkey-crawled into the darkened vent.

"Good girl," the AI said with relief.

Margo crouched in the air vent. Spinning to look back into the hold, she caught sight of her father lying motionless. Half hidden by the crates, he had taken the brunt of the concussion for her. As the vent slid shut, Margo caught sight of a figure in red armor step through the open hatch with an assault blaster sweeping the hold.

"There are ten of them," said Kozue.

Margo turned, stood up in the low vent, and started walking.

"Ten." Margo reached up and trailed a hand along the ceiling, while holding up three fingers on her off hand. "I'm Fiver."

The girl grinned up at her mother.

"I know, dear."

Trotting down the air duct, Margo began humming a haunting, old lullaby to herself. Kozue guided the toddler through the vent system and up to the bridge by illuminating the crawl-space with a soft glow in the direction to go. As the girl approached the final vent, Kozue opened the spiraling, metal maw.

Margo peeked from the opening.

"It's safe, Go. They are all down on the lower level," Kozue chided. "I need you to look under Shi's console."

"Shi?" Margo lit up with a beaming smile as she wandered to the empty pilot's seat. With a little shimmy, she clambered up into the seat and began tugging at the yoke. Staring out into the snowy twilight, a mock dogfight erupted in Margo's mind. The smile disappeared, replaced by intense focus as she pretended to blast enemy ships from the starry Black.

"Not that one, love," Kozue retained her mother's patience. "The other seat."

Margo stopped playing and looked behind her. She stood up in Daisy's seat and looked around. Surveying the narrow bridge like a lookout on an old sailing vessel, she spotted Shi's communication station and pointed as if she had spotted land.

"Chair." She grinned as she hopped down.

Galloping over to the chair, she spun the seat in a slow circle.

"Good," Kozue prompted. "Now, look under the desk. There should be a gun that's just the right size for you."

Margo spun the chair again.

"Look under the desk, Go," the AI goaded. "Quickly, look under the desk."

Bending sideways, Margo peered under the chair.

"The desk, Go, the desk," the patience in Kozue's voice betrayed her AI circuitry in the face of imminent violence. "You must move faster, my lovely. They are coming up the stairs.

"Desk, Go. Look. Under. Desk."

Margo righted herself and dropped to all fours to crawl under the desk. Twisting to look up, she found the gun strapped to the underside of the console. With a few jerks against the bindings, she pulled the arc blaster free and emerged from the cubby like a game hunter with the pistol cradled in the crook of her arm.

She hefted the pistol to her shoulder and approached the door in a childish crouch, imitating Shi's rifle stance.

"Careful, girl," Kozue whispered in her ear. "There's a pair coming up the fore stairs now."

"Yummy, pear." Margo dropped the muzzle of her gun to the floor.

"No, there are two enemies coming up the stairs."

"Oh." Resuming her scowling war-face, Margo hefted the gun and peeked around the corner to the galley hatch. "Bad men on stairs."

"They are moving slowly."

Margo shifted along the wall, doing her best to imitate a shadow. A dark ringlet drifted over her eyes and with exasperation, she dropped the gun to the deck and smeared her hair back with her damp palms. Then, retrieving the gun, she crept forward with renewed concentration. Hunching her shoulders, she aimed the gun at the corner by the galley hatch.

A head and an assault blaster poked up from the stairwell, forcing Margo to flatten herself into the doorway of the captain's cabin. With exaggerated intensity, she sighted down the barrel.

A second figure swept around the first with military precision and took cover in the storage-bay hatch opposite the stairwell.

Margo tightened her tiny hands on the arc-pistol and dug the grip into her shoulder.

"Clear," the first figure growled.

The second soldier ghosted into the hallway. His light armor glistened in the dim lighting of the upper deck. Moving with cautious steps, he shifted forward. His rifle drifted from alcove to alcove, three storage bays on the right and the cabin to the left. His feet moved by rote as his helmet swiveled with slow automation.

Margo leaned out, closed her eyes, and pulled the trigger.

A burst from the soldier's assault blaster ripped into the wall above Margo's head even as the electric bolt slammed into the man's leg and blue lightning danced over the surface of his armor. In a macabre rendition of the dancing death, the man arched his back and involuntarily squeezed off another burst from his rifle that bit into the floor at his feet.

Before the twitching body dropped to the deck, Margo vanished into the cabin she shared with her father, moving at Kozue's direction, fading back into the atmo system.

As the vent swished shut behind her, the toddler heard the rush of metal shod feet.

"Good girl," Kozue crooned. "Now you need to climb the ladder beside you."

Margo looked up into the darkness. Kozue raised the lighting enough to see the six rungs leading up to another low air shaft. Clutching the pistol to her chest, Margo made slow progress climbing the ladder and by the time she stood in the upper tube, the hallway below stood empty.

"Well, we missed that opportunity," Kozue said with simple recalculation. "Follow the lights, dear. There are a few of them in the galley."

With her words, a line of pale work lights twinkled left at the intersection.

"Think you can shoot more than one?"

Margo shrugged and hugged the arc-pistol to her chest as she clambered through the ventilation tube. Following the glow, she made her way to a vent in the ceiling of the galley.

With painful slowness Kozue eased the vent open.

"What in peklo took Merf out?" a voice seeped up from below.

"Burned if I know," a rough, woman's voice answered. "Bannie said it was a little shadow. Maybe this boat's got a wisp."

"Wisps don't kill folk." The man's voice hung somewhere between statement and query as Margo leaned forward to watch the two soldiers below. "Least I en't never heard of such. They might lead you into death, but en't never heard tale of them right ending a boke."

"That's an electro-bolt wound." The woman pointed down the hall toward the bridge.

The two soldiers, their light armor a matching, crimson hue that marked their regiment, stood facing each other beside the long booth set into the galley wall. With trained caution, they covered both entrances to the galley, their posture relaxed, but alert.

They stood ready, directly beneath the vent.

Indistinguishable from her counterpart buttoned up in armor, the woman flipped up the visor on her helmet to expose her face and take in her surroundings with natural eyes. "I don't like this," she growled as she brought her rifle to her shoulder and trained it down the dim hallway. "Toks didn't give us any hint we'd hit anything more than a root breach."

"She di'n give us nothing." The man flipped his own helmet open and thumbed a stim-tab into his mouth.

Margo watched in fascination as a shiver coursed through the man. She crouched in the darkness above, chin resting on her knees as she studied the pair below. Then she drew the arc-pistol to her shoulder. Her almond eyes narrowed as she sighted down the short barrel.

Before Kozue could prompt her, the toddler squeezed the trigger.

The gun chuffed and a burst of arc-bolts slammed into the unsuspecting soldiers below.

"Well done," Margo heard the nod of approval in her mother's voice as convulsions threw the pair into each other, igniting a secondary shower of sheet lightning as they intertwined.

Armor melted together, leaving a smoldering grotesquerie of flesh, metal, and plasteel for someone else to find.

"Ten." Margo beamed as she leaned back from the vent and turned her small body in the narrow confines of the duct.

"No, dear," Kozue corrected. "There are seven soldiers left."

"Ten," Margo reassured her mother's voice with a confident smile.

"You need to keep going, Margo." Kozue closed the vent with a soft hiss.

*   *   *

Rough hands jostled Atom.

He wandered the edge of consciousness. With rubbery legs dragging behind, he felt himself hauled across the floor.

His floor.

Drifting. Eyes rolling. Open. Cracked.

He watched the floor of the hold whisk by, flowing like a liquid dream.

Feet below. Four feet. Armored feet. Light armor.

They dumped him in a heap, tossing him against a wall like offal. Atom's eyes bounced open as he landed. The soldiers trotted back to round up the others, and like sacks of grain, piled them around Atom.

He tried to move, but found his hands zipped tight behind his back.

"Atom," Shi whispered without moving her lips. She lay with her face pressed into Daisy's ribs. "You 'live?"

"More than dead."

"I can't focus my eyes."

"Mine are floating too." Atom tried to blink some clarity into his vision. "I think they must have slipped us a trank after the conk. You bound?"

"Firm," Shi grunted. "Not sure why. I'm full gassed, no limb control."

A ripple of gunfire echoed from the upper deck.

"Who're they shootin' at? Ain't we all here?" Shi tried to look around, but only managed to slip her head into Daisy's armpit.

"Don't think so." Atom squinted. Moving his head with care, he counted four still forms mingled with them. "Margo's not here and we're missing someone else.

"Koze, is Go with you?" He strained against his restraints.

The only response came as a fluctuated ringing, deep in his ears. He tried again.

"Ain't gittin' nothin' either," said Shi. "Could the trank block Kozue? Or maybe a local jammer?"

Atom blinked and fought to drag his eyes back open. "The concussion probably scrambled our pans. I'd guess we'll need a hard reboot to align the interface, but that's on our end." He turned his attention to the hold, trying to keep his eyes in focus and half-closed at the same time."

Three soldiers stood near the side hatch. They huddled their heads, deep in discussion. All three wore crimson light armor. The tallest of the three—Atom judged her to be the leader based on tone and stance—stood with her helmet tucked under her arm.

Atom studied the woman. A familiarity tickled at his mind.

The woman turned her sharp featured face and caught Atom's stare. Before he could dredge the recesses of his mind, she raised her blaster and fired off a quick pair of stun shots. Pain arched Atom's spine as the mild electro-bolts slammed into his chest.

He recalled stifling a scream as the world faded to black.

*   *   *

A yelp jolted Atom back from that darkness.

Unlike the previous surfacing, Atom rose from unconsciousness to immediate and full alertness. He surveyed his surroundings with a practiced eye, tested his restraints, and formulated possibilities. The armored woman still stood beside the hatch, but she had donned her helmet. Atom recognized her height and stance despite the concealing helmet.

She stood alone, blaster held loose, but tense in her readiness.

Moving with subtle care, Atom kept his head drooped as he nudged Shi with his knee. The gunslinger remained motionless. Atom studied her and detected the slight rise and fall of her breath. He noted with amusement the drool-fall she fed down the side of Daisy's shirt to pool below on her bunched-up poncho. Relieved, Atom turned his attention back to his captor. Tension hunched the woman's shoulders. Even as the hold remained silent and still, the woman stepped back, her movements defensive and calculating.

Atom watched her with puzzled fascination.

Before he could act, another cry echoed from the upper landing of the aft stairs. A pair of troopers stumbled down the steps. Somehow, they managed to keep their footing as they fled some unseen terror.

As they sprinted across the deck towards their beckoning commander, the lead soldier thrust his hands out to halt his momentum against the inner hatch. But the hatch flashed open. Atom imagined the look of surprise as the man stumbled forward, overbalanced, to plow face-first into the outer hatch. A dull crunch reached Atom's ears as the soldier crumpled to lie motionless on the floor inside the hatch.

The outer door hissed open, unleashing an icy blast into the hold.

A few steps behind, the second soldier continued in flight. Just as she touched the boundary of the outer hatch, the doors snapped shut. Like a ship-shear in a scrapyard, the doors crushed into the soldier, catching her in the midriff and crumpling armor as easily as aluminum foil in the hands of a toddler.

Atom made to rise.

The crouching commander caught the motion and raised her blaster. Squeezing off a wild shot, she backpedaled and slapped open the hatch. The body of her trooper fell to the floor in a crumpled mess of flesh and armor and leaking fluids.

With a scowl, Atom scrabbled to his feet. He watched as the woman snatched the body of the first trooper from where it lay inside the airlock. With her back pressed into the corner of the lock, she cycled the outer door open and thrust the body into the hatch beside the first. Like darting a hand into the mouth of a beast, she held the body just right for the crushing doors to jam. The dead carved just enough space for the commander to slither through and make her escape.

Just before she disappeared into the swirling snow, she turned and took a final shot at Atom through the narrow gap in the door.

Instinct saved Atom. He threw himself to the side ... headfirst into a crate.

*   *   *

Light flickered in painful slices as Atom slipped one eye open. Vision blurred, he tried to make out his surroundings, but gave up as his disrupted equilibrium threatened to toss the contents of his stomach from his noodle-like body.

He tried to talk, but a strange croak leaked from his mouth instead.

With childish tenderness, a hand rested on his forehead, cool and soothing.

"Dada," Margo's soft voice fell like refreshing rain.

Atom croaked again.

Water dribbled on Atom's lips. His throat felt raw. For the first time, he realized the parched, scrabbled feeling of his throat as a spoon of water dripped past his swollen tongue.

Atom took a deep, rasping breath, trying to feel his body as his chest inflated a few grains at a time.

Another spoonful of water.

Atom swallowed more this time. Nothing seemed broken, but his head swam with the effects of the repeated head trauma. Gingerly, he flexed his hands, focusing on each finger and knuckle. His legs and feet followed.

"Atom," Kozue spoke with bedroom softness. "I detect no major damage to your system. However, you have suffered a moderate concussion."

Atom's eyes rolled. Then one drifted into focus.

Margo hovered. She held a small bowl in her hands with a deep soup spoon clinking in the bottom, a clocktower bell to Atom's ears. She smiled at her father and lifted the spoon with an undeniable look.

"Drink, Da." Her emphatic innocence brought a weary smile to Atom's face.

He sipped the trickle and dropped his head back to the deck.

"What the hell happened?" he mumbled through the groggy haze.

"Give it a moment, Atom," Kozue's voice took a firmer tone, but still remained soft.

Atom took another spoonful of water and lifted his head in an attempt to survey the hold. As he blinked like an inebriate, he frowned. The hold seemed untouched by the attackers, but a pile of still figures lay sprawled near the cargo ramp in an unceremonious mound. With more effort than he cared to admit, he pulled himself up to lean against the crate.

Margo helped in her tiny way, straining at his shoulder as he settled into a position that eased the pain throbbing in his temples.

"Are they dead?" He gave a vague wave towards the pile.

"Only the soldiers," Kozue stated. "Shi is still unconscious. Byron is vomiting in his room. He was also concussed. Daisy and Hither have tidied up the intruders. They wanted to dump the bodies, but I suggested it would be a good idea for you to look them over before disposal. Any information could prove useful for future encounters.

"Smart." Atom pinched the bridge of his nose and took a deep breath. "Wait, future encounters?"

"It seems probable. This is the same outfit you encountered on Gomori Alpha."

Atom closed his eyes and thought about the peace of unconsciousness.

"I thought you should rest longer, but Margo was anxious to have you up and about." Atom heard the shrug in her voice as she changed the subject. "So, I indulged her."

"You didn't think having the captain up first would have been the best course for the ship?" he grunted, massaging his temples with a wince. "I need to be able to run the ship and I can't very well do that if I'm taking a nap."

"I considered the options and studied your readings. You awoke in the earliest window to avoid adverse effects of a concussion."

"Such as?"

"You could be vomiting like Byron."

Atom nodded, his stomach queasy, either from the motion or the thought. "I'm good now. Fill me in on what I missed." Atom watched Margo scuttle over to Shi, cradling her bowl and spoon as if carrying liquid crystal. "Our daughter is disturbingly adept in your arts."

"Thank you," Kozue purred.

"Ten enemies breached our ship," Kozue's contralto flowed like the instrument of a fine musician. "They rode in on a transport from the small colony down the valley from the hab. We did not detect their presence because of negligence on my part. Having detected no arrivals or departures from this planetoid since our arrival, I did not have cause to believe our enemies would be waiting for us.

"I estimate that their first order was to neutralize the crew. They did this without fatality, which leads to the conclusion they were after information. They did not find what you did. They hoped to capture some, or all of you, alive.

"They used a bouncer."

"It was set to adult height, which means they weren't taking Margo into account." Atom pinched the bridge of his nose and squeezed his eyes shut as he processed.

"Yes, that was fortunate," Kozue's voice drifted, lending to the illusion of her ghost wandering the hold as she spoke. "Due to that miscalculation, Margo slipped beneath the main concussion ring, and from there I was able to lead her into the air ducts. I guided her to one of Shi's multiple weapon stashes.

"I chose the arc-blaster."

"Shorter range, greater hit radius," Atom mumbled. "Good choice."

"It was calculated …."

The words drifted. Atom's vision swam. Somehow, Kozue's voice lost cohesion and the words twisted into a melodic dance.

The world faded again.

"Concussion." The words danced at the edge of Atom's consciousness.

In the blackness, his mind shifted like a ship in a storm. It pressed through the swirling fog of war that clouded his eyes and carried him back to the beginning. The start of chaos ….

*   *   *

Atom slipped open his eyes and recognized the ceiling of his cabin. The problems flooded back. Pieces of a galactic puzzle twirled in his mind as he tried to fit them together, but now a new piece, a harsh angled fragment in a curving gap appeared. He had recognized Toks Marshall. The true question lay in her motives for attack.

Ignoring the dull throbbing behind his eyes, he rose and dressed.

"Kozue, he grunted, as he dropped back to his bunk to pull on his boots. "We need to figure out which planet in the Nemo System holds our ship."

"There are more pressing matters, Atom."

"Name one."

"An ordered list: the deaths of the Blonde family; we were attacked by unknown assailants; you and Byron are still suffering the latent effects of concussion; and Lilly is gone."

Atom dropped his half-booted foot to the floor with a startling thud.

"What do you mean, gone?"

"Immediately following the detonation of the concussion-grenade, a pair of armored troopers dragged her off the ship. As she is not one of the crew, I had not taken the liberty of implanting myself into her system. Therefore, my last data of her whereabouts is an image from our external cameras of the troopers loading her into a rover and heading spinward."

Atom wiped sleep from his eyes. "First order is to iron out the murders with the locals. I don't want the *Ticket* tagged because we burned before the law finished its process."

"I believe the bodies in our hold will help speed that process."

"Let's hope so." Atom wiggled his foot down into his boot with a scowl and rose to head for the hatch.

"I need a cup of bitter to twitch my bones." He smoothed his rumpled hair as the hatch hissed open and he stepped into the hallway. "And a shower and shave before I try to talk my way out of a pile of bodies."

"That you do." Hither wrinkled her nose as she slipped past Atom in the direction of the galley. "You set foot in town like that and they're liable to toss you right back out on your face. I'd prefer you de-stink first, but I imagine it would be a better call for us all if we figured out bearings first and cleaned up second."

Atom lifted his arm and whiffed himself. His eyebrows tried to join his hairline, but he followed Hither to the galley.

The crew fell silent as he stepped through the hatch.

Wearing a weary smile, Atom wandered to the counter. In a matter of moments, he filled a mug with steaming black bitter. He turned and leaned on the counter, closing his eyes to savor the steamy aroma.

A polite cough from Hither broke his reverie.

Atom sipped. "I hear we dodged a real mess." He held the warmth of the drink in both hands and willed its energy into his ragged bones.

"Understatement," Hither said. "We should be dead, every single one of us."

"But we ain't." Shi reached over and tousled Margo's loose curls as the girl climbed up into Hither's lap. "I know she had the help of her mother, but I ain't never seen a kit that coulda done as she did and saved 'er kin."

"As is." Daisy hushed the others with a wave of his massive hand. "Seems we have two issues to figure: how'd they find us, and what's our next play?"

"You're forgetting the locals and just who it was that attacked us," Atom said.

Daisy grumbled a curse. "I was hoping to just burn and avoid that whole bag of weasels."

"They tagged us inbound," Hither said with a shake of her head. "Atom's right, locals come first on that list. If we jump this rock, they'll tag us and pin the massacre of an entire family on us."

Atom nodded a distant grimace at the other.

"Don't forget that we have lost Lilly," Kozue interjected. "Without her, we only have a system and a name. There are thirteen planets in the Nemo System, seven of which are registered as inhabited. I can find no direct reference to Shepherd beyond a family name that seems fairly common in the system. The largest city is Stillwater, with a population of forty-seven thousand."

"One thing at a time," Atom said with a worn sigh.

"There are fifty-two cities with populations over ten thousand."

"Enough," Atom barked, slapping the countertop. "We need to dig ourselves out of one hole before we jump in the next.

Not to mention, we've added another group that wants to see us dead, and we don't even know who they are."

"The armor was military cut," said Shi.

"You don't think it's Toks?" Hither asked as Atom wandered to take his seat at the head of the table.

He stared into the depths of his mug for a moment. "I don't see a more likely candidate."

"I was afraid of that," Hither said.

"You mean we got imps on us, darl?" Byron's gaze drifted around the table, trying to gauge their trouble. "What's it mean fer us?"

"It means we've got somethin's bigger burnin' our tail than we've ever dealt with before." Shi leaned back and propped her heel up on the seat to hug her leg. "I reckin we gotta deal with marines and gun-ships and a shoot-sight list that'll pop a torp up our pipe 'fore they so much as say howdy."

"Kack." Byron deflated.

"But they didn't do any of that, to our knowledge," Daisy's calm tone settled the energy swirling about the table.

"But the bokes boarded us," Byron mumbled.

"Truth, but they only retrieved Lilly." The pilot slipped from the booth and stood beside Atom with his arms crossed. "They didn't kill us or take us into custody. That would indicate they haven't linked us to Lilly in any manner beyond a transport." He glanced down to Atom. "Cap, how do you know that the red armor links the imps with Toks?"

"I saw her face." Atom set his mug on the table and drummed a finger tattoo.

"And did she see you?"

Atom lifted his head with a thoughtful flicker in his eyes. "I couldn't say." He glanced over to Margo and studied her face for a moment. "I know she saw me, but I don't know that she knew it was me. I know she wasn't looking for me, but don't know that she had the time to register who I was. On top of that, our paths only crossed a time or two under my former employment."

"I can verify if you give me time," Kozue hesitated. "Yes, facial recognition and voice ID confirm that the woman aboard our ship was Toks Marshall. According to the open nets, she appears to be in command of the Blood Wolf Legion. Beyond that, I cannot say without digging and potentially alerting the Imperials to our interests."

"How'd they find us?" Hither asked.

"Maybs a tracer?" Byron replied with a shrug.

"Or they coord jumped us," Daisy put in. "It's not like we plotted a multi-burn to throw them off."

Atom studied Byron with a thoughtful expression. "Koze, you'd detect a tracker on our hull, right?"

"Most likely," she replied. "As long as it is programmed to send out a regular pulse. Although, military hardware is way beyond my paygrade. I imagine they have tech that's somewhat harder to catch."

"When did they slap us wiff a tracer?" Byron asked, glancing around the table.

Daisy and Atom exchanged a look. "The torp," they said in unison.

"I know we rattled some shrap, but it never crossed my mind that they would tag us that way." Daisy looked worried.

"I'd put my full chit on a vector drop." Atom pondered out loud. "If I'm right, they slapped us with a mag canister that drops a trail of breadcrumbs. They don't actually activate until we are out of normal scan range. We don't pick up any of their electronic chatter, and they are tuned to the pulse frequency. The imps just follow the dropped tracers and eventually find what they're looking for."

"Wouldn't Koze 'ave detected any 'ull anomalies?"

"Probably not. When Shi and I were in the fleets, we had similar trackers, but I imagine they've improved since then. I know the ones we had were made to blend with different parts of the ship to avoid detection."

"That's all well and good," Hither said. "But it doesn't explain how they got ahead of us."

Everyone sat in silence, turning ideas over.

Byron eventually broke the silence. "Lilly knew tha heading, seems waxy that tha Genkos wantin' 'er dead, shared all the info wiff tha bokes they's sendin' after her. Logic says they knew of Blonde, but weren't touched 'nough to figure it out."

"Most logical answer is most likely," Daisy said in appreciation.

"We have an idea of how they found us." Atom slugged down the remainder of his tepid drink. "But I don't have the foggiest of their next play."

"I imagine they got what they came for," Hither spoke up. "As we already covered, if they had actually wanted us for anything, they would have taken us too, and if they felt us a threat, they would have eliminated us."

"Why didn't they kill us?" Shi asked.

"She has a point," Daisy followed up. "They didn't seem to have any problem eliminating the Blonde family. I would imagine we are a loose end to be eliminated."

"I believe the answer to that question is sitting in Hither's lap," Kozue's fondness colored her words.

"Who'd a thought the imps'd be scared off by a wee gal?" Shi laughed.

"Then we only have one step to take at the moment." Atom rose and carried his mug back to the kitchen to drop in the recycler. "We need to clear our names of the murdering that's taken place in the Blonde homestead."

* * *

The ramp dropped and crunched through an icy crust, even as the massive doors grumbled shut on the hangar. Before the hydraulics ceased their whine, Atom plunged through the last swirling eddies of snow. Pain-killers eased the pulsing darkness behind his eyes, and even though the meds made his head feel off, he could at least focus.

"Play nice," Atom growled to Hither and Shi as he hopped the suspensor over the lip of broken ice at the ramp's end.

"I reckin'd it'd be warmer in here." Shi blew into her balled fists as they hurried across the wide hangar towards a distant hatch. "I can't think of a soul that'd agree to work in here. I'd lose toes." She tucked her arms inside her poncho and hunched.

"I told you to wear something warmer," Hither laughed as she snugged her puffy coat around her face.

"You look like an advert for a parade floater."

"But I'm a warm floater."

"I said play nice," Atom repeated as they drew near the hatch.

"I thought you meant with the locals," Hither said with a saccharin smile as she rubbed elbows like a playful flirt.

Three abreast, they stalked from the deathly cold into the arid chill of the domed community. With hands on pistols, they kept vigilant, expecting an imperial ambush to open up on them. Only silence, punctuated by the distant hush of air recyclers, met their ears.

The landing hangar sat at one end of the town's solitary street, which ran a half mile to a structure Atom guessed to be an atmospheric processing center. Above them, the dome seemed an exact replica of the Blonde's artificial habitat, but on a larger scale. Discarded shipping containers and pre-fab buildings lined the wide avenue in parody of civilization.

"Who looks a fluff now?" Shi joked as Hither fought to shuck her thermal coat.

Hither sneered back.

Atom picked out the dispensary, a solitary storefront, and halfway down the short road, what appeared to be a tavern. The tallest and broadest building, the tavern looked to be a reconstituted, heavy machine shop.

Atom stopped at the edge of the staging and storage area at the end of the street. Ever alert, he scanned the short, but broad avenue.

"Nothing here." He narrowed his eyes.

"You sure?" Shi flipped her poncho back and with gentle love, rested her hands on her pistols. "My ladies ain't so sure."

Only Margo seemed oblivious to the frigid silence surrounding them. She climbed down from the pram and scampered after a solitary snowflake that had slipped through the hangar and lock to dance on the cool breeze of the artificial circulation. Without taking her eyes from the right flank, Hither reached out and pulled the girl in close beside her. Even then, as she gripped the tail of Hither's long jacket and peeked out, Margo's eyes filled with wide-eyed curiosity.

"Margo has a sense about her." Atom flipped his brown coat down over the rail-pistol slung low on his hip.

Hither glanced to Atom and then shrugged as she turned Margo loose. As the girl stepped out from the trio, the ex-courtesan tossed her thermal jacket in the empty pram under Atom's hand and adjusted her long, sleek duster. "It's chillier in here than I would have anticipated," she said, folding her arms over her chest and shivering. "Seems you would keep things a little more comfortable."

"Compared to outside, I reckin this is a comfort." Shi tried her hand at a vapor ring.

"Why is this place so deserted?" Hither squinted into the chill breeze.

"Would you want to be out in this?" Shi barked out a laugh that turned into a fit of coughing as the dry air hitched in her throat.

"Let's get out of this." Atom pulled his coat closer at the throat. "Go, up."

Without hesitation, Margo clambered back into the pram and Atom tucked Hither's puffy coat over her.

Shi eyed the pram. "Think I'd fit in there? Last ride was a touch rough, if you want a chance at redemption, Atom. It's bleedin' cold out here." She cast a glance back at the hangar hatch. "I guess we move forward, that tavern's closer'n the *Ticket*."

Atom grunted and pushed the pram down the main street. He hunched his shoulders against the biting wind.

"Why the wind?" Hither asked as she fell into step beside him.

"Air needs to cycle?" Atom replied. "Although, I don't have the foggiest as to why you'd keep a breeze when the temp is already below freezing."

"At least I prepared," Hither said with a warm smile as she pulled a scarf up from her fur-lined duster to cover her lower face from the artificial chill. "Unlike some of us, who seem to try to make a show of toughness."

Shi clicked the hammer on one of her guns hidden beneath her poncho. "It's cold, lass," Shi said with a grin. "But not too cold fer a scrap."

Atom shook his head and shivered.

Leaving the pair, his long strides carried the trio to the front door of the tavern and without hesitation, he plunged through the atmo-field door. As soon as he broke the plane, a groan of relief escaped his lips.

A moment later, the ladies followed him into the warmth of the tavern.

"Evening, strangers." A portly man with a broad smile stepped from behind the bar and slapped a towel over his shoulder. He skirted several crowded tables and approached.

"We wondered if you were planning on joining us for a bit a kip. I've been tracking your ship since you dropped into orbit."

"Atom Ulvan," Atom extended his hand, palm up in greeting. "Captain of the *One Way Ticket*."

"Branimir Svitać." The man laid his hand atop Atom's and grinned up at the lanky captain. "I'm the mayor and tavern keep in this little town. I don't have much competition in the food and drink department."

The man laughed as he spread his arms wide. "Come, we'll find you a table. We don't have much of a choice in the way of a menu, but I'll put in for three dailies. First meal is on the house."

The man swept away, indicating a vacant table before disappearing into the kitchen.

Hither pulled down her scarf and shook out her long, auburn hair, eliciting a series of head-swiveling stares.

"How do you do that?" Shi asked.

"Do what?" Hither asked in mock innocence.

"Break necks."

"Practice." Hither flicked a coy smile at Shi. "Give it a try."

Shi dragged back her thin hood and her short, spiky hair sprang to attention. She shook her head like a dog drying off. Then with a grin, she flipped her poncho back and traced a lazy finger along the curving contours of one of her pistols.

The heads dropped back to focus on the tables.

"I'd say we make a good team," Shi grinned over at Hither. "You shock 'em and I knock 'em."

Atom chuckled. "I like keeping you around. With the two of you bobbing heads, nobody has time to notice me. That's good for business and livelihood." He pulled the coat off Margo and stashed it under the pram before pressing through the crowded dining hall to claim the table marked by Svitać. "I'll ask about the sheriff when the barkeep drops our dinner."

"That could put a damper on the meal," Shi drawled as she flopped into her seat.

"Needs doing." Atom flipped Margo into the seat next to Shi and pulled out Hither's chair for her. "And we look guiltier the longer we wait.

"Interesting place they've got here," Atom said as he dropped into his seat with a sigh.

"Head?" Hither asked with a touch of concern.

"It's just foggy. I'll survive," Atom deflected, looking up to the metal beamed rafters. "This place looks a lot bigger from outside. I thought we were walking into another hangar."

"It's classic frontier." Shi stifled a yawn. "They build a building inside another building to help with insulation."

Atom nodded and squinted as he examined the two-story room lit with soft hover-lamps. A broad balcony lined three sides of the room and drew focus to a stage dominating the far end of the eatery. Despite the plasteel walls and basic adornment, the citizens of the little town had gone a long way to make their gathering place feel warm and inviting.

"Beer," Svitać said with a broad smile as he thumped down three tall steins. "Local brew. And a cimn juice for the little princess." He set a small glass in front of Margo.

Atom nodded his thanks and raised the mug to his lips to take a small sip. He savored the sip and then raised an eyebrow to Svitać. "That is a well-crafted brew, Mr. Mayor. A cap tipper for your brewer."

"Call me Svit," the man said with a hearty laugh. "There is nothing out here in the nails that requires such formality. Unless we are called before the local court.

"And that never happens." He crinkled his eyes and patted Atom on the shoulder.

"About that." Atom frowned and looked up to the man.

Svitać's smile drifted from his face.

"I need to see the sheriff as soon as possible," Atom said, leaning closer to the mayor and keeping his voice low. "We stopped by the Blonde homestead and…. Well, I think we should talk to the sheriff before we get much further into the evening."

Svitać gave a slow nod and turned away from the table to wander back to the bar.

"Best course?" Hither asked.

"Only vector as I see it," Atom replied.

"We going to be troubled by this?"

"Not sure. We have a pile of dead we're floating into the village. Even if they know it wasn't us, we're the ones who brought the news that one of their families is dead. I can't imagine the folks in a small community like this will take too kindly to that kind of news."

A moment later, a stocky woman wearing a wide-brimmed hat detached herself from the bar and with a hitch to her gunbelt, ambled over to the table. Atom watched her approach with steady curiosity. She carried a mug. From the alert twinkle to her eyes, Atom guessed at a stim-drink of some variety.

"Howdo." The sheriff touched the brim of her hat with a single finger. "Svit said you folks was lookin' fer the sheriff and that's me."

"Atom Ulvan," Atom rose and extended his hand. "These are a couple of my crew."

Weathered creases radiated from the woman's eyes as she studied each of them with a slow, steady gaze. She nodded to Shi and angled her forearm just enough to reveal part of a regimental crest peeking from beneath a rolled sleeve. Then, with her mug raised to her lips, she patted Atom's palm.

"Name's Margie Coffey, I's expected ya a touch sooner." She hooked an empty chair from a nearby table and dropped to join the crew. "What kept ya?"

Atom studied the woman.

She met his gaze with a friendly mask of her own. A maternal smile quirked the corner of her mouth. "I've had my eye on you and yers for a couple hours now. Svity and I had a bet on whether you'd rabbit or stick put."

"Who won?" Atom raised his beer, but returned it to the table untasted.

"I've a better feel fer the shadier set a people." She measured Atom. "I said ya'd stay put. Ya ain't no duffer. That means ya killed ol' Blonde and his clan, and are smooth enough to stare me cold-faced … or you happened 'pon the aftermath.

"Which is it?" She sipped at her mug, her eyes never leaving Atom's.

He nodded. "Truth is, we were hoping to talk to Mr. Blonde. A client was aiming to locate him. I can't cash in if he's dead."

"Did you kill him?"

"No," Atom replied without thought.

"Truth, lie, truth." Coffey's face spread in a wide grin.

Atom stared at the woman for a moment and then realization lit his features. "A truther." His eyes widened in amazement. "This far out in the Fingers?"

"I got wearied of the Palm and moved home." The grin remained fixed on her face.

"The truth, then." Atom relaxed into his chair and folded his hands over his lean stomach. "I'm going to leave out a few things that touch on sensitive, but I'll give you as much as I can. Agreeable?" Atom cocked an eyebrow in question.

Coffey dropped a single nod.

"We were looking for Blonde," Atom spoke in a measured tone. "He had information we believe passed down from his grandsire. That may or may not have been accurate, but it was a lead. We had no desire to see any death in this matter. As a matter of fact, we were looking forward to a job without any evident danger."

"Guess that hope went out the airlock." Coffey sipped her drink.

Atom frowned in agreement. "I'm not sure who we are up against, but I think they have imperial connections."

"Ordered?"

"Doubt it. There's nothing done this way that couldn't be done better through official channels. That would lead me off the books. We ran afoul a merc group back on Gamori Alpha, and an imp ship dropped into the system just as we were burning for the Black."

"That the same merc group that destroyed the station?"

Atom glanced to Hither and Shi. Surprise lit their features.

"Ah, I see that's news."

"I doubt they destroyed the station." Atom turned back to Coffey. "We were ambushed by an assault detachment as we made our way back to our ship. They didn't have any regimental markings, but I recognize imp armor when I see it. The mercs were fairly wiped and scrambling for their ship by the time we uncoupled. Their command structure was gone."

"Imps then?" Coffey pulled at her lip in thought. "An imp ship would have the firepower to take out a station. Why'd ya take so long to make yer way to town?"

Atom anticipated the shift. "We had an unexpected party aboard our ship."

Coffey shook her head. "We've only had two ships in orbit in the past week and yer one of them."

"The other ship?"

"Players," Coffey said, gesturing with her mug to a loud group occupying several tables at the rear of the dining area, up against the stage. "They've been here off an' on all day. My read says they ain't the types to go assaultin' payin' customers."

"You're welcome to scan my ship's records to verify that we were attacked."

Coffey dropped her eyes, staring deep into her cup. "I know yer truthin' me."

"You sure?"

"I headed out to pay Blonde a visit when he didn't come around for his normal socialite breaker and cuppa perk. I seen how you laid them out, all respectable-like. That ain't the act a somekin doin' the killing and hopin' to get out with it. The fact a the matter is, ya turned yerselves up, and that paints you in an even better light."

"But that's not enough to clear me." Atom crossed his arms in thought.

"Naw," Coffey said as she slapped the arm of her chair with a laugh. "I played through his security feed."

Atom cast a glance to Hither. Coffey caught the look and her smile fell.

"What's the tale on the table?" she asked.

"Not sure what you're talking about."

"I don't give a care who ya are, ain't somethin' a body on his hob does when surrounded by the departed. I ain't never crossed a soul who would lay out the dead and shroud 'em, only to accidentally flip the table and give it a good rub down.

"I have ya in a tough spot." She leaned in close and dropped her voice. "Ya level with me, ease my curiosity, and I might see to let you burn."

Rubbing his weary eyes, Atom willed the pounding in his temples to the background. "I'm a trader first, and bounty hunter if the job is right. Times might be that I merc a little if money is tight.

"I was hired to track down a derelict." He opened his eyes with a dog-tired expression. "It was supposed to be a simple information trail for a client, but I've had the imps crawling up my back twice now, and I had to shroud a family that had nothing to do with the violence that's been hanging on my vectors. With this last contact, the imps took one of my own."

Shi flicked an eyebrow at the comment, but remained silent.

Sinking back into her seat, Coffey crossed her arms and fixed Atom with a steady glare. Then her eyes drifted to Margo.

Kneeling in her seat, Margo smiled at the woman and lifted her juice with both hands.

"I wondered." Coffey's eyes lit with amazement. "It's you."

"Excuse me." Atom cocked his head.

"I'd heard rumors among the merch ships that occasionally drop orbit," she said as a slight smile pulled at the corner of her mouth. "Then we had an ore hauler from Shelley, free-holders returning from a Palm run.

"They like to trade for our fresh produce." She raised her glass. "We have some of the finest hothouses on this Finger."

"Shelley?" Atom's face remained passive.

"Yeah," Coffey said, taking a long swallow. "They told us how they'd won the rights to their moon, told tale of a merc who stepped in with his crew and threw the corp off their back."

"How does that relate to me?"

"That merc had a little girl. And while I can't place that merc's name right now, Atom Ulvan sounds a touch familiar."

"I suppose you are in the market for a merc?" said Hither.

Coffey shrugged. "I've a problem that slipped through the cracks."

"We're listening." Hither flashed a pleasant smile.

*   *   *

The crew sat around the table in various states of attention. Daisy and Hither engaged in quiet conversation, while Shi sat with Margo perched before her on the table. The gunslinger handled an unloaded arc-blaster, going over the parts with uncanny patience. Margo looked on, occasionally interjecting with playful curiosity.

Only Byron looked up from his streaming data manual when Atom walked into the galley with Coffey. He grinned, bobbed his head at the sheriff, and dropped his attention back to the information scrolling across his screen.

"As you can see, we're a lively bunch." Atom rolled his eyes as he offered Coffey the lone chair at the head of the table and slipped into the booth beside Shi.

The other's fell silent as Atom introduced the crew to Coffey.

"So, you said you had a job." Atom gestured to the crew. "We work as a team, no lone wolfs here.

"Our usual rate is fifty-thousand, half up front, half upon completion," he stated, leaning back in the booth so Margo could slip into his lap and rest her head on his chest. "It's not exactly the kind of job you keep postings on, but I can assure you, we have an excellent record."

"I want to keep this off the boards." Coffey sat with military rigidness. "Let's just say it goes against my normal judicial stance."

"How so?"

"I've a firebug named Johan Kim who slipped through the cracks on a technicality."

"He's free?"

"Not exactly." Coffey gritted her teeth. "He's serving two to six months on a minor offense charge."

"And he warrants more? Are you asking us to dig up more evidence so you can request a retrial?" Atom looked around the table at the others. "I've never been much of an investigator. It might be more helpful to find someone with that unique skillset."

"It's past that," Coffey growled.

Atom stroked Margo's dark hair and waited for the sheriff to continue.

"There won't be a retrial. He had the best counsel in the system. He shouldn't have been able to afford her, but somehow he got her, and she got his charges dropped from death to a minor offense."

"What did he do?" Shi asked without looking up from the arc-blaster.

"Toasted a transport."

"As in destroyed it?" Atom furrowed his brow.

"No, he rigged the atmo-recycler to pump out pure O2 on the down shift. The watch didn't notice it until a spark tripped. The ship structure contained the explosion, but every soul aboard, all twenty-seven of them, crisped."

"Any proof to link it to him?" Daisy interjected.

Coffey shook her head.

"Then how are you linking this to Kim?"

"He left a half-slagged bottle of Svit's brew sitting inside the atmo control panel."

The crew stared at her, waiting for the link.

"I tried to nail him for a similar job a few years back, but he slipped the system before I could apprehend. The two hundred cycle limit on charging passed, almost to the day," Coffey placed a clenched fist on the table and tapped the metal surface a couple times before pressing on. "Facial recognition pegged him that time. He was smarter this time."

"But he left the bottle, just to let you know it was him." Atom weighed the information. "I understand. Could you step down into the hold and let us discuss this before we commit to anything?"

Sheriff Coffey rose to her feet and headed towards the stairs, but paused at the hatch. With a worried look she turned back. "There's one other thing, a matter of payment."

"And that would be?" Atom asked in a neutral tone.

"I don't have access to that kind of money, but I could pay in information."

"Words don't put fuel in my ship or food in our bellies." Atom hid his disappointment behind a stern look.

"It has to do with that table you were so interested in." Coffey turned and exited the galley, slapping the hatch shut behind her.

"Gamble," said Hither with a playful arch to her brow.

"I like a gamble." Shi snapped a fresh cylinder in her pistol, spun it, and sighted across the mess to a pot sitting on the galley counter.

"What can she know beyond what we already have?" Byron piped up.

"She's been living in the same town as Blonde far longer than we've been on this rig. And while we're chasing a wisp, she knew the man with the information." Atom looked down at Margo snuggling into his chest. Her eyes drooped. "All in favor?"

Three hands rose. Only Byron hesitated. "I en't 'gainst it, so much as I just don' know which point to pull."

"Why don't you hop and get her, By." Atom nodded to the hatch.

*   *   *

They walked back toward the town tavern with Coffey a short time later.

"We've never been paid in information for a completed job." Atom walked with his hands thrust deep in the pockets of his worn, brown coat as the pram glided a pace before them. "How do we manage the half up front?"

The sheriff, at his side, hunched a shrug. "I can give you half the riddle now and half when you finish up."

"A riddle?"

"It was something Blonde told me a while back. Actually, the first time he shared it with me was when we were kids. His va made him memorize it and I helped him out. Fortunate for you, I have a fair good memory."

"Fair enough."

Pausing outside the tavern door, Coffey turned and looked up at Atom with the squint of a range-rider used to snow glare. "Do you want me to write it down or can you remember it?"

"If I don't, Kozue will."

"Who?"

Atom shook his head, trying to hide a shiver. "My ship's AI."

"I'll send it over to her." Coffey blinked several times in rapid succession, her eyes unfocused and distant. "There, did she receive?"

"I did, Atom," Kozue replied with a distracted air.

"Firm." Atom waved for the trailing crew to head through the doors into the warm embrace of the tavern even as he stayed in the chilled dome-air with Coffey. "Can you read it to me?" he asked the AI.

"Inside, a man mourns long lost sheep, break. Walking nowhere, but continues to weep, break. No one descended from nowhere above, break."

"Sheep?" He looked to Coffey.

She quirked her mouth in a half smile. "I asked Blonde the same question and he said it floated straight down from his grandva. I looked into the old codger later and he definitely weren't from around here. We don't do sheep."

"I guess it really is a riddle, because I don't have any idea of what we're looking at. That's it?"

"Those are three of the six lines. The other three will backend our deal."

"I'll get your man." Atom extended his hand, palm up. "It seems your riddle at least touches on some of the other information we've gathered. How did you know to give it to me and not the people who came for Blonde?"

"Well," She hitched her thumbs in her gunbelt. "First off, I ain't never seen 'em, but even if I did, I ain't habituated to workin' with folks as kill my friends." Turning to the tavern with a sad droop to her shoulders, she continued. "Second, Blonde told me if anyone ever looked to his table like you did, they'd be in the know and would have already piece bits from the old story."

"Old story?" Atom followed Coffey into the warm interior of the tavern with a grateful sigh.

"The Blonde family had only been here four gens." Coffey shucked her heavy coat and hung it on a rotating rack beside the door, but kept her wide-brimmed hat on her head. "The first Blonde dropped out of the sky back long before my time. My va said he had worked a berth aboard a scavver. For some strange reason, he seemed to like the notion of the quiet hab-farming life.

"Simple as that." She waved to Svitać as she wandered to the table the rest of the crew had claimed. Atom parked the pram beside the coat-rack and followed with Margo in the crook of his arm. "He found a local girl and settled."

"That's the story?"

"Every once in a while, when I was just a kit, Ol' Blonde would tipple a touch and tell tales of an old war." She drawled as she dropped into a seat Daisy slid out for her, and tipped her hat back. "He never went into detail on which war, but he talked about his ship going down with almost all hands. He always drank a toast to the Mother's lost souls.

"I never heard of a warship called the Mother, and over the course of his youth there were half-dozen wars over the Hand and honest to the void, I never really looked too careful," as she spoke Svitać brought a round to the table.

Atom held up a finger as Svitać dropped a juice in front of Margo. "Could I trouble you for a red chi with a drop of nectar?"

The barkeep bustled away with purpose. Atom pushed his beer over to Shi and gave Daisy a look. "This isn't the time to cut loose," he spoke with quiet command.

Daisy knuckled his brow with a grin and sipped. "Slow and low," the giant grumbled.

*   *   *

Later in the eve, while Daisy sat nursing his third beer in as many hours and the rest of the crew had shifted to less potent drinks, the lights dimmed and the dinner crowd drifted in from their scattered habs and jobs about town. The tavern grew louder and cozier in the span of a few minutes.

After the first round, Coffey wandered away to greet her people.

Leaning back in his seat, Atom closed his eyes and turned over the riddle in lieu of worrying at how Toks Marshall fit into the big picture.

"Enough," Atom sighed. "We can't make headway on the lost ship until we get the rest of that riddle. In the meantime, all we can focus on is the next step. Our task right now needs to be finding this boke, Kim."

"You kin help with that, right Koze?" Shi slipped from her seat and shifted around the table to lean against the wall. Crossing her arms, she stared through the crowded room.

"Firm," Kozue replied.

"First off, who is Johan Kim?" Atom asked, closing his eyes and listening.

"And more importantly." Daisy stared into his glass and swirled the dark liquid. "Where is he right now?"

"Kim is a system skipper," Kozue said. "He has a long list of petty crimes, but nothing he's ever found long incarceration for. Longest he's ever been away is a thirteen-month stint for smuggling. He was just the transport, but he gave up the limited information he had on the sellers and buyers.

"Kim appears intelligent," Kozue hesitated as she sifted through information. "On that charge, he kept blinds on both ends of the deal. That meant he gave up everything he had, but the information ultimately led nowhere."

"How'd he go firebat?" Atom opened his eyes with a pinched look and squinted at the loudening crowd. "Seems everything I've heard has pegged this boke as a low-level mover. It's a big jump from theft and smuggling to taking life. And the method means it's not a passion kill.

"He rigged that ship to fire in flight." Atom massaged his temples. "Nobody there to see it. That fire wasn't about fame or recognition or even fetish. That jug meant it was a message."

"A hit?" Hither asked.

"Seems as such. Questions: who was the target, why the escalation, and why the taunt to Margie?"

"Does it matter?" Daisy drained his glass and thumped it down on the table.

Atom scowled. "It could tell us if we have bigger fists to worry about or if this boke is just drifting into psychosis."

"I'm with Daisy on this one," Shi said as her eyes roamed the room. "We stay quiet, slip someone in, an' pop the someduck. Exfil and away to the Black. Nothin' bigger and nothin' on us that ain't already there."

"I wish Lilly was still with us," Atom said with a frown.

"Easier at the anonymous?" Hither asked.

Atom nodded.

"I've been toyin' wiff some t'oughts on tha matter," Byron said in a chipper tone. "That darl's whirled me gig."

"Spill," Atom sat up, curiosity driving the headache to the background.

"Couple options, to slip in prison we need a way to skip-trip facials." Byron flashed his cocky, half-smirk. "Meanin' we flip yer face or ghost yer face."

The others stared at him, waiting for the scheme to emerge.

Byron relished the theatrics a moment longer than necessary. "We could reconfigure wiff the medoc, that would alter yer features 'nough to slip past scans. Then we cook a new ident to match the face.

"On the dark side." Byron leaned closer. "Remember that gear the Astral Points fused ta their spines? I've been toyin' wiff it."

Before Atom could reply, the lights of the hall gave a slow flicker, like a landing pad strobe. A hush fell over the crowded room as everyone turned their attention to the unlit stage. Svitać hustled up the side stairs and out into the center where a floating spotlight caught him.

"Folks, we have a few minutes until the show starts," he said as he squinted into the light. "If anyone wants eats or drinks for the first act, now's the time. Once the lights've dropped the players have asked that we stay sittin' down. I think there's to be some action out 'mongst us. So, keep the kits out of the main aisle."

Svitać bobbed his head and trotted down to resume his post at the bar. A low murmur arose from the townsfolk as they waited. A few souls trotted up for last-minute refreshments and returned to their seats.

Then, Atom watched the lights fall and silence follow suit.

For a moment, the tavern sat shrouded in a darkness only broken by the dim lights behind Svitać's bar. Then a faint aura rose on the stage like the predawn light of a cloudy morn.

The stage remained empty, but a flicker of fog seeped along the floor.

A haunting wooden flute broke the silence. For a few measures the flute danced and settled the audience back in their seats, weighing heavily on their spirits. Then pipes skirled in, jerking Atom alive with fear and passion.

His hand crept to his pistol.

Shaking his head to clear his senses, Atom leaned forward in his seat and watched a stout actor appear in the center of the stage.

Standing motionless, the player let his eyes wander over the audience with intense scrutiny. A line divided his face into smiling black and groaning white.

He gathered himself, drawing up to his full, short stature. "Knucklers," he began in a deep, attention drawing baritone. "The Globe Players present The Seven Samurai of Verona, a tale from the lost dark of time before time. We tantalize with a tale set in the mythos of our people's storied past."

"What's a samooray?" Shi whispered as she dropped into her seat and turned her rapt eyes to the stage.

Atom shrugged.

"Our story is one of good versus evil; of tragedy and romance; of unselfish sacrifice and death." The man paused, leaned forward, and craned his neck to sweep the audience with a hard stare. "In a time of distant strife, a small village lay besieged by vicious demons that terrorized the humble peasants, stealing their food, and even snatching the odd wayward child."

The man grinned down at a young boy in the front row, causing his mother to clutch him close.

"What recourse had these poor folk on the frontier of their kingdom?" The thespian stepped back from the edge of the stage and threw his arms wide. "What choice had they, but to fight or die? But did they fight with sword and arrow? No, these weak peasants chose to fight with their minds … their minds and their food.

"Because, remember this if nothing else today, it's not always what you can do, but who you know.

"I set the scene as two of the common-folk have left their homes and traveled to a distant city in search of brave warriors to protect them from the demon-spawn that plague their people. In fair Verona, at a poor inn, these two farmers begin their journey to greatness."

The lights dropped.

Atom looked around, suspicion crawling beneath his skin. Then, with a hiccup of a holo-projector a busy street appeared behind two men hunched over wooden mugs at a rough-hewn table. Atom shrugged and turned his attention back to the scene and studied the actors as they stared into their drinks with the dejection of the damned.

Clambering from her seat in silence, Margo bypassed Daisy's lap to drop in the cradle formed by Atom's crossed legs.

"Wherever shall we find salvation?" one of the actors wailed, throwing his hand to his face as he over-acted the measure of despair plaguing his soul. "Five days we have dwelled in this wretched hovel in the hopes that our savior might happen by."

Margo snuggled into Atom's chest, enraptured by the players.

The back door flew open with a bang. Several yelps skittered from the audience as heads jerked to follow the course of a rugged swordsman. Margo gripped Atom's collar and stood with concern on her face, watching the man saunter through the dimmed audience only to hop up onto the stage with graceful ease.

The man nodded to the two sitting at the table and walked over to the bar, where he ordered a drink with the flip of a coin.

"What of him?" one of the farmers asked in a stage whisper.

"Look at his coat." His companion pointed out the newcomer's ragged brown coat. "He can't be good with a sword if he can't afford better duds than that."

Margo looked down at Atom's coat, gripped tight in her tiny hand, and then back to the stage in confusion. The others glanced over to see Atom's reaction to the actor and stage and his uncanny resemblance to their captain.

Atom cradled Margo to his chest and studied the scene with furrowed brow.

A well-dressed dandy waltzed in from the crowded street upstage, one hand on a flashy rapier and the other holding a handkerchief to his nose. "I was told there were gentlemen here in search of warriors," he declared to the audience.

"Dos bokes," the mother-clutched boy yelled from the front row.

"These men?" the dandy played to the audience.

"Yep." The boy beamed despite his mother's attempts to rein him in.

"But they look so …." His dramatic pause drew a rippling chuckle from the audience. "Poor.

"Surely you must be mistaken, my good lad," he continued speaking to the audience. "These cannot be the benefactors in search of a swordsman of my caliber." The dandy shrugged and pranced on his toes back to the table.

"Good day to you, gentlefolk. I am Indigo Skapulette," he said to the farmers with a flourishing bow. "I am the greatest swordsman who ever lived."

The two peasants stared up at the newcomer in awe.

"I hear you are in search of swordsmen for a worthy cause." Indigo turned downstage with a jaunty toss of his head. "For the right price, you may purchase my blade to take part in your crusade of justice."

"How do we know you are any good?" the first farmer asked.

"Is my name not enough?"

"I've never heard of you before." The second farmer's timid reply brought a look of disdain from the swordsman.

"You, there." Indigo turned from the table and verbally accosted the brown-coated man leaning on the bar, lost in his own world of thought. For a moment he remained aloof, unaware that words flew in his direction.

"I say, good man." Indigo crossed to the bar and made to slap the rough man's shoulder. "Would you care to—"

Before his hand landed, the mute stranger flipped out an arm and deflected the descending blow. Indigo lost balance, but shifted a foot to steady himself. He studied the man's back.

"Would you care to spar? A demonstration of skill for these gentlemen?" he said, straightening the ruffles of his fine, white shirt.

"Nope." The man drank deep from his wooden mug.

"It would just be a quick bout, a demonstration." Indigo stuck up his nose in disdain. "A mere showcasing of my skills for my future employers …."

Before he could finish his sentence, the brown-coated player spun into a well-choreographed dance/fight sequence. Atom watched with fascination as the pair tumbled and leaped about the stage with flashing swords and acrobatic martial arts.

Atom lost himself in the story.

* * *

As the stage-lights dropped and the tavern lights flickered back to life, Daisy turned to Atom with a puzzled expression etched across his dark face. "Should we be worried?" he asked.

"About what?" Atom slipped Margo from his lap and watched as she wandered over to a group of children who had congregated in the center aisle of the ad-hoc theater. "Do you think that's somehow supposed to be us? I see what you're saying with the brown coat and masterful skills of death, but we don't use swords.

"Closest I've come to that was Shi's friend back on Oligump." He rose from his metal seat and stretched his back. "But there wasn't any real fighting with that, unless you count the grass Margo cut."

"Atom." Daisy shifted from his seat, mountainlike, and stepped around Shi to stand beside Atom. "I know there are seven of them, but don't you see any similarities?"

"It's a play, Daisy. Even if there are similarities, what are you worried about?"

Daisy frowned. He looked down to Shi and Hither. Atom glanced at them as well, waiting to see which side of the discussion they would fall on.

They shrugged and rose to push past the two men, making their way to join a growing line at the bar where the staff scrambled to fill drink orders and serve up snacks to the entire township.

Seeing the open bar, Daisy forgot his worries and grinned his way from Atom.

"Daisy," Atom caught the pilot's attention as he began to burrow his bulk into the crowd. "Moderation." Atom mimed a drink and although Daisy scowled for a moment, he nodded back in understanding.

Atom dropped back into his seat and turned his attention to the table.

"Thoughts?" he asked Byron without taking his eyes from the interlocking rings of condensation.

"What's to worry, darl? They pulled a few taskets leanin' towards you. Don't mean they know you is you."

"What if they're trying to get my attention?"

"You or us?" Byron sat curled in his chair with his knees tucked under his chin. He picked absently at a loose strap on his boot.

"Well, it's not often that you're the one lining up the jobs."

"I'd like to say overwise, but en't so."

Atom leaned forward, propping his elbows on the table as he watched Margo play with the other children. He marveled at children and their ability to find universal games to share in every port of call.

The children scampered about the hall, but kept their distance from the stage where a pair of players perched and watched the refreshment line.

As the line shortened, one of the thespians leapt to his feet. "Gentlekin," he called out over the hubbub. "It appears we are drawing close to the start of the second act." His gaze lingered a moment longer than necessary on Atom. "At the conclusion of tonight's rendition, we would welcome a chance to meet our audience."

Atom narrowed his eyes as the man moved on with his theatrics.

Led by Daisy, who carved a path as a human ice-breaker, Shi and Hither returned to their seats, slipping around Atom with their hands full of food and drink. With her eyes focused on the darkening stage, Hither handed Atom a chilled blue-chi and Byron a steaming bowl of fried onions smothered in a spicy sauce.

In the same moment, the tavern lights winked out, leaving the prattling thespian illuminated in the computerized spotlight.

"We left our valiant samurai in their distant village," the narrator spoke as shadowed players took positions in the dim background. "With a savage horde of foemen bearing down on them, our heroes stood as a stone bulwark before their peasant friends.

"Though they only numbered seven, history and skill strengthened their resolve."

"Bleh, bleh, bleh," Byron muttered. "Less talky, more flippy."

Atom chuckled.

Daisy cast Atom another look as the lights on the stage lifted to reveal the brown-coated hero squared off with a squatty villain with golden curls.

"Did you stab my horse, sir?" the brown-coat demanded.

"No, sir." The villain rested his hand on his sword. "But I did stab a horse, sir."

"I shall ask again." The brown-coat advanced. "Did you stab my horse, sir?"

"Nay, I but removed a leg, sir."

Swords flashed and, in the fray, one of the heroes lost their leg, leaving the brown-coat to drag that hero to safety as the others beat a defensive retreat across the stage.

Shi coughed.

The play rocked with action from the first confrontation between the seven warriors and the merciless marauders. Fight after fight rolled across the stage, each instance of acrobatic swordplay outdoing the previous. As the play reached its climax, the seven samurai of Verona faced down the frumpy dandy, and even though several heroes fell in valiant acts of self-sacrifice, the protagonists emerged victorious.

Then with final flair, the brown-coated hero wandered into a faux sunset with the daughter of the village chief riding the horse at his side.

As the final, virtual curtain fell, the audience erupted into cheers and applause.

"Still think that's us?" Atom asked before placing his fingers in his mouth and blasting an ear-rending whistle.

Daisy glanced to Shi and shrugged.

"None of ours died." Atom grinned as the players emerged from behind their backdrop to take their final bows.

* * *

Atom eyed Daisy with concern. Even as the captain sat at their table, the pilot threw down another glass of clear liquid and thumped his fist on the bar. Surrounding Daisy, a trio of burly farmers matched his drink and let out a group howl.

"Should we be worried?" Hither asked. She sat across the table from Atom, legs crossed, with her foot bouncing in time to the soft music that fluttered from the speakers hovering over their heads. Somehow, she projected an air of class despite her plain maroon dress and black furred boots.

"Reckin we're past that point," Shi chuckled and shook her head.

"Unfortunately," said Atom.

"Atom, why are we hanging around this place?" Hither asked. "Don't we have a head to collect if we're going to make progress on the Mother?"

"I'm waiting."

"For …?"

Atom shrugged.

"Trouble?" Shi pulled one of her pistols and checked the load and mechanisms with habitual efficiency.

"I'm not reading that at the moment. I'm waiting for the someone who wanted the word with us." He inclined his head to the bar where one of the players sat at the far end from Daisy and his crowd. "I'm just not sure if Daisy is going to complicate the evening."

As he spoke, a trio of thespians hopped down from the stage and wound their way through the near empty tavern. The families had long since departed and only a few of the single farmhands had remained behind. Making their way to the bar, the two men and lone woman laughed with each other, their words muffled by the artificial dampers hanging from the ceiling.

They leaned against the bar between Daisy's group and the solitary player.

Atom watched as Daisy's attention drifted to the female player. A small smile played over his face as he leaned over and slurred an offhanded compliment to the woman.

"Atom." Shi rolled the cylinder of her pistol as she cocked her head.

"Daisy may have bitten more than he can chew," Atom replied.

Across the dining area, Daisy slipped closer to the woman and laughed as he reached a hand towards the small of her back. Faster than Atom could register, Daisy found his face flat on the floor. Neither of the men had moved to interpose. The female player, all five feet of her, held Daisy's hand twisted and cocked at an angle that verged on dislocating his shoulder as she applied her foot behind his back.

Surprise and pain laced the roar erupting from Daisy's incoherent lips.

He pushed to rise with his other arm.

Atom winced at the pop that snapped across the room over the ambient music. As he watched, Svitać drifted to the far end of the bar.

Cursing as he rose to his feet, Atom paused and watched in amazement as Daisy reached over his back with his own viper strike and wrenched the woman's ankle, throwing her off balance and forcing her to release the hold on his damaged arm.

Daisy rose, a dark force of nature, and turned to face the woman. Behind him, the group of farmers had melted into the night as quick as rats before a fire.

For a brief moment, Atom hesitated. He looked into Daisy's eyes and found cold calculation. The drunken smile had vanished, replaced by something that sent a shiver down Atom's spine.

"Move," he hissed to his remaining crew.

Even as they sprang to action, a blade and a pistol appeared in the hands of the two men at the bar. The blade hovered at Daisy's throat while the gun trained with steady discipline at the center of Daisy's mass.

The female player, sensing the motion of the crew behind her, spun in a smooth pirouette, a blaster in each hand, trained outward.

"Nice toothpick." Daisy grinned as the tip of the blade tickled his Adam's apple.

Shi split left and Hither right with their pistols readied. They moved in silence, like gliding wraiths waiting for a moment to pounce on an unwary soul.

The player's blasters tracked their movements.

Atom stepped between the flankers. He stopped five paces from the player and flipped his jacket back from his own rail-pistol. Cocking his head with a slight, predatory scowl, he made eye contact with the woman.

She froze.

Daisy leaned into the point of the knife. He continued grinning down at the man who held him. The knife-wielding player stood several inches shorter than Daisy, and at least three of him could have hidden behind Daisy's broad shoulders. The man held firm as the tip of the blade parted Daisy's flesh and a trickle of blood slipped down the knife.

The player with the gun cast a glance over his shoulder to where the elder player still sat, sipping at his drink.

"Daisy." Margo stepped from behind her father. "Where's Mae?"

Daisy hesitated.

The spell of violence broke. The clarity of Daisy's vision drifted as a cloud scudding low over the sea. He rocked back on his heels, away from the knife and turned back to the bar.

Ignoring the others, he poured a hefty drink from the bottle and drained it. He closed his eyes and relaxed his back, cradling the wounded arm at an awkward angle. Then he flopped the arm across the bar, gripped the far side, and leaned back with agonizing slowness. With his off hand, he massaged at his shoulder.

Atom watched in amazement as the joint shifted, ground, and popped back into socket.

Daisy sighed and poured another drink.

Margo crossed the potential battleground and tried to climb the stool beside Daisy. After two unsuccessful attempts to mount the seat, she frowned and tugged at Daisy's pant leg. Without looking, he reached down and hoisted her by the back of her pint-sized coveralls. Depositing her on the stool, he poured himself another drink, but his time, he sipped at the contents.

"Mae should be back aboard the *Ticket*," he slurred.

"Mae come wiff us?" Margo leaned forward, kneeling on the stool with her arms and belly resting on the bar-top as she craned her neck to stare up at Daisy.

The others stood like an uncertain tableau. The three players flanked by Atom and his two Valkyrie watched the interaction with bated breath. Sensing the passing of the moment, Atom flipped his coat down over his pistol and stalked to the far end of the bar. He passed the three thespians with guarded steps as he slipped onto the stool beside the elder.

At a grunt from the woman, the weapons disappeared and the three actors drifted to the bar, giving Daisy a wide berth. Behind them, Hither and Shi eased up and backed to their table, never taking their eyes from the players.

"That's one way to make introductions." Atom waved to Svitać and a steaming mug of chi appeared with magical swiftness.

"Can't say I enjoyed any of it." The elder thespian sat with hands folded on the bar, his eyes unfocused on the long mirror at the barkeep's back.

"Name's Atom."

"I know," the old man murmured as Svitać placed a bowl of thick stew on the counter.

"Then why the test?"

"I've heard of you and your crew. I wanted to see how you reacted to threat. Evidence points to the stories being true. The crew of the *One Way Ticket* functions as a whole. That's not something to be taken lightly. You are a foe I would not care to face, ever.

"I know you had a mark on Lilly. I also know that the Genkos took it back and replaced you with Toks Marshall. They believe Marshall has a greater reach." The old man slurped at his stew without looking at Atom. "Do you know where Lilly is right now?"

Atom perched on his stool. He lifted the steaming mug without answering and held the drink to his face, savoring the dark, spiced scent of the chi as it swirled up to him. For a moment of silence, he studied the eddies of the caffeine-infused liquid. Then he cast a sidelong glance to the actor.

"Not at the present. We've crossed courses a few times." Atom shrugged and sipped at his chi. "She seems fair good at not being found if she doesn't want to be.

"First time I met her, I had no idea it was her. The second time, she put me down harder than anyone I've met in years. Third time we ran into each other, she hitched a ride out of a hot-zone only to ghost as soon as we were clear. Or Toks may have plucked her. I honestly haven't a clue as to where she is.

"I can't say I'm disappointed the Genko's pulled my bounty," Atom said as he set the mug down with a weary thump. "So, what is she to you?"

The man scooped a spoonful of his stew and looked over to Atom with an impassive expression. He took time chewing. "She's nothing to me personally," he said, studying Atom's profile for a moment before turning back to his bowl. "I'm just a lowly messenger, sent to find you."

Atom turned a suspicious glare on the old man.

"Easy, son." The thespian held his hands over his bowl, somewhere between warming them and showing their peaceful nature. "I just have a message for you. My master sent me to track you down and invite you to a sit down. Nothing firm, and it's not a setup. He just wants to see if you'd be interested in a job.

"Trouble is, he's not the sort that fancies showing his face unnecessarily. He's private, if you catch my vapors." The man eased another bite of stew from the bowl without taking his eyes from Atom. "He doesn't appreciate eyes on him."

"If you have interest, here are the coords." The actor slipped a small chip from a pocket and set it on the board beside Atom. "He will be at this point for seventy-two standard revs."

The man pushed his bowl away and nodded thanks to Svitać before rising from the stool.

For a time, Atom sat and stared at the chip.

Then he moved his attention back to his cooling mug. He brooded. Ignoring the tiny, blinking chip, he instead savored the last warmth of his bittersweet chi. Atom weighed the tumult of the past weeks and the path the crew seemed to blindly follow.

"What's that?" Hither's question reined his wandering mind.

"Custom wants a meet," he said, turning to her as his eyes quirked with question. "Not sure who they are or what they want, but the messenger mentioned Lilly."

"Genkos?"

He shook his head.

"New players then. They want to meet here?"

Atom shrugged and gestured to the coord chip on the counter.

"Nope." She squinted at the data popping up on the chip. "It's this sector, but looks to be on the far side of Klavir, in the planet's shadow."

"That place is death."

"You've been?"

"A lifetime ago." Atom slipped the coord chip from Hither's fingers and scowled at it in his palm. "I took a trip there on imperial orders. It's a water world. Grav is too high. It makes the surface like quicksand. Surface pressure is too high, but for some reason people keep on living there."

"Money?"

"Crab. Something about the high pressure infuses the meat with more flavor than any other planet in this Finger."

"But it's dangerous?" Hither asked.

"They die young down there." He pocketed the chip and dropped a coin on the counter beside his empty mug as he untangled his lanky legs from the stool. Spinning, he leaned back on his elbows and looked at Hither. "At least we don't have to go down to that planet. It's so wet and heavy, it's hard to tell the difference between above water and under.

"How far out from the planet do the coords take us?" he asked.

"Well beyond the grav-well." Hither's refined posture cast an interesting dynamic beside Atom's slouched form.

"Good," Atom grunted.

"Will this carry us closer to either of our goals?"

"Well, we'll be off this rock, which puts us a burn closer to both, but we're still in-system, so we won't be making much headway."

"I see." Dejection tinged her voice. "I was hoping we were planning on staying here a day or two. It almost feels like a vacation when I can do anything that doesn't involve me sitting on a ship." She slipped from her stool and cast a smile towards Daisy as the pilot sat listening to Margo's toddler dialogue with drunken intensity.

"Or involve getting shot at." Atom nodded to the three thespians nursing their drinks with open wariness.

"That's the dream, Cap." She patted his shoulder. "A sweet and very distant dream."

"We'll always have Vali."

"Too far away, and yet ...." A distant smile creased her face. "If I close my eyes and concentrate, I can almost feel the sun on my skin and my toes in the sand."

"La, that en't happenin' a'time soon." Byron wandered past on his way to join Daisy and Margo. "This 'ere rock's too murcked wiff snow 'n ice ta even dream 'bout beaches. Closest you'll get's windburn out on the pack."

Atom chuckled as Byron leaned a chummy shoulder into Hither's side.

"Who invited you to my dream?" Hither snapped, turning on the mech. She glowered at him with evil intent.

"I've the same dream most darks since we left Vali," Byron sighed and Hither relaxed. "I still can't get the picture a you glowin' in the sun out a me pan, laid out in next to nuffin."

Hither lunged for Byron, but the boy anticipated and slipped just beyond her fingertips with a sharp laugh. As he darted across the near empty dining-hall with Hither a step behind, the atmo-seal on the door parted.

Byron skidded to a halt at the feet of a severe woman.

"I don't aim to interrupt your game." The woman shook the cold from her greatcoat.

Hither slipped over to lay a protective hand on Byron's shoulder, even as she curtsied with deep respect. "Sorry, ma'am." She kept her head down in humble demeanor, but cast a sidelong glance to Atom as she turned and guided Byron back to their table. "Din' mean to cause no troubles, ma'am."

Atom, leaning back on the bar, took everything in.

"No trouble on my end," the woman said in a pleasant tone as she shed her coat and folded it over her arm with a crisp, minimalist touch.

Atom arched an eyebrow at the fresh-pressed uniform beneath the coat. With a dismissive sigh, he turned back to the bar and waved to Svitać for another mug of chi. Ignoring the woman's presence, he rested his weary head in his hand as he waited.

Behind him, the woman stared at Atom's lean form with a chill smile.

"Atom Ulvan," she declared. Her Cheshire grin failed to reach her eyes. "What a pleasant surprise."

"Toks." Atom took the fresh mug from Svitać and stared into its depths, but shifted his seat enough to free his pistol from his coat without moving his hands. "What brings someone of your prestige this far from the Palm?"

Toks Marshall draped her damp greatcoat over a chair as she approached the bar. As she drew close, Atom noted the worn nature of her immaculate, white uniform. Despite the old clothing, she projected a feral, if caustically thin image. Only her large, icy blue eyes, magnified by thick, square glasses presented a clashing perspective to the lines and angles that defined the imperial captain.

"On a bit of a treasure hunt." Toks sidled up to the bar, but kept her eyes locked on Atom as she raised a finger to Svitać. "Ice grass wodka, neat."

Atom sipped his chi and glanced over at the woman. "Sounds interesting."

Toks measured Atom as Svitać poured.

"This official business?" Atom asked.

"On the side, but above board. I cleared with Admiralty before committing. The Genkos pay well enough for the higher-ups to agree." She barked out a harsh laugh. "Does it hurt knowing I took over your contract after Lilly slipped past you on that back-channel dumping ground?"

"Hurt my business a touch, but pride's still intact," Atom replied.

"I know what she was getting into …." Toks left the statement dangling as Svitać slid the glass down the bar. "I know why she's so important."

"Just a mark, Toks. Genkos pulled my contract, so I've got no reason to care."

"I know you spoke with Johansen." She picked up her glass and with a spider's grace, slipped her long legs around the stool beside Atom. She sipped her drink. Then, appraising it with a pleased frown, she threw the liquid down her throat and tapped at the bar to regain Svitać's attention.

The barkeep wandered back from where he conversed with Daisy and poured a second dram of the local spirit.

"I can only assume the merc passed on information I could have used," she said.

Atom set his mug down and turned to Toks. "And what information would that be? And are you admitting to killing a civie without provocation?"

"No, of course not," Toks said with an easy laugh. "I studied the recordings."

"Then you know what he said. He rambled about his shepherd. I'm assuming he was trying to get me to save his soul or at least reach out to his priest. Beyond that, I couldn't tell you a shepherd from a cowboy.

"I was after that bounty on Lilly. It would have been a solid fifty-thousand ko. But thanks to you, that fell through and now I need to find another way to feed my crew.

"Is there something more to this that I should know about? Is there something you want to tell me that should get me upset? Because the way I see things, you just happen to be the boke that snatched a job from me. Beyond that, there's not a whole lot I care to be talking to you about." His hand dropped and he traced a finger along the grip of his pistol. "Is there a reason I should feel slighted on the way things fell out?

"You know me, I have no qualms about shooting first," he said with a dark grin.

Toks met his gaze. A smile tugged at the corners of her mouth. "Oh, you know, information that may, or may not, relate to the final resting place of the *Ave Maria*. I'm specking he let something slip with that dying breath.

"I can't imagine he would let information like that go with him to the Black." Toks leaned forward, taunting Atom with her closeness. "Would you?"

Despite her clean uniform, Atom caught the faint scent of sweat, an engineering bay, and an exotic spice. He narrowed his eyes. Then he pulled his hand from his gun, instead raising it to scratch his jaw in thought.

"*Ave Maria*? You don't say." A vulpine smile spread across his face. "So that's what he meant.

"Thanks, Toks." He spun and hopped to his feet before glancing back at the Imperial captain. Her smile faded into the bottom of her cup. "By the way, you know that legit merc died at the hands of imperials. I can only assume that as the only imperial presence in the sector, they were your troops. That means you must have approval."

Toks drained her cup and slammed it down hard enough to crack the base.

"Did you have a warrant to call in a death strike?" Atom watched the tension drain from Toks' narrow shoulders.

"I don't know what you're talking about." The smile returned to her face as a touch of humor crept into her voice, like an inside joke had flashed through her mind. "You know I arrived in system after the incident. In fact, I recall you fleeing the scene of the massacre."

"If you aren't involved, then what are you doing here?"

Toks rose to her feet and squared with Atom. She bristled. Staring him down for a moment, then the smile pinched her eyes behind their glasses. "I'm just patrolling my sector and following a knotted string in my spare time, Atom. Surely you remember the doldrums of the endless patrol?

"With Admiralty approval I'm tracking a known fugitive. The fact that she is just the end of that knotted string doesn't mean a thing.

"I'm touching the end of my cycle and I happened upon a distress call from Gomori Alpha. I responded. I reviewed the vids," she said as the smile drifted, replaced by something bordering on relief. "I just need to get through this, catch that fugitive, and end my loop without anything exploding in my face. We accomplish that and burn for the Palm.

"I know everything's more expensive up there, but I hate the way everything crawls out here. Life is too slow with too much black between the spots of life.

"I need more life around me, Atom." She leaned in, like an old friend and confidant. "That's why I'm following up on the incident and seeing where the information takes me. I'm pushing through as quick as a marcher. Ain't a thing in the Black will slow me down and keep me from taking my crew home.

"And I'm hoping to do it with our accounts a touch heavier." Her smile grew wider.

"Nothing to slow you? Not even a trail of death?" Atom crossed his arms. "You and I both know that complicates things. Paperwork takes time."

"Out of my jurisdiction." Toks shrugged in innocence. "Which I can't imagine them asking for. Nobody likes higher-ups interfering in anything. Locals are perfectly capable of wrapping up a few dead bodies far more efficiently than I could ever hope to do."

Atom stared, trying to plot her trajectory.

"Unless you have some information you'd like to pass on from your Lilly investigation," Toks said, crossing her arms with a shrug. "From one hunter to another, you know, professional courtesy. The bounty will be a nice little bonus, regardless of anything else we find on this loop."

"I had the bounty and had it pulled." Atom thrust his hands in his coat pockets, hunching in as a defeated look dragged his features down. "Not much I can do with it now and you have the same information I had."

"Then you aren't much use to me, are you?" Toks pouted, but her eyes flashed with an icy chill that mirrored the weather above the dome.

Before Atom could reply, Toks pointed a finger at his chest and a long, blue spark leaped across the narrow space.

Pain arched Atom's back.

With a jerk, his muscles contracted and he wiped out several stools as he flopped to the floor. There he spasmed and twitched like a fresh-landed fish. Tears stood out as his face locked in a mask of agony.

"Arrest this man," Toks announced to the room as she retrieved her greatcoat. She swung it around to set on her shoulders like a cloak of authority. "It is unlawful to threaten an imperial officer. Furthermore, he slandered the name of our righteous emperor and is wanted as a person of interest in the terror attack on Gomori Alpha."

Before she finished speaking, a double squad of armored assault troops in familiar red amor burst through the door.

Without thought, Daisy hoisted Margo over the bar into Svitać's arms. The barkeep looked stunned for a split second before he dropped to the floor, expecting violence. Behind the safety of the heavily reinforced metal of the bar, he tucked the child into a small cubby.

Margo stared at the barkeep with wide eyes, but remained silent.

Daisy had no such qualms.

With a drunken roar, the bear launched himself off his stool into the press of troopers.

"Non-lethal force," Toks called out in a pleasant, sing-song voice as a pair of troopers flew across the room to slam into the bar with a resounding crack. "We don't want any citizens of the empire to be permanently damaged."

She crouched beside Atom's still twitching form as Daisy carved a hurricane-like path through the troopers. She patted

Atom's cheek and wiped away a stray tear. With a mocking salute she rose to leave. Circumventing Daisy's scrum, she trotted to the door, pausing to scowl at the scattered occupants of the bar with a measured glare.

"When you're done subduing these terrorists, turn them over to the local constabulary. Less paperwork." She quirked a smile and swept through the doors.

Daisy fought on.

*   *   *

Atom fought the darkness again.

Flashes of restraints, scent of dogs, cold. Visceral emotions laced through the pinwheel images as they fluttered by.

Eventually, Atom's senses returned and he found himself slumped on a metal bench beside Daisy. A single, heavy gauge plastic shackle bound him to the seat. Atom jerked against the cuff as the sudden sensory rush threatened to overwhelm him.

"Easy, Cap." Daisy reached a steadying arm around Atom's shoulders. "You've been out a while. I'm surprised they didn't take you direct to the medoc."

"Where are we?" Atom squeezed his eyes shut, rubbing the grit away with his free hand.

"Processing."

Across the room, a fit-looking officer sat behind a small desk, plinking away, single fingered, at an archaic keyboard as he squinted at the monitor in front of him. The man scowled and looked as if he wanted to punch through the screen.

"I'll wrap as soon as I enter your information," the officer said, scratching his shaved head with a purple gloved hand. "Then I'll toss you upstream."

"But, where are we?"

The man's index finger hesitated as he tore his glare away from the terminal. Atom met the man's gaze with placid eyes.

"System lock-up," Daisy answered for the officer.

Atom eased back against the wall, his head ringing from the repeat trauma of the past days. He kept his eyes on the man, studying him, plotting. The man's short-sleeved uniform revealed a tapestry of glowing tattoos down his left arm. Skulls and shadowed figures slithered along the curve of muscle.

"What's the story with your art?" Atom asked.

Again, the words seemed to interrupt the man's thoughts as his finger froze over the keyboard. "We all face the reaper at some point," the officer growled, looking down at his arm.

"Have you?"

"Once," the office said as he rolled his arm, displaying the tattoo with a brash cockiness. "I faced down death and won."

"My name is Atom Ulvan." Atom leaned forward. "Meriwether."

"Thanks, I was just going to ask your name. I'll make a note that you're cooperating when I send you on up."

The man's face blanched and his eyes saucered.

"I see facial is matching up." Atom flashed a feral grin.

The officer, face a ghastly pale, rose to his feet and scurried from the room, careful to never turn his back on the seated Atom.

"What'd he see?" Daisy asked as soon as the door hissed shut.

Atom shrugged. "I'm guessing the part of my record that isn't sealed."

"Just part?" Daisy cast a sidelong glance at Atom.

"It was enough. Most of what I did in my past life is sealed up in imperial archives somewhere. Even disgraced, they don't want that information floating free." Atom chuckled as he closed his eyes and leaned his head back against the wall. "The only problem now is that facial gives us a countdown clock. They are going to be obligated to pass this further up the chain than they thought.

"System lock-up is where we want to be," Atom said as he glanced up at a series of cameras bracketing the room. "They should cut you loose on drunk and disorderly, but they'll call Toks back from wherever she is on her loop to take me into custody and transport me back to the Palm.

"I'm guessing she wasn't anticipating me revealing my ID. She just wanted us out of the way, but this might throw a spanner in her pipe.

"I just bought myself some time," Atom leaned in and whispered with a conspirator's ease. "When they release you, I want you to collect the bounty and head for Mei Ling's. When I get out, I'll meet up with you there and we can move forward. Just make sure you give the bounty to Kozue."

Atom sat back up as the door flashed open. He rested his eyes again.

The ashen officer stood flanked by a pair of armored assault troops. "Atom Ulvan of the Meriwether Han," his voice quaked. "You will be placed in solitary in the system prison until such time as the Imperial Governor sees fit to send an escort ship to retrieve you and return your person to the Imperial Court."

Without hesitation, the two troopers levelled their weapons at Atom's face.

"Any provocation will free us to terminate with lethal force." The officer swallowed on a dry throat and somehow managed to suppress a choking cough.

"Easy there, skipper," Atom said without opening his eyes. "I imagine the Emp might be touched if you didn't return his favorite toy in one piece. Plus, if I'd wanted you dead, I'd be walking out of here right now with your sidearm in my hand."

The troopers recoiled and the officer trembled.

Atom laughed.

*   *   *

Atom sat in his cell, alone and in silence. Occasionally, a faint voice echoed from the outside, from the open yard between the tiers of cells. Atom could have looked down on the congregating prisoners through the narrow window of the cell door, but he remained seated, cross-legged on his bunk.

He stared at the wall.

The silence proved oppressive.

Thoughts came to prison to die.

Alone in his head, he wandered and waited.

Time refused to pass.

Despite his words of bravado, Atom wilted inside. He estimated mere hours had passed, but with no way to judge time, his estimations proved as accurate as jump coordinates missing one of the four dimensions.

Eventually, Atom curled in on himself. He tried to craft a plan. Without thought he pulled the thin, plastic blanket up around his shoulders for comfort, not warmth.

"No blankets until lights out." A guard stifled a yawn as he peered into the cell.

Atom nodded and tossed the blanket into a loose pile at the foot of the bed. He waited, listening as the guard's heavy boots echoed away on the metal walkway. Rolling onto his back and lacing his fingers behind his head, Atom stared at the shoddy paint job of the ceiling. The footsteps disappeared within half-a-dozen steps, fading into a void of silence.

A whispered word floated up from the yard below, but nothing more.

Then a faint grinding drifted from somewhere above, like hard plastic on metal. A weapon being crafted or nervous insanity manifesting, Atom wondered.

The phantasm of sound ended.

Atom closed his eyes, listening to each breath, each beat of his heart, the soft ringing in his ears from years of combat explosions.

Somewhere around beat seven hundred, he drifted off.

*   *   *

Kozue stood over him, her silken hair drifting around her face as the soft autumn breeze stirred the embers deep in the fire.

She said, "I miss this every summer." She smiled and wandered around the broad stones of the firepit to rest a hand on his shoulder. "The first fire of the autumn chill is always the best. Fires in summer are fun, but they just make you hot instead of making you comfortable."

Atom leaned his head down, resting his cheek on his wife's hand.

"I wish I could steal this weather and pull it out for just the two of us to enjoy." A gentle kiss on her fingertips echoed his words.

"I wish we could steal this moment."

Striking like a panther, Atom snatched Kozue into his lap and enfolded her in his arms. He did not kiss her as expected, instead, he snuggled her into the fold of his neck and breathed her scent. Atom closed his eyes and savored all of his wife.

He locked each morsel of the moment away in his mind to pull out and reminisce.

"I love you," Kozue murmured, reaching up to cup a soft hand over Atom's cheek.

*   *   *

"Atom," Kozue whispered. "Are you awake?"

Atom took in a deep breath, opening his eyes from his nap and found Kozue astride him. She leaned forward so her dark hair canopied over them.

She smiled down.

With a languid stretch, Atom returned the smile. "I am now," he grumbled, his voice sleep deepened. "How long was I out?"

"Long enough," she said with a throaty laugh and leaned down to plant a kiss that bordered on violent. Atom's eyes flashed wide before drifting closed as he attacked the kiss with similar vigor.

"I needed that," Atom cleared his throat as Kozue reared back with her hands planted on his chest. "I miss you, Koze. You've been gone so long."

Atom lifted his chin and Kozue nuzzled in, leaving a trail of kisses.

"I'm here now, that's what matters," she whispered.

"Um, Atom," Kozue said with concern.

Atom's eyes flew open.

Kozue sensed the shift in tension and settled back. Her fluid, sensual movements tugged at a buried part of Atom's soul as she cocked her head. She bit her lip as her eyes narrowed with concern.

"Is everything all right?" she asked.

"That's not me," Kozue whispered in Atom's ear.

Atom stared up at Kozue.

"Who are you?" Atom asked, his voice low.

"I'm Kozue, silly." The woman traced a fingertip down Atom's chest with a grin. "Your wife."

Atom shook the sleep from his brain. "My wife is dead. I watched her die with my own eyes. And I know for certain that this isn't a dream."

"Are you so certain?"

"I wouldn't dream myself back in the prison cell I'd fallen asleep in."

With strong, firm hands, Atom gripped the woman at the waist and lifted her from him. Blowing out a deep breath, he sat up and swung his legs off the bunk. The likeness of Kozue stepped back to stand beside the cracked cell door and dropped her head.

"Have I displeased?" Her voice came as a faint plea.

"She is a very close replica," Kozue, the AI imprint of his wife, puzzled. "But the timbre of her voice is a touch lower than anything in my database."

"Lilly," Atom failed to hide the disappointment from his voice even as he took a deep breath to drag his desires back under control. "How did you get in here? And for the love of the Hand, why did you have to go and dredge up a memory like that?"

While the image of Kozue remained, her manner flipped like a page turned in a book. Her smile returned, but instead of Kozue's demure, controlled attitude a reckless flair leapt into being. Lilly flicked her long dark hair back over her shoulder. Then, with a playful smile, she spun and dropped to the bed beside Atom.

"Figured it would be a fun test." She leaned back on her elbows and kicked her feet out.

"Skirling my emotions is fun?"

"Maybe fun is the wrong word choice, but you must admit, it was a pretty solid test of my skills. I almost had you," she said, nudging Atom in the ribs.

Atom refused to look down at Lilly as he fought to control his emotions.

"Plus, you owed me for mucking up our first meeting. You weren't the one I was crying for." She sat up and flicked her lower lip with a fingertip.

"I owe you?" Atom growled.

"Well, I let those bokes follow me out of the bar and think they had the upper hand."

Atom swiveled his head at her in confused disbelief.

"I was planning on Gims coming to look for me. Find me crying. Then he was supposed to carry me back to the bar to play on the feeling of that other crew. My sources indicated that group had some connections to Johansen's merc crew. They were going to be my in with Johansen, but you got there first."

"You just let them rape you?" Atom demanded.

Lilly shrugged. "Trade secret. But I've done worse to get the information I needed." She gave a light laugh. "Remember, I got married."

Atom shook his head, incredulous. "How did you even get in here? I'm in solitary, waiting transport back to Toks."

Lilly, in Kozue's visage, shrugged. "Trade secret."

Atom shook his head in frustration. He thumped his head against the wall and closed his eyes with a sigh. "Could you please not wear that face?" he asked in a pained voice. "I can't focus when I'm looking into the eyes of my dead wife."

"I can respect that," said Lilly. Atom heard her take a deep breath. "It's ok now."

"Thanks." Atom cracked one eye and relaxed when he found Lilly tugging her green-tipped hair back into a ponytail. She looked at him, her face her own, but somehow plainer.

Atom cocked his head in question.

As if reading his mind, she rolled her eyes. "Looks get noticed. It's good to be invisible, especially in here."

"I'm sorry I can't look at Kozue's face."

"Don't fret it. I really just wanted to see how I stacked against the past." She left the bed and dropped to a crouch with her back leaning against the far wall of the narrow cell. "Now that I know a little of your pain, I'm on to the important bits. I'm guessing you made some headway on our little venture."

"Atom," Kozue interrupted. "I've just made a link between your nanos and Daisy's. He is on the move and headed in this direction."

"What is it?" Lilly fixed Atom with a puzzled look.

"I've a lot in my hold at the moment, the least of which is your half-cocked treasure hunt." Atom rose to his feet and passed Lilly to peek out through the open door. "The other items are on a tighter schedule than what you've brought me."

"Tighter than Toks trying to kill us?"

No guards patrolled Atom's level, but he heard voices from the enclosed yard below. "She's on the back end of a loop that should take her on an opposing vector."

Lilly rolled her eyes again. "And you believe that?"

Atom snapped his head back to fix Lilly with a questioning glare.

"I'm guessing you don't know as much about Toks Marshall as you think," she said, sliding herself up the wall with a strange, serpentine grace and padded over to stand beside Atom in the door. "She's a loose cannon that hides under the guise of an Imperial.

"Now we need to figure out our next move." Lilly poked her head out, glanced both ways, and then strolled out with her hands thrust in the waistband of her prison greens. As she walked away her hips and shoulders thickened. "I've a couple ideas tumbling around my pan at the moment, but most of them hinge on making contact with Ash.

"You coming or what?" She paused to glance back at Atom.

"I'm supposed to be in solitary."

Lilly scoffed and shook her head. "I took care of that as soon as I found out they had shackled you too."

"Took care of it?"

"I just tweaked your files." With a casual shrug she turned and continued her stroll. "You're a genny now. Come stretch your legs."

Atom stepped out onto the walkway and looked over the railing into the yard below. Several dozen men and women sat around one-piece table and bench combinations. Some talked, others played at holo-games, but most sat and stared at a stream of an imported sporty drama.

Both entrances to the yard lay behind pairs of heavily armored guards.

"I thought isolation would have been in a separate part of the prison," Atom said as he tracked several lightly armed guards who wandered about the yard, maintaining presence without forcing unwarranted confrontations.

"They're full up. From what I could gather, you're valuable, but not viewed as a danger to other gennies. You're here out of obligation, not on criminal charges."

"I guess that's reassuring."

"Atom," Kozue said in Atom's ear. "Daisy is approaching from the gate to your right."

Atom waited for Lilly to get out of earshot.

"Do we have communications? I didn't expect your extremities to survive the initial arrival at a facility like this." Atom leaned on the railing, trying to look as casual as possible as he stood talking to himself.

"Atom, you stole me," Kozue said with a playful laugh. "You know there's nothing like me short of the highest echelon of military black ops. The nanos in the bodies of each of your crew carry just enough memory for me to function at low-level while evading all but the deepest scans. Even those I can evade if I anticipate the sweep.

"And yes, you can talk to Daisy like normal, but I cannot pierce the null-electron bubble surrounding this prison."

"Meaning?"

"I can tell you where Daisy is when he is in range, but I am unable to give you a current location of the *One Way Ticket.*" Her voice sounded crestfallen, as if her mood somehow tied to being connected to her entire nano-bot self.

"Who are you yipping at?" Lilly demanded, her light steps had slipped Atom's notice. "Something you're not telling me?"

Atom snapped his head to her in surprise as she sidled up with a flirty look.

"Just working through things," Atom stammered.

"You have a plan yet, Captain?"

"I'm not sure," Atom stepped back from the railing and Lilly. "I don't have any way to contact my people, at least not that I've figured yet. I know Daisy was booked with me, so he's got to be here somewhere.

"I'd say, find Daisy and then figure the next step. You have anything?"

Lilly twittered a light laugh. "I always have a play or two." She smirked and turned back down the walkway. "Come on."

Without waiting, Lilly sauntered ahead and turned down the stairs.

"Koze, let Daisy know I'm in here," Atom mumbled as he followed after Lilly's ambling form.

Atom wandered down the steps, still unsure of his newfound freedom within the confinement of prison. He pulled at the ill-fitting, green jumpsuit as it bunched up in the armpits and crotch. Hitting the main floor of the prison block, he stopped to survey the scene. Thirty-odd prisoners drifted about the yard, most worn with the tedium of confinement, but a few seemed mentally restrained by a drug cocktail.

Atom tensed as one of the gate guards shifted to lock a shoulder turret on the center of Atom's mass.

"I wish Byron were here," Atom mumbled as he joined Lilly, leaning against the wall.

"Why's that?"

"I'd wager him a cooking shift that he couldn't hack one of those shells."

"Could he?" Lilly crossed her arms and scowled at the guard.

"Absolutely." Atom turned his back on the guard, even though every fiber of his being raged at him to meet the challenge head-on. "The kit's a master-mech. If it has an electronic pulse, he can manipulate it."

"But he's not here," Lilly pouted. "If you can wish for By, I can wish for Ash."

The near door hummed. Atom turned to look back. After several seconds, the actual locking mechanism spun to life, allowing a pair of thigh-thick bars to retract from their wall braces. With a deep grumble, the massive portal opened.

"That your man?" Lilly asked, pushing herself out from the wall to scan the line of inmates walking into the yard. Each prisoner carried a flimsy tote filled with general issue goods.

"Yeah." Atom gave Daisy a flicker of recognition before turning back to Lilly. "Leave him be for the moment. I want to see how the water flows around here. It's best that he not be tied to me in any way that could restrict his movements.

"I know you played one of your cards to get me out of that cell, but it's best if we don't have to do that too often," he said as he tucked his hands behind his back and wandered towards an open table in the corner. As he walked, he tried to adjust the crotch of his jumpsuit without using his hands. "How did you manage to get pants and a top?"

Lilly's playful shrug tugged at Atom's mind with a strange siren-song he had forgotten. "I have a way with people." She trailed along, scuffing her flimsy, plastic shoes on the ceramic plates of the floor.

Slipping onto the metal bench, Atom grimaced and tugged his sleeves down enough to free the constricting material from his armpits.

"We have a timetable?" Lilly sat sideways on her bench, propping a knee under her chin.

"I don't want to think about it."

"Why not?"

"I have a client meeting I might miss."

"Seriously," Lilly demanded, torquing her neck to glare at Atom. "We have the opportunity to find this ship and you're taking side-jobs?"

Atom studied the woman as he turned over his options. He debated on how much information she needed to know. "This is a continuation of an older job," he stated with a shrug. "It's bad business to disappear on clients. As to taking jobs, I'm going to keep my income stream open, otherwise the *One Way Ticket* is dead in the Black."

Lilly pondered Atom's words in silence.

"He's here." Daisy dropped into a seat at the table with force enough to startle both Atom and Lilly.

"He?" Lilly swiveled her glare from Daisy to Atom.

Atom kept his eyes on the table. He gave a slight nod.

Daisy leaned in. "Kim. He's in another block, but we crossed paths."

"Do we have watchers?" Atom flicked his eyes to the ceiling.

Lilly nodded. Her eyebrows arched in silent question.

"Kim's an old ... acquaintance," Atom scratched his scruffy jaw in absent thought, choosing his words with care. "Or, more an acquaintance of a client. It's a simple track job. We had a lead that he was in-system, but now we have a visual confirm to take to the client."

"Hopefully a visual is enough for the payout," Daisy grumbled, leaning on the table.

"It better be. If he wanted more than a track, we should have charged more."

"Wait." Lilly narrowed her eyes at Atom. "All you need is a visual to get paid? I really should sign on with your crew."

"Not as big a payout." Atom rapped his knuckles on the metal tabletop.

"Sounds a lot safer than my usual gig," Lilly pondered.

"Question is, how do we get visual confirm if we don't have access to our normal gear?" Daisy asked.

Atom glanced to the guards, then pursed his lips. "We'll cross that void when we come to it. In the meantime, we need to figure out how movement works in this place. Is it possible for us to recon our ... friend?"

"You're generally stuck in one place, unless you're a guard," Lilly said as she shrugged.

"Any of the guards solid?"

"Don't look at me," Lilly replied. "Toks dumped me in here a day ahead of you guys when she figured I was just a low-level deck scrubber from your ship."

"There are always a few decent bokes." Daisy laced his fingers behind his head and stretched his back until it popped. "The rest are either indifferent or chin-chins."

"Chin-chins?" Atom chuckled. "You've been spending too much time with Byron."

Lilly looked between the men with confusion written on her face.

"He discreetly called them genitals," Atom held back a laugh.

"Avoid them," Daisy followed up.

"Atom," Kozue whispered. "I have a thought. If Lilly is able to move about freely using her talents, she may have access to a communication device. If you could transfer a few of your nanos to her, I might be able to send a micro-burst that the *One Way Ticket* could track. I wouldn't be able to transfer enough to link her like the rest of the crew, but enough to interface with whatever system she hacks into."

"And how do you propose we do that?" Atom asked them both.

"They tend to find you," Daisy said, frowning. "If you notice any guard looking a little too happy or intent, things are usually about to drop out for you."

"Body fluid would be the easiest," Kozue said. "Sneeze in her face."

Before Atom could react to either comment, a small man with a tattoo snaking down his forearm sauntered up to the table and propped a foot on the empty seat. All conversation ceased and for a moment, he leaned on his knee, studying Atom while ignoring the other two.

Daisy growled.

"Easy there, big feller," the man drawled. "I'm just a noter, sent to touch base with the newts."

Easing back a touch, Daisy remained on edge.

Atom, however, crossed his arms and looked up at the man with a calm demeanor. "What's the note you're carrying?"

"Nothin' much at present. Just wanted to say welcome and if you need anything, Roop's the man to talk with. Just remember, no service comes for free, but we have payment plans and are more than willing to trade more than just goods. We'll also take info, action, and marks."

"What exactly does Roop deal in?"

"Anything: chow, alterings, tumbles …. You want it, he can make it so."

"Books?" Atom leaned forward.

The man hesitated, scrunching his face in thought. "Now there's a request we don't get none too often. I'd guess you'd need to talk direct with Roop to work that'un out. He's a businessman and would be happy to sit a meet with you."

"Is he free now? I don't know that I can stand the boredom of this place. I'm afraid it will kill me before anyone else would get a chance."

The angled agent looked over Atom's head and made eye contact with someone. Atom glanced over his shoulder and found a thick, intelligent looking man sitting at a table with several rough individuals and a mousy woman.

The man nodded.

"Looks like he has an opening," the tattooed man said. "Follow me."

"One touch." Atom rose to his feet. "I need to talk with Lil and see if she needs anything we can wrap into one trade. I'll be over momentarily."

"Suit yerself." The man strolled away, whistling a merry tune. "I'll keep a seat for you."

Atom watched the man walk and nodded for Lilly to follow him. He walked a few paces away from their table to the closest semblance of privacy he could find within the confines of the prison yard.

As soon as Lilly joined him, he wrapped her in his arms and slid into a deep kiss. She tensed at first, but melted into the kiss. Her arms snaked around his waist as he pulled her close. Slipping away from the kiss, he nibbled at her neck in a way that made her clutch at his lower back as he worked his way up to her earlobe.

A surprised moan escaped her lips.

"Use your tricks. Get to a terminal. Find Ash. Lock down an escape route," he murmured before pulling back and staring deep into her eyes.

"Is there anything I can get for you?" he continued in a normal, hushed tone.

For a moment she stared at him, then she shook the stars from her eyes and focused on his face. "See if you can barter for some hair suds," she said with a demur smile and dropped her eyes. "What they offer here isn't worth the wrap it comes in."

"I'll see what I can do." He looked away and found Roop staring at them with a burning intensity.

He started to walk away, but Lilly caught his hand. "What's the occasion, love?"

"I wanted Roop and everyone else to know you were under my protection. I know you've altered to keep a low profile, but that doesn't mean there aren't a few dirty codgers who don't care what a girl looks like."

An easy laugh slipped from Lilly. "Do I need to be marked as your property to survive in this hellhole? Seems to me, I should be the one marking you."

"Probably, not the worst idea," Atom said, casting a glance over the rough individuals lounging around the yard. "But I want the attention on me so you don't have to deal with any of the powers here breathing down on you. I'm the Captain. Daisy knows that, too. If you need any help, he's your man. Not that you will, but sometimes a little extra muscle can go a long way."

"I'll keep that in mind."

Atom flashed a roguish grin and left Lilly standing, staring after him.

"What do I call you?" Roop asked as Atom approached.

"Atom," he replied with a polite bob of his head before taking the seat indicated by the heavy entrepreneur.

"So, what can I do for you, Mr. Atom?" Roop leaned in with a smile that covered the predatory glint in his eyes. "My associate indicates you are in the market for something on the unique side. I believe he said you were looking to get your hands on some books."

Roop spread his hands in question.

"Among other things." Atom glanced around the room.

"Such as?"

Atom studied the man. "What will it cost me?"

"That's not how this works." Roop's slow blink reminded Atom of a stalking plains-cat from his childhood. "You tell me what you would like me to procure. I weigh the value of the item and find something of equal worth that can be exchanged.

"You're acting like a first-time visitor," Roop spoke with a languid cadence meant to relax and disarm. "What are you in for?"

"Politics." Atom grinned, matching Roop's level gaze.

"I see." Roop folded his hands across his ample belly and looked to Atom, waiting for the proper procedure. "Let's begin again. What is it that you are in the market for?"

"I'd like to get over to the next block."

"Long orders," Roop murmured, playing with his fleshy jowls as he studied the guards in thought. "Movings are tightly controlled. I would need to involve guards to make something like that happen. Are you looking for a transfer?

"I haven't heard of any danger to your body." His gaze drifted back to Atom. "You cross Gravix?"

Atom shook his head. "Not to my knowledge. They just dropped me here this morning. I don't think I've had time to cut anyone's nose off yet. And to be honest, I'm not looking to do so. I'm on a short list for a quick transfer. My aim is to keep my head down and slip out sideways before anyone notices I've been here."

"Interesting. If your goal is to lie low, why the interest in the next block? And which wing are we talking? Different wings mean different guards to talk to."

Atom glanced to the ceiling. "Aren't you worried we'll be overheard?" he hissed through a casual smile.

Roop slow blinked several times before a natural laugh slipped out, crinkling his face. "They don't watch me or listen to my words. It's more profitable for everyone if they don't. So, the business at hand, which wing are we talking?" He waited for Atom to nod to the door Daisy had arrived through. "And are you looking for a transfer or an afternoon visit?"

"Over the table, I need a visual confirmation on a target my companion and I have been tracking."

"Ah, I see." The plain-cat smile frightened Atom, making him feel like a barrow-rat being toyed with. "You are a political bounty-hunter. If that is the case, I question how and why you are here with us today. Are you more than you seem?"

"I'm a man of many ships."

"And all you need here is a visual pass-by?"

"What would it cost for a five-minute window? At this point, I don't have anything in the way of goods or information, but I'd be willing to trade action."

"A businessman," Roop roared out a deep basso laugh that hushed the room for a moment. "And you fooled me as a newt. I can get you the face to face, but it's going to take a little while, say an hour to line up. I'm going to have to pull some strings and trade favors, but it's doable.

"Anything else you'd like beyond a travel pass and a book?" He leaned in, his belly pressing over the table.

"Hair suds." Atom shrugged.

Roop laughed again, this time just a low shake of his flesh. "You are surprising. I'll see what I can do.

"Now." He hushed his tone and the jollity fled from his face. "In return for this movement, book, and suds, I'll need one action from you. It seems balanced in my ledger, an action for an action, with the rest tossed in as a perk and promise of future trade. I'm going to need that action being the delivery of a message."

"A message?"

"Well, things are a bit of a stalemate at the moment." Roop waved his entourage away from the table. He waited in silence as they did so and forced the vacating of all nearby tables. "The Gravixhan has been angling to take over this prison-station, but let's just say the Charnalhan doesn't see the profit in allowing that to happen."

"Why don't you just have one of your people deliver the message?"

"It's complicated," Roop said, dropping his eyes to the table where he traced invisible doodles in the metal surface with a plump finger. "The warden plays a third party, and while he's technically in control of the station, he also profits if he can play us against each other."

Atom clicked his tongue as he digested the information. Then he said, "I think I can help with this message. Just let me know when and where."

*   *   *

Daisy sprawled on the top bunk for the enforced quiet time following the midday meal. Below, Atom sat cross-legged on his new bunk, secured by Lilly's manipulation. On the ceiling of the cell, a synthetic sun dappled through the imaginary tree branches that swayed in a breeze Atom could almost feel.

"Why do they do the whole sun thing?" Daisy asked. Atom could hear the sleep creeping into his pilot's voice.

"Calming," Atom replied as he watched the synth-sunlight play on the floor. "They do the same thing aboard imperial ships. The sunlight helps the pan unwind. Think back to your earliest good memories."

Daisy spent a moment in silence. "Riding a suspensor-bike across the lawn with my mother watching from the porch," he said with concentration.

"Paint the picture."

"Green grass. A little long. It parts under the suspensors as I ride around a long track I marked out with glow-tabs. Mom is sitting at a wooden table, watching me ...." Daisy hesitated as he dredged. "She's peeling something. Fruit? Maybe dragon-pears. My two younger sisters are climbing the big tree across the yard. They're laughing and yelling to my mom."

"Was it warm?"

"Yeah, spring has sprung. It's the first warm day since the rains quit."

"And...."

"It's sunny," Daisy said with a laugh, vibrating the bunk with mirth. "Seems you know more than you let on."

"Sometimes I know a thing or two." Atom closed his eyes and rested his head.

"Tell me about the Meriwetherhan."

Daisy tossed the conversational bomb in such a silky manner, it took Atom a moment to register. His eyes flashed open.

"I didn't realize you'd picked that up." Atom slipped from the bunk and leaned against the wall where he could see Daisy. He crossed his arms and frowned up at the pilot with a look of deliberation.

Daisy rolled onto his side, propped a hand under his head, and met Atom's gaze. "I listen when people talk. It's a bad habit I picked up in my youth.

"It makes sense," he continued, stifling a yawn as he drowsed. "I don't know much about the Emperor's Fist. The little I picked up fits you. Everything you do has the feel of someone who could snuff the verse if they really wanted to."

"That might be a stretch, but I can do a lot of things that will keep Margo alive and safe for the time."

"That your only goal?"

Atom slumped and said in a pain-laced voice, "I would love to have life go back to the way it was. I'd even have stepped down if it would have saved my han."

"Past is past," Daisy sighed and shook his head in remorse. "We all have things we would change if we could, but then we run the risk of being different than we are today. I'm not sure if that's better or worse, but we have to press on with the memories and past that we've chosen."

"I'm an outlaw who was a general. Who are you?"

"A drunk," Daisy said without hesitation.

"Nothing's that simple."

"No," Daisy sat up, his head brushing the ceiling as he dangled his legs. "I'm a pilot."

He kicked his legs in a gentle rhythm and played with the ill-fitting jumpsuit with nervous fingers. He caught himself and folded his hands into fists, pressing down into his legs. Then Daisy sat in silence. He studied the scars lining his knuckles.

Atom could see the memories floating free, dislodged by each trigger of damaged flesh.

"Simple story?" He refused to meet Atom's eyes. "I came from a good family. Both my parents taught at a small prep-school on Atico. I scored high enough on my ap-tests to float to any school in system."

He ventured a furtive glance at Atom, but dropped his eyes back to his fists.

"I chose the naval academy. I've always wanted to be a pilot and even had dreams of captaining my own ship someday."

"Then why don't you?"

"Duel."

The solitary word breathed life into Atom's mind. "Girl. Honor. What brought the duel?" Atom peered up at Daisy, trying to see beneath the furrowed brow.

"Doesn't matter," Daisy growled. "The boke picked blasters."

"Who won?"

"I'm here, aren't I?" Daisy crashed down to the floor and lumbered to the door to peer through the narrow window. "I didn't really expect to kill her, but I did. Even though her family didn't press the honor issue, it cracked something in my pan. I washed out of the academy the next quarter.

"I had never touched alcohol before that. My family didn't drink. But it turned out to be a heavy part of the washing.

"I never looked back," he sighed as he turned away from the window and paced.

"Is that why you use your fists?" Atom returned to his bunk.

Daisy nodded and rubbed at the knuckles of his left hand. "I told myself I'd never use a gun again. I don't want the guilt of killing an innocent. It already weighs too much on my soul."

"It was a duel, Daisy," Atom consoled. "Whoever you killed could hardly claim innocence. To be honest, pistols would play to most girls' advantages. With your mass and the average mass of the female of our species, you should have died. She chose the weapon. It was her choice, Daisy."

"She couldn't back down without losing honor." Daisy snapped his ursine head to fix Atom with a death stare. "You, of all people, should know that you can't back down from a duel."

"So, set sum, you killed a girl in a duel and feel remorse." Atom paused to allow Daisy to counter, but after a moment of silence he continued. "How is that a problem now? You have the guilt, but being the best pilot doesn't burn on that trajectory. I know you have the occasional brawl, but you never kill anyone there. I don't see what weighs you."

"Atom, there is a piece of me that is primal violence," as Daisy spoke, a darkness shrouded his glare. "I can't avoid the need to hurt myself. It claws its way out when I try to drown the memories."

"What about your family?" Atom redirected, closing his eyes in peace.

"They turned their backs on me."

"Because of the duel?"

"Because of the true outcome of the duel," Daisy sobbed, dropping his head into his hands, his breath coming in short, sharp gasps. "Her name was Emma. We had a relationship that lasted through the first two years of the academy. In our third year, I broached the subject of marriage. She said no. She told me that my family name wasn't good enough to fuse with hers.

"Her words went beyond simple rejection." Daisy's eyes glistened when he looked up, imploring Atom to intercede, but Atom sat in silence. He waited. "She slandered my family name and flat out told me that my line and planet would never be good enough.

"She slapped me and walked away. Before she could leave, I challenged her."

"And you killed her," Atom said to conclude Daisy's tale. The pilot, tears streaming down his face, stopped his pacing and collapsed against the wall.

"But there was no vendetta," Atom continued. "A family of ranking could easily have circumvented the laws of the duel to pursue you for the death of their daughter. Why would they let you live?"

"Because she carried my child. I didn't find out until I had already washed out."

"Is the guilt you carry for your lover or your child?"

"Both," Daisy whispered. "It's the reason I agreed to work for you. Margo is the reason I've stayed on longer with you than any other ship I have ever piloted."

"And the drinking and fighting?"

"The drink helps me live in that instant where the past doesn't matter. All that matters is the moment and the fight. I have no problem pounding someone coming after me, but don't ask me to handle a gun. Nothing good comes from guns."

Atom quirked Daisy a look.

"At least not in my hands." A broken smile cracked Daisy's features.

"Where does Mae fit into your story?"

Daisy shrugged.

A soft knock at the door startled the two of them. Through the narrow window, Roop's man with the snake tattoo grinned. He glanced down the walkway and waved. Then, with a hum the locking mechanism turned and the door slid open.

"Roop talked it over with Charnal and found the boke he wants you to make an example of," Snake said in a hushed tone from the doorway. "I'll take you there and point him out. What you do with him is your business, as long as the message is sent. When you're done, you'll be happy to know that your boke is on the same block.

"Deliver a message, and you get your visual as payment. Then you're back here to sleep all peaceable."

"And the rest of my goods?" Atom rose and stepped to the door.

"They'll be on your bunk when you return." Snake grinned at Atom, then glanced down to Daisy. "He running light?"

"He'll be fine." Atom leaned and patted the pilot on the shoulder. "He just has a touch of the hanger. Give us a couple minutes to hydrate and we'll be square for a hard burn."

"I'll be down in the yard," Snake said before turning away.

Atom sat back down on the bed. "Koze, when you send that burst, ask Hither to either stall the next meet or get us a new set of coords. It's going to take us a few days to get free of this hole."

"Do you have time to dawdle?" the AI asked both men.

"Speaking of," Daisy grunted as he rubbed his eyes clear and rose to his feet. "What's the turn and burn on Toks ship? Will she even come back for the pickup if she's after the same long-game as us?"

"That's up in the Black. Honestly." Atom scratched his jaw in thought. "I could see her going either way. Although, if she was going to take us aboard her ship, I imagine she would have done that back at Lassiter."

"I agree with that assessment," Kozue calculated. "Probability points to her not believing that you have any useful information. She most likely views you as a liability. The safest place for you is to keep you out of the way. On that note," her tone shifted. "You'll have a larger window to complete the current tasks and formulate a proper escape plan."

"Just make sure Hither knows to push the meet back." Atom strolled to the door. "I don't want to lose that contract, whatever it might be."

*   *   *

"What are we going to do to this boke?" Daisy asked as they stood waiting for the heavy block hatch to cycle through the locking sequence.

"Just pass along a message." Atom glared at the back of the armored guard several paces in front of them. "I wasn't asked to do anything more than that. You know I try to fill the letter of the contract."

"Bet you wish your girl was here."

Atom's hand drifted to his empty hip. "Yeah, she tends to be useful."

Daisy looked over his shoulder to the second guard who stood motionless behind them. The lock finished its cycle and crawled open with the speed of a suicidal glacier.

"I meant Go," Daisy chuckled.

"I know."

With a final shudder, the gate ground to a halt, just wide enough for the two men to fit. On the other side, four more power-armored guards stood waiting, their hands empty, but lethal nonetheless. Behind the guards, a second gate stood closed, waiting for the cycle.

A verbal exchange occurred inside the armor. Atom recognized the moment of silence in the presence of power-armor.

He glanced to Daisy. "Any idea of how long you're in here?"

"They said they had to clear my paperwork. I can't tell you how many drunken brawls I've been in and never landed this far up the chain or discipline. Usually I'm just defragging in the drunk tank and cut loose with the rest of the rowdies."

"Yeah, but you never dropped fists with imperial troopers before."

Daisy nodded. He rolled his shoulders and stretched out his back. "They really did a number on me, but I'm surprised they didn't do worse."

"Toks gave a clear order. Non-lethal. Soldiers are crafted to follow orders."

"They sure toed that line."

Atom laughed and said, "But they didn't break anything or leave you damaged beyond recovery."

"Prisoners, move," one of the armored guards said after they concluded their conversation. The guard waved them forward through the gate. They waited through the cycle and as the second gate opened the guard recited, "Stay to the left and keep quiet while in transfer mode."

Atom and Daisy followed instructions with their heads down, but a dozen steps down the long corridor Daisy drifted. Without warning, one of the guards shoved Daisy with an armor augmented hand and bounced the pilot of the wall.

"Stay to the left." The guard sounded bored.

Daisy rebounded, looking startled. Atom read the tense set to Daisy's shoulders. He coughed a sharp warning that caught the pilot's attention. Daisy took a breath and settled back into their walk.

The guards relaxed from a readiness Atom only noticed after Daisy settled.

At an intersection a thin, bald man stood waiting. He adjusted the powder blue cravat adorning his immaculate suit with long, nervous fingers. Beside him a hard woman scowled at the approaching group. She rivaled Daisy in size and seemed overly eager to tear someone's arms off.

Atom and Daisy exchanged a worried glance.

"Sergeant, give us a moment," the bald man ordered.

The guards froze.

"You can wait in the next lock." The man adjusted his glasses and smiled, but his eyes grew hard at the hesitation.

"You know who this is, sir?" the sergeant stammered.

The slow predatory blink drilled through the guard. "He's just another prisoner and if you don't follow orders, I'll let Fresk sort things out." He stared death at the man as the woman growled behind him.

Without further hesitation, the armored guards thumped down the hallway, leaving Atom and Daisy with the two newcomers.

"Don't let them fool you," the man said as he unbuttoned the jacket on his simple, yet well-tailored suit. He smiled. Atom's instincts bristled. "I think the guards are worse than the prisoners here. You seem to understand how the system works. I'm in charge, but we want things to run as smoothly as possible.

"Warden James." He extended a hand, palm sideways, neutral. "I know you're new and only here on temp assignment. I also know your credentials are on lockdown, so in the system you're just another short-jock jumpsuit."

Atom tapped the Warden's hand.

"But I know who you really are."

Atom froze.

"In addition," the Warden continued in a business-like manner. "I know that you've been approached by Charnal's people. They need to be taken down a notch to maintain the status-quo. Make that happen and things will run a touch smoother for your end.

"I assume it's something your experience will sort out for you." The warden hesitated as information flashed along his glasses. "Daisy Hernandez." His eyes drew back into focus. "My, you are a specimen. Maybe I should give you an eve with Fresk here. Think of the offspring you two would create." A darkness fluttered in James' eyes. "I could get rid of the guards here altogether. What do you think, Fresk? Would that be enjoyable?"

"He might give me a run." The woman spoke for the first time, in a feminine voice that failed to match her hulking frame.

"So, what are you proposing?" Atom crossed his arms, a defiant tone on his lips.

Before he could follow up, Fresk's ham-fist slammed into his stomach like a sledgehammer. Moving faster than his eye could register, the woman had doubled him and dropped him to the floor.

Daisy nodded with an appraising frown.

"Care to join him, Daisy?" disdain dripped from James' use of the name.

Daisy shrugged. "I'll dance."

Before the words finished wandering from his mouth, Fresk moved. Daisy slipped the blow, ducking to let Fresk's fist glance off his forehead. The blow stunned Daisy for a moment, but he felt one of her smaller bones pop.

Daisy grinned and shook the cobwebs from his head.

The woman narrowed her eyes and circled, cunning caution in the placement of each foot.

She stalked.

Daisy danced.

"Atom, you yobo?" Daisy asked in a conversational tone. He flashed a charming, toothy grin at Fresk and rolled his neck. He continued to draw her attention away from his gasping captain.

With a grunt, Atom rocked himself up into a sitting position and scooted back to lean against the wall. "I think she may have crushed my innards." He worked to regain his breath as he studied the passive Warden James. "Are we sure this is the best use of our time on this rock? I mean, we might miss our hair appointment."

James turned an indifferent eye to Atom as Daisy slipped another lethal attack from Fresk with a playful deftness. He lashed out an open paw that caught the woman in the side of the neck.

"Darl, you'll need to move faster—" Daisy's banter cut short as her flat-footed heel kick caught him in the chest, forcing a stumbled retreat.

Fresk grinned.

Before Daisy regained his balance, she pounced. The pilot threw a heavy punch, but Fresk slipped inside his guard and wrapped an arm around his shoulder even as she pistoned her knee into Daisy's side. The maneuver crumpled Daisy inward as the ogrish woman continued to drive her mass up and through. Off-balance, Daisy rolled sideways, attempting to gain purchase, either with his feet or on Fresk's body.

He failed.

Their momentum ran the pair into the wall where they rebounded and crumpled into a heap of muscle. Fresk slithered like an eel, twisting about Daisy in a sinuous manner that placed his arm and neck at the mercy of her trunk-like legs.

Only a few seconds spanned the fight from start to finish. Atom, recovering from the gut blow, slipped up the wall, still fighting to regain his breath.

"Daisy," he gasped as he lunged toward his fallen friend.

James caught him like an intervening father. "Atom," he chided. "This is just a test to show where you stand on the ladder. I mean no harm to you and yours. In fact, you serve no purpose if you are too damaged to function.

"I say, Fresk." He released Atom's arm, but hesitated to make sure he could stand under his own power before turning his full attention to his goon. "Ease up on Mr. Hernandez."

Like a bear trap released, the pressure disappeared from Daisy's arm and neck.

"Easy, girl." Daisy spun up from his back in a defensive crouch, giving Fresk a wary glare.

"We're done." The thick-necked woman dismissed Daisy with an approving nod and moved her hulk behind Warden James again. There she came to an easy parade rest with her hands tucked behind her back and her eyes locked in the middle distance.

"As you can see, gentlemen," the Warden said with a playful smile. "I have no need to play petty games of violence with you. If I wished to be more permanently damaging than Fresk here, I could simply cut the atmo supply to your cell while you slept and never lose a thought over it.

"This." He glanced over his shoulder at Fresk. "Was simply a demonstration that you are playing a game on so many more levels than you are used to out there in the Black. Play my game and you might survive. Prove profitable and your chances increase exponentially. The two faux-hans exist because they bring stability to my prison and ko to my pocket.

"But," he sneered. "They both need to be taken down a level or two."

"I have your permission to achieve this?" Atom still held his side, but now he managed slow and even breaths as he straightened up to stand before James, proud, but less defiant. "I have your permission to terminate parties that I see as a threat to the functionality of your prison?"

James hesitated. He narrowed his eyes and gave Atom a thoughtful look.

"Atom." Excitement laced Kozue's voice. "The burst succeeded. I have contact with the *Ticket* and Hither informed me they move on your word and can be on location within an hour."

Daisy placed a heavy mitt on Atom's shoulder.

"What are your thoughts, Daisy?" Atom never took his eyes from James.

"Always up for a tussle," the giant grinned.

"This isn't a negotiation," James snapped.

"Isn't it?" Atom asked with mock surprise.

"Just give them something to think about." Warden James turned and strode down the side hall without care. "Send them my message."

Fresk continued to glare at the pair as James disappeared through the gate at the terminus. "Don't think to cross the warden," she squeaked. "If you dream it, I'll finish what I started here today."

Daisy bowed from the waist. "Any day, darl." He reared up to look down on the titan-like woman.

She bristled.

"Come on." Atom turned and sauntered along their original path, away from where Fresk stood in undecided rage. "We have business to attend to. Plus, there's that payment of reading material Roop promised us."

Daisy's grinning face brightened. "Brawls and books and brawls," he sing-songed as he trotted to catch up with Atom. "Could this day get any better?

"Side thought." His words became calculating. "James said he knew who you were, but then he said you couldn't handle the game within a game. Do you think he really knows who you are?"

Atom shrugged and laughed as they approached the monolithic hatch, "As I told that officer, most of my file is sealed. It's like an iceberg, they only see the tiny bit poking the surface. Most people have no idea what I'm actually capable of. My old boss knew … and maybe Hither and her sisters."

They reached the end of the hall and Atom banged on the sealed gate. Daisy stared at Atom as the gears and pressure locks whirred to life.

"Respect." Daisy ducked his head as the gate ground open, revealing four power-armored guards standing in an anxious arc. All four peered beyond Atom and Daisy to where Fresk still glowered.

Then, without a word they filed past, leaving Atom and Daisy alone.

The gate thudded behind them.

"What's that about?" Daisy examined the gate as they stood in the quiet embrace between the two massive gates.

"Maybe we're free to move about our business," Atom said with a chuckle.

The far gate hummed to life.

"I could have pounded her seven ways from a turnip."

"I know." Atom watched the gate inch open. "I know you were holding back. But they want to play games. James said so himself."

"So that's what we're here for, a sit down of crimps?"

"Seems that way, but we have business to take care of first." Atom stepped through the gate as soon as the gap allowed. Daisy followed him into a yard identical to the previous, with one exception.

"Where are the guards?" Daisy growled as they surveyed the block.

"Not sure," Atom puzzled. "Stay the course. We get paid, then we move on to our secondary job."

"And then the third?"

"Game within a game within a game," Atom muttered as he looked for a place to start.

Behind them the lock shuddered shut.

The yard flowed. Prisoners, men and women, wandered about with slow purpose. Occupied tables sprinkled the floor, surrounding an open row of showers that drew a line down the center of the yard. Three tiers of cells rose on both sides of the yard connected by sporadic bridges and symmetric staircases.

Atom looked up to the synthetic, blue sky.

"Kim first?" Daisy flexed his arm, rubbing at the strained elbow joint.

"How's the shoulder?" Atom asked. "You didn't reinjure it?"

Daisy stared at him for a moment. "Oh, from the players? They bonded it with an internal bone cast. Stronger than normal," he said with a grin, demonstrating the full range of motion. "Why you concerned about my hand, aren't we supposed to be using our eyes for this gig?"

"Firm," Atom replied. He studied the hundred or so cells. "I wish we had locked down a more precise location from Roop. Fishing for firebats could take a turn or two.

"Go make friends." He waved toward the busy floor of the block. "I'm sure you can find a game to join or someone with a tipple-pot. Keep your wits about and your ocs wide. I'll catch up with you when I've located our target."

Daisy tugged at his jumper and wandered away.

"I can help," said Kozue. "Lilly's tampering gave me a mousehole into most of the prison datasets. My access is passive, so I can't operate anything, but I can look.

"Our target," she paused. "Can be found on the second tier, cell 213."

"Daisy," Atom called before the pilot had reached the first tables. "We're moving faster than I'd thought. Let's go for a walk."

The block bustled with more energy than the one they had left behind. Atom surveyed the occupants as Daisy returned. All the cell doors stood open and people moved with purpose.

"Kozue, is the lack of guards normal?" Atom asked as he watched the swirling motion of the cell block. "What does security usually look like for this prison?"

"As I'm tracking," the AI replied, "the block you just left seems to maintain the second highest guard presence. The greatest concentration of guards appears to be the central hub, which is administration."

"What's the block we just left?"

"It appears to be a neutral ground between the Granix and Charnal factions."

"Interesting," Atom pondered, tapping the gun shaped void on his hip.

"What's our play?" Daisy asked.

"Two jobs," Atom picked out a mixed group sitting at a table off to the side of the main floor. "Why don't we divide and conquer. You go talk to those gentlefolk over there and get a feel for how operations run around here. Find what might send the message we've been hired to deliver."

"What's the schedule?

"Not sure, we'll stay liquid." Atom looked around, searching for something. "What do they use for currency in a place like this?"

Daisy shrugged. "Goods, information, favors …."

"Interesting." Atom's eyes lit on a man mixed in with the crowd. "I might have a touch of an idea. I'll catch up with you when you need me," Atom said with a nod. "Feel free to yell if that comes sooner. Take your time, feel the situation. In the meantime, I need to find a dispensary on my way to visit our friend."

"Works for me," Daisy frowned. "I wonder if there's a place to get a drink around here."

"I'm sure you'll work that out," Atom said with a laugh and wandered into the crowd.

He cast a curious glance behind him just before Daisy disappeared from view. "I wonder what kind of trouble Daisy will get himself into while I'm busy?" Atom mused to the alarm of several passersby.

"Depends on his ability to find drink," Kozue replied in Atom's ears.

Atom flashed a feral grin at the floor and a small, empty circle grew about him.

"What's your plan?" she asked.

"Find a bowl still."

"You don't drink."

"True, but it's polite to bring a gift when visiting an old friend," Atom said with a laugh that widened the circle. "I would hate to have our friend think we're rude and don't value his friendship."

"Interesting," Kozue sounded amused.

"Friend." Atom's hand snaked out and snatched the arm of a frail woman. With a rough grin and a twist of his wrist, he revealed a run of track marks.

The woman squealed with a mixture of pain and surprise.

"Where can I find a still?" Atom pressed his face close to the woman, ignoring the rancid, death-breath of the addict. "I'm new to these parts and have a thirst that needs quench."

"Second tier, outer," she managed to squeak.

"Many thanks." Atom released the woman and mockingly bowed, as if the woman embodied the empress in her skeletal form.

The woman shambled away, mumbling a few choice words.

Atom straightened his too-tight jumpsuit and made his way up the indicated stairs. He wandered down the walk, glancing into each cell as he passed. After half a dozen cells, a faint scent alerted him to the proximity of his goal. Several cells further down the trail, a pair of heavy inmates leaned against the railing in apparent conversation.

"Ho there," Atom called out, stopping a respectful distance from the pair.

For a moment the two thugs ignored him.

"An acquaintance pointed me in the direction of your ship." Atom leaned to the side without moving his feet, trying to make eye contact with the men. "I'm new and trying to figure out how this works."

With an annoyed grunt, the nearest man turned his glare to Atom.

"The way things work," the man growled. "Is you give us payment and if what you offer is worth it, we give you what we want."

"What do you take in payment?"

"What've you got?"

"Well, like I said, I just arrived, so I don't have much in material." As Atom spoke, the man crossed his arms and turned back to his companion. "But if you take information, I might have something you could take up the chain."

The man hesitated and glanced back at Atom with narrowed eyes.

"You guys are Gravixhan, correct?"

The man cocked his head, without replying.

"You have a Charnal over here." Atom shrugged. "Maybe he's on legit business, or maybe he's checking up on things. I'm assuming that this is your territory and your bosses probably aren't too keen on your enemies wandering around unescorted." Atom pasted a cheesy smile on his face. "For a bottle of your purest grain, I'll point him out to you."

"Just a tick," said the meat.

He leaned his head close to his companion. After a brief exchange, he trotted off.

Atom turned and leaned on the railing, mimicking the bigger man as he allowed his attention to wander over the flow of the floor below. It only took a moment to pick Daisy out of the crowd. The pilot sat at a crowded table with a hard-looking woman on his knee. Despite her evident lethality, she sported a broad grin. The rest of the crowd leaned in, hanging on Daisy's words.

The thin Charnal man proved harder to locate, but Atom eventually found him leaning against the far wall, engrossed in conversation with a pair of locals.

"Megi gave the nod," the Gravix guard called out as he trotted down the walkway to Atom. "Bottle of the purest if the information turns solid."

"That boke over there," Atom gestured with his chin and turned his back to the floor. "The lanky one talking with the other two. I don't know them, so I won't call them anything other than bystanders."

The first guard stood beside Atom a moment and studied the floor. "The one in the cap?" he asked.

Atom nodded.

"Get a bottle ready, but wait on it," the burly moonshiner told the other man before heading back the way he had come.

The remaining muscle disappeared into the cell and returned with a plastic bottle.

As the man leaned on the rail beside him, Atom turned and looked out over the yard. "I'm new here, so this might be a stupid question, but where are all the guards? I just came from a block over and the place was crawling with armor just looking to put a gauntlet through someone's head."

"Dunno." The thug sounded bored. "It's the way things run. I can't vouch for the other side of the ring, but here the guards give us free run most of the time. We know they could come in with the powers and we couldn't do a thing to stop them, so we just keep our heads down.

"I suppose the uppers have a deal with the warden to let business do its thing, but on the real, there's no difference." The man shrugged and stared down into the yard. "From here, things always seem to flow, no matter who's pulling shots."

"And everything flows down the well to the warden?"

The man grunted. "Grav pulls."

The pair fell silent. Below, Atom picked out a half-dozen people whose movement stood out. Atom glanced to the guard.

"You guys act quick," he said, gripping the rail and tracking the stalking pack.

"No sense in putting off what's coming."

The foot soldiers converged on the unwary target and in a brief tussle that drew little attention, they subdued the man and dragged him toward the far gate.

"What'll happen to him?" Atom grimaced as he watched the group disappear.

Before he could reply, the first guard crossed a bridge towards them. He nodded to his companion.

"Don't rightly know," the man answered and handed Atom the bottle.

Atom nodded thanks and sauntered back down the catwalk the way he had come. The bottle disappeared into his sleeve. He dropped his head to his chest in thought. His plans coalesced as he descended the stairs.

"What's the play now?" Kozue asked.

"Not sure," Atom grumbled as he hit the floor. "I'm thinking of taking the firebug out so we can get that off our deck. I'm still working on how to pull that off, but I'm thinking there might be a couple ways to tie it into something bigger, so it gets lost in the fray unless you're looking for it."

"Coffey was very specific about cause."

"Harder to pull in a controlled atmo."

"And you don't have enough accelerant to fully accomplish the job, unless you can somehow contain the fire in a manner to afford maximum exposure and catastrophic system failure."

Atom paused at the foot of the stairs lost in thought. A pair of inmates started to approach, but turned away when he looked through them.

"I need a spark. Just a tiny spark."

"Even with a spark, I'm estimating the worst you can do is second and third degree burns with your current arsenal."

Atom laughed and said, "I've got a plan."

He set out across the yard with a spring in his step, like a shopper deciding which storefront would best suit his needs. "I don't need to strong-arm the man or spit liquor in his face. I just need to convince him that my plan is what he really wants to do in the first place. And that's always easier when drink is involved.

"Daisy, I need a spark. You have any ideas?" Atom continued to study the room as he wandered in the pilot's general direction.

Daisy coughed.

"Can't talk?" Atom craned his neck, searching the sea of prisoners to find where his pilot had docked.

Daisy coughed again.

"Well, if you can come up with anything that could give us a spark and be ingestible at the same time, let me know."

"Ingestible?" Atom heard understanding creep into Kozue's voice. "That could work."

The cough deepened. "Gentlekins," Daisy's basso voice filled his head through the open com. "I think some of this drink has tickled the wrong pipes. I feel like I swallowed your pipe-light."

Atom's eyes lit.

"What's yer harbor, cap?" A willowy young man sidled up to Atom. "You've a need, I can make arrangements."

Atom started. The young man smiled up and ducked his eyes in a strangely familiar manner. Atom slowed his step and turned to face the stranger.

"You have that look in yer eyes that says yer searching fer something, Atom." The youth drifted away and looked over the crowded room as people grouped and congregated. "Yer searching fer a treasure amongst these here stars," the boy sang, waving at the throng.

"Wait." Atom's eyes grew wide in amazement. "Lilly?"

The baug laughed and gave a theatrical twirl. "One and the same." The boy winked up at Atom. "But I go by Thomas in this form."

Blowing out a breath, Atom shook his head in wonder. "You certainly take some getting used to. Although, you read me straight up. I'm looking to get my hands on an intake burner of a pipe."

"Done." Lilly turned and strolled away, leaving Atom alone in a state of confusion.

With hesitant steps, he began following the image of the young man, but soon lost the slender form among the green sea of prisoners as they surged and rebounded in a confined tide of humanity waiting to burst over the sea wall.

Shaking his head, Atom found his previous heading and began moving towards where he had seen Daisy sitting.

"Atom." The pilot's voice caught his attention and Atom turned to find his friend waving from a few tables away. Atom waved back and picked his way between the crowded tables to stand behind Daisy.

"What's the good word?" Atom asked over Daisy's shoulder.

"Won some and lost others." Daisy laughed and held up the thin, metal playing discs for Atom to look over. "Don't plan on making any cred, but maybe a contact or two amongst these fine pouge players."

The other prisoners around the table shifted their eyes between Daisy and Atom before a smile and a shrug from the pilot seemed to answer their challenge. "Well," Atom said. "That's why we came over. That and to say hi to Kim."

"You track him down?"

"Firm, and I traded for a present." Atom slipped the bottle from his sleeve and held it discreetly where the table could see.

"That en't cheap." One of the pouge players raised an approving eyebrow.

Atom slipped out an easy laugh. "You can't bring an old friend cheap still."

"I'll catch up with you after a few more hands." Daisy nodded back to the table. "I'm still good for a touch more before I call it a cycle."

"You can stay and keep feeding us your markers," one of the other players said, a woman with an angry, fresh scar running across the bridge of her nose, and jabbed a finger at the pot with mock severity. "Long as we all keep our hands above the table, it's all good here."

"I'll give a fair hail for you." Atom slapped Daisy on the shoulder and left. He turned his eyes up to the tier of cells as he headed for the stairs.

"Your goods, sir," Lilly whispered in Atom's ear as he slipped through the crowd.

"Back to ...." Atom turned to her voice with a smile on his face and rammed a shoulder into a passing inmate's chest, knocking the man off balance. For a moment the prisoner hesitated, then he bristled and stepped towards Atom with a fist raised.

Instinct kicked in.

Atom fell back a step and lashed out with a flat-footed kick that caught the inmate in the kneecap. The man fell with a pained grunt, taking out several bystanders. Before he, or any of the jostled prisoners could react further, Atom dropped his own knee into the man's face with fight-ending force and scampered away in the confusion concocted by the sudden outburst of violence.

Ducking and weaving, Atom fled for the stairs in the far corner.

"Kozue," he panted. "I need a little guidance to get to Kim's cell."

"Take the stairs ahead of you to the second tier," Kozue replied in a calm voice that offset the uproar below. Without hesitation, Atom mounted the stairs, taking them three at a time as he pounded upward to his goal. "His cell will be the fourteenth in."

As he left the stairs behind, chaos erupted below. Even as his pursuers plowed through bystanders with wanton disregard, Atom heard Daisy's voice rise above the murmured cacophony. With a roar like a cornered bear, the pilot unleashed a primal bellow of rage.

"Cheat," Daisy cried.

Atom chanced a quick glance over the railing just in time to see the hard-eyed woman soar over the crowd to land on another table, spilling drinks and scattering an assortment of gaming pieces around the room.

Turning back to the open path before him, Atom counted the passing cells.

He reached his destination just before his pursuers crested the top step. Ducking inside he found himself face to face with a slight, middle-aged man. The man reclined on his bunk reading a dog-eared book. Surprise spread over the man's face as Atom dove under the solitary bunk and pulled a dangling blanket down enough to cover his presence.

"Throw them off and there's a cut for you," Atom hissed from beneath the metal frame.

"Of what?" the man whispered back.

Atom swished the liquid around in his bottle and saw the man's feet touch the floor just as a cavalcade of thundering footsteps drove down the walk.

"What's the fuss?" Atom heard the man ask.

"Boke took a poke at Dilly," a new voice replied. "Busted his knee and face. I know he came up this way."

"Fellow dashed through. Caught my eye. That's why I wanted to see ...."

"You say he passed?" the man interrupted.

"Far as I know."

"He can't be far." The group ran on.

"You better be worth it," the man said as he returned to sit on the edge of his bunk. "Is the commotion in the yard your doing as well?"

"That I couldn't say." Atom shimmied from under the bunk and edged close enough to the cell door to peek down at the tumult taking place on the block floor. Daisy had done his work escalating. Atom assumed Lilly had played a part as well. The yard seemed a seething mass of motion. As Atom watched, the gate groaned open and four power-armored guards waded into the mess.

"I can honestly say, I'm glad I'm not down there," Atom said with a laugh as he returned to drop onto the far end of the bunk. "Name's Atom." He patted his chest with one hand and produced the bottle with the other. "I say we polish this off right quick before they decide to toss the block."

"Kim." The man held his hand out, palm up. "Arsonist by trade, artist by choice."

Atom uncapped the bottle and took a long pull, wiping his mouth with his sleeve as he passed the liquor to his new companion. "Merch and merc depending on the day," he said with a lopsided grin that sucked some of the tension from the air.

Raising the bottle in salute, Kim took a long pull. Atom watched half the bottle disappear like magic.

Atom reached into his pocket and found the pipe Lilly had stashed in their brushing. He pulled it out and started to dismantle the pipe. Wiping the bottle off with his sleeve, Kim passed it back.

"What have you got?" he asked.

"Pipe wouldn't work, I'm trying a quick clean to see if it's just jammed up." He took a quick nip at the bottle and as he wiped the mouth off as Kim had done, he dropped the ignition filament in the bottle. Then, with a grimace he passed the bottle back.

"Too strong for me, kill it," he said, blinking away tears. Kim shrugged and upended the bottle. Just as he finished the last pull, Atom asked, "Remember a law-bringer named Coffey?"

Kim sputtered. He narrowed his eyes over the bottom of the bottle, but continued to pull until he had drained every drop of the precious liquid. As the firebat lowered the bottle with a question on his lips, Atom slipped from the bed and edged towards the cell door.

"Hope this works," Atom said through gritted teeth.

"What are you talking about?" Kim coughed and thumped his chest. "Yeah, I remember Coffey. She had it out for me, but could never pin anything on me." Kim grinned.

"That drink's from her." Atom had reached the edge of the cell.

The firebug coughed again. Then he took a deep breath. The filament ignited the fumes of the grain alcohol.

The explosion launched Atom over the railing. Flame roiled around his feet as he flew through the air. A knot of milling prisoners softened his landing, but the impact still knocked the wind from his lungs.

For a moment, Atom lay in a crumpled heap. Wrenching convulsions wracked his shoulders as he fought to regain his breath.

"Atom," Kozue called through the haze creeping at the edge of his vision. "You need to get up. Daisy needs your help and the two of you need to get out of this block or you'll end up in lockup. As it is, they will probably lock down this block with you in it."

Blinking away the woozy effects of the impact, Atom staggered to his feet. Chaos swirled around him. Prisoners fought to escape the swirling smoke billowing from Kim's cell while trying to surrender to the onrushing guards.

A second later, all atmosphere from the block purged. Smoke, fire, and breathable air fled to the reaches of space as the system killed the fire.

Atom felt his lungs threaten to pull out through his mouth.

"Five seconds to purge end," Kozue said, her voice distant and tinny in the near vacuum. "There should be no lasting harm."

Five seconds felt like five levels of hell as Atom's body revolted against his brain.

*   *   *

When Atom came to, he lay sprawled on his belly on his bunk.

"What in the blazing Palm happened?" he demanded in a half-slurred attempt at speech. "I thought you said no lasting harm."

"You're fine, Atom," Kozue replied with a tickle of laughter in her voice.

Atom rolled over, trying to peel open his sand-gritted eyes. "How am I supposed to accomplish anything if I can't function? Did we at least eliminate Kim?"

"Firm."

"Now we just need to get out. I don't suppose there is any legal chance we walk?"

Kozue let out an actual laugh, which caused Atom to crack one of his eyes open in surprise. "Atom, you know you're on a military extradition charge filed by Toks. She's trying to bury you, even if you do have information. So, the probability of a legitimate, court-ordered release borders along the same lines as throwing an object out an airlock and having it hit something on the other side of the galaxy."

"Thanks for the encouragement," Atom groaned as he sat up. "We're on our own."

"Firm."

"How to get out of this one?" Atom mused.

"Well, as of right now, you still have the freedom of movement Lilly bought you. For some reason they haven't pegged Kim's death on you. It's possible that in accord with his record, his manner of death pointed to self-immolation of the accidental persuasion."

"Firebug got burned," Atom laughed, then crawled to the metal toilet and vomited.

"Well, there's a strange sight," Daisy said from the doorway to their cell. "Atom Ulvan, hungover. I've never actually seen you drink."

"There's a reason I don't drink. And this isn't a hangover." Atom hugged the bowl.

"I guess so." Daisy wandered over and settled down on Atom's bed.

"I don't like losing control," Atom croaked as he flopped back against the wall, shaking as cold sweat poured over him. "Bad things happen when I lose control. I have too many things to juggle to risk dropping something. People die when that happens."

Atom closed his eyes and pressed back against the cold plasteel wall, allowing the cool to soak into his cheek.

"That's why I'm just a pilot." Daisy grinned. "How much did you drink, anyway?"

Atom held his thumb and pointer four inches apart.

"Weak," said Daisy with a shake of his head.

"So, boys," Kozue sidled into the conversation. "What's the next step?"

"I think Atom's working on that right now," Daisy chirped.

Atom waved a weak hand in Daisy's direction.

"I'm doubting we can expect much help from the *Ticket*, but that would be nice." Daisy leaned back and thrummed a steady tattoo on his thigh. "Even if they could help, there's no real way to coordinate."

"The key is to stay alive between Charnal and Gravix long enough to find a way out," Kozue said.

"And don't forget about James," Atom groaned from the corner.

"I hope we sent enough of a message," said Daisy.

"You two sent the perfect amount of disruption," Roop said from the doorway. "Charnal is most appreciative."

Daisy scowled. "You have a habit of dropping eaves on folks?" he growled.

Roop spread his hands in innocence. "I was on my way up to congratulate you on a job well done." He stepped into the cell, making sure to linger in the door long enough for Daisy to catch sight of the two uniformed guards behind. "No lasting damage was done. That means no reason for punishment.

"That's straight from the warden." He leaned in with a conspiratorial wink. "Other than that lonestar, Johan Kim, there were no fatalities."

"Kim?" Daisy asked. "He the reason for the decomp?"

"Aye. Apparently, he was cooking something up in his cell that didn't handle too good. His death was ruled accidental, so no major investigation."

"Saw the explosion from the yard. Do they know what caused it? I imagine the prison is tight with anything that could compromise the integrity of the station's hull."

Roop shrugged.

Daisy eyed the heavy man as Atom groaned.

"What's the real reason for this visit?" Daisy climbed to his feet and faced Roop.

"Charnal wants a sit down." Roop frowned down at Atom. "Let me know when he's back on his feet."

"I'm good," Atom said without opening his eyes.

"You want to go now?"

"Better now than later." Atom took a steadying breath and pushed himself to his feet. Stumbling over to Daisy, he grabbed the pilot's arm to steady himself and managed to squint at Roop. "Any idea what it's about?"

Roop shrugged. "Maybe it's a personal congratulations on the job." He turned to exit the room. "Or maybe he just wants to throw something else your way.

"Any way about it," he continued after passing the guards. "My shop is open."

Atom followed on wet-noodle legs, falling in between the guards. He leaned on Daisy to keep himself steady. Roop parted ways as they reached the block floor, whistling a soft ditty as he returned to his table of business.

"You sure this is smart?" Daisy asked as they followed the guards towards the gate.

"Nope," Atom said as he took a deep breath. "But we need to figure out where we stand in this whole mess." The guards seemed to be turning a deaf ear to their conversation, but Atom didn't trust their words to stay private. "I do know we're stuck here until we get the recall orders. That means we need to find a way to play civil between two hans and a warden."

Daisy sighed. "So, we just need to ride things out?"

"Keep our heads on the deck and hope we don't skim too close to a grav well."

As they approached the gate, Atom heard the soft grinding of locks and decompression cycles. He took another deep breath, willing his head to clear. With each breath, he felt a touch further from death.

"I'm almost feeling human again." He winced as the door opened with a loud hiss.

In the portal beyond, Warden James stood waiting with Fresk at his side like a loyal hound.

Atom and Daisy swore in the same breath.

The warden smiled and straightened his glasses. Without a word, he motioned for the pair to join him in the hall. He turned without waiting. Fresk simmered as Atom stumbled through the gate with Daisy a step behind.

"Excellent, you sent my message." James led the way up the plain hallway and made a turn away from the next block. "I appreciate the speed with which you work. I can't wait to see the back half of this message for Charnal. Unfortunately, there is someone who wants a word with you before you can complete this task for me."

"Who else knows I'm here?" Atom asked as they approached the smaller, hub gate.

Warden James remained silent as the gate hummed to life.

In the station hub, they passed through a series of hallways that increased in comfort to the point where Atom questioned whether he still walked the halls of an interstellar prison. Casting a glance back to Fresk, he wondered at the purpose of the meeting. The ever-present guard glared at Atom and growled.

As they drew near the center of the prison station, Atom felt a shift in the soles of his feet.

"Cocked grav?" Daisy murmured.

"It's light," Atom replied.

"I find it easier on the joints," James spoke without turning his head. "Just know, whatever the outcome of this meeting, I expect our agreement to hold. I haven't seen any files on official transfer, so I'm assuming that means you're here for an extended stay."

"Warden, who is this meeting with?"

"Mr. Ulvan, I find your candor both presumptuous and stimulating." The warden stopped outside a door flanked by a pair of armored guards. "Whom you meet is at my discretion and frankly, it only concerns you once you enter their presence."

He waved to the guards and the door hissed open.

Inside the room, Atom found an empty sitting chamber with several low couches and reclining mats. As James stepped over the threshold, the low lights sprang to life. The warden waved to the empty couches and proceeded past them through one of several smaller portals.

"Make yourselves comfortable," said Fresk in her soft voice even as she flashed a hard smile.

Atom ignored the woman and settled onto one of the mats with a straight-backed grace. Daisy snorted at the formality and flopped onto one of the couches.

"You'd think with all the money this boke rolls, he could afford some comfier seats." Daisy grimaced and shifted in his seat to find a more comfortable position. "Hey, lass," he said, waving a hand in Fresk's direction. "Why don't you scare us up something drinkable? I could savor a brew right about now."

Atom fought a retch.

"Or maybe you grab some eats and join us." Daisy grinned at Atom's discomfort and patted the seat next to him. "I saved a seat for you, darl."

Fresk looked ready to explode. "I'm not your serving wench," she growled.

"Fooled me," Daisy said with a playful laugh. "Hey Atom, you have any idea what she's here for, if she's not a servant."

Atom took a deep, centering breath. "Maybe a secretary?"

"That the case, la?" Daisy craned his neck to look at Fresk from an inverted position. "You turning into a soft scribbler?"

Fresk took a step forward, but at that moment James cracked the door to his office. "Oh, Fresk, there you are. Run to my larder and fetch a platter of shaved quri steak with a sharp cheese." The warden waved at Fresk like an impatient schoolmaster and hissed in a low tone. "Now, woman, I have important matters to attend to. This could be a move for both of us."

For the briefest moment, Fresk hesitated. Atom watched with interest as her eyes flashed between Daisy and James. Something in the look gave Atom pause, then she disappeared through the far door and James ducked back into his office.

Craning his neck, Atom caught sight of a long wooden table as Fresk's door hissed shut to leave him alone with Daisy.

"You worried, Atom?"

"She knows her path," Atom replied, too much from rote.

"Go's got the rest of the crew watching over her." Daisy yawned and rubbed his eyes, fighting the sedate quiet of the sitting room. "She's safer there than here."

"That's always the case." Atom folded his hands in his lap and focused on his interlocking fingers for a time before turning his gaze back to Daisy. "Tell me how Mae fits into the story of Daisy."

"Not much to tell, she found me and sticks to me wherever I go."

"Cats are territorial. Your territory is the Black."

"I know, Atom. She doesn't make any sense. I figure I'm her territory."

"Fair enough," Atom said as he rose to his feet in a fluid motion and walked the circumference of the room with measured strides. "Tell me another story about Daisy."

The pilot watched Atom's wandering and registered the distracted air. He pursed his lips in thought. "I split a girl's head open once." Daisy frowned at the floor and Atom glanced over from the far side of his lap. Daisy leaned forward, elbows on knees, his former air of uncaring disregard gone. "I didn't mean to. But accidents don't mean a thing, because they still happen. It might have been a stupid mistake on my part, but that girl had to grow up with a scar down her forehead because of me."

Daisy lifted his eyes and Atom found the ghost of regret.

"What happened?" Atom asked.

"I thought she was cute."

"How old were you?"

"Seven," Daisy grimaced. "A mate and I stole the girl's hat and were playing catch with it while she tried to get it back. I wanted her to notice me, but hadn't figured out how to use my words yet. Like a dummkopf I used actions instead of words. She tripped on the leg of a chair and pitched head-first into the teacher's desk.

"There was blood everywhere." Daisy looked down at his hands as if envisioning the blood and the manifestation of the guilt.

"What happened?"

181

"We owed recompense." Daisy sniffed and lifted his eyes. "My ma sold six months of my life to the family of the girl. Every day after school I went to their house and did whatever chores they gave me.

"Realistically, it could have been much worse." Daisy rose to his feet. "They could have demanded financial compensation. That would have broken my family. I don't think her father ever truly forgave me, but the girl and her mother did. Girls aren't stupid. She knew exactly why I did what I did. In her way, she was kind to me after that. Every afternoon she would share her snack with me, even though she could have crushed me if she had wanted."

"Why do all your stories make me want to walk out an airlock?"

Daisy shook his head, slapped by Atom's words.

"I mean," Atom continued, ending his lapping of the room and returning to his place on the mat. "Something good or funny had to have happened to you at some point in your life. You laugh and smile too much for all of your stories to be doom and gloom."

"Most of those involve drink."

"Drink makes you happy?"

"Loosens me." With a shrug, Daisy rose and wandered over to the door to the dining room where he tried without success to open it. "I don't necessarily drink to forget. Most nights it's just to relax."

Atom closed his eyes and stretched his back upright.

"One time, at a cadet dance, back when I was in the academy, I carried seven friends across the room on my back." Daisy returned to his own couch, but ended up perching on the back with his arms crossed. He stared daggers at the office hatch.

"What do you value?" Atom asked.

"I used to value loyalty, but there seems so little of that in the Black these days. I don't have family. Money is money and while it keeps me floating, I don't need much more than a handful to get me to the next job."

"Seems you spit a whole slew of things you don't value," Atom said.

"I value," Daisy hesitated, "what you and the others have done for me. I value my place on the *One Way Ticket*."

"Remember that." Atom's voice carried a grim finality. "What we have is fragile. A moment's hesitation, the slightest mistake, a miscalculation and we all end. I will give my life to keep this ship-family together, but like everything else in the Black, this family could disappear in a whisper of particles scattered to the astral winds.

"Is that still acceptable to you?" Atom listed his eyes to Daisy.

"Aye," Daisy replied without hesitation.

A smile quirked across Atom's face as he examined the situation with stolid resolve. "Then let's figure out our next step. Margo needs us."

They waited in silence a few more minutes before Fresk came bustling back through the door bearing a platter of meats and cheese. Before the door hissed shut behind her, Daisy and Atom moved in a synchronized, if unrehearsed, dance.

The pilot lurched to his feet with a hungry grin on his face as he stepped towards Fresk. "My gut, I'm starving." He all but drooled at the assortment of savory offerings. "I'm hoping against my ship that those are for us."

Fresk dropped a hand to the stun baton at her hip. "Ain't got time fer your games," she said and slipped past Daisy's disappointed gaze.

Daisy watched her leave like an abandoned puppy outside a restaurant.

As the door hissed shut behind Fresk, Daisy whipped around to find Atom sitting in the same position he had before. The pilot's broad shoulders slumped as he realized their plan had failed.

"No dice?" he asked as he circled the couch and dropped back down in defeat.

"Why would you say that?" Atom grinned and rose to his feet, minus a flimsy rubber shoe. "I would say we are right where we want to be at the moment. Come on and give me a hand."

Daisy perked. He hopped to his feet and followed Atom over to the dining room door and found the portal wedged open by Atom's shoe. With the two of them working against the door hydraulics, they managed to pry the sliding wings back enough for Atom to worm an arm through and trigger the internal release.

Standing in the door, Daisy followed Atom's progress as the captain slipped his shoe back on and ghosted across the long dining room into the kitchen beyond.

Lights sprang to life as Atom stepped across the threshold into the kitchen. He wasted no time in searching, instead took in the room with a single glance, found a magnetic knife rack, chose four carving blades, and ducked back through the dining hall before Daisy had time to question how he progressed.

Without a word, Atom slapped the hatch closed. He handed two knives to Daisy, then slipped his own up his sleeves. Taking a last, surveying glance to ensure nothing had been missed, Atom resumed his seated position on the floor mat.

They had just taken a moment to steady their breathing when the door to Warden James' office hissed open and the warden stepped out. Atom started. Catching the look, Daisy whipped around to find the cause. Warden James stood looking at them with surprise on his face and his hand on his throat.

Blood pulsed.

He tried to gurgle a few words, then collapsed.

Atom and Daisy sat frozen, uncertain as they stared at James' twitching corpse. Swiveling without taking his eyes from the door, Daisy turned to Atom.

"Is that part of the plan?" he asked.

"We adapt." Atom rose and slipped one of the knives from his sleeve. With cautious steps he stalked to the door and pasted himself to the wall just outside. He motioned Daisy to the far side of the portal.

From within the darkened office, Atom made out the sounds of a struggle. Shaking his head as Daisy flanked the door, Atom plunged into the fray.

Atom slid to a halt two steps inside the office and took in the scene. The office lay in scattered disorder. On the floor, Fresk wrestled with Toks Marshall. Fresk used her mass to pin the wiry woman down and slipped a beefy arm around her neck. Slithering onto her back, Fresk threw Toks off balance. Her arm constricted beneath Toks' chin.

Toks thrashed, but Fresk used the frantic motion to work deeper. As Toks fought against the arm, Fresk snaked her legs about the commander's waist and arched back.

Atom and Daisy looked on, uncertain of what to do.

As they watched, Toks' scrabbling hand found a long sliver of glass from a shattered lamp. Without hesitation, she jammed it into Fresk's side.

"Should we ...." Daisy began to ask, but Atom laid a restraining hand on his arm.

Fresk let out a muffled grunt as Toks pulled the makeshift blade out and stabbed again. Despite having less force than the first blow, the second wound proved too much. Fresk's face rippled with shock and Toks squirmed out of the hold. Quick as a mongoose, Toks spun on her aggressor.

Only then did Atom release Daisy.

Without the grace of the grapplers on the floor, Daisy lashed out. With her attention focused on Fresk, Toks only registered her danger at the last moment. She tried to dodge, but Daisy's massive paw locked on her neck. A quick twist of his shoulders and Toks flew across the room, slamming into the wall, and sliding down in a stunned heap.

"Help her up," Atom tossed his knives aside and crossed the short gap to Fresk's prone form. He grabbed her under the arms and lifted her with greater ease than should have been possible for her solid bulk. Even with the lighter grav in the station hub, Fresk should have been a challenge for Atom to even sit up, much less heft to her feet.

Blood poured down Fresk's side as Atom hop-stepped her towards the door.

"We need to get her out of here now," Atom snapped at Daisy. "I'll explain later, but we need to get past those guards at the door somehow."

"The warden's dead as a class-3," Daisy said as he hustled to get an arm under Fresk's opposite shoulder and almost upset Atom's equilibrium. "She's too light."

"Because she doesn't have Fresk's mass."

"Because of the low grav?"

Atom shook his head as he laid Fresk down on the couch. Concern plastered his face. "Because she's not the real Fresk." Atom looked around the room for something to pack against the wound. "Find something to stop the bleeding."

"Wait, it's Lilly?" Daisy asked as he disappeared back into the study.

"That's my educated guess."

A smile broke through the grey of her wan face. "Am I that transparent?" Lilly asked in Fresk's high voice. Her breaths came in short, shallow gasps, but her eyes flashed with grim determination. "You move too slow. We need to be gone."

"Gone won't help if you're dead," Atom snapped as Daisy ran back into the room with several torn strips of cloth and Toks' jacket.

With the skill of a practiced medoc, Atom packed the wound and snugged the long strips of material around Lilly's thickened torso. A low moan escaped Lilly's compressed lips. Examining the dressing with detached concern, Atom nodded in approval and then turned his attention to the narrow-shouldered jacket.

He shook his head.

"I don't suppose you can shift under this kind of duress?" he asked, holding up the jacket.

Lilly tried to laugh, but her eyes rolled back and her head drooped back into the couch.

"How are we getting out of this?" A hard tone crept into Atom's voice. "If we could get her to shift into Toks' skin we could cover the wound and claim she came for a transfer."

"Atom, she's covered in blood," Daisy pointed out.

Patting Lilly's cheeks, Atom drew the baug back to consciousness. Lilly's eyes fluttered and continued to roll as she tried to curl herself into a ball on the couch.

"If we open those doors and the guards see us with her, we're dead where we stand." Atom rose and paced the room again. "Any chance we take those two suits with some kitchen knives?"

Daisy just chuckled. "You're the Left Fist, you tell me," he said with doubt.

"A power surge could cause a suit to reboot." Atom weighed the idea for a moment and then shook his head in disgust.

"No chance?"

"We'd have to pull all the power from the hub into one wire, and that would only reboot one of the suits. That might buy us 30 seconds with only one suit to worry about. Maybe if we could …."

"Atom," Kozue interrupted in a puzzled tone. "I'm detecting a disturbance down in the loading dock. For some reason, whatever is happening seems to be knocking out all the sensors in that region as well."

Atom perked.

"We moving on this?"

"Firm." Atom leaped to action.

Without instructions, Daisy scooped up Lilly. As she rolled her head into his chest, he found her familiar face staring up at him with a distant bleariness. Her body followed her face, slipping into the slender frame they had first met. Cradling the baug with gentle care, Daisy padded to stand beside the main door to James' suite.

"Koze." Atom snugged up the bandages before he took his place at the far side of the doorway. "Are the guards outside responding to the disturbance?"

"That's a neg."

"I think I might be able to help," Lilly murmured into Daisy's shoulder.

"What's your thought?" Atom asked.

Lilly cleared her throat and knit her brow without opening her eyes. For a moment nothing happened, and then she opened her eyes and gazed at Atom with lucid clarity. "Anything you can think to do with this?" Lilly's mouth moved, but a fair imitation of Warden James' voice sounded in the room. "I think we better find a way to talk to those guards without them looking me in the face."

Atom shot for the office like a seeker torpedo.

As he entered, he found Toks climbing to her feet with a woozy wobble. Swerving from his path, he took a moment to drive his knee into the side of her head. With a crunch, the imperial spun back into the wall and crumpled into a twitching heap.

Ignoring his fallen foe, Atom surveyed James' desk and managed to find his way into the station coms.

"Daisy," he called out. "Bring her in here, I've got things lined up."

The pilot hustled in, cradling Lilly in his arms like a sleeping child. With hesitant care, he settled her into the warden's seat.

Atom tripped the call.

"All guards," Lilly said in James' voice. "We are experiencing a glitch in our sensors. As a precaution all prisoners will be locked down for the time being. We will begin prepping for evacuation. Do not, I repeat, do not proceed with evac until you receive direct orders from your superiors.

"In the meantime." Sweat stood out on Lilly's forehead from the effort. "All excess manpower should report to your assigned staging areas."

She severed the connection and collapsed back into the seat.

"The guards outside the suite are moving," Kozue reported.

"That's our cue." Atom waved at Lilly and scowled over at Toks' immobile form. "Kozue, do you have any info on that disturbance yet?"

"Other than it is moving in this general direction, no," Kozue replied. "It seems to be killing the prison sensors as it progresses, almost as if it's kicking out an electro-magnetic field in a perfect sphere."

"What disturbance?" Lilly had assumed her normal voice. She held a protective hand tight to her wounded side.

Atom cocked his head, for a moment forgetting that she did not have access to Kozue's voice. "There's a blackout moving towards us," Atom said as he motioned for Daisy to pick her up again. "Kozue hasn't been able to determine what's causing it, but she said the disturbance originated in the landing bay. That fact leads me to believe it's a legitimate disturbance."

"It's Ash," Lilly closed her eyes and nuzzled back against Daisy as he cradled her against his chest.

Atom flashed her a puzzled look, then asked, "How can you be so sure?"

"Because he always comes for me."

"Always?"

"He's tied to me," Lilly murmured in dreamy shock.

"Should we try to find him?" Atom exchanged a concerned glance with Daisy as they stepped out into the sitting room.

"Mmhmmm," Lilly mumbled as her head drooped.

"What about Toks?" Daisy asked.

"I'll finish it, you get moving with her and I'll catch up." As Atom turned back to the office Toks staggered to the hatch and slapped it closed. "Or not.

"No time to waste, we move." Atom took a centering breath. "Kozue, show us the way."

*   *   *

They found Ash, or more accurately, Ash found them, ten minutes later as they hurtled through the byways of the prison. Under Kozue's careful guidance, they avoided rally points and guard posts. She alerted them to being in the vicinity of Ash, but the golem still caught them off guard as he smashed through a nearby wall with the ease of a farmer walking through a wheat field.

Atom and Daisy skidded to a halt and almost bolted like startled rabbits.

Only when they realized the metal monstrosity stood motionless did they register that they had stumbled across their savior.

"Lilly," the golem whispered in its mechanized hiss.

A barrage of blaster fire followed the golem through its newly-crafted doorway. The metal beast shrugged the attack off and without looking, pointed a fist back into the aperture. A pulsing energy beam erupted from the fist and hostile fire ceased.

Ash took a step towards them, bobbing its head in a subservient manner.

"Lilly," it whispered again. This time the golem opened its arms wide and as it did so, the center of the chest rippled outward to reveal an opening big enough to accommodate Lilly. Casting a nervous glance to Atom, Daisy edged forward and slipped Lilly into the golem's chest cavity.

If Ash had a face, Atom imagined a smile of relief plastered across it.

The golem's chest rippled again, like metal fingers closing over a precious gem. "Friend," Ash whispered and turned away to leave the pair staring wide-eyed at its retreating form.

"I suggest you follow the golem." Kozue broke the spell.

Without a second prompting, Atom and Daisy bolted after the receding figure. They struggled to keep pace with the long strides of the looming golem, but at a dead run, they managed. Due to the Ash-enforced communications embargo and Lilly's orders, they met light resistance as the golem forged the straightest path to the prison's docking bay.

As they followed Ash through the last wall into the bay, Warden James' voice echoed over the prison coms. "There has been a catastrophic breach." A tinge of panic laced James' voice.

"Execute evacuation protocol. Repeat: execute evacuation protocol."

"Koze, is there really an emergency?" Atom asked as he watched the golem clambered up into the *Hellkite*.

"Other than the security breach, no," Kozue replied. "That com came from Ash."

"That's what I thought." Atom stopped on the flight deck outside the *Hellkite* and watched the hatch shut. A moment later the ship powered up and launched from the hangar. "How did the golem manage to pilot the ship in here past all the prison defenses?"

Atom felt Kozue's shrug. "I didn't detect anything until the golem was aboard the station and kicking out the null readings on the system."

"That's impressive," said Daisy. "Now I suppose it's time for us to find our ride off this station. I don't suppose you have any suggestions for us, Kozue? Most of what I'm seeing here are prison transports that will get us flagged as soon as we enter any proper system."

"It appears Ash left the warden's personal ship unlocked for you," Kozue replied. "It has been fully prepped."

"Works for me." Atom sprinted across the quiet bay towards the gangway of the single ship tucked behind the boxy prison transports. The sleek ship hovered in a suspensor cradle on the far side of the bay. As they ran, the engines hummed to life and a soft golden-blue glow emanated from the main thrusters as the ship warmed.

"Tell me you can fly this thing," Atom panted as he pounded up the gangway into the small, but plush living suite.

Daisy, a step behind, did not bother with a reply. Instead, he slapped the hatch shut and hopped over the pilot's console, into the seat. A few buttons later, the ship detached from the docking locks and floated free into the Black.

"We good?" Daisy called over his shoulder.

"Stow and go," Atom replied.

Daisy punched the throttle and the ship burned hard for the Black.

* * *

A few hours later, Daisy coupled the warden's ship with the *Ticket*, and after plotting a course for a nearby asteroid field, they said farewell to their small escape vessel. Back aboard his home, Atom blew out a ball of tension he had failed to notice aboard the prison station.

He swept Margo into his arms and inhaled her innocent fragrance.

"I say we make it a point not to split up anymore, unless we can't help it," he whispered in her ear.

"Love you, dada." She grinned and squeezed his neck with all her tiny might.

"Good to have you back, Cap." Shi handed Atom his rail pistol as she flashed a sly wink. "I reckin green's a good color on you. It really makes yer biscuits pop. You might consider holdin' onto that there jumper."

"What's the course, boss?" Hither asked, failing to keep a smile from her lips as she focused on the far wall of the hold.

"We still have a rendezvous with the other client?" Atom asked as he tucked his pistol in the pocket of his jumpsuit. "I'm not sure it puts us any closer to that treasure, but it never hurts to have jobs lined up. After that meet, we'll head back to Lassiter to have our sit down with Coffey. Our end is complete and it's time we get paid."

"The contact understood your predicament and extended their stay at the coordinates. I'll punch the course now." Hither nodded for Daisy to follow, leaving Atom alone with Shi and Byron.

"You looked after my daughter and the *Ticket*," Atom said as he shifted Margo to his hip. "I think that might count for something special when all this settles out."

"Weren't nothin'." Shi bobbed her head, embarrassed by the acknowledgement.

"I made somefin fer the bobbin," Byron chirped.

"And what would that be?" Atom asked.

Byron whistled and a soft whirring buzzed about Atom's head. Margo laughed. Instinct hunched Atom's head and shoulders as the soft buzz passed again. Shi and Byron joined in with Margo's laughter as Atom tried to locate the sound in the dusky shadows of the ship's hold.

"What is it?" Atom squinted up, shielding Margo from the unknown.

"Ease up, Cody," Byron called into the air.

"Cody," Margo squealed.

The child held out her hand with timid joy and after a humming whir of mechanical wings, a tiny dragon landed in her palm. Wingtip to wingtip, the dragon just managed to drape over the edges of Margo's hand, but its long, sinuous tail snaked around her wrist for stability, even as golden eyes turned up to peer into her face.

"See, dada." Margo held the mechanized beast up for Atom's inspection.

"That's amazing," Atom murmured as he squinted at the intricate detail.

The dragon preened. Lifting a head no bigger than Atom's thumbnail, the creature twined with a serpentine grace that caught the hold's light along its black and gold flanks. Each scale looked to represent hours of synthesizing, weaving, and coloring.

The little dragon lifted its head and yawned as it studied Atom.

"Where did you come up with the name Cody?" he asked.

Margo shrugged. "Is Cody." She spoke as if common sense dictated it truth.

"Tell me about Cody," Atom said as he headed for the stairs and the commons above.

"Nuffin' special, 'e's just a toy I fabbed down in my shop." Byron trailed along behind Atom, his head dropped with sheepish pride. "I'd some time on me 'ands and I figured Go could use a touch a distraction.

"Got the idea back on Shelley on the ghosty-ship. I know it were a while back, but it got me finkin' we could use a scout bot 'stead a pu'in' us in 'arms way. So, I gots to finkin' 'bout what we could use to 'elp us out in that sort a sitch. It'd 'ave to be soemfin' lil an' fast. So's I'm si'in at the table and 'iver's tellin' Go a beddy-time tale 'bout dragons 'n such an' a lass who 'as to use 'er pan to riddle a dragon outta his heap a treasure.

"Got me finkin' 'bout dragons." Byron followed Atom into the commons and slipped into the booth without missing a beat. "An' Margo's all dreamin' 'bout dragons an' I says to meself, 'bet I could print a dragon' so's I did. I dreamt 'er and tinker'd 'er.

"An' poof." He mimed an explosion with his hands held wide. "Me pan pops an' out flies Cody."

"I'll bet Margo's excited about it." Atom laughed as he set his daughter on the counter and filled a mug with black perk. "It's only been a couple days and I feel like I missed an entire chapter of all the happenings."

"Yes and no." Shi wandered in from the bridge. "We've pretty much bin sittin' tight."

"I wish I could have been in better touch with you."

"We got your burst and knew your relative location." She hopped up to sit on the counter beside Margo, her brace of pistols chunking against the metal topper. "It came through a touch garbled, so we couldn't lock down a rescue mission, but we knew where to drift."

Margo held Cody out for Shi to stroke.

Atom nodded and turned his attention back to Byron. "What are the specs on Cody?"

"Well." Byron pulled his long, dark curls down over his eyes. "Problem is, I'm a right good crafter, but I en't so solid at the programin'."

"Meaning?" Atom sipped and grimaced at the heat.

"Meanin' he can't control the blasted thing worth a darn," Shi laughed. "He built the dragon and tried to program it, but it imprinted on Margo and won't listen to anyone else."

"So, we have a rogue dragon aboard the ship?"

"Sor' of." Byron searched his brain for the best way to present the problem. "It'll do wha'ever Go asks it to, but if anyone else commands, 'ere's an even chance it kacks in yer 'and."

"Koze, could you interface with the dragon?" Atom lifted Margo by the back of her canvas jumper and with one hand, hoisted her to the floor.

"Not presently," Kozue answered.

"I guess it's a cute toy." Atom shrugged in Byron's direction. "The craftsmanship is superb. I tip my cap to your attention to detail, but the question in my mind is how to make this more than a toy."

"Guess it en't nuffin' but a purdy bauble fer the kit."

"Work with it," Atom encouraged. "Work with Kozue on this. What if Cody could be a physical body for Kozue to join us on missions. I think if you two work together, something could come of it."

Byron's eyes lit.

"In the meantime." Atom turned his attention to Shi. "I do believe we need to get ourselves prepped for the meet with the new client."

"Any idea on who the client is?" Shi hopped down from the counter and fell in beside Atom as he turned for the bridge. "I picked up they was tied to the actor's guild."

"My estimation is the ties run deeper than that. From what I know about our situation and what we've faced off against up to now, I'd say we're meeting someone with links to the Tribes. The very fact that they are being so secretive as to give us expiring coords, points to darker contacts than anything we've faced to date."

"Danger to us?"

"There's always danger in our line of work."

"Truth." Shi ducked into the bridge ahead of Atom and nodded to Daisy. "Good to have you back, you lunkhead."

Daisy sat in his pilot's chair with Mae preening in his lap. He scratched under her chin as he broke off the discussion with Hither and turned to face Atom and Shi. A relieved smile creased his dark face.

"We on course?" Atom interrupted.

"Aye, Cap." Daisy mocked a salute in Atom's direction. "Lucky for us, our little jaunt didn't take us too far out of our target system. Hop, skip, and a jump and we'll be right back where we left off."

"I hate all these side gigs. They just distract us from our final goals." Atom leaned on the overhead conduits and sipped at his steaming perk. "I sure did miss this view." He stared into the nothing beyond Daisy's display. "What's our new arrival time?"

"Quarter cycle, give or take."

"Will we hit our window?"

"Just inside," Hither replied from her navigator's seat.

"Good, Margo needs a nap." Atom grinned at the crew and turned to leave.

"You mean, you need a nap?" Shi jibed.

"That's what I said."

*   *   *

The *One Way Ticket* dropped into the system just as Hither had predicted. Under Daisy's hand, they skirted the inhabited planets and made for the deep space rendezvous. Each member of the crew prepared in different ways as they tried to anticipate the unknown client and myriad possibilities of their docking.

Atom sat in silence on the bridge, watching as they approached the coordinates, trying to anticipate what sort of ship awaited them. He made idle note of Daisy and Hither's actions as they flew.

In Daisy's lap, Mae purred with unabashed contentment. Behind him, Hither's hands flew through the projected displays of the navigator's console.

"What are we looking at?" Atom asked.

"Large ship." Spooling information held Hither's attention to the boards in front of her. "I'm registering something with greater mass than a small moon. I'm not sure if it's actually a ship or a pirated moonlet."

Atom glanced over from Shi's com-station. "A moonlet?"

Hither flipped a hand and the initial readings on their approaching target sprang up on the console in front of Atom. As more information poured into the *Ticket's* scanners, the picture gained clarity.

It did, in fact, look very similar to a small moon.

"What kind of readings are we getting on that thing?" Atom asked, scrolling through the information with idle curiosity.

"Fair low EM projections for something that large." Hither's eyes pinched as she flicked through the incoming information. "They seem to be running silent, other than microburst communications with more than a dozen undesignated points throughout the galaxy. And I wouldn't notice those except I'm actively scanning the target."

"No outliers?"

"Not that I'm detecting, although there could be a few scout ships beyond our scan range. If they're there, they are running dark."

"I wonder why I've never come across anything like this before." Atom scowled at the projections, spinning them in the air with a flick of his finger. "Daisy, how close are we to visual?"

"Deep scans will give you a fuzzy, but nothing that will help us at this point."

"And we're sure this is our target?" Atom stroked his chin in thought.

"I don't see how it could be otherwise," Hither replied. "It's sitting smack on the coords you gave me. It's too far outside normal lanes to be a coincidence. And it's the only thing within two AU's worth mentioning."

Pulling the image up on Shi's console, Atom examined the grainy picture. With each second, the pixilation recalibrated, until Atom stared at a rough surfaced asteroid.

"You weren't kidding," Atom said. "She's almost a rogue moon."

"Think the client's ship is hiding in her shadow?" Daisy asked.

"I'm not so sure," Hither replied. "These EM bursts are coming from the moonlet itself. That's pointing to some sort of station on the surface, or just below the surface. Or perhaps a ship tethered to the surface."

Atom studied the moonlet. As they approached, a deep crater hove into view, revealing a line of recessed docking bays visible only as shadows through the scanners.

"You picking up the bays?" Atom asked Hither. "There are enough to haku an entire mid-sized fleet at once." The presence of man-made structures countered by the lack of ship traffic surrounding such a base ticked a warning switch in the back of Atom's mind.

He swiped the images of the moonlet off his screen and pulled up the coms.

"This is the merchant ship *One Way Ticket* requesting docking clearance," Atom called out, flashing the ship's transponder ID as he spoke.

For a moment, the only sound on the bridge was the soft hiss of the com system.

"Merchant ship *One Way Ticket*, this is fleet vessel Harvest Moon, maintain your current course. Once clear of our perimeter, you will be notified and guided into the correct docking bay via beam interface."

The connection blinked out, leaving Atom with a surprised look on his face.

"I guess we've officially been invited." He spun away from the console and stood. "What's our time looking like?"

"Rough estimate is twenty ticks," Hither replied.

"Daisy's got this, Hither. I want you geared and ready to float. Daisy, grab your gauntlets on the inbound, and then join us in the hold as soon as we touch down. I don't know what we're expecting here, but I want all hands, and prep like a hostile drop."

Hither closed out her station and hopped up.

"See you in a touch," Daisy continued to stroke Mae as he studied the fast-approaching asteroid.

*   *   *

The beam-supported docking proceeded as smooth as if Daisy had dropped the ship himself.

Atom focused on the upcoming meeting. As tricky as the search for the *Ave Maria* had proven, he wondered if the job might be better stowed in the back of his hold. As he strapped on his rail pistol, he smiled down at Margo. She sat in the little bunk he had rigged to the ceiling, swaying like a miniature Buddha.

"Best lesson learned on a job," he said as he straightened the collar of his shirt and slipped into his dulled brown jacket. "Look the best you can with a new client and play the honesty card, Margo. You'd be surprised the leeway you can garner from a little honest banter.

"We don't have time for another job at the moment, but talking one out can't hurt either side." He picked her up and set her on the floor with a loving tousle of her hair. "As long as they know where they stand in your docking order, most clients are more than willing to work with you and wait their turn. Good clients wait for good work to be done. And if they're in a rush, they can always move on with their second choice."

He guided her from their shared rack-room and towards the hold.

"Can't say I've been more impressed with a beam dock in all my time as a pilot," Daisy laughed as he fell in beside them. "I think the whole crew is ready to hit this one. We plan on sticking with you through hell or high water."

"Appreciate it." Atom picked up Margo and tossed her to the pilot.

Margo squealed with delight.

"It's nice to see you looking normal again. I can't say anything about prison agrees with either of us." Atom gestured to the pilot's attire. Dressed in his usual canvas work pants and snug, short-sleeved shirt, Daisy nodded in agreement. At his hip, hung like a pair of shackles, bounced his power gauntlets.

"Back there," Atom continued. "You said you've never killed anyone since leaving school. How can you be so sure with those gauntlets? They can liquify a man's innards faster than a rad-burst. I've seen you dust cement walls with ease. Seems a human's a touch squishier than cement."

Daisy patted his gauntlets as he carried Margo through the galley. "I always set them to the lowest level when I fight people. That should limit the damage to broken bones and concussions."

"Should?"

"That's what I tell myself," Daisy quirked a smile. "I still sleep at night."

As they stepped out onto the landing above the hold, Atom paused and looked down on his little crew. He marveled at the change from when they first set foot aboard his ship.

Atom swore Byron had grown a few inches in the months aboard.

As a whole, they seemed more a family than any crew he had flown with before. Shi stood in her customary heavy-weave poncho, her hands hidden beneath as she shared a quiet laugh with Hither. The ex-courtesan wore a simple dress that flattered her figure and complimented the spritely red curls framing her face.

Cocking an eyebrow at Hither's choice in footwear, Atom trailed Daisy down the stairs. "I hope we don't run into trouble," he said, gesturing to her heels.

"Why, Atom," she dropped a demure head bob to hide a shy smile, "You should know by now that I hide behind improbability. Nobody expects more than a pretty face when I wear shoes like this."

She held out her foot for inspection and then executed a perfect pirouette on the tip of her other shoe.

"Plus," she leaned in with a stage whisper, "I can always kick them off." She mimed a shocked look. "For some reason, that always surprises people."

"Don't ferget she kin use the heel as a lockpick, ice-pick, an' maybe even a toothpick," Shi said with a laugh as Atom and Daisy approached.

"Only if she wants them to lose a tooth." Atom joined the light laughter.

"Or an eye," Hither added.

"Where's By?" Atom asked as he set Margo in the pram and looked back to the closed doors of the workshop. "He knows we're all heading out, right?"

As if on cue, Byron trotted from the side hatch and joined the others.

"I miss somefing?" the mech asked.

"Not a thing," Daisy grabbed the sprouting boy in a headlock and roughed him up. "Just Hither flashing some leg. Nothing you haven't seen before or will probably see again."

"Ah, why I always miss the goods," Byron lamented as Hither slapped Daisy in the arm.

Daisy laughed and set Byron down.

"People," Atom called out as he powered up the pram and hovered it close to the hatch. "We need to focus up. This might be the first client meet I've had where I can honestly say I have no idea what lies ahead.

"We stay tight and we stay focused." He locked eyes with each member of the crew. "Until we understand who we are looking to take a job from, I want each of you to watch each other. I don't anticipate walking into any danger at this point, but the Walkers are far-reaching, so we approach cautious-like.

"Stay sharp, stay alive. And if things go null, fight for the *Ticket*. If you can't make it here, get to the Black and have Koze blast a pulse."

A round of affirmatives met his glare.

Atom turned back to the hatch, rolled his shoulders, and prepared for the final docking lock. The rest of the crew settled behind him as the familiar thump of a settling ship met their ears. They readied.

A surprising hiss startled Atom, causing his head to snap sideways as the main cargo ramp broke seal and whirred to life.

"Koze?" Atom shifted stance, his hand drifted to his pistol.

"I'm sorry, Atom." Kozue sounded perplexed. "I turned over nav-control of the ship for the docking procedure. I am trying to ascertain how they are controlling anything beyond that."

"Seems a touch hostile." Shi grinned and flipped her poncho back as she stepped up beside Atom.

"Simmer," said Atom.

The others turned their attention to the ramp as it fully cracked the seal and began to drop. They fanned out, their eyes sharp and senses heightened. From around the edge of the ramp a pale blue light seeped. Atom glanced at the others and then led them over to stand ready.

The ramp settled with a thud that drove a shiver up through Atom's bones. The crew stood ready in the mouth of their ship, looking out into an empty hangar. Dull metal walls framed the moon carved rock and while some ambient ship pops and hisses met his ears as the *Ticket* settled into her berth, the hangar hung in eerie quiet.

"Seems like we should have a little mist to set the mood," said Hither from Atom's left.

Shi snickered.

Daisy joined in, his deep basso echoing through the empty chamber. "Maybe they could pump in some gloomy music." The pilot continued to laugh, ignoring Atom's frown. Despite his face speaking otherwise, the relaxed, jovial nature of the group pleased Atom as they stepped off into the unknown.

Even Byron joined in, mimicking haunting reed flutes from a third-rate jump-scare vid.

"Easy, kin," Atom hissed as he fired up the suspensors on the pram and hovered Margo towards the ramp. "Let's keep our guns loose and eyes sharp. Just don't forget, we don't want to lose a paying gig."

A broad access hatch in the hangar wall opened to reveal a solitary figure.

"Atom Ulvan of the Meriwether han," the figure called out.

Atom recognized the player from the tavern. Atom nodded in greeting.

"Nice to see you again," Atom said in a business-like manner. "I never did get your name when we met back on Lassiter."

The man shook his head in disappointment. "I suppose that means you didn't pay too much attention to our play then. I understand I wasn't the headliner, but I did play an important role as the village chief in The Seven Samurai of Verona.

"Bronte, Alderon Bronte," the man said with a flourishing bow. He swept his long grey hair back as he rose to stand before the crew.

Atom introduced the crew with polite reserve.

Bronte nodded to each in turn before directing his attention back to Atom. "If you would kindly follow me, I will take you to our han leader."

Exchanging glances with his crew, Atom fell in beside Bronte and allowed the player to lead them across the empty hangar and into the interior of the hollowed asteroid. Beyond the hangar, a series of tunnels carried them past redundant air-locks and blast doors.

"Welcome to our village," Bronte said with theatrical grandeur as the last door hissed opened to reveal that the center to the moonlet had been hollowed out and a complete biosphere hidden within.

"Well, en't that somfin." Byron stepped past Bronte, amazement plastered over his face.

The group stood at the head of a cliff-side path dropping into a cauldron valley. Atom had to remind himself that they stood inside an asteroid, free-floating across the Black. At the foot of the switch-back path, rice paddies checker-boarded the flat valley floor. A river gushed from a cliff face on the far side of the habisphere and wound a lazy path through the paddies until it fed into a broad pool that lapped at the base of the cliff to their right.

Hither joined Byron at the edge of the cliff, resting a hand on the sturdy wooden rail marking the edge of safe travels. "I've seen small streams aboard luxury ships," she whispered in amazement. "I've even seen decorative ponds, but this is bordering on a lake.

"How did you do this?" She turned her wide eyes back to Bronte.

"Money," he replied with a matter-of-fact tilt of his head. "We needed a refuge that was safe and mobile, so we built this. It's a completely self-sustaining system. Everything recycles.

"I'm not saying that we're above bringing in outside food and materials," he laughed, stepping forward to offer his arm to Hither.

Without waiting for the others, he led the way down the easy decline of the wandering path. Falling in a step behind the pair, Atom nodded for the others to keep up. Not used to playing second fiddle, he spent the walk in careful observation of their surroundings.

"How you run the grav in this fing? Byron walked nearest the railing and ogled the scenery. "Overlappin' plates?" Wouldn't that frow external readings?"

"A very finely tuned plate," Bronte replied without turning.

"A single plate?" Byron stammered. He pressed on his temples with his fingertips as he tried to compute the power and precision necessary to manufacture anything of the scope Bronte suggested.

A few silent, awestruck minutes later, they reached the level floor of the synthetic valley and stepped out on the path across the lake of rice paddies. Following Bronte, they strolled past lines of stooped workers who sang a haunting song and planted to the steady tempo.

"How many people live here?" Atom asked, watching the sowers.

"Enough."

Atom nodded, calculating land area and trying to gather a rough estimate in his head.

Drawing near to the river, Atom felt himself lulled into a sense of calm. Cicadas chirped a steady rhythm. Across the river, a wall of tall pines rose to the skies above. The path crossed a simple wooden bridge and Atom marveled at the whole landscape as they stepped onto the sturdy wooden beams. Behind them, a synthetic sun bathed the fields in a golden light, while ahead a peaceful shroud of shade beckoned.

"Not much further." Bronte paused atop the arch of the bridge and turned back to Atom, ignoring the others.

Stepping up to face Bronte, Atom flashed Hither a glance. She returned the look with a serene smile. "Do you have any idea what this meeting is about?" he asked the player with a touch of concern. "Most jobs I entertain, I have a rough idea of what will be discussed. Being kept in the dark tends to point to something I'm not going to like."

Bronte gave a knowing, but sad smile. "I am privy to my lord's council, but it's not my place to pass along this information." He clapped a hand on Atom's shoulder in a friendly fashion. "Know this, though, if you choose not to accept the job, you will be permitted to depart without any interference. We have faith in our ability to disappear. We aren't worried about anything beyond this contact.

"Beyond that." He shrugged and turned to look up into the gloom of the forest. "You will need to speak with my lord."

Atom looked over Bronte's shoulder at the landscaped forest and narrowed his eyes, trying to see what lay hidden in the shadows.

"Lead on." Atom gestured to the woods, even as his hand rested at his hip for the reassuring heft of his pistol. "I personally don't feel the need to draw things out any longer than necessary."

Bronte laughed with hearty enthusiasm. "I heard you were a succinct man and tenacious warrior."

"The two flow in the same riverbed."

"Then onward and upward," said Bronte and with a sweeping gesture he led Hither on the downward sloped timbers of the bridge. "The sooner we reach the village, the sooner you shall have your meet with my lord."

*   *   *

The climb through the pines doubled their paddy-crossing walk. In and out of trees, the path wandered as if a child had laid the stones as whimsy carried her. Only after they paused at a dramatic overlook and continued through a thick and ancient stand of trees did Atom sense the approach of their destination. Just beyond the silence of the copse, they crossed into a well-tended cemetery.

Atom eyed the neat rows of simple wooden grave markers. On each, a name stood out, carved in a flowing, archaic script.

"How long have you lived here?" he asked. "Everything seems such an odd mix. I know this was all built by the hands of man, but there's a feeling that everything I'm seeing has been here since the beginning of time."

"I believe that was the original goal," Bronte preened. "I don't know how long this has been here, but I can tell you have multiple generations buried in this cemetery.

"This row," he said with pride as he rested a hand on a marker. "Contains my family, going back to the ninth generation.

"That would make me the tenth." He fixed Atom with a contemplative look. "That would put this village at roughly three hundred years old. But my family wasn't among the original occupants."

"Yer sayin' this place is been floatin' fer 'undreds a years?" Byron exclaimed, his eyes twitching as his mind overflowed with the information.

"Aye, lad." Bronte released Hither in order to wander down the row, trailing a hand with loving attention on several markers. "We've been around long enough to make a mark on this galaxy.

"But now my thoughts are slowing us up." He turned back to Atom, apology in his eyes. "I'll get you up to the village and up to the meet."

Without any further explanation, he turned, and tucking his hands behind his back, led the group on the far path, deeper into the woods. They walked with muted footsteps between the ancient trunks. The path, although carpeted with pine needles, proved easy enough to pick out from the surrounding landscape.

As they drew near the village, Byron leaped with surprise and excitement as he pointed to a doe and her two fawns grazing in a sunny patch of grassy meadow visible through the distant trees.

"There's a bleedin' deer in an asteroid," he hissed, his eyes wide as saucers.

"Yes, son," Bronte said with a paternal smile as he craned his neck to take in his own view of the majestic beasts. "As I said, we have a fully sustainable ecosystem here. That includes animals.

"Come now." He turned and continued along the path. "The village is just ahead."

Reveling in the whisper of a breeze swirling through the trees, Atom maneuvered the pram up a final set of stone steps leading into Bronte's village. He halted at the edge of a carved plateau nestled up against the curved side of the hollowed asteroid.

The village consisted of fifty or so immaculate, if ancient, wooden structures. Smaller thatch-roofed dwellings surrounded a wide meeting hall. Black tile shielded the roof and artesian shachihoko decorated the ends of the central beam. In front of the broad, pillared hall, a small packed earth square sat empty.

"Quaint," Atom said as the others fell into a ragged line at the top of the steps.

"It's home." Bronte shrugged.

As they made to cross the square, Atom noted several shadowy figures lurking in the doorways of the houses flanking the open space. The doors to the central hall opened at their approach, held by silent acolytes.

Bronte led the way inside.

Heavy timber posts ran in dual lines, creating a sylvan avenue terminating at a low dais at the far end of the room.

"Atom Ulvan of the Meriwether Han." Bronte's introduction carried Atom along with a thespian flair as the captain pressed forward with stolid curiosity. "And the crew of the *One Way Ticket*."

Atom halted halfway across the long room, studying the man seated on a cushion upon the dais. With one hand on the pram and the other stroking his holstered rail-pistol, he stood in calm silence. Atom's eyes slipped from the man, taking in the surroundings in a single, sweeping glance. Drifting between each pillar, soft glowing paper lamps hung on suspensors. Tight weave, rush flooring mats compressed beneath Atom's boots. Sliding doors lined both walls behind the pillars.

Atom shifted his head and caught the soft rustle of cloth as a guard or ambusher shifted.

"Crew?" The man upon the dais questioned without looking up from the book resting on a low table before him. "Or compatriots?"

Atom shifted forward a couple steps, swinging the pram to settle at his side. "They're my crew, m'lord." Atom's stiff bow brought a gentle chuckle from their host.

"I appreciate your formalities," he said. "But in my estimation, we are equals."

Casting a staying glance to his crew, Atom strode to the dais with a boldness that brought a gasp from Bronte and a tense shift from beyond the shoji screens. Atom studied his host as he and the pram halted just beyond the edge of the platform.

The man, older, but fit and wiry, sat facing the side wall with one hand shielded from Atom's view. Dark glasses hid his eyes and his slicked, white hair gave a sleek, predatory cast to his already lean features. As if Atom's advance gave no concern, the man traced words in his book with a finger that fluttered somewhere between fine and frail.

"Would you care to sit?" the man asked without looking up from his book.

Before Atom could answer, a servant whisked from a sliding door behind the dais with two cushions and, from her knees, bowed to Atom as she placed them on the dais at a civil distance from her master.

"Please," the host said as he closed his book and turned his gaze, "join me."

Atom lifted Margo from the pram and set her on the dais as the unburdened machine settled to the floor with a relieved sigh. Shepherding his daughter to her cushion, Atom dropped to a stiff-backed posture with his arms resting on his knees.

"To what do I owe the pleasure?" Atom asked.

The man tsked with a gentle shake of his head, reminiscent of a weaving snake. "Always in such a rush, Mr. Ulvan." The host shifted his low table aside so nothing sat between them. "You of all people should recall the civil formalities which must be observed when rank deserves it. Without civility we are little more than the beasts we hunt."

"What rank do I possess?" Atom quirked his head in amusement.

"Why, you are a high lord." The man sounded amazed.

"Was. I am nothing but a ship's captain now, a shadow of what I once was."

"A lord of shadows." The man clapped his hands together and pressed them to his lips. "Oh, how I like the sound of that. Atom Ulvan, the shadow lord."

Atom stared at the other's mirth with an impassive glare.

"Forgive me." The man's predatory smile revealed a dead front tooth that matched the cold, calculating eyes behind the dusky glasses. "My name is Alderon Pips. I am the head of this meager tribe of players."

Atom glanced down the hall to where Bronte stood beside his crew. "Alderon ...." he began.

"Is a family name," Pips filled in.

"And the Tribes aren't a myth?"

"Fortunately, no," Pips said with a laugh and some of the predatory tension fell away from his face. "We are not a myth, not completely. I will admit that we allow some of the stories of our prowess to spin on larger than reality, but we do exist. Generally, we keep to ourselves and take the odd contract to perpetuate the flow of ko. I can assure you, however, that the stories you have heard are beyond our capabilities."

"If you represent the Ghost Tribes, why do you need me?"

"To clarify, I only represent a single tribe. There are others out there. But, I am the head of my Tribe and I would like to hire you because there are times ...." Pips struggled to find the right words. "Where an outside contractor is needed to preserve the peace and structure within one of those Tribes."

A light of understanding drifted across Atom's face like a veil, but before he could voice his thoughts, Margo rose to her feet. She stepped close to lean on Atom's shoulder. "Hims funny eyes." She leaned her head sideways to study Pips.

"Hush, love, that's not polite," Atom chided.

A broad smile spread across Pips' face. "She is rare," he said and removed his smoked glasses to reveal blue eyes, pale enough to border on white.

Margo leaned forward and nodded in confirmation. "Yip, funny eyes," she repeated, looking up to Atom with a worried expression. Seeing her consternation, Pips replaced his glasses. Margo stared, but settled back against Atom's shoulder. She relaxed her body, but not her vigilance.

"Care to talk of the job?" Atom wrapped a comforting arm around Margo's waist.

"I am actually presenting a pair of jobs. The first is something of a test. We could handle it ourselves, but if we're already hiring you, why not use your skills.

"The Migori have taken up against the Adlerians. Simply put, they contest a system in the First Knuckle of the First Finger. The Adlerians have contracted us to remove an opposing piece, Admiral Leilani Motoki Migori.

"It would be a simple matter for us." Pips retrieved his table and once again began tracing a finger over information. "But it should give us a sound reading on your abilities."

"And the second job?"

"Kill Lilly Prezrakov Genkohan."

*   *   *

Back in the safe embrace of the Black, the crew mulled the possibilities.

"I feel as if we been over this one already." Shi had her feet propped on the empty chair at the end of the table. "Kill 'er, don't kill 'er, kill 'er agin. I vote, she ain't done nothin' wrong by us. Leave 'er be."

"Oi, darl, you forgettin' the cap's bleedin' conks," Byron chipped in from across the table.

"I've done the same an' he ain't put me down … yet." She grinned at Atom.

"That's 'cause I en't tickled 'is palm 'nough," Byron said into his bowl of spicy rice.

Blowing a childish raspberry, Shi returned her attention to slipping bullets into her gunbelt. Their relationship had evolved in the months aboard the ship. Coming from the same planet, the homeworld pair had grown into a sibling pair that sometimes amused, and other times grated on Atom's paternal nerves.

The captain stood with his back to the two, scooping his own bowl of spicy rice and topping it with a heap of saucy veggies. At his feet Margo sat, playing with Cody.

"She could be dead." Atom spoke without turning.

"You know 'er, Cap," said Shi. "I wouldn't wager a single shell on attending her buryin'."

"It was a deep wound."

"So you say, but she was alive when you put 'er inside that golem."

Atom shrugged. "Barely. She wasn't conscious and as uncolored as a body can get before hopping on to the other side." He pondered his way to the table and shared the chair with Shi's feet. "I didn't think she was going to make it. I didn't think to check her pulse, but her breath almost gone and she couldn't hold any form but her own."

"Why'd the golem want 'er inside?" Byron asked. "Get an 'unger or somefin?"

Cody flew over, and without landing, stole a strip of sautéed zucchini, and whirled back to drop the food in Margo's outstretched hand.

Giggling, Margo stuffed the food in her mouth. Atom shook his head.

"If I had to guess," he took his own bite, "That golem has a stasis pod installed."

"En't standard." Byron plotted schematics in his mind.

"Koze, is it possible to dredge prints for a golem?" Atom asked. He sniffed as he hit an extra spice bite.

"Unfortunately, no," the AI replied. "If I could worm into an imperial core, I might be able to find what you are looking for. But at the moment, I have no access to records directly addressing golems."

"We 'ave to assume she's modded that metal beastie so hard the imps would scrap him an' start over," Byron said with a distant shrug.

"But a stasis pod is possible?" Atom asked.

Byron licked off his spoon and used it to scratch his scalp. He scowled down at his bowl. "Jus' a trisky twist a space 'n power. Could 'er guts play 'at way? Sure...." He left off fishing his spoon through his thick, dark hair and took another bite of his dinner. He chewed in thought before looking up at Atom and Shi. "But, powerin' anyfing larger 'n a stasis cast makes portability improbable."

Atom pushed his food around in his bowl. "Possible, but not probable," he mused. "We need to bounce to the highest orbit first. We need to talk to Coffey and figure if her information holds air. If it's solid, have choices on the table."

"Whether to ride fer money or more money?" Shi grinned as she slipped the last bullet into her belt and closed up the ammo box. "You know my vote on that matter. Question sits, is there a time limit on the Tribe's job. Turnin' the matter, seems to be the Migori boke might be time-crunched, but the other?"

"Lilly?"

"I reckin' that's a touch more open. We gotta track the trail first. We can't kill what we can't find ... and that's if she's still breathin'."

Atom dropped his spoon in his empty bowl and rose. "We hit Coffey first. Tie up that intel loop. Then we move on the Tribe job, first part first. Sounds like there is a window there and we'll aim to shoot that gap.

"We miss that window and we lose the bounty, and that's bad for business.

"We'll see how that job and the treasure ship line up." He rinsed his bowl in the sink and tucked it in the cabinet. "We'll vote on our course when we get to that point."

*   *   *

Atom stood behind Daisy in the cockpit as Klavir's moon crested the horizon. Leaning on Daisy's seat, he lost himself in the possible avenues life presented. The moon, icy white, fully rose as Daisy guided the *Ticket* towards the distant haven.

"They aim to betray," Atom said, grimacing at their fast approaching destination.

"You plucked that spirit from the air of that meet?" Daisy drummed his hands against the yoke. "I didn't hear much of what was said, but nothing in that place struck me as solid grav."

"Hole?"

Daisy bobbed his head. "Class three, the kind that hides until you're in it."

"They're sucking us in?"

"Not so much as hiding and waiting to grind us to atoms."

"And getting us to toss their kack in the meanwhile," Atom growled. "How do we go about meeting our ends and theirs on a path that gets us where we need to be?"

"You ask too many questions," Daisy replied with an easy laugh as he reached up and adjusted a few switches overhead. "You're the cap. You're the one that gets to make all those tough choices."

Atom opened his mouth to speak, but Daisy continued. "But if I know you, we're headed to fulfill the contract. Something about the code." He held up his hands to mime a person talking. "Blech, I think you just get your jollies putting yourself, and us by association, in harm's way. It has to be about the code, because it's not about the money."

"How about you just get us to Lassiter in one piece, and I'll worry about the killing." Atom slapped the back of Daisy's seat.

"Better you than me," Daisy grumbled in reply.

"Let me know when we're on approach, I want to check in with Byron on the state of the ship. It's been a couple months since anything went wrong, and I've that feeling in my gut that we're due."

"Last thing we need at the moment."

Atom ducked out of the bridge and trotted straight through the commons and quarters, only stopping after ducking into the upper hatch of the mech bay. Machinery hummed in pulsing rhythm that always made Atom think of what a baby heard in the womb. As a young commander, he had spent many hours among the ship's mechs, finding it the most relaxing part of any ship.

"By, you in here?" he called out over the thrumming.

Not hearing a response, he headed deeper into the inner workings of the ship. Life support, recycling, and eventually the power-plant intertwined with the ease and charm of a writhing snake-pit.

Atom cupped his hands to his mouth and called out, "Byron, where are you?"

"Here, darl." He emerged from a tangle of pipes and tubing like a grease smeared xeno. "I've been torquin' on this 'ere converter an' I en't likin' what I'm seein'. I've slipped a bypass, but that puts strain on the scrubbers.

"See these burners tracin' the seam." He held up the part for Atom's inspection. "I'd recommend a full switch-out on the rack or we'll watch a cascade roll the line."

"We're coming up on Lassiter." Atom took the part and traced a finger over the corroded seam. "Think they'll have what you're looking for?"

Byron shrugged and smeared grease around as he tried to wipe his face clean. "I'd assume. If 'ey don't 'ave it exact, I'll try a 'and at ticklin' a couple dirtside converters." He took the piece back and threw it down the open well to land on the floor between his worktables below. "Might even be, I can salvage some of what we've got, if'n they en't been chewed up too bad. I'll clean 'em up and see.

"If 'ey work I'll toss 'em in store fer a rainy day on the Black." Byron thrust his hands in the pockets of his coveralls and closed his eyes to listen to the heartbeat of the ship.

Atom watched the boy, sensing a communion between man and machine. He turned and slipped from the mech bay. Taking the aft stairs, he headed for the hold. As he reached the empty floor, he stopped and looked around.

"Koze, we need to pick up a legitimate run, sooner than later. People might start getting suspicious." He smiled as a soft buzz whispered through the air near his head.

"Will that interfere with our current goals?" the AI asked.

"You mean treasure?" Atom looked around, trying to follow the faint sound of the toy dragon.

"Presumably."

"We don't even know what the treasure is." Atom wandered toward the far end of the hold where half-a-dozen storage crates sat tucked under the edge of the fore stairs

"I've accessed the limited records and can find no manifest for that voyage."

"I know. It was either scrubbed or never logged to begin with."

Kozue changed tack. "Why are you so intent on finding this treasure?"

Atom slowed as he approached the crates and peered between them. Margo rested in the protected cubby, curled in her pram with a cocooning blanket. Above her head, the tiny dragon whirled and soared.

"I'm intrigued," Atom whispered as he backed away from the nest. "Any time people are willing to shed so much blood, there is usually a reason for it."

"But nothing on record."

"Exactly." Atom grinned as he mounted the far steps to head back up to the living level.

*   *   *

Daisy tucked the ship down in the same hangar they had occupied on their last visit to Lassiter. A small, battered rock-hopper sat dusted in icy crystals on the next pad over. Atom stared at the craft from the cockpit canopy for a moment before a smile crept over his face.

"I want you and Shi to watch the ship." Atom pulled his pistol out, checked the load, and reholstered it. "I'm sending Byron and Hither out to pick up a few parts and some fresh supplies from the local hothouses. You two will be back-up in case anyone needs it.

"If not, sit tight, because I'm fair certain we aren't long for this rock." He tugged his brown coat snug about his shoulders and strode from the bridge. As he trotted down the hallway, he relayed his instructions to the others.

"Got a funny twitch in my gut." Shi sat in the shadows of the stairwell, a motionless shadow herself.

"Me too." Atom stopped a few steps below and gave her a sidelong glance.

"I should come with."

"That's why I need you here. If things go sideways, I need to know the *Ticket* is primed and ready to get us out of here. They've gotten onto our ship before and I need to know you and Daisy can handle it."

Shi stared through Atom. "I should still be going with."

"Margo and I can handle whatever floats our way, and if we don't, you make the call to cut the umbilical. No sense in wasting atmo on a lost cause." Atom's shadowy grin flashed in the dim light of the stairs. "But the way I see it, my gut's kept us alive long enough to give it mass. Plus, I'm taking Go and the pram with me. Things always seem better when she's around."

"Fair enough."

"If I need you, I'll call in the marines for a drop."

"Count me for that one." She extended her hand, palm up.

Atom laid his atop hers. "When the time is right, we'll all drop together. Just don't count on that being tonight.

"Are the others of your simmerings?" Atom waved for the gunslinger to follow as he turned and trotted down into the hold. "I know the situation has been steering for tension, but I need to figure where we're headed without burning this whole colony to the ground. They're just caught in the crossfire, and if I can slip in and out without stirring the embers, I plan on doing so."

"They're firm. Not a body moves without Hither's say-so." Shi grimaced. "Doesn't stop us from wantin' it, but your word first, then hers."

"Good." He dismissed her with a nod and crossed the hold to find Margo still slumbering in the pram, tucked behind the crates. For a moment he wondered how she had managed to wedge the pram into the cranny, and then the answer came to him.

"Give me a moment," Kozue purred.

Of its own accord, the pram rose on humming suspensors and drifted out to settle beside Atom with a contented sigh of machinery. Atom thrust his hands deep in his pockets and jerked his head for the pram to accompany him as he headed for the side hatch.

"Why do you and Shi have trouble with your stomachs?" Kozue asked as they cycled open the hatch and stepped out into the blustery evening. "Was some of the foodstuff spoiled?"

Atom laughed. "No," he said, hunching his neck down into his coat to ward off the chill of the frigid biosphere. "It's just an old soldier's nerves creeping out. The body senses surroundings and picks up on things our eyes don't see."

"Nerves?" Atom heard the thought in her voice. "You mean instincts?"

"Firm." Atom cycled through the hangar lock and scanned the near empty street running from the tiny space-port. A few bundled figures trudged along the ice crusted road, their attention locked on their destination. "Call it instinct or intuition, or even superstition. Most soldiers have it to some degree. They know when something is looming over the curve of the horizon. Can't exactly say why, but they know it's there.

"Sometimes it's pure spec." He crunched through the rime as he pushed the pram in the direction of Svitać's tavern. "Other times there are little tells that we pick up on. Sometimes they're big. They call it a soldier's intuition because we don't always register that we've picked up on the tells."

"What do you mean by 'tells'?"

"Well, it can be little things, like a quiet forest when there should be noise, or a dust cloud that doesn't sit right, or a floor creaking wrong."

"I see: indicators that the natural order is being disrupted by the presence of something outside the normal parameters of the situation."

"Call it what you will."

"Tells, then," Kozue sounded amused. "Are you gleaning something here?"

"Something big. That's Lilly's ship back there, which means she's here somewhere." Atom approached the tavern. "That would lead me to believe Toks is also in the vicinity. She is searching for the same information we are and has to know that we made it out of her trap. Logic dictates circling back to the last point of contact and searching for the new trail.

"She's like a pit-hound." Atom stopped outside the hatch and scowled "When she's on the scent she won't back down. And if the Tribe's after Lilly, they're here too."

"With those numbers, I estimate a resolution in the near future."

"I hope not," Atom muttered and pushed his way into the ice-melting warmth of the tavern. "Koze, has Hither left the ship yet?"

"Neg. Why?"

"Another hunch." Atom scanned the scattered patrons of the tavern. "Patch me through."

A moment later Hither's hurried response chirped in Atom's ear.

"I need you to pull the *Ticket* back to a low orbit of Klavir. I want you to stay low enough to avoid all but the closest scans. I'll have Koze let you know when I'm ready."

"Trouble?"

"I'm not sure, but I want to handle Lilly with care and if anything else pops, I don't want to cause any more commotion than necessary. There shouldn't be trouble yet, but I'll let the crew in when the time comes."

He listened for a moment and then the distant hum of the ship's engines vibrated through the soles of his boots.

Only then did he wander over to the bar. "Chi, blue and a milk." He tapped the bartop and gave a pleasant nod to Svitać. "What's the daily?

"Capy stew," the barkeep replied.

"I'll take a bowl. Count it as a tip for a job seen through to completion."

Svitać's eyes lit. "Up in a mome."

Atom made his way to the same table tucked against the far wall and sat just in time to catch the hiss of the door and the atmo-trap slipping around Shi's lean, ponchoed frame. He frowned, but settled into his chair without comment and lifted Margo into the seat beside him. Shi scanned the room with professional ease and wound her way through the tables to join him.

"I thought I told you to wait on the ship," he said, motioning for Svitać to add a meal.

"Trustin' my gut, Cap." She kicked out a chair and slouched down into the seat. "One more company will make you stand out less and give you a couple more guns when this drops in our lap. Plus, with the *Ticket* in orbit, I don't need to kitsit 'er.

"Only thing." She locked her eyes on the front door and stared it down. "I ain't goin' to jail as you did. Been there once and I ain't goin' back. I'll end every sumbitch who tries."

"Fortunate for you." Atom leaned back and smiled up at the waitress approaching with a tray full of food. "They won't take us.

"Thank you." He bobbed his head and dug in his pocket for a tip.

"Drink for you, miss?" the waitress asked as she deposited a steaming bowl of vegetable heavy stew in front of Atom.

"Perk. Black. Strong enough to chew." Shi flashed a lopsided grin.

"Just a mome."

"So, what's the scam?" Shi propped her hands behind her head and surveyed the room over Atom's shoulders.

"Eat," said Margo with a serious nod.

"Like the way you think, lil' miss." Shi scooped half a spoon and blew on it with care. Flipping the spoon around her held it out for Margo. "Won't do you no good burnin' yerself on your kip."

Margo took the spoon and shoved it into her mouth. As contemplative as a food judge, she held the food in her mouth. Then she swallowed and her face split into a wide grin. Disregarding the heat, she grabbed Atom's spoon and shoved another mouthful in. Her eyes flew open and teared up. Then using her tongue as a plow, she discarded the stew back into Atom's bowl.

"Hot," she said in amazement.

Atom laughed and pushed the small glass of milk towards Margo. She hopped up from her knees and leaning with her full weight on the table, sipped the milk through a straw.

"As to the plan." Atom took a bite of his stew and savored the flavors. "We wait and see what floats our way."

"Any idea how long?"

"A day and a night." Atom shrugged. "More or less."

*   *   *

And they waited.

At the end of the night, Atom yawned and climbed to his feet. "I'll get us a room," he muttered as he wandered through the maze of empty chairs to the bar.

Svitać eyed him with concern.

"No trouble." Atom held up his hands as he perched on a stool. "I just want to book a room for the night. It might turn into a couple nights. I'm waiting on a contact."

"Last time you waited, my tav got tossed by the imps."

"Unforeseeable circumstances."

"It's strange." Svitać snapped a towel from his shoulder and began polishing an imaginary spot from the glossy wood. "You and yours don't strike me as aiming to misbehave, except for that pilot of yours. But outside of his scrap with the players, I don't think he was looking for more than a quiet drink."

"Sometimes trouble has a way of happening by," Atom apologized.

"Is it following you now?"

"I'm hoping not. At the moment, I'm just looking for that contact. I noticed a new ship out there in your hangar, but I haven't seen anyone looking like a traveler."

"Da." Svitać gestured up to the balcony that circled the second story of the tavern. "A woman. She looked ill, but swore up and down that she just needed a few days of rest. She took a room and hasn't come down since."

"Shame, I'm looking for a boke. He runs on the chubby side of life."

"Then this is not your contact," Svitać said in his heavy accent.

Atom's shoulders drooped in clear disappointment. "I guess I'll just have to take that room then." He slipped from his stool and stretched his back. "Do you have private baths?"

"Da, each room has a small wash cubby, but there is a larger communal in the corner if you want a more relaxed soak," said the barkeep as he pointed out the corner. "Payment must be up front for each night stayed."

Atom pulled a blank chit from his pocket and clicked it down on the bar. "Just keep my tab open. I'm hoping we will only be here a day or two, but you know how the lanes run."

Svitać nodded, slid a key chip across to Atom and said, "Keep the chip on you and it will open your room. The tab covers room and board." He connected Atom's chit to his register and nodded in approval. "Your credit is good here. Stay as long as you like."

"Do you have any broth soups in stock?" Atom asked.

The barkeep nodded.

Atom flashed a tired smile. "As a favor, send a bowl up to that sick traveler. Put it on my tab. And make sure you toss some of your fresh bread, too." Atom rapped his knuckles on the bar and snagged the key chip.

He turned back to Shi and strolled over to join the gunslinger as she rose and maneuvered the pram out from behind their table.

"We got a room." Atom squinted up into the dusky rafters as Margo wandered after Shi. The girl rubbed her eyes with sleepy fists and reached up to Atom. He grinned at Shi and scooped his daughter into his arms.

"Don't be expectin' nothin' from me," Shi skewered Atom with a frosty glare. "I'm as cuddly as a porky-pine and I only sleep with my ladies, so the bed might get a touch crowded. You ain't makin' a play fer me, Atom?" Shi placed a hand on her chest and feigned astonishment.

Atom barked out a laugh.

"No insult meant," Atom said as he wiped a tear from his eye. "You just caught me off guard."

Margo looked from Atom to Shi and then nuzzled into Atom's neck.

"Not easy to do." Shi grinned.

Pecking a light kiss on Margo's head, Atom said, "I'm more worried you would take advantage of a poor old soul, such as myself. Luckily for me, we have Margo to chaperone our engagement. I would just rather you and I stay close," he dropped his voice as he leaned in, but left the smile on his face. "In case anything were to happen."

"I know." Shi matched Atom's smile. "It's what we do in the field."

Atom turned and carried Margo to the stairs. Shi followed behind with the pram. The smirk remained.

As they approached the stairs the serving girl bustled from the kitchen with a small tray. She bobbed her head at Atom as she mounted the stairs and led the way. Atom trailed behind, watching as she brought the bowl of soup around to the far side and knocked on a door.

Atom made note of the room before heading for their own room.

"What was that about?" Shi asked as their door clicked shut behind them.

"I'm fair certain Lilly is the other guest. Unless she is holed up on her ship." Atom looked over the simple but comfortable arrangements of the room.

Before he could say anything further, Shi flopped on the double bed and kicked off her boots. She closed her eyes and with a contented sigh laced her fingers behind her head. With a yawn she stretched out and cracked her toes before melting into the bed.

"How do you sleep in a poncho?" Atom settled Margo on the far side of the bed.

"I don't, unless I'm in the scrub."

*   *   *

Once Margo had drifted off to sleep beside Shi, Atom slipped from the room. The gunslinger cracked an eye and cocked the gun resting on her stomach as she dozed. Seeing Atom, she relaxed and he closed the door with a muffled click.

He felt naked without his coat, but Margo had insisted on snuggling into it instead of the blankets on the bed.

Standing on the balcony, he surveyed the quiet tavern below.

A pair of late-night drunks still perched at the bar. They murmured to each other. Svitać leaned against the liquor shelf like a piece of the tavern's furniture. He looked up and noted Atom's emergence and then drifted back to half listening to the familiar drunken tales of his clients. The rest of the tavern tables sat empty and forlorn.

Taking the steps with casual grace, Atom descended.

"Any chance you have a coat I could borrow?" he asked Svitać. "Margo stole mine."

Without a word, the barkeep pulled a heavy, fur-lined jacket from a hook behind the bar and tossed it over. "Just don't tear it. There's no supply ship scheduled for a few weeks."

"I'll be careful." Atom slipped the warm coat over his lean frame.

He left the warmth of the tavern behind and plunged into the dim light trickling through the dome. Cool blue light reflected from Klavir's turgid surface and did little to ease the meat-locker chill that pervaded the little town. Atom stood for a moment and searched out the sheriff's office. The frigid, recycled air tugged at his legs, but did little to penetrate the fur lining of the jacket. The cold, however, pained through his sinuses, freezing shards of snot through his face and brain.

Just as he feared he would lose feeling in his face and legs, he noticed an illuminated sign hanging in the window of a squat building half a block down the road. He hustled for the building, keeping his head tucked low.

"How do you live here?" he demanded as he slipped through the porous membrane of the door. "Every step out there is just an exponential ball of pain . . . and that's not even outside."

Coffey, who sat behind a battered metal desk, looked up from a data-scroll with amusement. She spun in her seat to pour a steaming cup of black perk and set the mug on the far edge of her desk. With a weary yawn she waved for Atom to take an empty seat.

"What brings you back so soon?" She crossed her arms and drooped back in her chair.

Atom shed his furry second skin and lifted the mug. He cradled it in his hands like a miraculous, life-giving elixir.

"I heard a little story through some of the back channels about a prison riot and eventual break-out. Sources won't disclose, but I've even heard rumor that a firebat took a swan-dive off the second tier after lighting himself on fire during the riot. Reports are hushed on the cause of the riot, but word is the scuffle and flaming dive set things in motion."

"That the word?" Atom stared into his mug.

"So, how'd you get out?"

"Warden signed my early release papers."

"Funny, official statement claims he was assassinated by his second-in-command. Then she must have got herself in a scrap and offed by the prisoners trying to escape herself. Funny thing is, they've tracked the vids and can't figure out how she got from the killing to the getting killed.

"And to top it, several prisoners disappeared during the evac." Coffey leaned forward and steepled her fingers as she snared Atom with a studied glare. "So, we have a dead warden. Can't say I liked the man, but he was appointed.

"Can't say I approve of your methods," she harrumphed.

"I had several stimulating conversations with him," Atom said with wide-eyed innocence. "And Daisy took a shine to his thug, excuse me, second. I wouldn't have wished him to end. It certainly appeared he kept that prison running smoothly."

"And he signed your papers?"

"Well," Atom drawled with a sheepish grin. "Not officially."

"Died first?"

Atom's silence told Coffey everything she needed to know. "But our deal is taken care of?"

"If I take a job, I always finish it," he replied.

Coffey nodded and fished in the breast pocket of the heavy jacket hanging from her chair. She pulled a small, folded piece of paper out and held it gingerly between two fingers. Through the whole process she kept her eyes skewering Atom.

He met her gaze.

"This is our agreement." She held out the paper, just out of Atom's reach. "I can't say I like what happened up there."

"You don't have to like it." Atom did not play Coffey's game, instead he awaited payment with an open palm. "You just have to be satisfied with the achievement of your goal. When I take a job, there's a desired conclusion and the path to that conclusion isn't always pleasant."

"But I'm having second thoughts."

"That's not how it works," Atom said with simple directness. "A job is a contract and unless you call it off before the conclusion, there is no way to avoid the outcome."

Coffey narrowed her eyes.

As she contemplated, a roar of ship engines washed over and through the thin walls of the town's hab. As Coffey glanced up, Atom snatched the paper from her fingers and hopped to his feet.

"I can't say it was a pleasure doing business with you," he said with a wistful smile. Her hand snaked to her gun, but Atom held up his hands. "Transaction's complete."

Coffey stayed her hand on the butt of her gun. Her eyes darted from the vibrating ceiling to Atom and back. "I didn't hear any tell of an arriving ship. Our skies were clear until our supply drop, sometime beyond next week.

"Are these friends of yours?" she demanded, her accusing eyes bore into Atom she rose to her feet. Her knuckles whitened with tension as she gripped her pistol.

Atom shook his head.

"So, who are they?"

"Not a shade," Atom said as he tucked the paper into his pocket and turned for the door. "But I can almost guarantee they aren't friends of anyone here."

He paused, his hand hovered over the hatch control, and he looked over his shoulder with concern framing his eyes. "If you can, get everyone to the outlying habs. This trouble started with Blonde, but I won't say it hasn't jumped to me now." He scowled at the closed hatch, as if he could catch a glimpse of the ship settling into the hangar at the head of the town. "But that trouble has everything to do with the information you just gave me."

Her face blanched. "If I know the poem, am I in danger?"

"Does anyone else know about the poem?"

She shook her head.

"Then you should be safe, as long as you make yourself scarce."

"One last piece of info," she said as she rose to her feet. "Your girlfriend came in and reviewed the tape of the Blonde incident. She seemed a might interested in your findings on the table."

"My girlfriend?" Atom looked puzzled.

"The one with the glasses."

Atom turned, slapped the hatch, and leaving Svitać's coat behind, plunged into the bitter wind. He held one hand to shield his eyes against the recirculating breeze. The other hand hovered above his rail-pistol.

He stalked into the night.

"Koze, any idea what we're looking at?" he growled against the wind.

"Based on engine signature I would estimate a dropship," Kozue replied. "I don't have the scanning abilities without the *Ticket* in a closer position.

"Margo and Shi?"

"Shi is awake."

"Tell her to load Margo up in the pram and sit tight for the moment." Atom halted in the center of the road and glowered at the broad, hangar hatch. "I want to see what we're up against before I bring them in."

"Be careful," Kozue sounded worried.

"When am I not?" A dark grin pulled at Atom's cheek as the pale planetlight drifted between the scudding scatter of clouds above the hab.

"Always," came the reply.

The biting wind skirled around Atom's legs.

Framed by the snow-glow of the icy ground, the drop ship sank beyond the boxy bulk of the hangar like a squat hound hunkering down against the evening chill. The whine of engines fell momentarily, only to scream as the dropship burned from the hangar's pads.

Atom's pulse quickened as he stepped out of the hangar hatch.

Without any solid information, he assumed at least one squad, if not two, had disgorged from the darkened maw of the beast.

As he drew near the tavern, the hatch hissed open. Light spilled into the street. Atom halted, his toes just shy of dipping into the warm, golden pool. He tore his glare from the hangar and watched as the atmo-skin slipped over a shadowy form ... and a pram.

"Rekin you'd miss this." Shi sauntered into the street, pushing the pram with Margo snuggled up, still asleep, inside. Shi tossed Atom his coat. "She's still tuckered, but I ain't feel comforted sittin' this tussle out."

"You listen to suggestions like a marine," Atom growled. Nonetheless, he slipped into his worn brown coat.

"I'll take the comp. Or ya could say a marine scentin' blood's like a wolf on a wounded stag." Shi grinned as she stood in the warm tavern glow and surveyed the empty street. "You'd think a town this size'd have more lights to ward the dark."

"It could work to our advantage," Atom stepped into the light and took the pram.

"How you reckin?"

"Dark gives us more shadow to hide." He led the way into the dim light from the planet above, leaving the tavern behind. The hatch shut, closing out the last true source of light.

"You know they've gear to null that."

Atom shrugged as he said, "We can't do much about it in the present."

"You could wait," Kozue interjected.

A shot rang out from the darkness, a blaster-bolt. In reaction, the pram's shield flashed into existence and deflected the bolt up into the night.

Both Atom and Shi drew and fired. Instinct split the pair. Atom winged several shots into the darkness as he side-walked into the cover of a nearby alley. Shi fired twice and scurried to tuck into the cover of a parked rover.

The pram sat alone in the blue-green light of the night.

"What should we wait for?" Atom asked Kozue.

Kozue remained silent. Then, with a flickering surge, the scattered lights along the street glowed brighter until each building cast a wide arc of light into the night. "It will only last a few minutes before the system overloads, but this may prevent the enemy from using the darkness to their advantage."

"Level the battlefield?" Atom hazarded a glance out into the street.

As the street exploded in a ruddy glow, Atom caught sight of the lightly armored soldiers advancing against the backdrop of the buildings. The soldiers scattered in the light, like exposed cockroaches.

Atom stepped into the street, pulling his pistol and dropping the last stragglers.

"With me," Atom called out.

"On you." Shi rose, flung her poncho back, and brought both guns to bear. In a steady tattoo, she fired into the artificial twilight. Some shots hit, others forced the enemy into scurried retreats, but most important, the fusillade allowed her to shift positions and advance up the street into the cover of a nearby building.

"Loading," she yelled, kneeling in cover to run her ladies through auto-load.

Atom took the lull as an opportunity to shift forward, calling the suspensor-pram to his side as he walked the street with stolid steps. A shot barked from his rail-pistol with each step until he ran dry and ducked into cover.

"What's the count?" he yelled to Shi.

He held his pistol to his belt and the auto-reloader.

"Put down two. Winged a third," Shi replied.

"A moment," Kozue murmured and from the pram, Cody rose to disappear into the black above the golden burn of the hyper-illuminating buildings. The moment passed. "It would appear five have fallen between the two of you. I count eleven more, four of who are wounded. There is also a reserve of four waiting near the hangar.

"I don't believe they have connected Lilly's ship, despite the fact that a record should tie the ship to the prison break. Interesting," Kozue puzzled. "Either Lilly has scrubbed her connection from the operation or you have done a wonderful job of getting under the skin of Toks Marshall. If the information on the treasure ship is the ultimate goal, I would assume Marshall has associated the two of you and so should have her ship pinged."

"And this concerns me how at the moment?" he grunted.

Snapping the cylinder home, he peeked from cover only to be driven back by a spatter of blaster fire.

"We're a fresher meal." Shi leaned low and fired off a pair of shots.

"It'd be my play." Atom pulled his secondary pistol.

He kicked the pram out into the street. Harmless fire splashed off the shield. He ducked out into the street after the pram, firing a rapid salvo. Shadows flitted beyond the edges of the building lights, drawing his fire.

The pram coasted to the center of the street.

Running dry, he spun back into the alley.

"Firing," Kozue called out and the turbo-laser dropped from the bottom of the pram. Guided by Cody's eyes in the sky, a brilliant pulse of light ripped from the underside of the pram and flew in short, staccato bursts. Leaping from target to target, Kozue drove enemy troops to ground.

"Flank," Kozue called in alarm, just as a squad of armored troopers slipped into Atom's alley.

Throwing himself sideways, Atom managed to avoid most of the attack, but a stray blaster round ripped through his left shoulder and punched him back into the gutter.

Rolling to a stop with his back against the metal wall of the building, Atom snapped off a few rounds with his good arm. Even as he drew attention to himself, Shi sprinted at an angle, bypassing the pram and slipping into the alley. Without wasting breath, she emptied her pistols into the enemy.

Her shots ripped through the light armor of the four troopers.

Atom watched. Pain laced his vision as he fought past the cold burning of the blaster bolt.

Centering his breath, he dropped his rail-pistol and pushed himself up the wall.

"You solid?" Shi asked as Atom poked at the singed hole in his brown coat. He stooped and retrieved his fallen pistol.

"I'll manage," he grunted as he struggled to holster his off-hand pistol with his right hand. Panting to control the pain, he picked up his rail-pistol and tapped it against his thigh to knock the icy crust from the barrel. "It's time to end this," he growled.

Without waiting for a reply, he strode out into the street and past the silent pram. Vengeance burned fierce in his eyes. As each enemy appeared, they fell. Atom's pistols could not miss. His right arm extended and fired, even as his left hung limp and useless at his side.

Like Death, he stalked the street.

Behind him, Shi scurried to keep up. The gunslinger threw lead at every shadow to catch her eye.

Atom ignored the pain.

He fired by instinct. Soldiers died at his hand and burned before his fury.

Only when he reached the supply depot outside the hangar did Atom slow. His breath frosted the air like an agitated bull.

He swayed.

Shi caught him and eased him to the ground as the pram floated up behind them and settled to the ground allowing Margo to look on in concern.

"Dada," she whispered.

"Just a scratch, girl." Atom kneeled, supporting himself with the gun barrel of his good arm jammed in the icy ground.

"Sorry bunch we seem," Lilly said from a pool of light a dozen paces behind.

Atom twisted his gaze up from the road. Shi's gun leaped like a snake, beading on Lilly even as she slipped between Atom and the baug.

"Peace, slinger." Lilly held up her hands, but remained motionless. "He ok?"

"Are you?" Shi asked Atom without taking her eyes or gun from Lilly.

"I've had worse," Atom grunted through gritted teeth. Sweat stood out and froze on his forehead. "Shot missed anything vital, but it may have burned a chunk from my blade." He reached up and poked at the wound. "No bleeding, which is good. It's a blaster burn, which isn't good. It hurts a hell of a lot more than a bleeder."

"We should get him back to the tavern." Lilly stepped forward.

Shi tightened her grip on her pistol.

"She said peace," Atom whispered, his head lolling forward and breath coming shallow. "She'll stand by that word." Taking a deep breath, Atom forced himself to his feet where he stood swaying beside Shi.

"Will she?" Shi whispered back as her eyes tracked the shadowy figure slipping through the flickering light.

"I believe the lights may be reaching their threshold," Kozue said.

Most of the lights followed her words and winked out, leaving Atom standing in the dark of night. Here and there a few tenacious lights continued to glow in scattered pools, but the noon-bright illumination had passed.

"You can trust her." Atom closed his eyes against the pain. "I can make it."

Shi backed off a step, but remained close. On the other side, Lilly stood with a concerned expression as she watched Atom sway like a thin tree in a winter breeze. He clenched his eyes. Breathing in short gasps, he gathered himself and fought the pain.

"Nice to see you again," a voice called out from the darkness of the supply depot. "Where's your man?"

Atom froze.

"Show yerself," Shi called out, shifting again to place herself in harm's way. Her pistols strained to see into the shadows.

Lilly slipped in close beside Atom. She wrapped a supporting arm around his waist.

Lights sprang to life, revealing Toks Marshal, clad in heavy crimson battle-armor. She stood just outside the hatch to the hangar. The lights shone from her armor. Without a helmet, Toks' short hair whispered in the wind. Her glasses reflected the blue light of the armor's HUD. A thought of a quick shot and a quicker death flitted across Atom's mind, but vanished. Toks played to her advantages. He knew she had an angle.

Maintaining his best, level stare, Atom waited for Toks to speak.

She remained silent.

"What do you want?" he asked after a few uncomfortable moments. The chill breeze bit through his coat, but he burned with an inner fire.

"You know what I want," Toks laughed. Her face seemed unnaturally smooth, almost porcelain in the soft blue glow of her armor's HUD lights that continued to feed her information. "I'm a seeker of knowledge. I guess that makes me a scholar. I know you have the knowledge I'm looking for. I aim to collect.

"And I've a score to settle with your man." Toks grin drove some fire from Atom's gut.

"I have no men. I left that behind when I resigned my name."

"Pity." She pouted. "Guess I'll just have to settle for your women."

Shi bristled.

"I'd have your lady-friend stand down," said Toks.

"Why's that?"

A shot ticked the side of the pram, jolting it sideways. The suspensors whined in surprise, fighting to maintain balance and position. Margo grabbed the sides with a fearful expression as her deck wobbled beneath her. Her fortress lay compromised.

Shi kept a gun trained on Toks while the other searched the darkness.

"I have nothing Atom," Kozue spoke in a hushed tone. "I calculate a sniper in thermal cover. He's good. I'm not detecting any irregularities anywhere in the dome.

"Even running numbers, I can't drop below six possible locations." She sounded at loss. "Too many options." Panic flowed through her words. "That's a high velocity rifle. It will bypass the shield and punch right through the pram."

"Stand down." Atom laid a hand on Shi's shoulder.

Emitting a soft growl, the gunslinger lowered her pistols with aching slowness, but refused to return them to their holsters.

"That's better." The predatory smile returned to Toks' glowing face as she looked to Lilly. "You know he's contracted to kill you."

Atom felt Lilly's breath catch.

"Oh, he failed to mention that, did he?" Toks shifted forward, her cockiness radiating through the augmented power of her servos. "My birds told me of a meeting he had with your father.

"That has to hurt." Toks crossed her arms and looked down on the group with smug superiority. "Your dad wants you dead and your partner's the one to do it."

"He's not my partner." Lilly glared back defiantly, but shifted away from Atom.

"If you're a free player, what say you hop over to this side of the trench and I will slap a truce. You and me find this treasure and I'll split sixty-forty your way. I'm not greedy. Way I see it, you fly with Ulvan and nobody gets the goods.

"Fly with me and you get two things." Toks nodded, feeling the flow and effect of her words with a fisherman's caution.

"Yeah?" Lilly dropped her arm from Atom's waist and took a step towards Toks.

"You get the treasure and you keep your life. Don't think Ulvan can promise you either of those things."

"And you can?"

"Kill him and we have all three parts of the map." A shadow flitted across Toks' face.

"Kill me and nobody has anything." Atom's wan smile reflected his wounds.

With deliberate and casual air he lifted his rail-pistol and aimed at Toks. The smile never left his face.

Toks straightened. Her weight shifted back. "You know I have a bullet with your daughter's name on it." She shifted her gaze between Atom and the pram. "Even if you put me down your daughter dies. Can you live with that?"

"We've made our peace." Atom's gun held steady. "We live every day like it was our last because, to spit the truth, we died with our han."

"You're ghosts?"

Atom's smile grew hard. "We're on the Ghost's Road."

Toks' eyes darted to Lilly and the imperial cocked her head. "Seems one more good reason to slip sides in the matter. I wouldn't want to fly on a death ship."

"Wrong again, Toks." Atom clutched his wounded arm to his side as he stepped out from behind Shi. "I have a piece of this puzzle and Lilly has the other half. And while you're just twiddling out in the Black, riding our vapor trails, we actually know where we're headed.

"What do you say, Lilly?" he asked without taking his eyes from Toks.

"I say," she deliberated, looking first to one and then the other of her suitors, "I'll stick with the enemy I know."

At her words, the night exploded in a heartbeat

The broad hangar hatch slid open and her ship flared to life like a bright, evening star. Heat and light drove through the hatch in a blinding fusion.

The pram juked sideways as a wild shot whispered through the void. In that moment of chaos, Atom fired. His shot, unsteady through his pain, punched through the armor where the leg joined the torso, driving Toks back a step.

Shi's ladies began barking at the armored figure.

Anticipating the assault, Toks whipped her arms up to shield her face from the barrage. The bullets bounced harmlessly into the night. As if in response to the gunfire, her gunship dropped on the bubble, punching a hole in the roof and crushing down on the depot outside the hangar hatch. Toks lurched towards the ship just as Atom's second shot missed and punched through the dropping ramp of her ship.

Controlling the pram in its wild slide to the side, Kozue dropped a missile from the undercarriage. The pocket rocket hovered for a fraction of a second as it oriented on the new arrival and then flared to life in a short streak of fire.

The explosion tore one of the four engines from its mount and threw everyone from their feet.

In that moment, assisted by her power armor, Toks managed to stagger up the ramp. Without waiting to button up, the pilot lurched the ship into the night sky. Like a dragonfly missing a wing, the ship scraped through the hab hole and wandered toward the horizon where it lifted through the thin atmosphere and disappeared into the Black.

Lilly's ship powered down.

Atom lay on his back, allowing the icy soil to dampen the fire within.

From her back, Shi continued to fire into the night sky until her guns ran dry. She continued to pull the trigger, hammers falling on empty chambers with a sharp click in the silent night.

"Easy, girl," Atom mumbled. "They're gone."

She continued to pull, her face locked in a grimace of agony.

Only when Margo laid her small hand on Shi's cheek did the gunslinger's eyes drift back into focus.

"How'd y'all git outa yer pram, lass?" Shi sat up and looked around in confusion.

"Climb," Margo stated. "Dada hurt."

"Aye, lass." Shi clambered to her feet and extended a helping hand to Lilly. The baug took the assistance and then shook her head to clear the explosion. "Gimme a hand with him. It'll take two of us to git him back to the tavern. I don't s'pose the people'll be too happy about a hole in their sky.

"Koze, call in the *Ticket*," Shi said as she and Lilly managed to haul Atom to his feet. "We're going to need to fire up the medoc again."

*   *   *

Atom grimaced as he flexed his arm and rolled his shoulder. The knit skin pulled against the stretching. Sitting on Byron's workbench in the bowels of the *One Way Ticket*, he looked over at Hither. She ignored the questioning glance, instead focusing on the range of movement and the readouts scrolling across her handheld screen.

"It would seem the medoc knows its business," she frowned. "The shoulder will be tender for a week or so, but the muscle has knit nicely and the machine replicated the lost bone.

"Be careful with it." She locked eyes with him. "It's fragile."

"What's the worst that could happen, the muscle tears or the bone fractures? Isn't that why we have the medoc?"

"It is, but remember, it's not so much reinjuring the shoulder as what you're doing when you injure it again. You could be climbing and rip it. That shoulder won't support you. What happens if you pull with your injured arm and it's a touch slower on the draw than it should be?" Hither laid a warm hand on his bare skin. "You have to keep that in mind. Also, what happens if you are trying to lift me from a bottomless chasm? Would you drop me?"

"I'll just use my right hand." Atom grinned.

Hither glared and shoved him back as he tried to rise. "If you get me killed because you didn't listen, I'm going to come back and haunt you."

"Will you be wearing clothes?"

He yelped as she grabbed his shoulder and dug her thumb into the freshly healed wound. "Don't play." Her sweet smile bore an underlying hardness that gave Atom pause.

"Fine," he grumbled. "I'll take care. Can I put my shirt on now?"

Hither nodded.

Slipping down from the bench, he pulled his shirt over his head and hissed as the muscles protested. Hither reached up and helped, trying to ease the shirt down with the least amount of torque on his shoulder. She held out his over-shirt and helped

231

him slip into it before worrying at the buttons in a distracted manner.

"What's on your mind?" Atom took over for her and finished running the buttons.

"Just thinking on this job." She stepped back to survey the upper level of the workshop, dropping her voice. "I don't trust the direction it's heading. I know we usually have people gunning for us, but this feels different. We don't usually work with those that mean us death."

"I know." Atom shrugged into his coat with a grimace. "But the other option is walk away from potential."

"Level with me, this isn't the haul to end all?"

"I don't think there's one of those in all the Fingers."

"Then you're on this boat to the death?"

"Mine or theirs. I don't know that there is a real alternative. I know things can't go back to the way they were, but I need to eliminate that threat before I can have any hope of normalcy for Margo."

"And you don't think this life is damaging?"

Atom's face warmed with a sad smile. "We are all damaged, but we can choose to rise above or let the damage drag us down. Someday that will be her legacy.

"Back on this job, I don't full trust Lilly. I know she's in this for the money and she'll take that vector at any cost, but I don't see her turning on us unless we come between her and that goal. She's a merc. There isn't anything personal about it."

"And the contract?"

"It's on the table now. We'll cross that void when we come to it." Atom motioned for her to follow as he headed for the hold. "In the meantime, we know Toks has it in for us. She wants the money, but I think she genuinely wants to eliminate us at this point. We've compounded the personal for her with the knock out and shooting."

"Our best bet would be to eliminate her before she gets her real chance at us." Hither linked arms with Atom and wandered. "But we need to wait until she takes off the captain's hat. She's under imp protection when she hides behind her uniform. I don't need to tell you what happens if we attack her unprovoked.

"Universal death," she said with a chuckle.

"It's a good thing we've never had to deal with that before." Atom grinned.

"What's the play?"

Atom shrugged and said, "Complete the job we've been hired to do and see where it takes us."

As they entered the hold, they found Lilly and Byron running around the parked *Hellkite*, playing with Margo. The girl's delighted giggles echoed through the empty space as she tried to catch the other two. Dancing just out of reach, they both grinned with the joy of forgotten worries.

Atom watched with a relaxed smile playing over his features.

Looking at his face and realizing the good there, Hither reached over and squeezed his hand before mounting the steps to the upper level. She hesitated on the upper landing for a moment before nodding and disappearing into the hallway.

Atom absorbed.

The game continued a few more slow laps as Margo's toddler legs sought to keep up with the other two. Lilly noticed Atom standing near the doorway first and even though she continued the game, her stance stiffened. Byron remained oblivious to Atom's presence until Margo caught sight of her father.

"Dada," she squealed and ran into his arms.

"Fiver." He closed his eyes and breathed in her scent. He relaxed.

"Atom, what's our next jump?" Lilly approached like a skittish deer, hesitant to break the moment of familial embrace.

Atom opened his eyes like someone rising from a pleasant dream.

"I have a job I've committed to." He shifted Margo down to sit on his hip. "It's not too far off our course to the Nemo System, so I figured we earn some coin to cover the fuel costs."

Pursing her lips in thought, Lilly studied Atom's face. "You're serious," she stated with slow understanding. "We have potential limitless wealth at our fingertips and you're sidetracking to cover fuel? What if Toks beats us to the coords? Are you willing to pass up a head start?"

Lilly kept her voice level and despite the emotion that strained at her stance, Atom sensed her willingness to understand before acting.

"Walk with me," Atom said as he turned towards the stairs and called back to his mech. "Byron, round up the others for a quick meet at the table."

The captain kept silent until he took his seat at the head of the table. He nodded to the narrow galley, but Lilly shook her head. When she declined, he turned his attention to Margo. He seated her on the edge of the table with her feet resting on his legs. Margo grinned and reached over to tickle Atom under the chin.

For the moment, Margo encompassed Atom's universe.

Lilly looked on, her expression somewhere between disbelief and longing.

She coughed and Atom glanced over to her, the spell of solitude broken.

"About what Toks said ...." she trailed off, her eyes on the table.

"About the contract on your head?"

Lilly puzzled a slow nod. "Where does that leave us?"

Atom stared at her long enough that Margo turned to look at Lilly as well. "It leaves us in the same position as when we met. There is a second bounty on your head."

"And you took it?"

"I didn't turn it down. Figured it was safer than doubling Toks' reason to come for you."

"I'll ask again," said Lilly as she narrowed her eyes to study Atom's face. "Where does that leave us?"

"Stand-off. We both have reasons to kill each other and reasons to let the other live. For the moment, none of those reasons seem to outweigh our mutual interest of trying to track down this ship. There's a treasure that could make all our contention moot. Plus, way I see it, we find this ship and you buy out the bounty. Problem solved."

Lilly sat in silence, her eyes locked with Atom's.

After a few moments, the crew filtered in and seated themselves around the table. More than a few questioning glances rested on Lilly.

"You all know the score." Atom spun Margo and nestled her into his lap with a protective arm draped across her middle. "We have a treasure, a job, and a potential score docked in our hangar. You also know our routine.

"Except you Lilly," Atom said with a nod to the baug, but held up a hand for patience. "To settle things up for you, on any matters of money, we vote. If there is a tie, Kozue votes, otherwise, our path is settled at the table. I'm captain in matters of combat and the ship, but we are a unit outside that.

"It might seem odd, but I figured from the moment I brought this crew together, that they were here for a reason and as their lives rest on the block too often, they should have a say in how that's to play out.

"That said, we have a decision to make here and now." Atom paused to take stock of his crew, finally resting his gaze on Lilly. "Unfortunately, you aren't crew so you don't get a vote on our course, but I will give you time to plead your case should you see fit. I can't rationalize putting my crew in a position to not have their trajectories covered, so we all hear what the options are and then we decide where to fly."

Lilly scowled, but nodded in understanding.

"Three options sit out in the Black. They're waiting for us." As Atom spoke, his eyes dropped to the table and a frown tugged at his mouth. "Our first option is to burn straight for the treasure. It's not a bad option and I'm sensing it's the most appealing option for Lilly.

"Table is yours, Lilly," he said.

Lilly rose from her seat and paced out to the center of the galley before turning to face the others. "I've been after this treasure for years now," she began, crossing her arms as she chose her words with care. "If I had a choice, I'd rather not split it with any of you, but seeing as the Maker saw fit to pass on vital information to your captain, I don't have much choice if I have a hope of seeing any of the treasure.

"That said, I don't see why we waste a single cycle without grabbing what's ours. I'll not force your hands, but with or without you, I'm heading for that treasure.

"Do you have any notion of what's on that ship?" Hither asked.

Lilly straightened and glared down at the table without making eye contact with anyone. "No." Her whisper lifted just over the air cycler.

With slumped shoulders, she drifted from the galley.

"Do any of us?" Hither demanded, turning her attention back to the others.

"Does it matter?" Shi leaned on the table, cupping her chin in her hands. "Way I see it, no harm in sketchin' the layout. Worst we see is a new system, scout some stock in trade. I hear this Nemo System's a glut on scrap."

"Especially 'at far outside the lanes," Byron chirped with a juvenile grin. "Low prices."

"What are the other two options?" Daisy leaned back, folding his arms and fixing Atom with a steady gaze.

"Second option, we take the first job offered by Alderon Pips. That should bump our accounts and leave us a cushion in case the trip out past the skins leave us empty hold. Third option is we ignore the siren call and carry about our normal business."

"I hate to say it, but there's still the fourth option." Daisy dropped his eyes to the table.

"I don't want to cross that void yet."

Byron looked back and forth between the two. "Say it negs," he pleaded.

"We could cash the bounty on her head," said Daisy.

"Atom," Kozue interrupted the discussion. "The airlock has cycled."

Atom looked to the others in alarm.

"Don't worry, she is using one of the void suits and her ship remains powered down. Ash has not departed the *Hellkite* either."

"You should talk to her," Hither said, looking to Atom with concern. "I think she's caught in a lonely situation with hostiles on six vectors. Even though she doesn't trust us, I think she is trusting that we are at least allies in this search for the treasure.

"We need to decide what we're doing and not string this girl along any further than she has already been led." Hither slipped from her seat. "With all the options floating around this table, I'm going to vote for the second, fill the coffers and burn for the treasure. I don't think we can pass up the possibility that something there sets us for life. If we load up before we head out, chances are we don't get caught without pants in the Black."

Hither swept her gaze around the table, then with a nod, she plucked Margo from Atom's lap and strolled from the galley.

"Any other thoughts?" Atom asked.

"I's shootin' fer a straighty burn, but 'ivver makes a point." Byron shrugged. "All I knows is we en't entertainin' Daisy's pan drippin's, are we?" Byron's eyes widened as he searched the table for a negative answer.

Nobody met his eyes.

"We'll park that in orbit for the time," Atom said, lifting his gaze. "In the meantime, how do you vote?"

Daisy held up two fingers.

Shi waited for Byron to hold up two fingers before she followed suit.

Atom slapped the table. "Two it is. Daisy, plot a course for Kafiristan, but wait until we're off the float to burn."

*　　　*　　　*

The airlock in the ship's belly always plagued Atom with a sense of vertigo as he stepped from the ship's gravity into the null-g like a swimmer dropping into a pool. His momentum allowed him to drift down the ten feet to the far hatch, where he doubled over to grab a handhold and swing about.

Settling into the directionless land of the Black, he took a deep, steadying breath and listened to the hiss of air as the hatch cycled behind him.

"She's still out there?" Atom asked on a private channel.

"Firm," Kozue replied.

"Am I doing the right thing?"

"Speaking as your wife, I believe you are approaching your decisions cautiously. That is the best course of action for the protection of Margo. As your ship's AI, I would disagree. Calculating probability says there is likely no treasure to be had and therefore you are needlessly putting all lives at risk by venturing beyond the safety of the shipping lanes.

"Furthermore, there is an even higher probability that Lilly betrays you after the knowledge that there is another bounty on her head."

"I meant going after Lilly right now," Atom replied. "I was asking if she needed the alone time and if I was stepping over an unspoken line."

"Oh, in that case, most definitely. But she also needs your reassurance at this moment. In fact," Kozue hesitated. "Chances of betrayal significantly drop if you go out and demonstrate that she is an ad hoc member of this crew."

"That's reassuring," Atom chuckled as the outer doors slipped open in null-silence.

"Lilly," he called out on the open channel. "I'm coming out. Do you mind the company?"

No reply came over the coms. Atom clipped to a handhold just outside the door and floated out into the Black. He spun in a slow circle a couple inches above the ship's skin, searching until he found Lilly. In silence, she floated near the prow of the ship, her boot tips poised against the hull.

Atom floated towards her, using the ship's myriad handholds to climb in the right direction. As he approached, he clipped into her hold and remotely disengaged the previous line.

"You solid?" he asked, turning to face her inside his helmet.

For a time she continued to stare into the void surrounding them. She floated motionless, velocity equal to the ship on the float.

"I don't know whether I feel more alone out here staring at the nothing or dirtside surrounded by people I don't know." Her voice sounded low and tinny in Atom's helmet. "I've spent so much of my life alone or pretending to be someone I'm not, I'm not really sure who I'm supposed to be inside."

"Sometimes alone is a good thing," Atom replied.

"But not all the time."

Atom held up his hands in a suited semblance of a shrug.

"I don't want to change who I am. I just need to find a place that I fit. I need to get to a place where I can stop listening to others tell me who I am and who I'm supposed to be.

"My family tells me one thing, society tells me something else. I'd rather they all just mind their own business. I want to make my own decisions, listen to my heart, settle down somewhere and just be myself. Maybe I'll get married and start a family, or maybe I won't. None of that is for someone else to tell me.

"Maybe I'll continue on taking lives, but only if I want to. That's easier when there are no connections." Lilly pivoted her space suit to meet Atom's eye. "It's easier to kill what I don't know. Although, that's never really stopped me.

"Do you have trouble killing?" she asked.

"It's happened a time or two. I actually found it easier with the people I didn't know. Granted, I've never had to put down a friend, but I've had to end acquaintances. I knew their darkness, which made it easier to pull the trigger."

"Are we friends?" Lilly's bluntness caught Atom off guard.

Before he could reply, she continued. "I suppose I best watch myself."

She turned and began floating back towards the hatch. Just before she swung herself into the ship, she turned back to Atom. "I know how you float. I've put you down, but I also saved you a couple times."

Then she cut the connection and the hatch cycled, leaving Atom floating alone in the Black.

*   *   *

The *One Way Ticket* dropped into the Kipling System without fanfare and slipped into the scattered inbound traffic. Answering a trade call, Atom dropped the ship on Seeonee. The planet's broad, fertile plains and shallow seas provided the majority of the system's foodstuff and with a thinner atmosphere, the planet sat as the system-hub for larger planet-bound transport ships.

Daisy dropped the *Ticket* to the surface with barely a shudder.

Without ever leaving the ship, Atom brokered a hold full of corn that stacked neatly about the *Hellkite*. The magnetic crates cocooned the baug's ship in a shroud of corn.

Almost as soon as the hold sealed, Daisy kicked the engines to life and lifted from the surface.

Within a day, they dropped on Kafiristan with legitimate trade papers.

"I go alone for the time," Atom said to Hither on the stairs to the hold. "I have a contact to make and, in the meantime, I want you to line up a buyer for all this corn."

"I don't like having the hold this cramped." He reached up and rapped his knuckles on one of the crates stacked to create a low ceiling to the stairwell. "Plus, I feel like it sends the wrong signal to Lilly. I don't think she could leave without serious damage to her ship and probably ours as well."

"Done and done." Hither grinned. "What's the next step?"

"Depends on what this contact has up their sleeve. I don't think we can just walk in and shoot Migori without slamming our escape route shut."

"Isolate and execute?"

"Seems the best approach from here." Atom snatched Margo up by the back of her jumper as she rounded the corner and attempted to dodge past the pair. "If that turns out to be the case, I'll either attempt alone, or bring on Shi as a possible snipe option.

"Realistically, I have no intel. That means I need to go collect."

Hither wrinkled her brow in thought. "Not much to go by." She closed her eyes and smoothed her countenance with a deep breath. "Just keep me posted. I'll run things smoothly on our end. You need more, just relay through Kozue and we'll be on the spot."

Atom mocked a salute and trotted down the stairs with a wriggling Margo in one hand. He followed the corn tunnel to the side hatch and plunked his daughter in the waiting pram. After a quick check of his rail-pistol and backup weapon, he straightened his brown coat and slapped open the hatch.

"I hope this meeting involves food," Atom grumbled as he powered Margo out into the brisk mountain breeze.

The city sat surrounded by a ring of processing plants and crowded landing pads. Beyond the border of civilization, a line of craggy hills gave the impression that the *One Way Ticket* had landed in the bottom of a wide, flat bowl. In the midst of the productive turmoil, the planet's capital city spread in a mix of stone and plasteel buildings, business and residence interspersed with commercial districts.

Atom frowned as he exited the landing pad and slipped onto a conveyor walk. "Where am I supposed to meet this boke?" He glanced around at the scattered drift of pedestrian traffic hopping on and off the conveyance.

"I have coords," Kozue said. "Looking at them now. It appears to be an office building, belonging to a shipping company. I'll guide you. Just follow the pram."

With half an eye on the pram's trajectory, Atom wandered along the bustling streets. The section of the city adjacent to the port overflowed with warehouses, offices, quick-stop diners, and four-seat noodle vendors. The surrounding swirl of humanity consisted of porters and mech-loaders, although the occasional pairing of uniformed security officers, or a group of riotous spacers stood out from the bustling throngs with their wandering saunter.

Atom wove after the pram. Kozue guided at an easy pace that flowed with the general traffic.

"What's our timing look like?" Atom asked as he lost track of the number of warehouses passed. "I feel like we're stuck walking in a straight circle here. Or maybe I just get uncomfortable not knowing what I'm walking into."

"Twelve minutes at our current pace." Kozue hesitated. "That's interesting."

"What?" Atom perked up.

"Every passing security detail has had two members, but there is a group of seven approaching on a rough intercept vector."

"Trouble?"

"I'm not sure. I'm jumping surveillance feeds and it would appear that they are more worried about what's behind them. Although, the woman I estimate is their commander appears to be using her handheld pad to track you."

"Why would you say that? Have you hacked her system?"

"Unfortunately, she is using a high security system that would take more effort to get into than I care, or need, to tie up at the moment."

"How then?"

"Geometry," Atom could hear the shrug in his wife's voice. "Her vector has continually arced to track and intersect your own."

Atom hopped forward a couple steps and caught hold of the pram, wrestling it from Kozue's automated propulsion systems and dragging it out of the surging tide of traffic. He stood motionless, watching and measuring. Margo shifted in the pram, sitting sideways so she could see her father and the street. Her serious demeanor mirrored Atom's.

"Take Go back to the ship," Atom said after a moment of reflection. He keyed a sequence into the controls and closed up the protective shield. "I know I usually take her with me, but I usually choose my own jobs. This feels so out of my control, I don't know where she will fit into the plans."

"Understood," Kozue replied without hesitation, pulling the pram from his hand and guiding it out into the flow of foot-traffic.

"How long before the trackers find me?" He watched the pram disappear.

"They are around the next corner. If you move forward and meet them on the side street, there will be more freedom to act as you see fit."

"Firm." Atom reached under his coat and popped the straps loose on both pistols. Then, cracking his neck with a slow roll of his shoulder, he stepped out into the traffic and made his way toward the corner.

With purpose he strolled around the corner, whistling a light melody as his eyes skimmed the surroundings. The traffic died at the corner, leading Atom to surmise the byway offered access to a row of warehouses and little more. No vendors lined the streets. Atom's ditty fell silent as a feral grin spread across his face.

The trackers rounded a corner a hundred or so yards away, caught sight of Atom, and froze.

"Afternoon," Atom called out as he kept his pace and drew near.

The uniformed guards looked to the woman standing several paces in front. She waved them back, tucked her pad away, and advanced. Confidence leant gravity to her expression as she approached Atom with her hands held wide, away from her gun.

"Atom Ulvan?" She stopped several paces away.

"Depends on who's looking," Atom replied with a friendly nod.

She took a deep, calming breath. "I received word from Alderon Bronte that our plan was in motion. We have a simple task for you, assassinate General Lelani Motoki Migori. His loss should throw the Migori advance into enough chaos that we should have time to launch a counter-strike."

Atom thrust his hands into the pockets of his coat and stared at the woman.

"Why don't you just do it?" he asked, rocking on his heels.

"Honestly," she lowered her voice and stepped closer. "If it looks like it came from outside our han, it should cause more confusion for the Migori. We're hoping that the confusion will force them to halt their attacks long enough to figure if there is another player on the board …."

"And that buys you more time." Atom nodded in understanding.

"It buys a window for that counterattack to work. This system is rightfully ours and we plan on taking it back."

"Have you applied to the emperor?"

"And received the reply that it will be looked into."

"Meaning …?"

"We're on our own." The woman bowed from the waist. "And so, we have sought the aid of the Tribes."

Atom looked over her shoulder at her contingent. "And the plan?" he asked.

"Take these." She pulled a small package from a pouch on her harness. "They will identify you as a Migori inspector. You will use them to gain access to the orbital platform they have taken as their forward operating base."

Atom studied the woman in silence. Her dark features masked any hint of emotion. She held out the package to Atom. He shifted his eyes from her narrow face to the package.

"Before I take this on, there are a couple things I want to clear up. Why do I have to jump through all these hoops when I could just take my ship up and dock at that station? I could work out a supply run angle and have my mech rig something that would make all the kids dirtside ooo and ah. And speaking of that, why wasn't I stopped on my inbound drop?"

The woman looked at the unaccepted package and then sighed. "First off, you weren't stopped because the Migori don't want to damage the infrastructure of the system. It's the highest yielding system in the sector. Even though leaving trade open makes their job more difficult, they see the disruption as more economically harmful in the long-term.

"They have opted to keep most of their operations in the black. The Migori have landed a police force, but have kept their planet-side operations to small-squad engagements.

"As long as you pass their customs inspection on any trade transactions, you are free to come and go as per usual business. Granted, your everyday inspections are going to be a touch more thorough, so take that into account if you plan to up or download any goods from your ship.

"And to answer the first part of your question, the orbital platform is a no-fly zone for civies."

"That makes sense." Atom reached out and took the package from the woman. He popped it open to reveal a palm-sized, bifold pad with a rough printed badge tucked in a leather sleeve. He examined the badge which sported an unflattering headshot and the name Flynn Mosby stamped below. "How do I get past their security?"

"Press your thumb to the key of your new pad."

Atom did so and the pad sprang to life. With a flash of light the screen adjusted and displayed Atom's face along with alias information. He flipped through different screens, looking over his new credentials. Passing through the work screens, he found several personal folders, one of which contained pictures that had been altered to include him.

"Nice touch, with the pictures." His eyebrows climbed in appreciation.

"We tried to be as thorough as possible." A sad smile crept to the corners of the woman's mouth. "This task is of utmost importance to us all."

"Appreciated, I'll just be on my way then. I have a fortress to find a way into."

"That's not all." She caught his arm as he turned to go. "You must kill us."

"Come again?" he asked, turning his head back to her.

"We are Adlerians, known to Migori intelligence." She gripped his arm, her fingers digging in like talons. "Killing us adds credence to your identity."

Lights exploded behind Atom's eyes as her fist caught him in the side of the head, just above the ear. With her gripping hand, the woman spun Atom, throwing off his balance, even as his hand flipped back his coat.

Stumbling to the side, he lashed a foot out that connected with her leg.

The woman dropped with a grunt.

In that moment, Atom spun to regain his balance and as he rose, coat swirling, his pistol barked out in rapid sequence. Three members of the patrol dropped before they could draw their guns.

The other three scattered.

The woman scrabbled back towards the gutter, her leg dragging at an odd angle.

Without thought, Atom put a round through her chest.

Seeing their leader mortally wounded, the others charged with a suicidal tendency. Atom dropped them before they had covered more than a couple steps.

For a moment he stood, motionless except for his whispering coat. He looked over his shoulders to see the busy street behind him turn into a chaotic surge as the locals fled the sound of the gunfight.

A pair of security personnel rounded the corner with guns drawn, yelling for him to drop his weapon and get on the ground.

"Hold up." He held his gun skyward. "We're on the same side here."

With guns trained on him, the pair approached, as if drawing near a wounded wolf. The two officers flanked Atom and halted several steps away.

"On the ground," one of them growled. His gun quivered in his hand.

Atom stared down the barrel longer than necessary and then he knelt with exaggerated slowness. Raising his eyebrows and maintaining eye contact with the officer, he set his rail-pistol on the ground.

"My badge in in my pocket if you'd care to check." Atom leaned to the side, nodding toward his coat pocket. "I'm a plain. I followed a trail to these Adlerians. They were on course for an infil. I got 'em before they could." He grinned.

The grin remained even as the second officer circled behind and kicked him down to the ground. Kneeling on his bac, she patted him down with rough hands. The woman maintained the pressure even as she flipped his coat and pulled his secondary from his back holster. She tossed the weapon out of reach and fished in his pocket.

"He's proper," the woman said after overriding his pad to pull credentials.

Atom strained to look at the man standing over him. "See, like I said, I'm a plain."

A ragged cough snapped his attention back to his surroundings. A few feet away, the woman still lay in the gutter. Her hand slipped into her pocket. Fighting against the officer on his back, Atom managed a glance in time to see the Adlerian grin.

Blood stood out against the whiteness of her teeth.

"Too late," she gasped out as the standing Migori officer whipped his gun from Atom's head and placed two more rounds in her chest.

Before the light seeped from her eyes, Atom heard a soft click.

"Bomb," he yelled and tried to curl in on himself in spite of the other officer's weight on his back. He remained curled with his eyes squeezed shut for a few breaths before the standing officer's laughter alerted him to the fact that their surroundings remained quiet.

"You're a twitchy one," the woman laughed as she rose from where Atom had bucked her off. "I'd say she just had a suicide switch to make sure we didn't take her alive."

"She was already dead." Atom sat up and looked over the dead woman.

The guard pulled the woman's hand from her pocket and pried a small cylinder from her grip. The Migori's face dropped as she revealed the trigger. "What is it?" she asked, holding the device out for Atom's inspection. "If it was a bomb, wouldn't it have gone off when she popped the trigger?"

"Not necessarily," Atom said, holding out his hand for the device.

The woman tossed it in his direction.

Atom caught it and held the simple trigger with exaggerated care. He rolled it around in his palm.

A sudden silence tickled the back of his mind and he perked up like a dog hearing a distant whistle. The hubbub of the city had fallen quiet. The only sound to reach his ears came in the form of distant murmuring of human voices.

He cursed.

"Let me see my pad," he demanded, rising to his feet and holding out his hand. The guard shrugged and handed it over. Atom examined it for a moment and then looked up in frustration. "It's dead. I'm fair certain she just set off an EMP."

As if in response, a ship in a decaying orbit streaked across the sky to slam into a distant hill. A geyser of flame erupted from the wooded slope, followed by a roil of angry, dark smoke. Seconds later, the shockwave rattled the buildings around.

Atom's eyes widened with fear. "Go," he whispered. "Kozue, is she ok?"

Only silence replied.

* * *

The hum of the pram drifted away. A moment later the internal glow flickered dead, leaving Margo cocooned in darkness. She sat in confusion as the pram settled to the ground with a solid thump.

"Da?" she called out. The change unnerved her. "Ma?"

Silence met her queries.

Not since the night of their flight had Margo gone without the soothing sound of her mother's voice filling her ears. Now, however, only the muffled murmurs of people beyond the safety of her pram broke the stillness.

The pram jostled and Margo let out a yelp of fright.

More dampened sounds met her ears as people argued beyond her confines.

"Da," she called louder, banging on the inner shell of the pram.

The motion returned to the pram, accompanied by sharp taps against the metal outer shell. Margo braced herself as the pram began to rock.

A sliver of light appeared at the seam as a pry-bar worked into the joint.

"Da?" Margo leaned down to peer from the crack.

In the daylight beyond her prison, a pair of worn, work pants came into view. Beside the work pants, a young girl bent her eye to the crack. "We'll get you out in just a mome," the girl said and shifted back with a smile. "Just don't get too close while we work this open."

A second pry-bar slipped in, widening the crack enough for Margo to slip her fingers out.

"Careful, darl," a rough man's voice grunted as his calloused fingertips grasped Margo's and pushed them back into the darkness with as much care as possible. "I don't want you pinched if these bars slip. I should have this nut cracked in ten ticks. Just need to compress the rod a touch."

He grunted again and with a shift of the pry-bars he opened the cover a few more inches. As he did so, several sets of hands gripped the sides and with a heave, the pram split like a ripe persimmon.

Margo sat blinking in the bright sunlight.

"Do you know where your parents are?" the young girl asked, extending her arms to Margo.

"Ma's the ship." Margo stood, crossing her arms and scowling at the small crowd of people surrounding her. "Da's walking." Margo craned her neck, trying to see past the press of people, searching for Atom.

The girl shrugged. "I don't know how to find your Da, but maybe we could track your Ma if we can find your ship." She leaned to Margo's eye-level. "Is that what you want?"

"I want Da," Margo replied.

"It's time to go," an older woman called out from the edge of the road. "Leave her. Authorities will be along to find her soon enough. We have our own worries with this outage. Last we need is being late for work."

The girl held up a pleading finger, placating the grumping woman. "What's the name of your ship, lovey?"

"*Ticket*," Margo said with a confident nod.

"The *Ticket*?" The girl frowned at Margo's emphatic grin.

"Ain't getting much from that," the woman growled as she grabbed the girl's arm and hauled her from the press. "There's probably a dozen skiffs in port at this moment with the word 'ticket' painted on their bow. Plus, we don't have time to wait for the power to come back so you can run your search.

"And," she said with a cuff that mussed the girl's neatly parted hair. "We need to get to work. We ain't got time to waste on no lost lamb."

The girl frowned back at Margo as the woman dragged her off.

Margo waved at the receding forms.

The girl waved back.

Margo turned and looked up at the small ring of people gathered about her. For a moment, she scowled at them. Then, crossing her arms in mock gruffery, she thumped down and stared into space.

Time passed and the crowd dispersed. As they left, one of the workmen hefted the pram and set it up on the sidewalk in the shade, out of the way of the heavy foot-traffic.

The sun drifted and Margo sat, a still little statue carved from alabaster. In mimicry of her father, she focused her attention on her senses. With half-closed eyes she listened to the pulsing sound of the crowds. She felt the heat of the mountain sun waft into her pram to caress her cheek with soft zephyrs. Lifting her head, she scented heated plastic, industrial lubricant, unwashed bodies, and the distant smell of pine.

She breathed deep, taking in her surroundings, searching for the faintest trace of the familiar.

"Ho, lass." The voice startled her. "I'd guess someone's lookin' for ye."

Margo opened her eyes, confusion and surprise at the friendly tone the short man used. "Not Da," she stated as she crossed her arms and glared from her seated position.

"Cocky brat." The man laughed and tipped back his hat as he glanced over his shoulder to a pair of hulking shadows who loomed like overgrown boulders. He leaned down and Margo caught a glimpse of a shoulder holster tucked beneath his jacket.

Margo rose to stand in her pram, but maintained her scowl.

"I wonder who she belongs to," the man tugged his thick sideburns as he craned his neck to look up and down the street. "I don't see a body close enough to call on. Think there'll be a pot on this one?

"You know." He shed his hat and held it over his heart as he preached to his mountainous acolytes. "It would be out of the goodness of me heart that I'd look after a lass who had lost her poor da in all this confusion. And if he just happened to show his duff, I think it would be in the best interest of the lass for there to be a heavy transfer into my coffers."

He settled his hat back atop his bald head and smiled down at Margo. "I'll take you home with us and take care of you until your da floats on back."

The man scooped Margo from the pram with a flourish. As she nuzzled against his chest, he grinned. The smile lasted until she slipped a hand into his jacket and pulled the trigger on the gun nestled against his ribs.

The gun barked.

One of the hulks grunted as a slug ripped into his thigh.

Margo jerked her head away from the man's chest. As she pushed away, she threw her tiny fist of fury into the man's eye. The fist of a two-year-old missed the bone and flexed the man's eye like a deflated rubber ball.

Squealing in pain, he dropped Margo. On the ground, she took the time to kick the man in the ankle and then scurried away.

As she gained the walkway, she spun and stared down the trio with her best gunslinger glare. In perfect imitation of her father, her hand hovered above her hip. With a lightning-quick motion, her hand snapped up with her finger pistol.

"Grab her," the man roared, clutching his eye as Margo scampered into a nearby alley.

*   *   *

"How bad is it?"

The runner bent double, heaving as she fought to regain her breath.

Atom left her for the moment and wandered over to where the two officers stood at the mouth of the sideroad. They stood with arms crossed, frowning and talking in hushed tones. None of the heavy traffic on the main road attempted to step down the alley.

"I never got a chance for a proper introduction," Atom said with the calm of experience. "With the exception of your knee."

The female officer glowered and extended a palm. "Mir, Katarina Mir," the woman said as Atom slapped her palm with a light touch. "And this is Andre Toby. He's technically my senior, but he's actually a solid guy. We're military police, sent to pacify Kafiristan with minimal involvement. We're basically just observers."

"Flynn Mosby, we can't be looking at anything good here."

The man, Toby, shook his head as he patted Atom's extended hand. "What's it been, less than five minutes since we took them down." Toby put his hands on his hips and looked up at the sky. "Some sort of electro pulse to knock oot coms. Although, this seems a touch more powerful."

Atom cocked his head and said, "I'm not hearing anything mechanized. She has to have detonated something bigger than a com-bomb. I can't believe I didn't find any intel on that."

The runner staggered up and still panting managed to get words out. "The Adles left a dead-drift EMP net in orbit when they retreated," she said between deep breaths. "Coms are down. The up-ups haven't figured out what set it off, but as soon as it popped, the orbital stations got a good look at it. They dispatched an info-torp into the center of our compound, nearly killed Riley, but it got the info in our hands and Pico sent out runners to link with all the patrols."

"An orbital net?" Atom joined Toby in frowning up at the sky. "This is ten-fold bigger than a com-bomb."

"I couldn't say anything on those lines," the woman said with a final deep breath. "I'm just a runner at the moment. You all are to head back to base." She grinned like a cadaver. "I have the joy of tracking down three more patrols."

She nodded once and sprinted out into the busy road.

Atom sucked in his top lip and looked to Toby and Mir with his eyebrows cocked, then he said, "Looks like we're in a tough spot. We need to report in, but we've a byway full of bodies."

"Think we'll have any more loose drops?" Toby continued staring up into the sky.

"Your guess is as good as mine," Atom glanced up and then back to scowling Mir. "Most ships are shielded, but there are moments of exposure. I would guess a ship needs to be flying with faulty containment for anything to happen."

Mir shook her head at the pair and wandered back to the dead. Atom watched her poke around the scene with her pistol in stiff little fingers. Her aim darted from one body to the next, as if she expected their deaths to be a sham and the bodies to leap up in ambush at any moment. She circled once and then backtracked through the field of dead.

"Go float, Mir," Toby called to the woman. "Not a thing to be had by burnin' hot now."

"They're dead," Atom chipped in. He flipped his coat back and turned his attention to reloading his rail-pistol.

"How can you be so sure?" Mir called out as she trotted back to join them.

Toby shrugged and grinned. "Experience." He watched Atom's actions with calm approval. "If they were planning something more, they would have done it by now. No sense in lyin' aboot if they've a plan that'll save blood."

Mir deflated. Atom watched her shoulders slump and feet thump, almost like a young child having a silent tantrum.

"Rookie?" Atom asked in a low voice that wouldn't carry.

"Near enough," Toby said with a nod.

"What do we do with the bodies?" Mir asked as she holstered her pistol and stepped between the other two.

"Leave 'em for now." Toby looked over the narrow sideroad. "We'll drag 'em up on the walk so they don't impede traffic, but we don't have a way to call it in and I'm sure not aimin' to wait around for you to run to the station and back. We'll make a note and send someone to pick up the bodies."

"Suck job with no power," Mir replied.

Tucking his pistol back in his holster and dropping his coat, Atom looked back and forth between the two officers. "I'll take care of it. I put them down. Least I can do is get them out of the way."

Toby looked at Atom and crossed his arms, impressed, while Mir just looked relieved.

Atom straightened his jacket as he headed for the bodies.

"Kozue," he whispered. "Kozue, come in. Do you have a read on Margo?"

Silence met his inquiries.

A moment of panic set in as Atom grabbed the first body and dragged it over to the side. He took the time to lay the man on his back and fold his hands. He stood over the body for a moment, head bowed as rage and fear and adrenaline surged through his body at the thought of losing contact with Margo.

He rested on the precipice of abandoning the job and bolting for the *One Way Ticket*.

"What are you doing?" Mir asked.

Atom started, his thoughts disrupted.

"Moving the bodies," he said, regaining his composure as Mir stepped closer to watch.

"Not that I have much against them at this point, but why do you care enough to say a prayer over them?"

Atom smiled the sad smile of wisdom and said, "You have to learn to fight a war without hate. It is possible to fight as equals and respect your adversary. A fallen enemy is to be respected, because if you hate them, the hate will eventually consume you and destroy you."

"Whatever, grandpa." Mir looked on in disbelief as Atom followed the ritual for each of his fallen foemen.

"They fought bravely for what they believed," Atom said as he laid the woman beside her brethren. He bowed his head for a moment and assured himself that Margo had made it safely to the *Ticket* and did not need his help. "I would have shared a meal with them as easily as a fight."

He raised his eyes and walked toward Toby, wiping sweat from his brow that tickled in the cool mountain air. "Back to the depot then?" he asked as he approached the senior officer. "I hope those blasts didn't knock out the perkolator. I could sure use a cup."

"I hadn't thought of that." A look of alarm crossed Toby's face.

"Don't worry, old man," Mir said with a grin. "I'll build you a fire."

Toby rolled his eyes and turned to the main street.

"Lead, the way, I'm newer here than either of you," Atom said. "Even if everything is fried, we can't be too far off a cup of perk."

Following Toby's lead, Atom and Mir wandered through the aftermath of the EMP blast. While the city showed no physical signs of the blast, other than the occasional accident caused by an out of control vehicle, the citizens pulsed with nervous energy.

Atom absorbed it all.

People gathered in the streets, their words and conversations muddling into a background cacophony that almost rivaled the usual noise and hubbub of a port city. The roar of engines had been replaced by the cries of the lost calling out to each other in lieu of the usual com network.

For the first time in his memory, Atom looked around and saw everyone engaged in direct contact with each other. No pads adorned hands. No projected HUDs wreathed heads. Instead, without the electronic haze of modern society, people spoke with each other face to face. For the moment, word of mouth proved the only form of communication.

A smile creased Atom's face as those about him tried to understand their current situation. He listened to wild theories as fear lurked just beneath the conversations of the addled populous.

"I'm not sure how you recover from this," Mir said as she glared through the thronging people. "I know most sensitive gear is shielded, but if things can't connect, it won't matter."

"And the fact that it wasn't really our network," Toby laughed.

"Not our problem," said Atom as he pulled his dead pad from his pocket. "Think they'll be able to salvage this?"

"I'm not sure." Mir stepped closer to Atom and held out a hand. "Let me take a look."

Atom shrugged and turned it over.

"Now, I'm not exactly an expert, but …." She smashed it against a nearby wall. "But I would have to say, it's beyond slagged."

Mir doubled over laughing. Atom froze, uncertain as to what had just transpired. For a moment, he stood with a dumbfounded expression plastered on his face. Only when he noticed Toby grinning as well did he relax.

"Oh, your face." Mir wiped a tear from her eye. "You should see it."

"That had all my files, all my evidence."

"Everything's fried," Toby replied. "Nothing any of us can do. Like Mir said, there's no way to shield a whole network. Mine's dead too." Sighing, he pulled his own pad from his pocket, dropped it on the ground, and stomped on it.

Squinting up at the sky again, he glanced to his wrist before realizing that his wrist-com had also succumbed to the blast. "We need to move." He snapped his sleeve down with a frown. "No telling how long it'll take us to get back to the depot with things in this chaos. I wonder how they're going to debrief you. With no systems to pull up, you might have to wait a few days before they can start reconstructing our grid."

"It would probably be easier if they just popped him up to the platform," Mir said. "They'll have all the files on hand up there. You and I saw his creds and can rough vet him down here.

"In the meantime, I need to make a quick stop." She jerked her thumb at a public restroom where a hunched, old woman sat keeping watch.

"Just make it quick," Toby replied. "I want to figure out where we are needed."

"I won't even sit." Mir chuckled as she tossed a ko in the woman's plastic bowl. As she headed for the door, a middle-aged woman with several bags of produce waddled towards the restroom with a panicked look.

"I'll pay on the way out, dear," she called out to the elder caretaker as she cut in front of Mir, almost losing her groceries in her haste. "Excuse me, emergency," she said to Mir as she disappeared inside.

Mir rolled her eyes with an exasperated sigh as she cast a glance back to Toby. "That might be motivation to be faster than planned." She followed the woman into the restroom, leaving Atom and Toby in awkward silence.

"So, what's your game?" Toby eased out of the foot-traffic to lean against the wall of the public facilities.

"Most of it was top end." Atom joined Toby and watched the passersby with a curious eye. "We knew this planet would be the lynchpin for the system because of the ore coming out. The uppers slipped me in a few weeks before our incursion into the system in the hopes to prevent something like this from happening."

"Fat job you did of that."

"Could have been worse. Those could have been nukes in orbit. They could have glassed this planet and left the system useless.

"Problem is," Atom puzzled. "The attack tells us two things. One, the Adles know the worth of the ore coming off this planet. They aren't stupid. Two, they're in this for the long haul. EMPs in orbit mean they plan on coming back. Nukes would have made it useless. EMPs make it challenging."

"Not to mention, nuke use on population is banned under the accords."

"True." Atom's sad, slow smile split his face. "But when have the accords really affected anything outside the Palm?

"Realistically, that wasn't an option in the long game. They would have nuked their own people," Atom said, stepping out from the wall and looking to the door of the restroom with concern. "She's been in there a while."

Toby hesitated. Atom read the officer's attempt to jump thought-trains midstream.

"I don't like being here," Atom continued. "We're sitting on an unstable core. These aren't our people. And even though we are the lightest policing touch, I don't trust them out of my sight."

"Same." Toby's hand drifted to the pistol holstered across the chest of his armored vest. "Mir has been in there a while longer than usual. Think we should check on her?"

Before Atom could reply, Mir strolled from the door and tossed a few extra ko into the attendant's bowl. "I don't envy your cleaning of that place after what that woman just did," she said to the elderly woman. "My condolences."

Turning to the others, she adjusted the straps on her vest as they dug uncomfortably into her shoulders. "We ready to float out?" she asked with a grin. "Quicker we get away from this stink the better."

The cadence and lilt of her voice struck a chord with Atom. He studied her face with a calm intensity.

"You sure it was the lady in there and not you?" Toby's good-natured smile proved infectious and after a moment, Atom burst out laughing. Mir grinned and winked at Atom. "The downside to being your partner, Mir. I know way too much about your bodily cycles and functions."

He turned and led the way down the street. Atom and Mir fell in behind.

"How long you two been together?" Atom asked.

"Too long, evidently." Mir rolled her eyes.

They fell into a light banter as the trio wove their way through the crowded streets. Toby carved the path, but the other two walked on either side and the three exuded a light, jocular mood despite the chaos surrounding them.

Atom turned his attention from Mir and marveled at the people swirling about them. The Adlerians ignored the invading Migori military police and tried to figure out how to reboot their daily lives. The upside to the catastrophe seemed to be limited casualties. Beyond the single ship shorting and crashing into the distant hill, Atom only noted a few minor injuries sustained from the crashing of vehicles and lacerations from broken windows caused by the crashing ship's shockwave.

Confusion seemed the most common reaction. Atom assumed there might be problems with looting, but all the shops they passed seemed to be functioning as close to normal as possible. Patrons and shopkeepers worked around the power-outage.

"Seems the plan backfired," Atom commented.

"Say again," Toby said over his shoulder as he guided them through a press gathering around a dark pub nestled between two silent warehouses.

"I said, I'm not sure what the Adles were playing at with this EMP, but it seems it hasn't disrupted much of anything."

"It's shut down production in the warehouses." Toby gestured to the two towering warehouses flanking them with silence. He glanced at Mir. "But I'd guess they'll have some sort of power grid up and running within the day. You're right, it might cost them some money, but nothing much more beyond that."

"What's the purpose?" Mir asked.

Atom stopped in a small eddy of the foot-traffic and squinted up from their boxy, artificial canyon at the wispy clouds scudding across the green-touched sky. He looked to Mir and said, "They could have used the electronic gap to slip in a ship. Spies, saboteurs, or maybe assassins came down in the blast."

Toby joined Atom at the side of the road.

"You think?" Mir pulled her long, dark hair into a tail and glared up into the sliver of sky with defiance. "I don't know about you, but I haven't noticed any ships, other than that unlucky hauler on the hill."

"We'll check in when we get back to headquarters," Toby said. "They'll have a better idea of the possibilities and what we're to do."

Atom nodded. "I caught wind of something big in the chamber, that's what I was following up on when you guys stumbled on me. Unfortunately, all I could get before they pegged me was that they were prepping. Ammo, fusion cells, supplies were being stockpiled, but I never picked up what they were for or when they were to be used.

"Honestly," he said as he spread his arms wide in an exaggerated shrug. "I was under the impression that the counterattack was coming at Seeonee and we were just an off-world staging point."

"That's good to hear." Toby grimaced. "Maybe the group was just supposed to make a power grab after the main strike had neutralized the system hub."

Atom nodded with slow realization. "Logistically, that would make the most sense. Almost nothing ships direct from Kafiristan, it all runs through Seeonee. It would explain why they never received any orders to move.

"So, I moved," Atom rubbed his face with weary vigor, trying to wake himself from a heavy dream.

Toby grinned and thumped Atom on the shoulder. "It's above our grade. Let's just get back to the depot and let someone else try to make some sense of what's going on." He glanced about and slipped back into the crowd with worry in his step.

*　　　*　　　*

Margo made it to the first corner of the alley before the undamaged thug caught her up in his arms. He made sure to keep her well away from his weapon and clear of his face. Like a cornered honey-badger, she thrashed about, but eventually settled into a scowling impression of her father as the man hauled her back to the pram and his grumbling leader.

Beside the dead pram, the second guard sat pressing on his wounded leg.

"Hit me like that again and I'll break your arm," the short man growled as the thug held her up by the back of her tiny jumpsuit. He clutched an arm to his side, trying to hide the hole burned in his jacket and the raw burn beneath.

Margo stared in stony silence at the leader.

"What should we do with you?" The man stepped closer, his watering eye twitching as he tried to glare down Margo. "You aren't from around here. Spacer's kit?"

Margo lashed out with a tiny foot, missing the man's nose by a hair.

"None o' that, lil' miss," the thug holding her soothed in his deep voice, even as he held her a little further away from his boss.

"Come on," the little man snarled, kicking over the pram in a simmering rage. "She may not know our han by sight, that doesn't excuse what she's done. I'm sure your folks will come looking for you. They can redress the afront. If not," his lip pulled up into a sneer. "We can always sell you to cover damages."

"What about the pram, boss?" the guard asked.

"No way it survived the blast. Leave it." The little man turned to the street with fists on his hips. He glanced back at the wounded guard seated on the ground. "Get off your lazy goose and leave coords so her folks know what they owe us."

Without waiting, the leader fled down the street at a fast walk, parting the seas of idling citizens who had gathered to watch the show. Behind him, the guard carrying Margo shrugged at his companion and followed. The wounded man, pale and sweating, clambered to his feet and hobbled to the downed pram. Glancing over his shoulder, he righted the metal basket and set it against the wall. He frowned and tried to wipe away the smear of blood from his wounded leg, but only succeeded in making it worse. Pulling a blank chit from his pocket, he keyed in the han name, but left the total blank. With a shrug, he tossed it onto the bundle of blankets in the bottom of the pram.

Keeping his breath slow and even, he limped after his companions.

As he drew away and the crowd began to disperse, the blankets shifted and a small dragon head poked over the rim of the pram.

"I'm coming, Go," Kozue whispered.

*　　*　　*

Atom studied the layout of the compound as Toby led them through the gates into the hubbub beyond. Migorihan troops hustled in ordered chaos as they scrambled to react to the attack.

Stepping to the side, Atom and his companions dodged an outgoing squad of lightly armored security squad.

"Seems like they haven't lost too much initiative." Atom paused to watch the group disappear into the thronging streets beyond. The gates cranked shut behind them, blocking out most of the noise from the street.

"For as peaceable as things have seemed, you know that we're sitting on a powder-keg of a war zone," Toby replied as he skirted around the assembling squads in the courtyard. "Even if most of the people here aren't planning on rising up, they're Adlerianhan to the colors they bleed.

"I know you've been on the deep, dark side of the planet, but don't go wrong-thinking that because they aren't a direct threat that the populous won't be edging to help out where they can when the next attack comes."

"On that note, I do have some information that needs to trickle up the chain."

Toby nodded. The safety and relief of their surroundings washed an unwinding sense of weariness over the officer. "Mir, do you mind running him up to the captain. I need to turn in our own reports."

Mir shrugged without a snarky comeback. "Should I catch up with you after?" she asked.

Toby looked at her in confusion for a moment and then said, "No need." He turned away and ambled for one of the two-story, cinderblock buildings that comprised one wall of the compound. "We're done with our shift. When you're done dumping him, grab a shower and rest up. We're back out in the thick in six."

"Firm," she grumbled after his receding form and headed for the central building. "You coming?" she asked when she realized Atom had not followed.

"Sure." Atom watched her with hawk-like eyes, uncertain of her intentions.

"Well, come on then. You're standing between me and a hot shower." She turned and glared at him. "I've spent the last twelve wandering these dusty streets and I want a bite and a lie down before I have to float back out."

"Fair enough," Atom sighed, and trotted to catch up.

They wove through the crowds of arriving and departing soldiers. Winding, but always making their way towards their goal. Once Atom began following her lead, the surly officer ignored his presence. She nodded to a few officers and guards in a familiar manner, but for the most part seemed lost in her own thoughts.

"He's with me," she grunted at a pair of guards flanking the front door to the building, and again at several checkpoints as she wove them deeper and higher into the building.

Only when they reached the top floor did a ranking officer bar her way.

"Who is this?" the officer demanded from behind his desk. His two raccoon eyes and packed nose made it hard for Atom to take seriously

"Mosby." Mir's sour expression did little to reassure Atom, but he fixed his eyes on the officer and waited with a placid expression.

"He's not one of ours." The man leaned back in his seat and crossed his arms.

"His creds say otherwise."

"And those are …?" the man trailed off, locking eyes with Atom.

"They were on his pad, but that got wiped when the EMP detonated, just like every other piece of electronic equipment. He's got his badge, but nothing deeper." Mir dropped her chin, hardening her glare. "Look, Frederickson, I've less than six hours to my next shift, probably a lot less with the way things are floating. My orders are simple: escort Mosby up the chain, and drop him. I don't have clearance for a debrief and last I checked, neither do you.

"Not that I'd know, since he wouldn't tell me much more than his name and show me his creds. Now would you stop your toothless barking and run along to tell your master that Mosby is here to see him. Tell Pico that we picked up a plain out in the street who says he's under direct orders from the lord's son back at court and the rest is buried in his files."

At her words Atom's thoughts faltered. Lord's son ....

"So please, for the love of a shower." She crossed her arms and seemed to loom over the hapless Frederickson. "Figure out how to make your feet function so I can get on with the little bit of a break. Once he's settled, I can burn on with my life."

Officer Frederickson bristled then flinched at the pain in his face.

Mir grinned, as if daring Frederickson to strike. "Deflate," she whispered, a feral look in her eyes that amplified her intimidating air. "Do your job, so I can be done with mine."

The tension hung thick in the room. Atom felt the strange urge to slip out sideways. Instead, he straightened up and waited for the exchange to resolve itself.

"Fine," Frederickson said, choking on a dry throat. "Captain Pico is in his office trying to sort this afternoon out. I'll let him know you are here."

Without waiting for a reply, the officer rose and slipped into the office.

"You do that to him?" Atom asked.

"Nope," Mir replied. "Although, he's such a pain, I wish I had. If he doesn't get out of my way, I might be tempted to rebreak his face."

"Breathe through it. That would just put off your shower a long while," Atom said, stretching his back as he glared at the door. "How long you been down the well?" He asked without looking at Mir.

"I dropped right after the assault on the platforms." She wandered over to Frederickson's desk where she perched on the corner and started casually sifting through his loose papers. "Realistically, it wasn't anything of an assault down here. The Adlerhan defended the system long enough to evacuate key personnel and then pulled back to the gate station just inside this system. Their fleet is poised just within range of the shipyards, but those have been evacuated. We're sitting on the other side, but haven't made a move yet."

"That means we really are in a stalemate?"

"Other than the EMP I haven't seen any real action." She frowned at a memo, turning her head to read it in a darting glance. "Fact is, those bodies you put down were the first sign of violence I've seen on this planet. Granted, I'm just military police. I don't fight, I just keep the peace after the drop."

She returned Frederickson's desk to order and stood up, stepping close to Atom. "I guess things are peaceful enough for the real peacekeepers to be here," she said with a weary smile. "But I suppose you knew most of that, seeing as you've been here longer than I have. Way I see it." She tucked a strand of dark hair behind her ear and fixed him with a knowing look. "You should be telling me all of this stuff."

"I only asked how long you'd been boots down." Atom's pleasant smile disarmed her.

Shaking her head, Mir wandered away from Atom to stare out the wide window. "This is all wrong," she said, glancing over at him. "I've been doing this less than ten years, but I've never seen a planet pacified this fast. It feels like they know we're just visiting and are just waiting for us to leave. It's like they're all in on it, but forgot to tell us."

"War is never what we expect," Atom replied.

Mir turned from the window with a puzzled expression, but before she could continue, Frederickson swept through the office door.

"Captain Pico will see you now," he said without looking at Mir.

Straightening his shoulders, Atom nodded to Mir and stepped through the door with accustomed confidence. Inside, he looked down on a man poring over maps and loose-leaf paper. Mir followed in Atom's footsteps with trepidation.

"Who the hell are you?" Pico demanded without looking up from his cluttered table.

*   *   *

Margo found herself tossed into a small storeroom in an unceremonious heap. For a moment, she sat in confusion, trying to process the path to her imprisonment.

"Don't worry, Go, I've got you," Kozue purred from above.

Taking comfort in the sound of her mother's voice, Margo climbed to her feet and wandered around the confines of the room. A shelf occupied one whole wall. Above the shelf a small window allowed a spear of aqua-marine sunlight to illuminate the room. Margo wandered through the stacked crates and boxes that occupied the rest of the room.

"I sent help," Kozue said as Margo picked her way through the maze and back to the one open space in the room. "Look up."

Margo followed her mother's voice and squealed with delight as she caught sight of Cody poking his head through the grating over the window. Without hesitation, the girl clambered up a small pyramid of boxes to a point where she only had two shelves left to climb. Shoving small boxes and some tarps out of the way, she carved a small space on the top shelf to crouch and look out the window.

Cody flexed, sunlight reflecting off his oil-dapple wings.

With a smile, Margo poked a finger through the grating to scratch the dragon's chin. The dragon preened and then opened his mouth to allow Kozue's tinny voice to escape.

"I'll send Cody for help. I must also operate on the assumption that they do not know that you have been separated from your father."

"Where's Da?" Margo whispered. Her little fingers clutched at the grate.

"I am uncertain. I can't talk to him. But I will find him, love." As Kozue spoke, Cody looked about, searching for something.

Hugging Margo's finger with both foreclaws, the dragonette peered through the bars at the girl. "Hold fast, Margo. I'll be back with help as soon as I can locate the *Ticket*. With my network down, I don't have a precise location, but from altitude, I should be able to run a grid search of the landing pads and find our home."

"Hold fast," Margo repeated, steeling her eyes as her face slipped into a replica of Atom's.

Cody bobbed his head and disappeared into the sky with a flurry of leathery wings. Only when he had flown did Margo look beyond the window into the wide courtyard. The window sat level with the ground and Margo studied the low porch lining the rooms that opened onto the courtyard.

Even without the training possessed by her father, the girl recognized the buildings as a home.

A cry rang out from one of the adjacent rooms.

"It hurts," whined a familiar voice. "And she got blood on my new shirt."

Margo bared her teeth.

"Somebody's going to make that girl pay," the whine continued.

"Hush, lord," a woman soothed. "It's not fitting for the head of the regional house to speak so. What if the soldiers hear you?"

"Oh, let them. It burns."

"That's the unfortunate side-effect of a gun discharged against the skin," a deeper voice stated. "What do you plan on doing with this girl?"

"Blatt, I'm going to punch the girl," the whiner replied.

"But she is just a child, sir."

"Doesn't matter, she hurt me." A sharp intake of breath preceded a burst of sobs. "If she thinks she can do that to a han elder, she's in for a rude punching."

Margo continued to crouch as she turned from the window to survey the room. She wished for her father. She wished for her father's strength, his knowledge, she wished for him to hold her.

The latch rattled on the door.

Margo froze, her eyes locked on the door.

With measured slowness, the door eased open to reveal Blatt. Muscles strained against the thin fabric of his shirt as he swiveled his head in search of Margo. "There you are, Mite." A relieved smile creased his broad face when he found her crouched atop the shelf. "Careful you don't fall."

Margo remained motionless, her eyes hard.

"That's quite the glare." Blatt stepped into the room and clipped the door shut with a quick heel. "I need to know where your da is and if there is a way I can reach him. I don't suppose you would know either of those things?"

Blatt sat on a stack of crates and leaned his elbows on his knees. Tilting his head, he stared up at her. "Anything you could give me would help move the process along and keep Kon from doing anything stupid. Between you and me," he dropped his voice conspiratorially, "I can think of a dozen other folks who should have gotten the seat ahead of him. But ho," Blatted sighed and then smiled like a sad, faithful hound. "I serve the han, and he's what they gave me.

"You got a name, Mite?" The muscle's tone remained level. "You help me out now, the faster I can get you home to your da."

Margo hugged her knees tighter as she crouched. Her flinty glare answered Blatt's words.

For a time, the bodyguard sat and studied Margo with his sad, wide-eyed gaze. Eventually he cleared his throat and rose to his feet.

"I had a feeling this was going to float this course," he said as he opened the door.

Margo remained silent and still as the door thudded shut behind him. She listened to see if he would return, but when the room kept silent, she relaxed. Shifting her position, she sat cross-legged with her back resting against the wall beside the window.

She closed her eyes and waited.

*   *   *

"Captain Pico." Atom met the captain's glare with his own. "All you need to know is that I've been sent by our lord's son after a closed meeting with the emperor. I have been tasked with a private matter for Admiral Motoki."

"You'll need clearance."

Atom spread his hands in a wide shrug. "With the current state of things, I'm not sure how to provide that information."

"Then how are we supposed to vet you?" the captain growled, rising from his seat like a shark from the depths. "You think we would let you through to the admiral? I've never met you personally."

"Do you personally know everyone who works for our heir?"

Pico gritted his teeth and leaned with his knuckles on the table. "No," he hissed.

"Then you are outside this one," Atom leaned closer to the confrontation and lowered his voice. "There are political wheels turning in court and this attack is not helping our cause. As a result, I have a pertinent message for Admiral Motoki's ears only on how things need to play out.

"If you insist on standing in my way, there will be heavy repercussions on all of us." Atom looked over to where Mir stood staring out the window. "She's the closest thing to a vet I'm going to find on this piss-poor rock we are losing blood over."

"Mir." Pico never took his eyes from Atom. "Will you stand in for this agent?"

The woman turned with a surprised look. "I thought I already did that." Her eyes darted back and forth between the men. "Isn't that why I'm here instead of enjoying downtime?"

"I thought so." Atom raised an eyebrow to Pico.

"Fine," Pico grumbled, dropping back into his seat in weary defeat. "I'll put you on the next transport up to Motoki's flag. You'll have to skip through the platform, but it shouldn't be too much of a wait.

"Frederickson," Pico said into the com on his desk before recalling the EMP. "Frederickson," he yelled loud enough to be heard outside his office.

In a flustered scurry, the officer slipped through the door. "Sir?" He knuckled his forehead.

"Send a runner and find me a transport to lift these two up to the admiral's flag."

"Sir," Frederickson gulped, and disappeared like a frightened woodland sprite.

"I guess we have a little downtime." Atom turned to Mir. "Do you guys have a lounge or rec area I could crash for a touch? Maybe you could grab that shower while I close my winks."

Mir sighed and rubbed her eyes with weary indifference. "Yeah, I'll show you. Cap, with your permission we'll be down in the squad lounge until you have that transport lined up." She looked to Pico with deference and then a smile tugged at the corner of her mouth. "And if you could see fit to take a little extra time on that transport, I wouldn't mind resting my ocs to get the grit out."

Pico nodded and picked up a paper file, dismissing them without another word.

*   *   *

A switch flew and a loud snick filled the cramped storeroom, like a fly-fisher on a quest for pain.

Margo's head snapped to the side and a tear slipped down her cheek, but she remained silent in the face of her aggressor. She pushed herself up from the floor and settled back into her cross-legged, straight-backed seat. Grim determination steeled her expression. A long, red welt rose on her cheek.

"Who are you?" Konstantine Markins Adler spat. "What is your family name?"

The switch snapped out again, this time catching Margo on the arm. The girl sat naked to the waist with her jumper pulled down to expose her arms and back.

She folded her hands in her lap and glared.

"You might want to ease, boss." Blatt sounded calm, bordering on bored, but a touch of worry crept to the corner of his eyes as he leaned against the wall just inside the door with his arms crossed. "We don't know who she is. If she has connections to one of the major hans, or gods forbid, the Adlerians, we could be in a world of hurt."

"This doesn't concern you," Markins snarled without shifting his eyes from Margo.

In rapid succession the switch caught Margo on the shoulder, the back of her hand, and the insole of her bare foot.

Margo narrowed her eyes. She focused on her father. She allowed her mind to drift.

"This is not a child," Markins screamed, spittle flying from his lips as he raised the switch over his head. Before the tool descended on Margo's unflinching form, the door opened. Blatt stepped forward and shielded the girl, taking the switch on his broad back.

"Love," a soft voice intervened before Markins could lash out further at his bodyguard. "I thought we discussed this. There is more to be learned from this girl than brute force could ever hope to uncover. She is a beautiful mystery." The woman slipped past Markins, soft as a cool spring breeze, and traced a finger over the welt threatening to seal Margo's eye.

"What child is this that refuses to cry out in pain?" she murmured with theatrical flair as she lifted Margo's face and searched. "These eyes haunt me. They haunt my dreams.

"Husband, I have seen these eyes before." Her voice grew chill. She turned from her crouched position and looked up to Markins, the look bore such commanding force that the man shrank down before his wife. "There is much more to this mystery than we can plainly see. She carries death in her eyes. She has the look of a man who has passed through the crucibles of the damned and emerged on the other side. Yet she can be no more than three.

Rising like Aphrodite from the sea, she towered over her husband and asked, "Where did you find this lovely urchin?"

"She was in a pram." Markins shrugged. "It looked like someone had jimmed it open after the EMPs hit. She was just sitting there, kind of like she is now, with her eyes closed. I thought she was sleeping."

"She is separating herself from pain." The woman spoke just above a whisper as she turned and studied Margo's face. "What did she do when you removed her from the pram?"

"She shot Tonsy with my pistol."

"How did she know you had a gun?"

Markins shrugged.

"Safety off?"

Markins hesitated. "No," he said with slow puzzlement. "I never float without safety unless I'm expecting trouble."

"And there was no trouble in sight?"

"Just a girl in a pram," Markins laughed.

"What happened next?"

"Well, the shot burned my side." He held up his arm and gestured to his wounded torso. "So, I dropped her and she bolted."

"Straight away?"

"Yeah, headed for an alley."

Blatt cleared his throat.

"Something else?" The woman's eye drifted from the girl up to the towering guard.

"Ma'am, she stopped just before entering the alley and stared us down." The big man closed his eyes and grimaced in thought as he tried to imitate Margo's posture. "She kind of floated on her toes for just a second, like she was ready to throw on us, but she had no gun."

The woman zeroed in on Blatt, like a cat spotting a mouse, all attention turned to the guard's stance and words. She took a moment to absorb the imitation of Margo's posture. Then she hissed and spun on her husband. Her hand darted like a serpent to strike the top of his head. The clap startled Margo from her reverie.

"Fool," the woman spat. "Do you have any idea what you've brought into our home?"

"Just a girl." Markins blinked, startled by his wife's blow.

"How many gunslingers have you heard of that wander the Fingers with their daughter in a pram?"

Markins shrugged and shook his head with genuine ignorance.

"I've only heard of one." She narrowed her eyes and swiveled to study Margo.

"Atom Ulvan."

Margo's eyes widened a touch.

"I thought so," the woman whispered, her shoulders slumping. "Even if I'm reading this incorrectly, we can't be in a good place. Too many things wrong with this girl. Too much danger. Too much, too much." Her head drifted in a slow shake as she pressed her knuckles to her lips. "So many things I have been able to guide and manage, but this is beyond me."

"I could dump her somewhere," Markins said, trying in vain to sound helpful.

"No," the woman spoke without malice, as one resigned to her fate. "That would only make things worse. People saw you take her. They know we are at fault. Ulvan will follow the trail like a wolf that has scented the blood of his pup.

"At least we have a chance to plead our case with her alive." The woman spun and swept from the room. "We must plan to placate.

"Blatt, lock her in the study. We cannot give the appearance of ill treatment, but we can't let her wander from our custody."

Blatt hesitated. "What do we do about her face?" he asked Markins.

"Don't know." Markins' ashen face betrayed his mental upheaval.

"Go rest, boss. I'll take care of it." Blatt lifted Margo from the floor and carried her from the storeroom with distracted care.

As the guard walked down the hall, he passed three servants in livery who stepped to the side to allow Blatt room to pass. From her cradled vantage point, Margo caught sight of the girl who had helped pry open her pram to rescue her from the darkness.

The girl's face first broke into a genuine smile and immediately slipped to a scowl as she caught sight of the bruised lump forming below Margo's eye. The girl opened her mouth to speak, but her companion placed a restraining hand on her arm and the pair dropped their eyes to the ground. Blatt swept past without a comment and left the group to return to their business.

The stoic look returned to Margo's face.

"What's your story, Mite?" Blatt prattled as he strolled down the hall, his focus elsewhere. "Seems the mistress knows your da and she's none too thrilled at our chances. He a famed slinger or such? Probably," he continued, not expecting a response. "Any which, it can't be good for us." He seated her on a low couch, and with a sad smile, left her alone again.

*   *   *

"Which helped more, the shower or the winks?" Atom asked Mir as the pair shuddered through the upper atmosphere aboard a light shuttle.

She winged a two-fingered salute his way and dropped her head back against the padded rest. The vibrations of the shuttle jostled her back and forth, but that seemed to do little to interrupt her repose.

Huffing a sharp laugh, Atom stretched his legs out and propped his feet on the seat beside her. All the other seats lining the walls of the shuttle remained empty and Atom wondered at their situation. He tried to rationalize the deployment of an empty shuttle with the chaos of the EMP attack visibly straining the entire Mirogi transport system.

That alone should have been a disruption for the Adlerians to launch a counterattack. Minimal planetary transport should have given them the needed window.

Or had his ploy delved into deeper roots than he had anticipated.

Had he stumbled into a preexisting power-play?

Atom leaned back into his seat and studied the resting Mir.

Something set in his mind, an irritating grain of sand, rubbing a raw spot, that left him uneasy in the presence of the woman. She appeared simple, straightforward, and aggressive in her military authority, but he made a note to never turn his back to her.

Slitting his eyes like a cat, he relaxed his body into the vibrations of the journey into the Black.

The first leg of that journey only lasted an hour, and ended as the shuttle docked at a run-down waystation more accustomed to ore than passengers. The *One Way Ticket* had bypassed the station on the inbound flight, so the dinginess caught Atom by surprise as he stepped off the spotless military shuttle into the flickering light of the transfer bay.

Several sullen porters sat on a bench against one wall. As Atom and Mir disembarked, a few of them lurched to their feet like the undead and wandered over to the craft.

"Any portage?" one of them asked, his eyes flickered up from the floor.

"Just the two of us," Atom replied with a grin, gesturing to Mir. "She's tired enough that she might not mind if you tossed her on a cart."

The porter studied the floor plates in sullen silence.

Atom's grin faded. He studied the men with a puzzled expression. Only when the docking doors hissed shut and Atom felt the station's clamps disengage from the shuttle did Atom grasp their solitude. Realization set in that he had stepped onto a small factory city with an indigenous population who viewed him as the enemy.

"Peace, chomps." He held up his hands. "I'm not looking for any trouble. I'm just a boke trying to get from one point to another. Could you point us to the relay? We should be catching another flight out of here on the short."

The spokesman grunted and jerked his thumb towards the lone exit from the bay.

Only when Atom and Mir approached the hatch did the man call out after them, causing Atom to hesitate. "Watch yerselves up here," the porter said. "You might'a conked us, but that don't mean all Adlers'll take it on the float. We en't lookin' fer troubles, but don't want nothin' comin' back on us if you cross anykins."

"I'll take the advice." Atom waved to the man. "Nothing on your heads."

"Think we should take them?" Mir asked as she ignored the men and scowled at the hatch. "Technical speak, that was a threat and we're in enemy territory."

The hatch cracked and Atom took several steps in silence. "No," he said with a shake of his head. "The information I have to relay is too important to delay with low-level malcontents. I should have been talking with Motoki yesterday, but the chain of command keeps beating me down."

"Fine, but I'm going to have to put it in my report."

"It may save lives up here."

They continued down the hall to the central hub for the dozen docking spokes radiating outward. The entrance hatches staggered about the hub to conserve space and Escher-like stars dropped to the floor below.

Atom mapped the room in a single glance. On the main floor, a pair of clerks sat behind a wide desk. One of them played on a screen with idle boredom. Her eyes flicked up and registered Atom and Mir before retreating to her repast. The other clerk slouched with his head bobbing on his chest to the rhythm of his slow, slumbering breath.

Trash spilled from a silent recycler mounted in the wall near the hatch to the main hab. Iridescent graffiti danced over the door as station power pulsed enough to cause a low-level flicker.

"Seems hard times are come to this station," Atom said as he headed down the stairs.

Reaching the bottom, Atom breathed a weary grunt and trudged across the floor to lean his elbows on the counter. Neither clerk moved. Only when Mir joined him at the counter and rapped her knuckles in a sharp cadence on the grimy board, did either of them acknowledge the newcomers.

"Help you?" The slumbering man coughed as he blinked with startled bleariness. He smoothed his beard and grinned through the fur. "Apologies, I didn't hear you come in."

"We're to catch an outgoing transport to the flag, snap." Mir glared daggers.

"Give me a touch," the man said, rubbing crust from his eyes as he scrambled to wake his system. "It takes a minute for these systems to boot. The Adles didn't seem to care much about staying on top of the tech curve.

"No wonder we walked in here and snagged the system from them." He grinned as he smoothed a greasy tuft of hair down into some semblance of order.

The man's companion remained glued to her own pad with one leg curled up in her seat, affording her chin a resting spot as her fingers danced over the keys of her entertainment. She yawned and glanced up, catching Atom's eye. She seemed surprised to find Atom staring at her and dropped her eyes back to her glow.

"Security seems ...." Atom hesitated, "lax."

The man shrugged. "Well, the station's on lockdown." The man frowned at his own screen. "There are roaming squads that keep people in their quarters when they're not on the clock. Everyone's on lockdown except cooks and a pair of meds and those porters you passed on your way down."

"What's the usual pop on this spinner?"

"Runs around 1500, give or take. Most are mech-loaders who make their meal transferring ore from hoppers to long-haul transport ships."

"And they're all just sitting?"

"Until we can get this rock spitting out ore again." The man scooted his chair back and rose to grab an info tag issuing from a printer. "Here's your slip. It looks like you'll have a few hours before your transport floats out."

"Anything to do on this hoop?" asked Mir, pushing herself up from the counter.

"There are a couple food counters open on the main ring and an entertainment suite we keep running for off-duty personnel." The clerk shrugged as he handed out the tags.

Atom nodded thanks and headed for the hatch.

Trailing behind, Mir seemed more interested in adjusting her armored vest.

"You solid?" Atom asked, slapping open the hatch as he fixed his partner with a puzzled look.

"Yeah, I must have put on some weight. This rig is digging in more than it should."

"Weight in your chest?"

"I must have used too much water when I took my shower." She smirked.

Atom smiled, understanding creeping into the back of his mind. "That's why I've always worn mine on my hip. I strap it up every morn and it always sits just right."

Mir rolled her shoulders and neck. "As soon as I'm out of this gremlin band, I'll make that switch. Until then, I have to fit in regs."

"Someday, if we're so lucky. In the meantime, you fancy snagging some chow while we wait? Or maybe just a cup of perk?"

"I could eat."

Before they cleared the corridor, a klaxon sounded and the lighting dropped to emergency levels.

Atom, hand on his pistol, edged up to the far hatch and peered through the window with an eager calm. Seeing only an empty stretch of hallway, he glanced back to Mir and found the security officer stalking towards him with her own gun drawn.

"Looks like we might need to put that snack on hold." She slapped open the hatch with unrestrained energy and stepped through to survey the hallway. "Maybe there's entertainment."

With a dark, half grin she trotted towards the elevator banks at the end of the hall.

*   *   *

Margo sat on the table. With legs crossed and eyes half open, she could have been a meditating monk. Sturdy bookshelves lined the walls and framed the wide picture window overlooking the garden in the center of the courtyard. Margo studied the light snowfall that left individual flakes dancing across the swirling wind to grace the trees and stone ornaments with a painter's delicacy.

As soon as Blatt had closed the door, the girl had abandoned her couch and made a quick tour of the room. She had tried the drawers of the heavy wooden desk and found them locked.

With the grace and delicacy of a dancing ninja, she climbed to the desktop and inspected everything there. She poked at the controls for the desktop system, but found it dead after the EMP. She tried a few more switches to no avail. Only after fiddling with the desk lamp and trailing her finger over several baubles did her gaze stall on an ornate letter opener.

Glancing around with the furtiveness of a ferret, she rocked forward, looking to any observing eye as if she stumbled to her feet, but as she rose, the letter opener disappeared into her sleeve.

Clambering back down to the floor, she pushed the chair into place and made a slow circuit of the study.

For a few minutes, she stood at the window with one hand pressed to the glass. She leaned her forehead on the window and surveyed the garden. Her eyes drifted between the trees and the pond, the wooden bridge and matching pavilion, the stone benches and ornately carved lanterns.

She wished to be outside, running in the garden.

Sighing in frustration, she turned from the window and climbed up to sit on the conference table that balanced out the bulky desk at the far end of the study.

Margo reflected, thinking about Mae and the trouble a cat might find on her own.

A slight smile pulled at the girl's eyes as she imagined Mae sitting next to her on the table, as regal as any tawny lion. Margo imagined the cat. She heard the purr and felt Mae nuzzle her leg in an attempt to steal a scratch behind the ears.

Sitting in imaginative silence, Margo forgot about time. She defied the norm and sat, as a two-year-old Buddha, spending the afternoon with her feline friend.

A scratch at the door dragged Margo from the comforts of her imagination. Her eyes drifted open as the door opened a crack under a tentative hand.

The girl from the street peaked through the crack.

"Good, you're alone." She slid the door open a few more inches and slithered through like an otter, shutting the door behind her with noiseless care. "I was afraid you might have a friend or two in here."

Margo kept her face calm, but her head swiveled in curiosity.

The girl danced on tiptoe over to the table. "I thought you might be hungry," she said, pulling a small bundle from a pouch at her belt. "It's been more than six hours since they locked you in here. I know I'd hunger." The girl bobbed her head and unwrapped the pack to reveal a small handful of raisins and some crude-cut blocks of cheese. "I know this en't much, but I figured you could use it. My name's Tanny; I'm ten." The girl pulled one of the chairs out and sat down facing Margo. She pushed the food over as if making an offering. "En't right, them keeping you bundled like this. I said so to myself. It en't right that you got left all lonesome-like in your pram on the road, but it's even worse that someone who en't yer kin took you up.

"I don't know their game," Tanny pushed a raisin in Margo's direction. "They just round and body-snatched you. I hope that en't their usual business, but it seems it don't really add on a small world like this. Body-snatching don't work if they 'em as done the snatching.

"Sorry," Tanny said with a room-lifting smile, "I'm rambling. I'm new. My mom just signed me over fer a two-year run with the Markins. I guess I'm already doing my best to not fit." Tanny glanced at the door and her smile drifted down a notch. "Not that I aim to buck. No sir, I aim to fit, snug as a bug. Do my tour. Then head fer home. Hopefully things will be a touch better when I get back there, seein' as the kins git my sum added to one less mouth."

"Tanny." Margo picked up a couple raisins and held them out for the girl.

Tanny's lip quivered, but the smile remained, as she accepted the offering with a nod. She tucked the raisins into her mouth individually.

"You remind me of my lil' sister." Tanny leaned her elbows and scrutinized Margo as she sucked on the raisins. "I always call her Micro. I don't miss her yet, but I'm sure it'll happen sooner 'posed to later."

"Sister?" Margo tilted her head to look at Tanny. With dark, curly hair pulled back into a tail that spilled over one shoulder, the serving girl bore a passing resemblance to Margo.

Fear drove the smile from Tanny's face as the hiss of the sliding door sliced through their conversation. "Sisters?" Markins' wife slipped into the room, moving in silence on the balls of her feet as she glided towards the girls.

"No, ma'am." Tanny lurched from the chair and prostrated herself on the floor.

Margo maintained her seated posture. She looked up to the woman with an unnatural calm and folded her hands in her lap.

"Up, girl," the woman commanded. Tanny rose, but kept her eyes downcast.

The woman grabbed Tanny's chin and lifted her face. Studying the curves of Tanny's cheeks and slight slant of her eyes, the woman shifted her gaze between the two girls. She scowled and pursed her lips in consternation.

"There is a resemblance, but it isn't a strong one." The mistress dropped Tanny's face and the girl sagged in on herself. "If that isn't the case, what are you doing in here? Girl, you are new to this household, but that doesn't excuse you from knowing your place. It brings me no pleasure." She raised her hand to strike. "But lessons must be taught."

Before her hand could descend, Margo sprang into action. She pulled the letter opener from her sleeve, and despite the dull edges, the metal point easily punctured the woman's hand as she brought it down. The knife did little more than break the skin, but it caused the woman to flinch back from the girls.

"Go." Margo jumped from the table and sprinted for the door on her tiny legs.

Behind her, Tanny hesitated, deliberating between the girl and her family, duty and escape, the now or the future.

She froze, trapped between the possibilities.

The woman struck with rage; her bloody backhand sent Tanny sprawling.

"Blatt, get that urchin," the woman screeched as she spun back to the door.

The burly guard stepped in from the hallway just in time for Margo to scamper past his feet. He tried to slip his foot out to catch her, but ended up throwing himself off balance and impeding the woman's rush to pursue the child.

Margo raced down the hallway, juking past startled servants and guards who looked on in confusion.

Without knowing the layout of the house, Margo kept moving, hoping for the front door.

Footsteps thudded behind her.

Margo, on her stubby little legs, pumped forward. She rounded a corner on nimble feet and shot down the new hall like an arrow from a longbow. A dozen sliding doors flew by on both sides, all closed.

"Stop, Mite," Blatt called out as he slid around the corner, balanced as the polished floor offered him little traction. "There's nowhere to run, but in circles."

Margo ignored him.

Blatt stopped at the corner, watching the receding toddler. Margo glanced over her shoulder as she pumped for escape and found Blatt standing at the corner, breathing heavily, watching her.

As she neared the midpoint of the hall a familiar voice reached her ears.

"We're looking for a little girl." Hither's voice floated along the corridor like a soft ocean breeze.

"How little?" another voice countered. "The youngest we have here are around ten. They're servant girls. Are you looking for one of them? We did sign on three new girls this morning."

Margo slowed at the exchange. She looked back again to confirm Blatt's stationary stance. Then she crept to the door and peeked around the corner.

"No, she's younger than that. Just under three." Hither stood in the entryway.

"I'm afraid …."

Margo did not give the man a chance to finish as she bolted around the corner and scooted past Hither.

"Daisy," the girl squealed as she launched herself at the giant.

The pilot caught Margo with a familiar grace and settled her into the crook of his arm.

"You were saying." Hither turned her frigid ire on the doorman.

His hand flinched for his gun.

Shi's pistol barked. "I don't reckin I like liars," the gunslinger grunted as the man stumbled back to collapse in the doorway, gun falling from lifeless fingers.

Like a disturbed anthill, the household responded to the sound of the shot. Footsteps echoed down the hallway like ball-bearings bouncing across a wooden floor. As the bannermen thundered down the main corridor, heavy bolts slid home on the doors behind the crew.

With Blatt leading the charge, the han soldiers rounded the corridor and spread across the entryway.

"Who are you?" Blatt demanded, his eyes cold and calculating as he measured the crew of the *One Way Ticket* standing in a protective circle with Margo in Daisy's arm, as close to the center as possible. The Markinshan soldiers edged wider, flanking the group with intentional steps.

"We're her family," Hither snapped. She slipped a foot forward and rolled her weight to the balls of her feet.

Blatt studied the group. "Not blood. I'd wager a month's pay on that."

"That is not your concern." Hither shifted sideways to shield Margo with her body. What does matter is that you've taken one of ours, and from what we gathered when we found her pram, the taking wasn't done with the best of intentions.

"And," she cast a glance to the welt along Margo's cheek. "She was not kept in the best conditions."

Blatt frowned and said, "That's above my grade, Miss."

"So, where does that leave us?"

Blatt looked down at the corpse bleeding at his feet. "If you hadn't just killed one of ours, I'd say you were welcome to a sit-down with the liege and his lady." He hesitated, tapping at his jaw in thought. "But Brond here leaves a wrinkle in that plan. Blood for blood, it's the law of the land. You surrender those that perpetrated this killing into our custody, then maybe we see what the lord has to say about your claim to the abandoned girl he took under his protection."

"Yer man aimed to pull on me," Shi growled from Hither's flank.

"Be that as it may, this is the law," Blatt replied.

Hither measured the man. "You're stalling. Why?"

"I'm the head of han security; do I need a reason to keep you here?" Blatt took a deep, cleansing breath and dropped his hands to his sides. "I am offering to let you go in peace with the exception of the murderer and ...." He cocked his head, listening, "The girl."

"No," Hither spoke without hesitation. "We all leave or we have trouble."

"You would risk escalating this situation and the wrath of the Markinshan?"

"I'm not terribly worried. First off, I've been all over the Fingers and I've never heard of Markins. That leads me to believe you aren't an official han. Second, if this were a situation your family actually took seriously, I wouldn't be chatting with a retainer. If I read this situation, you aren't acting on the orders of a han-lord." A slow, predatory smile spread over Hither's face as Blatt puffed his chest just enough to validate her words. "Fact of the matter, someone gaffed. Folks I spoke with said it was the lord himself who took the girl.

"Funny thing, they didn't call him the han-lord. I would peg him as a low-level retainer or maybe even a boke playing at a kuza. That means you don't have that power. And if I had to guess, this so-called lord is the gaffer and someone else is trying to cover things.

"Am I getting close?" Hither narrowed her eyes and lifted her chin as if scenting the air. "The lady is the brains in this family. You're listening to her right now. She knows her husband crossed someone you don't want as an enemy."

"I suspected as much." Konstantine's wife stepped around the corner, gliding between the guards to take a position a step in front of Blatt. "A child of that nature is an anomaly. She does not fear when she should, and not out of ignorance.

"I've looked into her eyes." She stepped to the side to where she could scowl at Margo nestled in Daisy's arm. "She has seen death's angel. She has faced it in a way a normal child should never be asked to."

"She reflects her father," Hither agreed. "Now, I would say it would be in the best interest of your family to let this walk away. Leave Margo in our care and we act as if this never happened. I guarantee it will be in the best interest of your people. The way we care about her? The captain cares a thousand times more. Where we will kill to escape, he will kill to destroy.

"He is already at war with a han that sits on the emperor's council. That war may kill him, but if you make the mistake of harming his daughter, then I would compose your death poems now."

The woman studied Hither. Nodding in thought, she turned and with slow steps, drifted back through her wall of men.

"I suppose there is only one course of action left to us then," she said in a mournful tone. "If you were to escape and bring word of the damages done, our name would be revealed to this captain of yours. That would not be good for my people."

She cast a sad smile over her shoulder as she paused in the doorway. "You mustn't be allowed to leave. Blatt, do what you must to ensure nothing implicates the Markins name."

"As you must." Hither bowed in understanding. "If you would give me leave to compose my own death poem. Unlike my companions, I come from a family where it is expected. Perhaps you could honor me and hide it away so that my soul doesn't pass into the void without someone to remember it."

The woman nodded her assent.

"Thank you." Hither's sorrowed smile melted the hearts of several of the soldiers encircling them. "Byron, if you would do me the honor of finding me something to write with."

"Sec, bosslady," Byron unslung the pack from his shoulders and knelt as he set it on the ground. Moving with measured ease he rummaged, eventually pulling a handful of wooden pencils from the depths of the pack. "This 'nough?"

"That should do," Hither replied as Daisy set Margo to the ground and tucked her behind his tree trunk of a leg.

Without warning, Byron cast the pencils into the air and the tension kicked up.

The 'pencils' hovered above the heads of the group long enough for the Markins guards to exchange a nervous glance.

"What is this?" Blatt demanded, shifting into his lady's line of sight.

Hither smiled and bowed her head. With a wave of her hand the 'pencils' flew like javelins. Although not extremely accurate, the darts impaled themselves in whatever flesh happened to line up with their trajectory.

Cries of pain erupted in conjunction with a volley from the soldiers.

Daisy stepped forward and slapped up his shield in time to absorb most of the energy bolts winging in their direction. Only one bolt managed to slip through before the shield fully charged. The crimson lance ripped into Daisy's shoulder, leaving a charred furrow in his shirt and flesh.

The hit did little to slow the rumbling giant, instead it sparked his fury.

Slipping hands into the power gauntlets hanging at his waist, Daisy slammed his fists together with a cry of rage and plunged forward. Behind him, Shi and Hither spun outward. Shi's ladies jumped into her hands and began to sing songs of death. On the far flank, Hither leveled an auto-blaster and fired bursts into the press of enemies.

Byron gathered Margo behind Daisy's shield and pressed into the recessed door housing.

As they curled together, Cody poked his head up from Byron's pack. The mini-dragon caught sight of Margo and wove himself sinuously around her shoulders like a serpentine cat.

The two children watched the battle with frozen anticipation, knowing that their lives hung in the balance of warriors driving a wedge into the enemy phalanx.

Daisy charged towards Blatt, his power gauntlets destroying flesh with precision blunt force. His shield caught the scattered shots, but a few of the enemies shifted their attacks to non-energy weapons. The raging giant managed to deflect a knife thrust enough to escape with a long gash along his upper arm. He pulped the attacker's face with a lashing backhand that launched the soldier sideways into another cluster of attackers.

In front of him, Blatt backpedaled, guiding his lady behind his bulk as he poured a continuous stream of blaster-fire into Daisy's shield.

"Keep firing," he roared as Daisy dismantled a pair of guards who stepped between their liege and the intruders. "Overload his shield. He doesn't have long. Keep shooting."

Daisy roared forward, opening up the flanks and forcing Shi and Hither to spread wider. Ducking and weaving through the carnage, the Valkyrie pair flowed forward on an uncharted course in defiance of the Markins. As Hither gained the wall, she snatched a guard in a chokehold and used him as a human shield to press on towards the main entryway to the house.

Shi slithered forward in a serpentine route that dodged and darted through the enemy, dropping them where the opportunity afforded itself.

More soldiers poured from the innards of the house, streaming past Blatt and his lady.

The tables had shifted, if not turned, and the new guards found themselves caught in a pincer with blades to the flank and a shielded battering ram plunging up the gut.

Behind the human wave, Blatt guided his lady to safety and turned to look back at the crew as they minced through the guards sacrificing their lives in return for time. The look on his face conveyed an understanding that he could only prolong the inevitable.

Daisy missed the look as his ursine rage consumed him, leaving him to devour those before him instead of driving for the true enemy.

In the entryway, the crowd thinned. Shi paused to reload and several of the remaining guards turned their attention her way. Hither used the opportunity to press forward and take the small group in the flank.

Daisy smashed into the last soldier, driving the man to his knees.

The rage slipped from the bear's eyes to be replaced by cold calculation. "You know why we're doing this?" he asked, his chest heaving as he fought the aftermath of adrenaline.

"No," the man gasped. His arm hung dead at his side. "Just following orders."

"Family," Daisy growled. "You stole a member of our family."

As Daisy leaned over the kneeling man, the two women slipped past. Shi paused to put a bullet in the man's head.

"It's humane to put a wounded critter down," she said with a grimace.

Daisy stared as the man crumpled. It took a moment for his primal mind to comprehend. Then he nodded to Shi and turned back to Margo and Byron. He strode through the battlefield to scoop the girl into his arms. He snuggled the girl close to his chest.

"I'm sorry, Go," he whispered, his voice gruff as he fought back tears. He touched her welted cheek with a tender finger.

"Daisy," Margo pushed back and pressed her tiny hands to the pilot's cheeks. "No sad. Daisy smile. Where's Da?" She looked around, peeking over Daisy's shoulder as if her father might materialize from thin air.

"He's still out on his gig," Daisy sighed as he set the girl down beside Byron.

"Daisy." Hither poked her head back into the wide entryway. "We need to press this home. If they escape, you know it'll float around on the back orbit and catch us in the pipe."

Daisy nodded in weary assent and picked his way back through the carnage.

"Shi swept right," Hither said, glaring down the hallway to their left. "You and I will be the wall to her sweep.

"By," Hither commanded. "Keep Go with you and tail us. I want you to keep near, but out of the line of fire. If you have any little surprises in your pack, feel free to keep anyone from creeping up our back quadrant."

"Oi darl, I can start right 'ere." Byron grinned as he reached into his pack and pulled a handful of what looked to be metal juggling spheres.

He tossed the spheres around the room, mixed in with the dead, and joined the others. "Anyone who ain't us is in fer a tight s'prise if they come a tipsy-toed frough 'ere. An' I fink it'd be prime if'n we let Cody fly a touch and let us know what be's ahead."

Byron whistled and the mech-dragon sprang from around Margo's neck and flapped up into the air.

As the four slipped into the hallway, Daisy popped a new battery pack into his shield and fired up the half-sphere that protected his front. Hither slipped along as Daisy's shadow, half a step to his right. Behind them a dozen paces, Byron and Margo followed in an exaggerated crouch-walk.

Cody glided ahead. The dragon swooped up to cling to the wall near an approaching corner and inverted, using his claws to crawl across the ceiling like a gecko.

Behind the slithering scout, Daisy and Hither slowed.

The width of the hallway allowed them to walk side by side, with room to spare, but working together, they stacked to optimize the protection of Daisy's shield. The power-pugilist strolled, his fist ready and his feet light. Behind him, Hither kept her gun on the corner.

As they progressed down the hallway, the first of several closed doors drew near.

The cautious assault pair slowed and Byron drew Margo to the wall.

A head peeked around the corner and Hither snapped a shot that caught the unfortunate guard just above the eye with a burst of blaster bolts.

Cody eased his head around the same corner at the joint of the wall and ceiling.

"They are stacked around the corner waiting for you," Kozue told them.

"Daiz, check the doors." Hither crouched against the wall several paces ahead of Margo and Byron. "I'll keep them checked at the corner. I don't want any surprises slipping up behind us.

Daisy nodded and stepped up to slide the nearest door open. He poked his head in, surveyed, and moved to the next with the same result.

"Looks like they executed a fancy bug-out." He shrugged and stumped to the third and final door before the corner. He paused and grinned back at the others. "I could sure use a drink right about now."

He slipped the door open.

The hallway erupted in one cacophony of sound and motion. Just as the door opened, a slug ripped from within the room, sending Daisy sprawling back against the far wall in an explosion of flesh and blood.

At the sound, several Markinshan guards darted around the corner, only to be cut down by Hither.

Margo screamed and tried to dart forward.

Sensing her movement, Byron lunged and dragged the girl down by the back of her jumper.

"Daisy," the girl screamed, her juvenile voice cutting through the chaos.

Hither slipped forward and pressed her back to the wall beside the hostile doorway as Daisy, blood pulsing from a fist-sized hole in his back, lurched sideways and clawed out of the line of fire. A few agonizing feet down the hall he collapsed to the floor with a strange mewl, and continued to try to scoot away from the danger, his movements clumsy and garbled with pain.

His eyes widened as his breath came in short, bubbled gasps.

"Byron," Hither snapped the boy's attention from wrangling Margo as she fought towards Daisy with more determination than any child should have mustered. "I need one of your little friends."

He shrugged at Margo.

"Leave her," Hither commanded.

Byron released Margo, who promptly scampered to Daisy. The mech swung his pack and fished inside for a moment. Then, finding his prize, pulled another fist-sized ball bearing from the depths.

"Back," he commanded Hither as he tossed it sidearm, past her.

The ball landed in the doorway and defied physics as it refused to bounce. The metallic sphere vibrated. A series of shots rang out from within the room, heavy slugs tearing up the wooden floor around the ball, but failing to hit the target.

Sensing the violent intentions from within the room, a rippling series of legs thrust from the carapace and a metallic creature that seemed a fusion of spider and centipede erupted from within the plain metal. Faster than the eye could track, the mech-creature skittered into the room.

A scream of terror followed.

Hither's wide-eyed glance found Byron staring into the void.

"Is he ok?" the courtesan asked Kozue.

"He is interfacing with his mech," Kozue replied. "It would appear we have time for you to attend to Daisy. The enemy has fallen back to the next intersection. I cannot see them from Cody's current position, but estimate from building size and probable layouts that there is a defensive room on the left."

"Where is Margo?" Hither hissed, looking up and down the hall, but failing to locate the child.

"Unknown," Kozue replied in her technical AI voice. "Her nano connection was severed during the EMP and I have not had time to replenish her system. I estimate that she is in one of the side rooms, but cannot say for sure."

As if on cue, Margo emerged from the nearest room, hauling a wad of bedding in her arms. Unable to see over the burden, she walked with searching feet until she bumped a toe into Daisy's leg and dropped the sheets atop the curled pilot. Without hesitation, she packed the entire bundle against Daisy's wounded back, using her whole body to apply pressure.

"Daisy is approaching shock," Kozue continued with clinical indifference. "Margo is right, you need to attend to him now. I will scout ahead and alert you if anything changes with the enemy."

Margo held Daisy's immense frame as much as she could. Her efforts looked more like a hug that struggled to hold the giant in place as he writhed in agony.

Daisy's eyes fluttered as he fought to look over his shoulder at Margo.

Covering the few steps to the collapsed figure, Hither accessed his med stats through Kozue as she held a hand to his forehead.

"By," Hither called the boy out of his rapture as she nudged Margo out of the way and leaned into the packing with all of her weight. "I'm going to need you to pull the med-kit from your pack and stabilize Daisy. He's bleeding in and out, so you're going to need to pull that field-triage I taught you. Interface with the nanos to help you stop the bleed and slip an internal stasis ball inside the wound to help slow things down until we can get him back to the ship.

"Set your little buggers at all the nearby chokepoints and set them to sentry so you don't have to worry about anyone sneaking on you.

"I'm taking Go and I'm going to finish this." She eased off, allowing Byron room.

"Got it," Byron said as he dumped his pack on the ground next to Daisy and half a dozen spheres sprang to life, darting away like exposed cockroaches.

"Good." Hither knelt and waved Margo onto her back to clip into a reserve harness.

She wiped Daisy's blood from her hands on the front of her tan jacket like warpaint and rose to her feet like Shiva carrying the daughter of man on her back. She checked the charge on her compact auto-blaster and drew a second energy pistol from the shoulder holster beneath her jacket.

"Koze, you said they were regrouping at the next intersection?" Hither walked into Death's doorway and surveyed the aftermath of Byron's creation.

"Firm," the AI replied. "I'm along the ceiling as before. They are not moving. I'm assuming they fear death in the open and are content to wait for you to come to their prepared defensive position."

"Peachy." Hither's eyes hardened. "Let me know if they move."

"Firm," the AI repeated.

Byron's mech looked up from the remnants of the man who had shot Daisy. It looked as if the tiny machine had crawled inside the man, through his thigh, and erupted from his chest. The insectoid mech sat nestled in the wreck of the man's chest cavity, covered in gore as messy and innocent as a child in a mud puddle.

The mech cocked the multi-oc head protruding from the chaotic splay of razor limbs.

"Rule of thumb." The devilish grin that split Hither's face would have forced any human to step back in concern and fear, but the machine simply acknowledged her presence as a non-threat, and turned back to its gory bed. "Don't walk into an ambush if you can walk around it."

She crossed the room, careful to avoid the offal puddle surrounding the corpse, and slipped open the courtyard door a crack.

A pair of guards stood together on the bridge, using the arch to give them a slight vantage point. Hither did not give them a chance to react. Ripping the door wide, she erupted from the darkened room with her auto-blasters belching forth a fusillade of crimson energy.

Hitting the ground at a sprint, she made it to the foot of the bridge before the first guard realized death had passed. The second guard, shielded by the body of the first, managed to lift his rifle before a burst caught him in the face and snapped him over the railing to plunge into the pond below like a sea burial.

Hither flew past.

She took the walkway steps in one leap and put her shoulder through the light paneling of the door to erupt into Konstantine's office.

The lower-lord whipped around in surprise. The gun he had trained on the office door trailed his eyes. The lord's wife ducked behind the desk as a wild shot ripped a burning trail across the wall near Hither.

The Valkyrie pulled her trigger.

A triple-shot burst caught Konstantine, trailing up his arm in a muscle purging explosion of energy.

The man's gun dropped from fingers severed from muscular control.

"Milady," Hither said, bobbing her head to the wife peeking from the cover of the desk. "I will say that we gave you every opportunity to walk away from this situation."

Konstantine staggered back from Hither, clutching his dead arm.

"I believe the life of your guard in return for the fact that you kidnapped a member of our family would have been extremely fair." Hither stalked Konstantine. "This all should have been avoided."

Without further preamble, she thrust her blaster against the lord's throat and fired. He sank to his knees.

The woman squeaked and dropped back behind the desk.

As the sound of the shot faded, Blatt burst through the door with his own blaster raised. He froze when he caught sight of his lord on the floor, clutching at the missing side of his neck. With the burn of the close blaster fire cauterizing the wound, the scene presented very little blood.

In a convulsing heap, Konstantine collapsed.

Hither shifted her pistols to target Blatt. "Your lord is dead," she said in a hoarse whisper. "He has paid for his sins.

"Do you need to follow?" Hither remained motionless, calm, calculating.

Blatt swallowed. Sweat beaded at his temple. His gun centered on Hither's mass as he said, "We both go with him if you follow this path." His eyes drifted from her face to the barrels staring at him and back.

"I'm already on the path."

"She ready to take the path as well?" Blatt's nod in Margo's direction gave the courtesan pause. "No way I miss her taking you out.'

"Blatt good," Margo chirped, peeking over Hither's shoulder.

The bannerman's tired smile sealed the accord.

"Then we walk away." Hither's blasters dropped enough to demonstrate her willingness to entertain peace without fully removing mutual destruction.

Blatt lowered his gun.

Following suit, Hither relaxed. Margo beamed over her shoulder.

"I can't say the han won't file grievances up the chain, but I say we let the uppers sort things out." Blatt holstered his pistol and crossed his arms.

"It won't come to much. We don't have a han for you to negotiate with."

"Mercs?" Blatt seemed surprised. "I've never seen a hired gun carry their kid into battle."

"We didn't exactly bring her. I seem to remember our whole being here revolves around trying to get her back before our captain found out you had taken her. If he had been the one to retrieve his daughter, not a one of you or your men would be standing now. I consider myself to be more …." Hither paused, searching for the right word. "Civilized."

Blatt's laughter shook his impressive frame.

"You consider sending two dozen of my soldiers down the path to be civilized?" He shook his head in amazement. "If that's your perspective, I don't want to meet this captain of yours. What's his name anyway?"

"Atom Ulvan."

"I knew it," the wife screeched as she rose from behind the desk with an assault blaster trained on the pair. "I've heard of your captain. He never fails when he has taken a job and he always takes his child with him."

Hither's off gun drifted towards the woman.

"No, I don't think so." The woman's mind spun. "I have the child of one of the deadliest guns in the Fingers. There is no way I let this chance slip away. You will give me the child and you will return to your master. Explain the situation to him, his people have accrued a debt that he will need to pay off.

"Yes," as she spoke something popped in her mind and a grin split her face. "I will hold his daughter as a marker for that debt. Now that I know who she belongs to, I will use that to the han's advantage."

"Mistress." Blatt held up his hands in deference. "I don't know that continuing to hold the child is in the best interest of any of us. You have seen first-hand the lengths his crew will go to protect what they see as family. How much greater will the father's wrath be?

"To what lengths will the father lion go to protect his cub?" Blatt dropped to a knee. "I humbly advise against making this mistake."

A burst of gunfire erupted outside the door.

The woman flinched at the sound so close and unleashed a torrent of vivid green blaster fire across the room.

Sensing, more than seeing, the indiscriminate spray, Hither dove to the side, her guns skittering away as she tried to cushion Margo's impact. She hugged the floor, seeking what little shelter she could muster from the heavy ash conference table. Keeping her body between the woman and Margo, she tried to scoot on her side towards the smashed courtyard door.

A cry of anguish brought her up short.

"You will pay," the woman screamed from the desk.

Uncertain as to the meaning of the woman's words, the courtesan ducked her head to peer between the legs of the tables and chairs.

Sprawled a few yards away, Blatt gasped for air, clutching at a gaping blaster wound in his chest. The guard turned his head to Hither and even as his eyes glassed over he pointed to the open door behind her.

A final breath rattled from his throat and he lay still.

"Blatt?" Margo asked with concern, even as the gunfight continued in the hallway.

"Get up," the woman cried, panic driving her from the cover of her desk. "Get up before your companions come in here and murder me."

The woman fired another burst that scorched deep gouges into the wooden tabletop. "Get, up," she screamed with hysterical urgency. "So help me, I won't let you be the one to take the message to your captain. I'll send him your head in a box to let him know not to take me lightly."

Margo and Hither watched the woman's feet as she stalked around the table. Hither scrabbled on hands and knees to match the woman's stride, keeping the table between them.

Just as the woman stopped and ducked to grin at them through the legs of the table, Hither heard a metallic tinkling behind her.

"Help is arriving," Kozue said in a calm, efficient voice. "Byron has stabilized Daisy. Using his machines, he was able to pull Daisy from the hallway. He has pulled most of his machines back and has hunkered down in a room near the entrance to this building. He has sent four of his mechs to help you."

"Last chance to back down," Hither said to the woman.

The woman stared at her, a maniacal grin distorting her features.

Just as she lifted the rifle and aimed at Hither's face, the far door slipped open and Shi entered with a silent step. In an instant, she assessed the situation and snapped off a shot from the hip.

The bullet caught the woman in the shoulder, spinning her around and knocking the rifle from her hands.

In that same instant, the four metallic centipedes swarmed from beneath the table and slithered up over the woman. In a flurry of spidery limbs, they carved into the screaming woman.

Hither turned her back and climbed to her feet, leaving the woman to her fate. With the table shielding Margo from the carnage, she retrieved and holstered her fallen blasters. Rubbing the sweaty crust of battle from her face, she wandered to the wooden walk outside and sat, waiting for the cold sweat that always followed the adrenaline of a fight.

In the room, the woman fell silent with a final gurgling croak.

"Fancy timing," Hither cast a weary look to Shi as the gunslinger joined her on the veranda.

"I aim to make an entrance," Shi growled.

"What's the rest of the house look like?'

"Quiet. I think I eliminated all the real threats."

Margo began to squirm, trying to unclip herself from the harness. "Tanny," she called out, craning her neck to look back into the building.

The women exchanged a questioning look.

"Who's Tanny?" Hither asked.

"Sister," Margo stated.

"Wait, she has kin?" Shi stepped back to the door and looked into the study.

"She had two older sisters." Hither furrowed her brow in thought. "Neither of them was named Tanny and I don't recall any nicknames of the sort. I only met the family a couple times, Atom tended to keep his private life away from the court as much as possible. It's like he didn't want his children to be tainted by what happened there."

"Well, I reckin if he has kin here, it ain't no good to leave her behind," Shi drawled and pulled her pistols as she swept across the study.

Margo managed to unhook one of the clips and found herself sagging at an odd angle.

Hither unfasted the rest of the clips. In one fluid motion, she swung her young charge around and set her on the floor. As her feet hit the ground, Margo flew after Shi.

Hither closed her eyes and sighed. Then she hauled herself up and followed.

"Tanny," Margo hollered into the silence of the abandoned battlefield. She looked up to Shi, who stood scanning the hallway with guns drawn.

"Careful, Go," Shi said as Hither joined them. The gunslinger stepped out towards the rear of the house. "These bokes're dead, but I ain't speakin' fer anything beyond this hall. Why don't you stay back'n tell me which way to be headin'?"

Margo trailed along behind Shi. The gunslinger paused at a branching hallway leading deeper into the rambling mansion.

"Shi," Hither said in a hushed tone. "I'm going to head back to help with Daisy."

"Smart. We're gonna have a hard burn gittin' outta this town with our heads held tight. As soon as Go finds 'er sister, we'll float yer way and burn for the *Ticket*. Think he'll be ready to move?"

"I'll find a way to get him moving." Hither's dark chuckle gave Shi pause. "Although, I don't know that you and I will be able to carry him, at least not far."

"The man weighs as much as the ship he flies."

"Well, maybe as much as Lilly's ship," Hither's tone lightened as she turned and trotted back down the hallway.

"Just figure a way, and I'll be along to help," Shi called after her.

Shi turned back to the hallway in time to see Margo scamper away. The girl stopped by the first door and slid it open just enough to peek through. Shaking her head, Margo trotted to the next door and inspected the interior in the same manner.

When Margo approached the third door, Shi hissed a warning. Something drew the gunslinger's attention, sending warning flags. She motioned Margo back from the door. Only when the girl had slipped past the door and crouched down against the wall did Shi move.

Ghosting with silent steps, the gunslinger slid up and leaned her shoulder against the outer edge of the door jamb. She pressed her head against the wood and listened.

Her eyes moved as if tracing a map of the room's interior.

Margo watched with childish amazement as the gunslinger readied one of her pistols and pressed the barrel against the door. Shi listened and shifted her gun.

Then Shi waved Margo away. The girl looked at Shi, at the door, and then fixed the gaunt merc with an understanding gaze. With exaggerated care she tip-toed away. She made her way to the next room and cracked the door.

"Tanny," Margo exclaimed. She looked back to Shi as her face lit up with radiant beauty. "Tanny inside."

Shi fired. Margo jumped.

Inside Shi's room a man cried out in pain and began shooting holes in the wooden walls in a haphazard manner that drove Shi back from the door. Cursing, the gunslinger stumbled back down the hall, moving away from Margo with her head tucked low. Shi took cover at the corner and held up a hand, signaling for Margo to stay and crouch low.

The shots continued to rip through the wall.

Down the hall a hand reached out and pulled Margo into the room. Seeing her charge disappear, Shi waited half a breath for the gunman to reload before charging. She kicked the door off its track.

The Markinhan guard froze like a startled deer. The energy pack slipped from his fingers and dinged the wooden floor. Shi waited just long enough for him to register his looming fate before putting him down with three tightly grouped shots.

Before the body had time to hit the floor, she moved on to the next room. Without taking time for caution she slid the door open hard enough to rattle the frame. In the dim interior, a group of servants huddled behind several metal shelves of supplies. As one, the group recoiled from Shi's violent intrusion.

With pistol raised, the gunslinger entered the darkened room. Her military training drove her motions as she cleared each narrow aisle and pressed into the back of the room, each step closer to the terrified group.

"Margo." Shi lowered her pistol, but kept it out. "It's time to git home. Grab yer sister and let's skiddle."

"Sister?" asked the girl holding Margo in her lap.

"Tanny." Margo looked up to the girl as if the subject had already been discussed and concluded. "Tanny sister."

The girl stared at Margo. Sensing Shi's brooding power, she glanced up at the gunslinger and shrank back. "Honest, Miss," she stammered. "We aren't really sisters. I just said she looked a touch like my little sister back home. I felt bad for the lass and was trying to offer her a touch of comfort when there was none to be had."

"Go, we need to git," Shi commanded.

"Tanny, come," Margo said as she rose, tugging the girl's hand, willing her to join them.

"So, your name is Margo." The girl remained seated, but cupped Margo's hand in both of hers. "It's a mighty fine name and you do remind me of Micro more than you will ever know.

"But." She cast a worried glance up to Shi. "I can't be going with you. I signed on to this job and if I welch, I'm an outlaw with a bounty on my head. Then they'd shift the debt back to my family and they sure can't handle that."

"Come on, Go," Shi appealed to the girl. "We need a trail behind us before han reinforcements arrive. We caught them by surprise the first time, but I doubt we could handle even a small contingent, if they came expecting us."

Margo looked at Shi, heartbroken. She looked back to Tanny.

The girl smiled and nodded, dropping Margo's hand and pointing to Shi. "Go with your family. You have them now. Take my advice, don't let them go, ever."

Shi rested her hand on Margo's head.

"Family?" Margo reached up to take Shi's hand.

"I know we ain't blood, lil' miss, but we're kin. Thank you fer lookin' out for her, Tanny. What's yer family name?"

"Hyde, Miss."

"I'll pass that along to the captain." Shi scooped Margo into her arms and settled the girl on her hip. "I'm sure he would be happy to know of your kindness to his daughter."

Shi nodded once and swept from the room as if the hounds of hell bayed at her heels.

*   *   *

The klaxon fell silent as the elevators disgorged them at a lower level.

Atom and Mir made their way towards the main hub of the station. Despite the alarms sounding, nothing appeared to be locked down, which surprised Atom.

"I feel like nothing good ever happens aboard stations," he said as he covered a corner for Mir to dart for the next cover. "The past couple visits have brought me nothing but trouble. Come to think of it, I can't remember the last time I actually set foot aboard a station and someone didn't die."

"That's comforting." Mir chirped a light laugh that seemed as out of place coming from her mouth as it did echoing down the empty hallway.

"I'm hoping this is just some sort of drill to keep our people on their toes."

"You can hope, but you know as well as I that there's not a situation in the book where we run a drill like that in a hostile theater of operation. If I had to toss my dice, I'd say there was some sort of sabotage and they are locking everything down as precaution. The station is a natural choke-point for the ore."

She trotted ahead of Atom, her gun out and down at her side. She jogged without moving her arms, which seemed unnatural to Atom, but also seemed to conserve movement. "We didn't see anything down on the surface because it wouldn't have served any real purpose. Up here, they could hypothetically eliminate the orbital stockpile with a couple well placed explosives."

"I didn't feel anything like an explosion," Atom said in his hushed tone as Mir covered another abandoned crossroad, allowing him to leapfrog her position.

"Hostage situation?" she asked and trailed along, hugging the far wall.

"Seems more likely." Atom halted as a hatch slid open to reveal the main concourse. "I sure wish our coms worked."

"You're right. Seems like they should've replaced them when we got up here."

"I didn't think to mention it to those two bokes at the desk." Atom waited for Mir to flank the far side of the hatch and then he poked his head out, darting like a lizard as he quick-scanned for anything out of place. "I mean, they were so busy anyway, I doubt they would have had time to sort that out for us."

"Above their grade," Mir said with a smirk. "How we looking?"

"It's completely empty. No patrols, no people." Atom searched his gut, trying to isolate anything that stood out in the fleeting glance.

"Just empty?"

Atom pulled his second pistol from the holster at the back of his belt and stepped out into the open area, guns relaxed, aimed out into the nothing. Mir slipped behind, mirroring his movement to the flank.

The concourse sat eerily empty and silent. Two stories, with shops lining both floors, the common area stretched out to disappear at the distant curve of the station. Kiosks lined the center, alternating with wide, square planters full of atmo-scrubbing hybrids that stretched to the curve like dotted lines along a moonless back road. The shops lay shuttered. The small restaurants, bistros, and pubs sat dark and empty.

The synth-sky above radiated a beautiful dusk that illuminated the central track of the concourse, but left the periphery in shadow. Atom swept the area, careful and cautious as his guns slid across the dim storefronts, searching for any sign of life in the tomb-like stillness.

With concern furrowing his brow, Atom holstered his weapons and straightened his coat. He glanced to Mir and said, "I feel like we should be concerned by all this, but realistically, there's nothing that I can see that could potentially constitute a threat. It feels wrong putting my guns away, but there's no reason to keep them out."

"Sometimes you have to trust your gut." Mir dropped her gun to her side, but kept it in hand. "But sometimes you just have to play the odds."

"Statistically speaking, there should be minimal threats here." Atom thrust his hands in his pockets and with a self-assured nod, he sauntered down the ring. "If all viable threats have been removed, what you are left with is a façade of security."

"Façade?"

"Just because you can't see the threat doesn't mean it doesn't exist, but it means you'll spend more time looking than preparing."

"It'll kill you if you don't root it out."

"It could kill you if you do." Atom glanced over his shoulder as Mir trailed along in his wake. "I'm good with it either way. If you live your life afraid of death, it will seek you faster, but those who accept that they are already dead will find life."

"What's wrong with you?" Mir picked up her pace and trotted next to Atom. She took one last nervous glance around before holstering her own gun.

Atom laughed. "People are too busy trying to stay alive. They try to find happiness in money or success, but they're already dead in that life." He pulled out his rail-pistol, flipped it to present the grip to Mir. "I expect the bullet, bolt, or explosion with my name on it has already been produced. But what happens if I fixate on it?"

"You stay alive?" Mir took the offered gun and appraised it.

"No," Atom shook his head and closed his eyes. "You miss being alive.

"Take right now, for instance." He took a deep breath, reaching out with his ears. "I could focus on the probability that something is cooking and we'll most likely be caught up in whatever is happening. But if I kept that in my sights, I would miss the soft cadence of your words, the familiar rhythms of your breath, the lifting nature of your laugh."

He opened his eyes to catch Mir studying him with her eyebrows arched in confusion. Her words came soft and short, "And that gets you what? It doesn't keep you breathing if something pops."

"Maybe nothing." Atom smiled and held out his hand for his gun. "Or maybe it buys me a moment of lightness in the Black. Or maybe it helps me notice something I would have missed if I was trying to find some boke looking to jump out of the shadows and end my days. Either way I've filled the void with a moment of beauty."

Before she could respond, Atom held up his hand to halt their steps. He cocked his head like a hound and took the gun from her hands.

"Someone's coming." He holstered his gun.

Mir listened. "Sounds like a patrol," she said, her eyes darting as her ears worked. "Too uniform and heavy to be scouts or spec-ops. Patrol squad in skirmish armor …."

"Best be out in the open." Atom looked around, located the vector of the patrol's approach and placed himself in a conspicuous position with his hands held wide. He glanced at Mir and waived her over.

They did not have long to wait. The patrol seemed intent on completing their circuit in record time. Atom had seen it before. Low-threat patrols looked the same everywhere.

Laughter fizzled as the squad rounded a corner to find Atom and Mir watching them.

"Hands stay," the squad-leader barked as half-dozen assault blasters glared at the interlopers. "ID. Now."

"Easy now, cap," Atom said with a slow calm as he raised his eyebrows and hands a touch higher. "We just checked in upstairs and have some time to burn before we catch a shuttle out. In case you haven't heard, there was an EMP strike down on the surface that torched almost all our electronics.

"Things are wrapped in mingo at the moment," he continued with a knowing chuckle.

The six soldiers tightened their grips on blasters, but kept their fingers off the triggers. The leader stepped out to the flank, his blaster trained on the center of Atom's mass.

"Names?" he demanded.

"Flynn Mosby, Inspector Special Unit," Atom said in a low, even voice. "Badge is in my pocket, but I'm lacking in digital credentials. Mir has been able to vouch for me to this point."

"Lieutenant Katarina Mir, 2nd Division MPs," she said with a straight face. "Still cleaning up the messes you boys leave behind. I'll vouch for this spook. He's on a special assignment and if you need any further info, you are welcome to have a chat with Pico.

"I'd only go that route if you want a blood-pissing, desk-drop cap to rip into you because he's got rifle envy." Her dour expression broke, replaced by a beaming grin.

For a moment the squad-leader just stared at her. Then he grinned back and let out a dark chuckle. "Not that you're one to talk, you mip. Names Haveer, Sergeant Newt Haveer." He dropped the muzzle of his assault blaster and tipped his helmet back at a jaunty angle. "Most of our transports come in at the main depot. I'm surprised they dropped you at the top spinner.

"Come on." He waved for Mir and Atom to join him. "We'll take you down to the stockpile and depot. You'll probably have to wait a while, seeing as the transports are running low numbers with the Adlerian fleet sitting out beyond the yards."

"Yeah," Mir said as she fell into step between Atom and the squad-leader. "Up at the info desk, they told us it would be several hours at best."

"You'll be lucky if that's accurate. We haven't seen a packet in two watches."

"Sorry for being such a heavy burn." Atom stared ahead into the dim curve of the station hub. "So, sarge, this seems a pretty light job for obvious drop-jocks. Are we expecting things to go sideways up here or did you just happen to spin up the commander's daughter?"

One of the soldiers behind them laughed.

"Not quite that simple." Haveer scowled over his shoulder. "This ride is beyond punishment. I'd expect a mip like you to get stacked with this gig, but I did open my mouth and got us saddled with hall-monitor duty."

"Sounds like a story," said Mir. "And I hear we've time to burn."

"Not a long story."

"Well, it'd be better than nothing, since you don't have any Adles to shoot up."

"Stupid desk-humper named Frederickson has the high g's for Shea back there." Haveer jerked a thumb over his shoulder. "He was leaning and I won't stand for anyone crashing the orbits of my squad if I have a say. I don't care who he is, he messes with the combat effectiveness of my squad and you'd better believe there will be more than words thrown about.

"I should have scorched a bolt through his pan, but that would have had the same effect on the squad. The kacker doesn't actually have any say over operationals, he's not high enough up the chain, but he had enough pull with that Pico of yours to have us humping deck instead of dirt. We're stuck up here on civvie patrol while the rest of our division is down there in the mountains."

"We haven't even got to loose a round," one of the troopers in the rear mumbled. "Thanks a holdful, Shea. If you'd had the stones to break that boke's face instead of Haveer we might have gotten tossed on the front-line as punishment."

"Sorry to disappoint," the woman replied with laughter in her voice, then she punched the other trooper in the arm, a love-tap to the armored soldiers that would have left Atom bruised.

Atom shook his head at the pent-up aggression. "So, things are quiet up here?"

"Nothing happens here," the first soldier complained. "The civvies just sit tight in the quarters and wait. They don't even complain. They've got food and access to the network, so they don't even seem to mind. It's like ...."

"They're just waiting for us to leave?" Atom finished his sentence. "I've been hearing that a lot."

"Should we be worried?" Haveer looked eager.

Atom shrugged. "It's the same down dirtside. You really aren't missing much up here except for true atmo. The scuttle is a counter at some point, but I haven't heard or seen anything definitive along those lines. I'm guessing the strike is coming at the yards, but be ready for anything.

"How many troopers you have aboard the station?" he asked as they drew near a junction. "And how many civvies are left on permanent station? Are there enough that you would be worried?"

"Give or take fifteen cents on the civvie pop. We have four squads. I managed to drag our whole fireteam along with us on punishment brigade."

"Just twenty-four to handle a whole station?"

"You don't think we can do it?" Shea cut in from the rear as they turned and followed a new corridor to the center of the station."

"If you had some power-armor I don't doubt you could handle it. Fifteen hundred on twenty-four is a tough mountain to climb. You isolate the hab rings and hold choke points and I'd say you have a fighting chance."

"Seems solid," Haveer sounded impressed. "We also have a dozen flight techs and mechs who could back us up."

Atom shook his head. "Problem as I see it, the only way you lot can handle any kind of real rise-up is to put it down hard before it pops. There aren't enough of you to preempt anything large, but if there is confirmed activity have your lute hit first, and hit hard. Pop 'em in the nose so hard they don't want to get back up and take a swing at you."

"Kind of like Frederickson," one of the soldiers said with a snicker.

"I'll talk to Motoki when I see him." Atom quickened his pace, as if making it to the hangar would speed anything about the flight out.

"Wait, that's why you're routing to the flag?" Haveer asked.

"Not necessarily, but that doesn't mean I can't pass a word about what I'm seeing. I'm assuming our goal is to use the local population to get the economy up and running, to get the ore flowing again. We need to have enough of a presence that things move smoothly without being oppressive enough to warrant resisting.

"We want a simple power shift, not destruction and repop."

They approached the elevator at the central hub. As they paused outside, Haveer held up a hand and listened to orders coming through his armor's internal coms.

"You might be in luck, Mosby," he said. "I just got word that the admiral himself is expected to arrive in hangar 52 within fifteen minutes.

"Evidently you must have something he wants." Haveer reached out and tripped the elevator doors. "That seems like it makes you someone worth noting. If you want to put in a word, that could get us reassigned to the drop, I wouldn't complain. Frontline is where we belong."

"Careful what you wish for." Atom stepped into the elevator and shifted to the back as the armored soldiers crowded in. "If we aren't careful, this might turn into a front faster than you can vent a lock."

They descended in silence. The elevator hummed as it dropped from the main hab rings, down through the processing plants, and all the way to the loading docks. There, refined ore from the planet below shipped out to the yards in orbit above the Seeonee, the system's main planet.

The ride down seemed to last forever, but as the doors split onto the main loading bays, Atom found they preceded the arrival of the admiral's skiff by several minutes.

Another squad of armored drop-troops lounged near the control hub at the center of the full circle of bay doors. Just like Haveer and the troopers with Atom, these six wore light skirmish armor with their helmets strapped to their small packs. They hung about the open door to the hub, chatting with the techs inside who presided over the empty hangars that usually bustled with dozens of ore ships at any given hour of the day.

Following Haveer, Atom and the others headed over to join the laughing group.

The soldiers fell silent, but their relaxed attitudes remained.

"What's the touch down on the inbound?" Haveer asked. "This boke's got to hitch a ride with the top floater."

"No other traffic?" Atom sounded surprised. "I expected more ships here."

One of the techs in the hub looked up. "Four and a half on the AD. Traffic is shut down, for the most part, until we get things up and running dirtside. There's no other reason for ships to float through, other than supply lighters which dock a couple times a day."

"This is worse than you let on," Atom said to Haveer. "You droppers must be floating out of your pans."

Haveer rubbed his face with a gloved hand. "Maybe worse," the squad-leader sighed. "We might actually start fighting each other, just for something to do. Sound like a good plan, Meeks?"

The leader of the second squad shrugged. "I won't complain, but I ain't givin' you no warning." She laughed and turned to Atom. "You seem to be the highlight of the week for all us drops. Please tell me, you got a good tale to tell. Break my boredom before it breaks me. Please, I'll settle for a funny bit, or even a bucket of scuttle."

"Unfortunately, I don't have much in the way of news until I talk to the admiral," Atom replied.

"He let drop there might be a pushback, sooner than later." The eagerness in Haveer's voice reminded Atom of a kid the day before her birthday.

"That so?" Meeks demanded.

Atom glared at Haveer as if trust had been broken.

"Two minutes to touchdown," the tech interrupted.

Atom turned from the troopers and walked out into the wide, empty hangar and stared into the Black, hoping to catch a glimpse of the incoming ship. At two minutes, the braking burn of the ship seemed a bright star in a sky full of pinpricks.

Crossing his arms, Atom watched the ship grow larger.

"Think that'll make a difference?" Mir stepped up beside him, thumbs hooked in the arm holes of her armored vest.

"Hmm?" Atom scowled at the ship.

"The information you passed, will it make a difference?"

Atom shook his head. "Not for them. It might save lives if that was the direction the attack was really coming from. It might make a difference if bokes like that found themselves in a straight up fight. It might make a difference if they had power-armor and not skirmish.

"No promise though." He caressed the grip of his pistol with an absent motion. "All the armor in the 'verse won't save you if your time's up."

"That's reassuring." Mir's quiet chuckle seemed to drape a heavy blanket over the open atmosphere of the bay. "I was hoping for something along the lines of, 'everything's going to be wonderful, Mir',"

"This is war, kid. Nothing is wonderful. Migori invaded and spilled blood. Right or wrong, the die's been cast by those as sit in their ivory towers. You and I are the ones who have to live or die by the way fate lands. We fight because it gives us a better chance to make it home than if we didn't."

"Thanks, old man." Mir's light slap gave Atom hope that the galaxy might hold.

As Mir turned and sauntered back to the hub, the shuttle broke through the atmo-field at the mouth of the bay. In a blast of thrusters, the ship halted and, kicking up suspensors, settled to the floor with a hydraulic hiss.

Haveer and Meeks ordered their squads into line and settled at parade attention, waiting for the side hatch to cycle open.

Atom strolled forward to meet the admiral as he disembarked. Mir joined him.

A final blast of compressed air split the air as the hatch opened and a fit, middle-aged man stepped forth followed by a pair of guards. He surveyed the eerie silence of the hangar bay with a quick eye and turned his attention to Atom.

"I surmise I have you to thank for pulling me from the front, Agent ...?"

"Mosby, sir. Flynn Mosby of the Special Service, working in conjunction with han heir Malcolm." He glanced to Mir and stepped closer to the admiral, dropping his voice as he did so. "I've been sent to inform you that our ranks have been infiltrated by the enemy. They are waiting for the opportune moment to counterstrike."

"And how do you know this?"

"Because." Atom jerked his pistol from his hip and leveled it at Mir. "She is one of them."

The two guards had only managed to get their hands to their service pieces before Atom had drawn and aimed at Mir with steady confidence. They froze in uncertainty, looking to the admiral for direction.

Mir's hand drifted towards her shoulder holsters, but at Atom's headshake, they continued up in surrender.

Seeing the opportunity for action, Haveer and Meeks rolled over their armored phalanx of twelve. They took up flanking positions and trained their rifles on Mir with eager anticipation.

"And how do you know this?" Motoki asked, nonplussed.

"I infiltrated the enemy, sir," Atom replied. "I've been on the plain for several months now in preparation for our movement. Several days ago, I received valid intel that there would be a move on your life."

"My life, why?" The admiral looked to Atom in confusion.

"Disrupt our forces, sir. The Adlerhan planned to move on the announcement of your death."

"Very interesting." The admiral tucked his hands behind his back and took a step towards Mir. "It would be a wise move on their part. My death wouldn't stop us by itself, but I surmise it would provide just enough chaos in our ranks for a counter-attack to gain traction."

"Who is she really? Is she an Adler?"

"No, sir. Outside contractor. Hired from the Tribes." Atom kept his pistol trained on Mir, but shifted with measured steps to position himself beside the admiral.

"The Tribes, now that's a surprise. Their services do not come cheap. The Adlers must calculate that my death will be the tipping point of our border war. Do they believe they will be able to push back into our territory and make gains to offset what they must be expending?"

"I don't know that, sir. I only know what I've been able to gather from their frontline cells."

Motoki nodded. He studied Mir with a distracted, if thoughtful air.

"Do you have a name, girl?" he asked.

Before she could reply, Atom answered. "Lilly."

Lilly glared at him through Mir's eyes.

Atom took one more step, then shifted sideways like a serpent and put a rail round through the side of Motoki's head.

Everyone froze in surprise.

Atom used the lapse to pull his second pistol, spin, and drop the two trailing guards. Ducking back, he hopped up into the open hatch of the transport, dropping several armored troopers in the process.

Before they could turn their rifles on Atom, Lilly drew her own blasters and began ripping into their ranks at close range.

"Lilly," Atom shouted from the transport. "Get in here." He leaned out and dropped another trooper with a headshot.

Lilly crouched and sprayed around her with indifference as she scuttled to the ship.

The remaining troopers drifted into a firing line after their initial surprise, but the seconds it took to organize allowed Lilly to dive into the open hatch.

Atom fired a couple more rounds without leaning out and slapped the hatch closed.

Lying on her side, Lilly glared up at Atom. "How long did you know?" she demanded.

Atom shrugged. He holstered his weapon and surveyed the interior of the ship with a studied eye. Satisfied that no surprises lay in store, he loped through the small cabin, towards the cockpit. He glanced back from the door and said, "Lock down that hatch before they think to crack it. We need to be in the Black before they dredge up some weapons heavy enough to scratch this little firefly."

He hopped into the pilot's seat and fired the engines. Outside, the troopers continued to pour blaster fire on the ship, hoping to damage something enough to prevent lift.

A moment later, Lilly slammed into the co-pilot's seat. With a practiced hand, she pulled up her screens and began scrolling through data. "We just lost port thrusters," she growled. "We need out or a turn before they fully kill that flank."

Atom scowled at the controls and slammed open the throttle. The landing gear tore gouges in the flooring. Whipping away from the troopers, he jerked hard on the yoke and scraped a wing along the hub at the center of the hangar. Under Atom's delicate touch, the ship continued to accelerate, punching through the atmo-shield and into the Black, clipping the frame on the way.

"I don't suppose you have a good escape plan?" Lilly asked without looking up from her displays.

"We just escaped, didn't we?' Atom glanced around with a mock startled expression, surveying their cramped lifeboat. Built for quick hops between ships and planets in-system, the skiff didn't afford much more than a series of seats lining the outer walls, a central rack for storage, and a cramped head at the rear of the narrow cabin.

"You know what I mean." Lilly refused to look at Atom. "We don't have the capability to make the jump-gate ahead of any pursuit. I don't see anything on the scope yet, but you better have a good next step to this little charade." She pulled up a second display in the air above the previous pair and began scrolling through details. "We don't have any weapons on this ship. It's purely transport."

"Not a problem. I don't aim to fight anyone at the moment, we just have to run the gauntlet."

Lilly snapped her head sideways to stare at him. "Gauntlet?"

"We're either going to the shipyards or need to look like we are. I haven't decided yet?"

"Haven't decided?" Lilly verged on panic. "Was the shipyard the plan from the get go? I thought you just had to take out Motoki."

"That was the assignment from your people."

"My people?"

"Your tribe."

"They're not my people anymore."

"If you say so." Atom pulled on the yoke, lifting the skiff into a gentle swoop that pointed them away from the gate and further into the system.

"Are they sending you to the yards?"

Atom shook his head. "That's all on me. After neutralizing Motoki, they would expect us to either head back to the planet to hook up with my ship, or burn hard for the gate and hope we outrun any pursuers."

"So, you float for the spot they wouldn't expect?"

"Firm, right through the heart of their fleet and on to the stalemated shipyards. If we can mosey this shuttle up their tailpipes, we might be able to fool them long enough to slip it through their wall and then I'm hoping they won't risk any kind of shot that might damage the yards."

Leaning back in her seat, Lilly whistled as she processed his plan. "You're hopped out of your pan."

"I think I did that a while back."

"What's the play if we make it to the yards?"

"I have an idea, but I need to work that out." Atom flashed a cocky grin as he locked in the coordinates for the fleet and relaxed their acceleration to an acceptable in-system pace. "We have about an hour before we hit our event horizon. Can you relay a tight-beam to the *Ticket* so I can try to line up the next step?"

Lilly's fingers began flying before she said, "I think so."

A moment later, Hither appeared on Atom's console.

"You're alive." Relief swept away worry like clouds after a storm. "We've all been wearing holes in the floor waiting for word. Kozue said an EMP went off and killed all unshielded planetary electronics. And we couldn't figure a way to reach you or even figure out where you went." The words swept out in a torrent. "Please tell me, for Margo's sake, that you're safe."

Atom bobbed his head. His smile softened his rugged features. "Yeah, things seemed to have worked out in our favor. I completed the job, now we just need to work the back angle, contact the client, and get paid. This is the first time I've had to figure out how nomads settle their accounts."

"That would explain the visit we just had from Bronte."

"Bronte was there?" Atom asked in amazement. "We just completed the job, not even half an hour ago."

"We?"

"I discovered Lilly decided to tag along."

"That explains why we haven't been able to locate her around here.

"Worrisome?"

"No, we just figured she had ducked into the city. She's not crew, so we didn't even give it much thought." Hither frowned. "We just thought of her in passenger terms, until we started wondering if we were going to have the pop the bubble and leave her behind. We took a vote and decided that if it came to a premature lift, we would leave the pad on a credit with the *Hellkite* parked for her."

"Much appreciated," Lilly said from her seat, out of Hither's line of sight.

"It's the least we could do." Hither shrugged. "Seems moot at this point. What are we up against?"

Atom stared at Hither in silence, his mind turning and formulating.

"I need you to lock this trajectory and burn hard for an intercept." Atom punched a few keys on his screen and sent the information. "Did Bronte bother to settle while he was there?"

"He did. Fifty-thousand ko, on a chit. He asked about the next job."

Atom looked up from the screen, focusing on the spread of stars gleaming through the Black. "I don't know that I've made a final decision on that." His eyes pinched at the mental discomfort. "I know how the crew voted last time, but I don't know that I want to worry that one right now."

"Then we move on the treasure?"

"The potential treasure," Atom corrected. "We just landed the ko that will cover our expenses, there and back again. Even if we don't find anything out there, we know we'll be covered enough to float to our next gig."

Hither stood and stepped back from the screen to grab the bridge com from the ceiling mount. "Shi, bridge it. Everyone else, prep for lift in two." She stepped off camera, but left the connection live. "I'm prepping the burners now, Cap. We should be off the ground and out of the well in ten.

"And then we're looking at …." She dropped back into her seat, but shifted her attention to another screen. "Probably four hours to intersect. I have the coords punched in the nav-system and a flight path locked, but I'll crunch numbers and see if I can't shave time."

Shi trotted by in the background. "Hiya, Cap," she called out with a friendly wave as she swiveled into Daisy's seat and dropped down to begin fiddling with the controls. "Thanks fer preppin' the engines, Hither. Firin' now."

"Lift time?" Hither asked.

"Lift in sixty," Shi replied.

"We'll be on our way to you, lifted and burned, momentarily." Hither turned back to Atom. "I'm looking at the numbers. If you ease off the accel, we can make it to you in under four hours."

"Where's Daisy?" Atom demanded in a hushed tone. "He's not on one of his benders?"

Hither shook her head and said, "He's a little dinged up at the moment. Should be fine, but he's not really in a spot to fly right now."

"You guys had trouble?"

"Nothing we couldn't handle, sir."

Atom stared at her through the screen, trying to measure her words. She played the game well, but he noted Shi stiffen in her seat in the background.

"I'll be home soon," Atom said, keeping his own voice and face level. "I want to keep our flight uninterrupted. Not that it will fool anyone looking closely, but it will keep people guessing as to who we are and where we're going. I'm hoping the nest I stirred on the station will set them back on their heels long enough for us to slip the system sideways."

"And the reason for the shuttle instead of just waiting for us to scoop you?"

"No sense in sitting at the scene, waiting for someone to figure out we're there."

*   *   *

"Atom, we're on approach." Strain flexed Hither's voice. "Our vectors will overlap for ten minutes, but we'll overshoot unless you want us to alter velocity."

Atom growled to himself. "We don't have suits, you'll have to brake and match. Unfortunately, that'll throw some of the ambiguity out of the lock about what's happening to us."

"We don't have much choice, do we?" Lilly had shifted back from her escapade as Mir and sat coiled in her seat, dozing as she half-watched the monitors.

"Maybe it made them wonder at our course."

"If they're even looking." Lilly sighed and punched a black monitor to life. "There's nothing popping on the feeds about this, military or civ. There should be something somewhere, but I'm not catching any chatter anywhere.'

"Is there a chance they don't know yet?"

"It's been hours. We didn't kill everyone, not even everyone in the bay. I didn't get a good count of everyone we left alive, but there were a few marines and the techs in the control room. That doesn't count the two patrols somewhere else in the station that should have found them by now, even if we'd managed to kill all witnesses." Lilly shifted in her seat and hugged her knees to her chin in thought. "There's no way someone hasn't discovered the present we left and sent the info up the food chain."

"And don't forget the admiral had to be on the radar," Hither said from the open com. "People had to know where he was in case something needed to be brought to his attention."

"Unless there's nothing to pass along and they assume he's aboard this lighter." Atom rubbed his eyes and sighed with resignation. "We have a better chance of falling in a black hole than slipping under their scans."

"Maybe you should have brought the admiral aboard and eliminated him there," Hither quirked a shrug.

"I don't think Atom understands a knife in the dark." Lilly's laugh fractured the tension.

Atom cursed, even as he grinned and shook his head in disbelief. "I can't believe I didn't see this playing out like this." He rubbed his hands through his hair and leaned back to stare up at the ceiling. "I anticipated a hot pursuit that I would take to the planet, or that I would have thrown them for enough of a decayed orbit that they wouldn't notice me long enough to slip the system."

"You didn't anticipate me either." Lilly grinned.

"And that was a pleasant surprise. I could have pulled the job without you, but you pulled their attention in a way I couldn't have by myself."

"I don't suppose you want to cut me in on a portion of the payout?"

Atom slipped his hands from atop his head to cradle his neck. "We can discuss it when we are safe aboard the *Ticket*, but until then, I say we worry less about the money and more about how we're floating out of all this intact."

They sat in silence for a moment, contemplating their situation when a tight-beam communication lit up Lilly's console.

She glanced to Atom in alarm. "That's not from your people."

"Nope," Hither said from her screen. "We've the open channel already."

Lilly's fingers flew across her board. "That's a direct link from the admiral's flag. If we don't take this, they'll know something's afoot."

Atom nodded and muted Hither's feed. "Can you do that voice thing again?" he asked.

"No, I didn't have enough of a sample," Lilly said as she patched the transmission through.

A young captain popped up on Atom's console. "Admiral Motoki, we just received a trans …. Wait." The man registered Atom looking back at him. "You're not the admiral. Who are you?"

"Liaison from our office at the imperial court, Flynn Mosby." Atom gestured over his shoulder. "The admiral is closing his eyes for a few. If you think this is important enough to wake him, I can do that. He did seem pretty adamant about letting him rest, but if you think this is important enough …."

The captain hesitated.

"Or you could just relay it through me and I'll tell him when he wakes," Atom said.

"Just let the admiral know that we received a transmission from Kafiristan orbital regarding a disturbance in the hangar bays. The information is minimal at the moment. Apparently, there was a rapid decomp in the bay. We know there have been casualties, but nothing as to the timing of the incident. We believe an attempt was made on the admiral's life, but they must have mistimed their attempt.

"I'm waiting on the full incident report and if there is anything of importance I will be in touch with you." The man seemed relieved to unload the information.

"I'll pass it along as soon as Motoki wakes up. I've been picking up rumors in my digging about some sort of attack. I assumed it was another act of sabotage along the lines of the EMP that took out our coms relays all over the planet.

"Perhaps a saboteur blew a lock." Atom looked at the captain with concern. "Hopefully casualties weren't too high. The good news for us is that we seemed to have skipped out before the admiral could be in danger. On that note, we are anticipating an arrival time just under three hours from now."

"Very good, sir," the captain nodded and cut the connection.

Lilly slumped in her seat. "I don't know what I expected there, but you talking your way out of things didn't seem high on the list." She flashed a weary smile. "And they didn't mention the *Ticket* in any of that."

"Interesting turn." Atom pulled Hither back up on his console. "They're dealing with a massive decomp in the bays. That probably means no bodies, or time-consuming retrieval on the outside orbit."

Lilly perked. "That means no admiral."

"They don't even suspect he's missing at the moment," Atom replied. "I wonder if we clipped a stasis projector during our escape?"

"Nothing kills atmo like lack of containment," Hither said.

"That leaves us slipping out just ahead of the attack with the most important Migori man aboard our ship. Hopefully, that buys us enough time."

"And the *Ticket*?" Lilly asked.

"She's an indie merch on a straight shot to the jump-gate. That our paths cross is purely coincidental."

"They'll figure it out eventually," Hither said with a distracted air as she looked over her screens. "The good news is we are set to shift our course momentarily and link in just under ten. We're extending the umbilical now."

"We'll be ready." Atom closed the coms. "Lilly, let's wipe this place down."

"What's the play? Are we leaving them a surprise or spreading more confusion?" Lilly uncurled and leaned into her screens. "Or should we just slip out and leave them with absolutely nothing?"

Atom stared at his own screen in thought. "Let's leave them a mystery." His grin brought a low chuckle from Lilly. "I'm wiping all traces of this dock, but let's set the lock to vent atmo after we've left. That way when the shuttle arrives, it'll be empty and they'll have to piece everything together.

"Hopefully that will give them even more of a riddle to spin their pans and it gives us more time to slip into the Black." Atom punched a final key and initiated manual override as he brought the ship into line with the *Ticket*.

In the Black, two ships drifted closer together and the docking umbilical locked over the skiffs hatch. A slight thump tapped through the hull as the magnetic ring engaged. Atom watched a green light pop on his screen signifying a positive seal.

"Time to go." He rose from his seat and initiated a final system purge.

Lilly scowled at her monitor a moment longer, finalizing the ghosting of their ship before joining Atom at the hatch.

*　　*　　*

Seven jumps and the respective system crossing put the *One Way Ticket* closer to the Palm than the crew had been since coming together. It also made their discovery and apprehension exponentially more unlikely.

After they reached the Pinky, Atom settled. He knew the chances of the Migorihan tracking their ship after the first jump-gate calculated to the distant decimals, but something in the way the hit had played out, and the involvement of the Tribe left the feeling of a heavy blade hanging over his neck.

They knew his identity, and while the Tribe might not be able to actively track his movement through the galaxy, he knew they had eyes in every system.

Two weeks passed in quiet.

Only then, when they floated on the Black, deep between two systems, did Atom pull the crew into the mess. He chose a time when Lilly worked in the hold on Ash's weapons systems. He closed and locked the doors before joining the others at the table.

"The haul is divvied," he said, taking a seat at the head of the table with seven even piles of square ko coins in front of him. "I've pulled an extra share for Lilly. Whether we asked her to or not, she put herself on the line to complete the job. I can't say whether she deserves this or not, but I want to put it to a vote."

"Is this a permanent arrangement?" Hither asked.

"No." Atom shook his head. "One-time payment for services rendered."

Daisy studied the piles. He had healed from his wound, but the slow recovery worried Atom. The pilot's usual glowing dark complexion still seemed wan and waxy. His eyes, though, maintained the alertness. "How does this affect the back half of the Tribe's job?" he asked.

"We tabled that. We never voted on it and honestly, the more I think about it, the more I don't think that's something I need to put on all of you. I won't ask any of you to pull the trigger and I don't plan on putting you in that position."

"I'll do it," Shi said, her voice flat, calm, deadly.

"I know you would," Atom replied. "But it's my call at this moment.

Shi nodded. "Jist let me know when you change yer mind."

"You 'ate the biddy that much?" Byron glared across the table at Shi.

"Got no feelin's one way or 'nother." Shi shrugged. "It's a gig an' she ain't one a us. You float outside our family an' it makes no differ whether you live or die. 'Less yer a danger to one a us, thin you die."

"Back to this cut on the table. I don't want this to be a hire," Atom said as he turned to watch Margo stalk Mae around the thin kitchen island. "Think of it as a contractor fee for a job."

"I've nothing against it," Daisy said and held up a finger. "I'm for."

With the exception of Shi, the others each raised a single finger in approval.

"I ain't aginst it." Shi shrugged. "I jist don't like seein' my ko go to others when it could be in my pocket."

"Fair enough," Atom said as he pushed a pile to each of his crew. "We all take that bite on this. On to the next order, the treasure. We've made it far enough that I'm not worried about the Migori, so let's put that behind us. We know we need to make it to the Nemo System. How are we looking on that, Daisy?"

"I'd have to plot it in the nav-comp, but rough estimate is less than a week," the pilot said with a frown as he plotted the maze of jump-gates in his head. "I'll let the comp pull the fastest course through the maze, but I can guarantee it won't be much more than a week."

"Let's rough plan on a week to be prepped and ready for whatever we might come up against. We each have a separate role to play in this, and a role as a group."

"Do we have any idea of what we need to be prepping for?" Hither asked.

"Table that for a moment." Atom lifted his eyes to the ceiling. "Kozue, could you ask Lilly to join us?"

"Just a moment," the AI replied. "She will arrive momentarily."

The crew exchanged glances and Atom took note of their reservations. They shared a ship, but Lilly floated in an orbit outside their own. Despite the back and forth, and the prospect of a haul to retire them, she still had not earned their trust.

Atom smiled and turned his attention to Margo.

Trotting around the narrow island, she sang to Mae. The cat humored her childish song and led her on a merry chase, stopping to look back at Margo to keep the girl interested.

"Koze, play some music for her," said Atom as he watched the interplay.

Margo froze for a moment, then her eyes lit up with delight and she started to bounce with a rhythm that changed the mood around the table. The crew seemed to forget their dark mood and smiles broke out as Margo bobbed her head back and forth to the beat of an unheard melody.

Mae sat on her haunches and watched Margo with a placid expression that belied the underlying spirit of cat.

"However this goes, we'll always have Go to keep us entertained." Daisy smiled.

"We do this fer her." Shi watched the girl, the corner of her mouth curling. "Whatever floats our way, we remember what we all owe her our lives.

"At first, I'd've said we's jist crew." Shi pulled her foot up on the bench and leaned on her knee. "But, I ain't never been tight with a crew like I am with y'all. I rekin Margo is what sets it. Plus, I ain't never bin saved by a wee kit 'for. That'll be a story to tell when she gits older."

"Imagine telling that story at her wedding?" Hither said with a reserved laugh. "You're marrying a girl who took out an imperial assault squad … as a two-year-old."

"She's almost three." Atom joined her laughter.

"Because that's the important part of the story," Hither countered. "Anyone who marries her better stay on her good side. If she can do that when she's almost three, what is she going to be like as a teen?"

"Didn't I tell you, that's why I hired you and Shi."

"You ain't said nothin' about that whin you hired me," Shi drawled. "Might's well jump ship now."

The whole crew joined in the laughter. The mood soared.

"And don't forget, anyone hitchin' 'er will 'ave to keep us in mind," Byron chirped.

"They might have a rougher nuptial with us as family than any han could offer," Daisy said as he slipped from his side of the bench with a hiss of pain. He wandered past the dancing Margo to pour himself a mug of broth. "Speaking of her future, do you think this score will set her up with a real one?"

Atom sighed and his smile slipped a touch. "I'm hoping it might be something to leave her."

The door slid open to reveal Lilly. Margo stopped dancing and looked up at the baug. Sensing the tension fluttering beneath the surface of the room, Lilly bobbed her head as if entering a library full of studying students.

The attention turned to Lilly, and Atom gestured to the open seat next to Shi and the pile of ko sitting on the table.

"We're moving on Nemo," Atom said as she sat. "The Tribe paid up as soon as we completed the job and that's your cut of the affair. Although, I'm still not certain how they knew we had completed our task."

"They have eyes everywhere," she said as Daisy finished heating his broth and rejoined the table. "That's why I've had to be so careful."

"Understandable." Atom leaned forward on the table and studied his hands. "That puts us in an uncomfortable position. I'm fair certain they're looking to back us into a corner and they know we've been in contact with you."

"And they still have that mark on my head."

"If they've made that public, Toks will be double gunning for all of us. I think all we can do is try to get ahead of this."

Daisy and Shi exchanged a look.

"What?" Atom asked, glancing between the two.

Daisy cleared his throat and took the lead. "Even if we manage to get ahead of the Tribe, there's no way we stay there. We're racing Toks and we have no idea where she is at the moment."

"Then we push for Nemo." Atom shrugged.

"And what about when we reach the end of this here ride?" Shi squinted at Atom.

"We cross that void when we get to it," Atom replied, looking to Lilly. "In the meantime, together we have enough of the puzzle to get us where we need to go. Toks has part of it, so we have to assume she knows to head to Nemo."

"We just need to get there before she does," Lilly said. "Otherwise, she'll spot us on the inbound and just trail us to the treasure."

"You're right on that front." Atom pushed up from the table and began pacing the mess deck from hatch to hatch. Margo watched him for one cycle and then trotted over to climb up into Daisy's lap.

"According to Daisy, we have around a week, give or take." Atom turned to the table with his hands tucked behind his back. "Time is not our friend. Daisy if there is any chance you shave a day or two off our inbound, that might prove the difference between finding this treasure for ourselves, and digging it up for Toks."

Daisy nodded and rose, shifting Margo to his empty seat. "I'll see what I can crunch. I might have to skirt safety," he said as he left the mess deck with Mae weaving about his feet.

"Byron," Atom said, shifting his gaze around the table. "I don't know what we're going to face when we get there. We have the treasure ship on record, but we don't know where it'll be or how we're getting into it. I want you to put together the tech to bypass security, physical and tech side. We also need to get to the ship whether it's in the void, some place on land, or even underwater. On top of that, we need rigs that can punch through the hatches of a warship."

Lilly raised a hand and waited for Atom to nod at her. "Ash can help with that. I could have him interface with Byron and see if we can load him up to tackle that problem."

"Good, that'll help. You up for it, By?"

"Absolutely." The little mech looked as if he wanted to scamper away to his workshop right then.

"One last thing." Atom held up Byron with a finger. "I want you to get together with Hither and plug up the rigs to couple with the void-suits so we can function in any of those environments I just mentioned. I know they'll be bulky, so just rig breach suits for Shi and me. I don't think Daisy can handle that stress now and I want you and Hither nimble for tight spots.

"Lilly will be suited, but working with Ash," Atom said to the rest of the table.

"Righto, darl." Byron leaped up and shot for the door.

"Hold up." Atom stopped him as the hatch hissed. "Do the same for Margo's suit. She'll be with me, like usual, but instead of clips, could you rig a light rack that can attach to any of the suits? She might need to jump us at a moment's notice."

Byron blinked several times as schematics fluttered through his mind. "I reck I could build you somefin 'long them specs."

"Git." Atom grinned as the mech disappeared down the hatch like a startled rabbit.

"Shi, you good for breaking at my side?"

Shi cracked her knuckles and smirked. "Fittin' that we'd be first in."

"Problem?"

"Naw, it's right where we should be."

"But it'll mean you might have to man a holding point."

She didn't look at the other women at the table, but Atom sensed her confident spirit. "You need the others to follow their assigned paths. I'll hold the path open for you when things go sideways inside a hostile ship."

"That's my thought. I want you to do an inventory of our weapons. I know we aren't an Imperial Marine ship, but you've stocked us quite nicely. You know our preferences, so put together an assault package in case we have to deal with Toks climbing up our pipes."

Shi knuckled her forehead and looked to Lilly. "Scuse me, miss. I got a list to make."

Lilly slipped out from the booth and let Shi saunter off into the ship, mumbling and counting on her fingers as she disappeared.

The baug looked to Atom as she dropped back into her seat. "I suppose there's some way I fit into your outfit. I just don't want to get in the way."

"You'll fit." Atom gave a thoughtful half-smile. "I just need to figure out where. I pulled this crew together because they fit, not because I was looking for anyone specifically. We work perfectly, and while you're an extra cog, we should continue to function.

"In the meantime, I have a couple questions." He studied Lilly from different angles as he resumed his slow pacing. "How small can you get and is your suit built to handle shifting?

Lilly laughed. "The smallest I've ever reduced is maybe twenty inches in height. It comes in handy for infiltration. The only problem is my mass is packed into the tiny frame. Meaning, don't expect me to be faster or lighter, just because I'm smaller. I just have to be careful about where I'm placing that mass.

"Don't even dream that I would fit in the palm of your hand, although, I could strap into your shoulder harness if you were prepared for the weight.

"As to the second question, I have several suits on my ship geared towards different sizes." Lilly paused to run inventory in her head. "I have a child's suit on hand that would drop down to that size, but I doubt I could stretch it out too much larger than a small child, so I'd be stuck at that size if wearing the suit."

"Just be ready for whatever comes." Atom stopped at the table and leaned on the back of his seat, looking at Margo. "You and I will see this to the end. Figure what you want to do with Ash. We'll stay together as long it's feasible.

"What I don't want," he turned his gaze back to Lilly, "is there to be any question once we get in. If we have to separate for any reason, I don't want to have to think about who is going where or worry about whether you'll change your mind. Those decisions need to be made before we even drop in the Nemo System.

"The way things are floating, I don't know what kind of lead we have on Toks and even though we burned time completing the job for the Tribe, I say it bought us time with them."

"And what if Toks beats us there?" Lilly frowned down at the table.

"Then we re-evaluate the situation."

Hither cleared her throat and said, "It's possible that if they beat us there, we can just drop in with the usual system traffic."

"If they are there, they'll be looking for us," Atom replied with a shake of his head.

"Do we even know what kind of traffic a system that far outside the Fingers gets? It could affect what our possibilities might be when we arrive."

Lilly looked up from the table and asked, "Would it be a good idea to pick up a cargo so we could pass as a legit merch? You know, similar to what we did with Seeonee and Kafiristan? I could probably dig and figure the best trade route for us to take."

"No need," Atom replied. "Kozue, can you get me trade info on Nemo?"

"They export scrap," Kozue said. "Their imports tend along the lines of manufactured goods. They seem to produce most of their own basic needs, but don't have the production capabilities to fill those demands. I would suggest items such as monitors, smaller farm equipment, suspensor-bikes. Any of these items would trade for scrap at a very profitable rate."

"And where is the best place to pick up a hold?"

"Daisy is still playing with our route, but I believe I can line up a hold full of replacement monitors with very little deviance from his course. It may add six hours travel time, plus whatever it takes you to haggle a good price, but it would give us a solid cover should we find Toks awaiting us."

"Good, pass the information on to him and have him build it into our route."

"I'm going to talk to Byron," Lilly said and she rose and headed for the rear hatch.

After she had left, Atom poured himself a mug of green chi and tossed a pinch of cinnamon into the steaming liquid. He closed his eyes and scented the drink before wandering back to the table.

"What am I missing?" he asked Hither as he sat down and blew a wisp of steam in her direction. "Everyone has a task to keep them busy while we wait. Most will probably be unnecessary, but it'll keep their minds off what's coming. We can only plan for possibilities right now. I guess we could look at that poem again and see if we can pick anything out that might help us."

Hither slipped around from the far end of the table to sit next to Atom. With a smirk, she took the chi from his hands. "Thanks, love. Why don't you get yourself a cup?"

Atom flipped an eyebrow and retreated to the kitchen.

Hither cupped the mug, savoring the heat seeping into her hands. "We can go over the poem," she murmured as she stared into the mug. "I honestly haven't thought about it since we first picked it up. Things have been chaotic."

"Isn't that normal?" Atom chuckled as he filled a second mug and joined her at the table.

"Depends on the season."

"Kozue, could you throw the riddle up on the wall screen?" Atom took a steaming sip.

The poem appeared on the wall screen that dominated the far end of the table.

> *Inside, a man mourns long lost sheep*
> *Walking nowhere, but continues to weep*
> *No one descended from nowhere above*
> *Guiding the sheep out beyond the Glove*
> *The man takes solace turned into himself*
> *Then buried her beside him, asleep on the shelf*

Atom and Hither stared at the words.

"Where do you think this came from?" Hither asked, tilting her head to the side and leaning on her fist with a frown.

"Blonde."

"But the story from Lilly is that each one of the navies on that pod had a single piece of the puzzle. One each for the system, planet, and location."

"If that was the plan, then why did one of them seem to have all three of the pieces and hide them in a stupid jumble of words? I'm not saying he didn't do a fancy job of hiding the info in there, but I've never been one for word puzzles."

"You think Blonde concocted this puzzle?" Hither asked.

"Probably not, but who wrote it is irrelevant. We have to assume Lilly's basic story is true, and that each sailor had a single piece of the information. Each of them was ordered to carry that single piece of the puzzle into the Black. Either the poem came along after, or perhaps the captain sent it along without actually telling Blonde it was important." Atom paused to sip his own chi. "What we do know is that we have two pieces of this puzzle, and Lilly has the other. We know from Johansen that the name Shepherd is important in some dimension and that claim seems supported by the poem."

"What if the poem is something else?"

Atom stared at Hither.

"We have the system name and Shepherd," she continued.

"Just to rule out," Atom interrupted. "I had Kozue reference the name Shepherd and there are seven hundred and twenty-three planets with Shepherd in their name. There are fifty-two systems with some derivative of the name. Unfortunately, none of them line up with the Nemo System in any way.

"Come at it from the other side and we are left with a Shepherd in the Nemo System."

"Then Shepherd is the treasure ship?" Hither asked.

"It has to be."

"Then we are on the right course?"

Atom shrugged. "There's only one Nemo System. It doesn't seem like a very popular name. Plus, Lilly said her clue was a planet, so I can't see any other vector."

"In the entire galaxy, only one Nemo? Not that I'm fighting it. I've never even heard the name before. It still seems unlikely."

"If there are any more, they aren't in the planetary registry."

"So, Nemo System it is." Hither took a breath and turned her attention to the poem. "I see shepherd referenced in there. I mean, they mention a guy with sheep, that's pretty straight forward, but where do you get Nemo in that jumble?"

"Well, Nemo is a name meaning nobody, or no one, but I don't know that I would have picked that out of the poem if we didn't already have the clue."

"Maybe the poem isn't a clue, but more of a key."

Atom studied the words and drained his mug without tearing his eyes from the wall-screen. "You think that means we won't be able to pick out Lilly's clue from the riddle?"

"I'd guess not." Hither slipped from the booth and took Atom's mug from the table. She dropped it, along with hers, into the recycler. "Have you asked her?"

"Nope," Atom said with a chuckle as he joined Hither.

"Are you going to?"

"When the time is right." Atom scowled at the riddle.

"You know she's going to try and cut us out."

"Yeah, but how is she going to do that if we hold all the pieces to this puzzle."

"And you think we can bypass her clue?"

Atom shook his head in dejection. "How many habitable planets can there be in one system?"

"Who says they need to be habitable?" Hither leaned on the counter, crossed her arms, and studied the words. "Koze, how many planets are there in the Nemo System?"

"Thirteen," said Kozue.

"That's too many to search." Atom pinched the bridge of his nose. "How many inhabited?"

"Seven, but only three to any degree of consequence."

"Would you hide a treasure ship on an inhabited planet?" Hither asked.

"Probably not," Atom agreed. "But we can't rule them out, and we'll need to start somewhere. Dropping into the system and immediately burning for an uninhabited planet would kick up klaxons for anyone watching. We'll have to hit the system-hub first and then find a reason to spread our search outward.

"Can we pick anything out of the poem that would help? Weeping or shelves, anything we could tie to a location? Maybe there's a shelf of some sort on the planet, like a mountain range or something?"

"Kozue, can you cross the poem with geographical locations from the system?" Hither asked.

Kozue replied in a neutral voice. "There are several worlds that might extrapolate from the given wording of the poem. In

323

addition, there are several words that might fit with manmade locations.

"One of the major townships is named Daybreak, which could be a loose reference to morning, or as in the poem, mourning. Sheep are the major protein source in the system, so we could look for the greatest concentration. That would be on Stillwater, the system's capital planet. One of the smaller inhabited planets is Solace, which is also in the poem.

"There is a seasonal waterfall on Stillwater known as the Weeping Sister. There is a moon orbiting Stillwater named Guidance, and another called Squam, which could be a corruption of the old word for nowhere.

"I can't make any connection to the last two lines and so I must surmise they were either added to balance the three-part rhyme scheme, or they pertain to something not accessible to my digital probes." Kozue's human tone drifted back and Atom smiled at the puzzled sound. "I find the last two lines most intriguing. They cannot just be to balance rhyme scheme. There must be more, but I just can't see the direction."

"And the first four give too much direction." Hither rolled her eyes with a quiet chuckle. "I'm not seeing anything that will help us."

"Hopefully, we'll find something in system that sparks a thought. Close it down, Koze." Atom rubbed his eyes as the mess wall sprang back into existence. "I'm going to get Margo down for a nap. Maybe a little sleep will pop something in my pan."

*   *   *

They dropped into the outer reaches of the Nemo System ahead of schedule with a hold full of crated replacement monitors. Atom stood in his usual spot behind Daisy as the pilot eased into the system at a relaxed pace.

"Anything on the scopes?" Atom asked Hither.

"Neg." Her eyes flew over data as it streamed across her station screen. "Usual traffic, but nothing that I'm registering as imp."

"Good for now," Atom said with a smile pulling at his face.

Daisy grunted as he guided the ship towards the center of the system. "Where we headed first?" he asked as he monitored the secondary feedback flowing up from Byron's station in the shop.

"Stillwater," Atom said without hesitation. "I know we talked about scouting the system a touch, but it looks more natural to drop our cargo first."

"Firm," Daisy eased on the yoke and punched the coordinates to pull up a vector that would curve them into a high orbit around the system capital. "I'll try to line a path that might give us a scurrying glance at some of the outer planets as we make for landfall."

Atom remained silent and looked out at the distant specks circling an old orange star.

"Well, that's strange." Hither leaned back and pulled on her bottom lip as her brow knit. "Atom, you need to take a look at this. I don't think I've ever seen anything like if before."

He turned and leaned over her shoulder. "What am I looking at?"

"This." She tapped the screen and highlighted Stillwater. "Notice anything?"

He squinted at the screen and said, "Nothing stands out." As he reached out and pulled in tighter on the planet. "Low water planet with grav a touch below standard. Small seas, but eighty-six percent landmass.

"It would be tough to cover any major crash site from the past two centuries." He paused to tap a few commands. "And I'm counting hundreds of them."

"That's in line with a massive orbital battle." Hither swatted his hand away and pulled out to show the planet and surroundings.

"I didn't realize the battle was that big."

"Me either." Hither glanced up at Atom with arched eyebrows. "Look at the moons."

"Three satellites."

"There are only two according to system records."

"What's the third body we're looking at?"

"It's artificial," Hither said with a puzzled smile as she punched in closer on the smallest moon. "That all appears to be wreckage from the battle."

Atom whistled. "I see how these bokes could make a living as scrappers. There's enough metal and tech to last a dozen lifetimes." Atom played with the screen to pull in tighter to where the shapes of individual ships and ship fragments could be discerned. "This battle was massive. I'm talking entire imperial fleet massed in one place and squared off against a force of equal size.

"Koze, what can you tell us about the engagement?" Atom rose and glared out the canopy to the pinprick of the planet.

"According to the histories there was no battle here. There are references to a limited skirmish between an imperial scout force and a few rogue han ships. The imperials supposedly eliminated the rebel fleet with minimal losses and destroyed the han. There are also folk tales of the final stand of the Afkin Rebellion.

"That does not compute," Kozue sounded puzzled.

"What doesn't?" Atom asked.

"First off, there is no reference in the official histories to what han the imperials were pursuing and second, there is enough wreckage there to fill the recorded engagement a thousand times over. It looks to be an entire han on the move, and a major one at that. Many of the ships I'm looking at are not military vessels.

"What we're looking at is not what was recorded in the Imperial Annals. Something happened here that the Empire didn't want to be remembered. That could explain the relative obscurity these scavengers have managed to exploit."

Hither spun her seat around to face Atom. He exchanged an overwhelmed look with her and whispered, "Thousands of ships, not all military, we're looking at an exodus of a han."

"And we're supposed to pick a shepherd from this mess," Hither sighed.

Atom backed up and dropped into Shi's empty seat. He leaned on his knees with a heavy spirit.

"What if the ships are the sheep and the shepherd is something else." Hither pulled her legs up to sit cross-legged. "Like a planet, or maybe one of the moons?"

"That's not helping," Atom said to the floor.

"Helping what?" Lilly asked as she stepped through the hatch and made her way up beside Daisy to stare out the canopy at their distant destination.

"This whole treasure hunt," Atom replied as he looked up at Lilly with a worn, befuddled expression. "I'd say it was time we put our chips on the float. We both know the system from

Blonde's table. We've followed that, and here we are on the outskirts of the Nemo System, at least three gates from the closest civilization.

"I have a name and you have a name." Atom crossed his arms and turned toward Lilly. "I don't think we have time to hold back now."

"Do you think Toks is that close?"

"I have no idea, but it's not really something I want to dicker with if we can avoid it. She's demonstrated the ability to make me look warm and cuddly."

Daisy's snicker cut short as he fought a coughing fit but managed to gasp out, "You're about as cuddly as a porky-pine, Cap."

"I know, but I wouldn't destroy a station because it suited me."

"We both ready to lay out?" Lilly ignored the laughter and stared hard at Atom. "I know I haven't been full-up honest and straight with you throughout this whole mess, so I'll make it up and go first. I pull and then you and we'll be square with our agreed upon split.

"The name I got from my source was Stillwater." Lilly's gaze softened with hopeful intent. "Does that mean anything to you?"

"We've already laid course," Daisy said. "It's the closest thing to a civilized planet in this system. There are a couple others that pinged on our charts, but they are little more than frontier processing facilities."

Lilly's shoulders drooped. "You already had the info?"

"Just a lucky guess," Atom stared up at the baug.

"Probability," Kozue interjected.

"We have to start somewhere," Atom spoke over his AI. "The piece of the puzzle I picked up from Johansen is Shepherd. We are guessing it's a ship, although it could still be a town or some other location."

"Wait," Lilly asked in confusion, "Aren't we looking for the *Ave Maria*?"

"That's the treasure ship from the legend, but there may be some wrinkle and we have to assume that there's just as much fiction to the legend as actual fact."

"Do we actually have specs on the *Ave Maria*?" Hither asked. "We've been wandering after this ship for all this time and I don't recall anyone actually knowing what the ship looked like, or if it even existed.

"I mean, are we looking for a fat cargo ship, a sleek personal yacht, or maybe she was a warship, armed to the gills." She paused and rocked back in her seat.

Atom's gaze grew distant. "That could influence where she was hidden and also what we'd be up against when we try to board her."

Lilly glanced back and forth between Atom and Hither.

"How do you know there's even treasure on the ship?" Hither continued. "For all we know the reference to Shepherd could be a clue telling us that they unloaded the cargo from the *Ave Maria* and now we should be looking for some hiding place that doesn't actually include a ship."

"Or what if the ship crashed on that planet and broke up?" Daisy asked. "That could mean that Shepherd is a debris field."

"On that tack, it could be a debris field used by shepherds," Lilly said with a sigh.

"We will need to get that sorted," Atom said in a calm tone. "But for now, we need to get down on that rock and hope we get to cover before Toks comes burning in hot. Once we're tucked away we can start digging for a trail."

*   *   *

They burned for the planet, slipping in among the scattered system traffic. Daisy kept a course for Stillwater while Hither logged their plans with system flight control. As they drew close, a berth opened and Daisy dropped the ship towards the surface on a gradual descent that afforded a panoramic view of the planet.

Broad rivers veined dusty brown plains with dark, muddy waters that flowed south toward an equatorial sea, girding most of the planet. From the poles, thin shards of deep green forests plunged towards the sea like shark's teeth.

"Nice looking place," Atom muttered as he held onto the overhead piping against the buffeting of the atmospheric descent.

"Looks dusty," Daisy said with a grin.

"Speakin' a which." Shi sat at her station on the left side of the bridge with her eyes closed and feet up on the console. "Y'all ever git the feelin' that we frequent the dust bowls a tad too much? Remember, ya found me on a rock with some moisture? Ever stop to think it might be that's what I prefer?"

"I thought you followed the ko," Atom said without changing his posture.

"That's fact, but I sense a trend in yer planet pickin'."

"Well, if that's how you feel, maybe we should try to see what kind of work we can hustle on a swamp."

"That's be fine by me." Shi stretched her arms up in the air and yawned with feline ferocity. "The dry wreaks havoc on my sinuses."

Below them, the planet grew in size. As they drew closer, they found sporadic clumps of cobalt lakes sprinkled across the ferrous brown streaks of the plains. Darker patches solidified into mountains. From their descending course, altitude proved tricky to judge. Wispy clouds circled the equatorial seas in eerie bands.

"I'm wishing I could see more green." Daisy adjusted the vector with a tap of the yoke. "I wonder what they eat?"

"Besides sheep?" Shi planted her feet and pushed up to stand beside Atom on the bucking deck. "I'd wager they've acreage to keep their veg an' mins up. I know we ain't seein' huge greens, but there must be enough scrub to keep them sheepers in the ko."

"I hate to burst your seal, Atom, but I'm detecting a massive energy spike back at the jump-gate. We have multiple ships entering the system," Hither spoke with the dead-pan efficiency of a naval officer.

Atom responded to the tone. "We're close enough to Stillwater to blend into the natural traffic. Daisy, just keep her steady and stay our course. We need to avoid anything that would draw attention to us. If we're careful, we'll be able to put the planet between us in short order.

"Hither, keep scopes on the ships and gather as much intel as we can," Atom snapped as he reached up and snatched the hardwire com. "Byron, get to the mech-deck, there is the off chance you may need to fiddle about.

"Shi, grab Go. Make a sweep and lock the ship down for the unexpected.

"And Lilly." Atom hesitated a moment as he worked through his plan. "Get to your ship and get her prepped. If Toks pegs us, I'm going to open the hatch and dump you. If that happens, we'll meet up on the fly."

Atom didn't wait for a response. He clipped the com back above his head and gripped the pipes with both hands as the turbulence increased.

"We're hitting atmo," Daisy called out.

"Any more on the new ships?" Atom asked Hither.

"Looks like the *Graff* and four support ships," she replied, scowling at her screens as the scopes supplied more information. "Two destroyers and two corvettes. They don't have a ton of firepower, but they have speed for days.

"And let's be honest." She glanced over her shoulder at Atom. "They don't need firepower against us."

"What are they doing now?"

"Fanning wide. Burning on system center."

"Hard burn?"

"No, they're bordering on a leisurely stroll. It's just plain strange. You'd think they would want to pin ships to the planets."

Atom shook his head, staring at the growing planet as he tried to crawl inside Toks' head. "No, it actually fits perfectly. She knows there's only one jump gate in this system, which means she controls the choke point. A ship from here could cross the Black, but you're looking at months on the burn. There's no reason to rush into things. She can take her time and spread her ships while running a deep scan of the system to peg traffic patterns and hope to glean something on the location of the treasure ship.

"The upside to that is there's no rush to get to the surface. We're inside the atmosphere, mixed with a planet full of ship traffic," he said, turning his attention to Daisy. "Take us in as easy as laying a babe in the cradle. No sense in standing out because we're sloppy."

Daisy didn't reply, instead he adjusted the controls and the powerplant eased back. The *One Way Ticket* rode the gravity well and slipped through the planet's atmosphere, each second drawing her deeper into the meshed traffic lanes of the system craft skirling about like bees in a disturbed nest.

"Control, this is the *One Way Ticket*," Shi drawled as she dropped back into her seat. "Are we still locked fer our assigned pad?"

"You have seen our newest drop-ins." The woman's thick accent did little to hide her annoyance. "They have thrown our operations into confusion. We must now reroute you to secondary docking location."

"If that location could be discreet, we'd be much obliged."

"Are you carrying anything that could prove problematic?"

"That's a negative, control. Our haul is completely on the upper." Shi glanced over her shoulder at Atom. "But a couple of our crew ain't in the good graces of the imps. I reckin a run-in with them imps would be more than an annoyance."

"I understand," the comptroller replied. "Sending you new landing coordinates now. There will be a local trade officer to meet you at your berth. He will assist you."

"Much appreciated, control." Shi said flipped the new coordinates to Daisy's HUD.

The pilot adjusted his control of the ship as they buffeted through the atmosphere and dropped into a long, graceful swoop. The *Ticket* diverted from the center of the main city, instead aiming for a rocky shelf that curled around the southern sprawl of low housing blocks and industrial complexes.

Keeping a feel on the air flow around the ship through the tug of the stick, Daisy dropped down below the level of the rocky shelf and drifted the ship sideways into one of a series of hangars carved directly into the rock face of the cliff. Following the guiding beacon of their assigned berth, he nosed the ship around to ease into the hangar and set her down with a gentle hiss of compressing hydraulics.

Behind them, the hangar door ground shut, closing them in a coffin of plasteel and stone.

"Let's go see what the locals have in mind." Atom nodded to Hither and Shi. "Daisy, why don't you take it slow and make sure we're shut down proper. I have no idea how long we'll be on this rock, but I don't want to get back aboard and find we've let slip the charge to jump the reactor."

"On it, boss," Daisy said with a grimace as he leaned forward to run through the shutdown sequences.

"And Daisy," Atom said with a pat on the big man's shoulder. "I know you're far along the mend, but why don't you lock down and lay up. Regular treats on the medoc so you keep on that road. We've something ahead of us and I don't want you slowing us or getting reinjured because you aren't full charge."

"I'm good to go now," the pilot said through gritted teeth.

Shaking his head, Atom squeezed the shoulder. "I know you could scrap if you needed to, but you don't right now, so heal up. I'll keep you posted and when you're needed we'll let you know."

Atom turned and led the women from the bridge. As they passed through the mess deck, Atom checked the load on his pistols, more from habit than actual anticipation of danger. While a rock full of smugglers and scrappers could prove dangerous, having an imperial fleet in orbit diverted that danger. In the hold, they met up with the rest of the crew and Atom pulled the retrieved and refurbished pram out from its spot beside the hatch.

"I don't know what we're getting into," he said as he hefted Margo into the pram. "Follow my lead and let's feel out the situation."

"Do we have a goal?" Lilly asked. "Or a contact?"

"An imp fleet dropped through the gate after us. It has to be Toks." Atom cycled the hatch. "Our goal should be finding a way to keep our heads down. Avoiding contact is the primary objective. Once we've figured that, we can worry about finding the next step in the clues."

"But you know she's going to be squeezing anywhere she thinks she can find us or that treasure."

Shi laid a hand on Atom's arm. "Boss, what are we doin' with Daisy? His gut ain't healed up. I rekin we're headed to scrap and he sure ain't gonna handle that. You ain't serious about callin' him in?"

"He's on ship detail for the moment." Atom turned to find concern written clear across each face of his crew. Only Lilly seemed oblivious to their need. "We need to figure our play. If I can get him to a safe-house, I will. Otherwise, he'll stay home aboard the ship until the last moment.

"For the time, we're running light." He looked to Shi and Hither. "Keep that in mind if something goes sideways."

The women nodded. Atom turned and slapped open the hatch.

A cool, dusty scent hit them in the face, carrying the bittersweet, earthy smell fused with oil that Atom assumed leached from the stone. A pair of uniformed men trotted across the woven mesh of the landing pad.

Hopping down from the side hatch, Atom and the crew watched the men approach.

With a tired smile, Atom rocked the pram while the others fanned out just enough to have space without appearing to have threat read in their actions.

"What's the word, gentles?" Atom asked as the locals drew within earshot.

"Word is you have a couple contras and want to avoid the ocs of the imps burning for orbit," the taller of the two men said as he held out a hand, palm up. "Name's Bextiple. I'm the fore on this dock level. I'll take care of the unload and load of your ship.

"You have a need for the ship, let me know." He recited his litany as he handed Atom an info chip. "You can reach me, or one of my subs, at any time. Most things, legit or no, can be had for the right price. I'll be the one to put you in contact with the right parties for the right goods. As you can see, Stillwater's far enough outside the lanes that we run on our own system and that ain't always the up-up.

"Let's start on the right hop," he drawled, crossing his arms as he looked up at the ship with an appraising eye. "Right peachy burner you got here. Looks to be you keep her fair. What are you looking to swap out? And I'd appreciate you being upfront with any …." He hesitated, rocking his head back and forth while smirking. "Complications.

"Ain't nothing wrong with under the table deals, I just like to know how to broker your goods."

"I'm not carrying anything special." Atom shrugged. "Replacement monitors. Differing sizes. Two-fifty crates. Stasis sealed."

"You did your research." Bextiple grinned. "Monitors always fetch a fair price."

"What's your cut?"

"I take an honest five on all transactions I set. Nothing else. No sliding scale. It's the standard rate and it keeps most of us trade officers honest. I won't say no to a tip at the end, but everything in the midst stays aboveboard."

"You seem fair calm with the imps bearing down."

"I'm guessing it's just a routine shakedown." Bextiple played with the saggy skin of his neck. "We'll keep you tucked.

In the meantime, we'll just go about our business and keep the unders out of their ocs.

"You mind if I take a quick visual of your cargo? I want to get it processed and on the boards to see if we can line up a good trade."

"Not a problem," Atom replied as he pulled Margo from the pram and set her on the floor. "By, why don't you run Margo a touch while I handle this."

Bextiple followed Atom into the hold and scanned a couple random stasis-crates to verify their contents. The only pause to the cursory inspection came when Bex rounded the stack of crates and found the *Hellkite* parked beside the main cargo ramp.

He lifted an eyebrow, but otherwise remained quiet.

"Looks solid," Bextiple said as he returned to the hangar floor. "I just tossed your goods on the local boards. I would guess you'll have an offer within the hour, or at least a potential based on local trade.

"Here you go." He pulled out his pad and flipped through a couple screens before shooting something off into the ether. "You can find the link to your board posting through the tag I just gave you. Anyone posts a bid on your goods will show up there and you can work out the deal. I'll reach out to a few of my contacts and let them know what you're offering.

"I'll work at earning that five."

"Sounds grounded." Atom walked over to his crew and scooped Margo into his arms. "In the meantime, is there a place we could stack up, get some eats, and perhaps find some local intel on what we should haul out of this system?"

"You can find most trade info on the boards, unless you are looking to carry something a touch more contraband." Bex scrolled through his pad and flicked a few more times. "There are a couple port-side inns tied into the top portions of this stack of the port. They tend to be a touch pricier than some of the places further in town, but they're close.

"If I had to choose one of them, I'd go with the Cozy Cavern. It's only two levels above where we stand now and their cook throws a tasty dish."

"Many thanks." Atom reached into his pocket and pulled a metal chit. He locked in an amount and flipped it to Bextiple. "Hundred for you to keep me in the loop on what the imps are after. If possible, I'd like to steer clear and keep my crew safe."

"Absolutely," Bex grinned. "You aren't alone in that concern, so there are back page updates on what we have to look out for."

"Good man," Atom said and he waved for the others to join him. "We're headed up to that inn and hopefully we can use the downtime to rest up. It's my hope we'll decompress from the time in the Black. I'm sure we could all stand for a rockbound meal and pint or two."

Despite the inbound imperial fleet, the crew managed to look excited at the prospect of fresh-cooked food and the freedom from the confines of a ship.

*　　　*　　　*

The walk to the inn covered several floors carved into the living rock of the hollowed ridge. The *One way Ticket* sat docked one level below the lowest living areas, but a healthy buffer of stone helped to somewhat shield life from the reverberations of lifting and landing ships.

The crew managed an exhausted light-heartedness as they wandered up the circular ramp that wound through the rock like a meandering miner's tunnel.

Only Daisy's absence seemed to dampen the moods of the others, but knowing how close to death the gut wound had taken him, they allowed him the respite. Beyond thoughts, however, they kept their chatter light and eyes observant.

They passed an open market with every commodity a spacer could need: hawkers lauding the variety with their drinking establishments; front offices for mech shops offering ship repair and part replacement; and an intermixed smattering of sleeping establishments. For a frontier planet, Stillwater presented a clean, relaxed waystation for weary spacers.

"We should be there soon," Atom said, consulting his data-pad.

The soft glow of a recessed, track-light conveyed the illusion of surface light to surround the crew as they wove through the light foot-traffic of the warren. Just as they rounded a corner and Atom pointed out their destination, the lights dimmed, flickered out and then surged back to life with a squint-worthy flare.

A moment later, a low rumble shook several streams of dust from the ceiling.

"What was that?" Hither asked as the party came to a halt among the frozen flow of startled pedestrians.

"Power fluctuation," Atom said with concern.

"Should we be worried?"

Atom shrugged and turned to a man, a grease smeared mech, who had come to a halt beside the party and asked, "Is that normal?"

"Not in these parts," the man said with a shake of his head as he stared up at the overhead rock. "Our grid is top end. I've never seen a flicker like that. You might find something like this in some of the outliers." He pulled his pad and started scrolling through screens. "Or maybe in a mass duster, but it's the wrong season and there haven't been any alerts."

"Anomaly?" Atom exchanged a darting glance with his crew. "Could it be the imps?"

The man swore under his breath. "Looks so," he replied. "According to the local feeds, they just dropped a K-bomb close enough to our plant to shake down the power."

"Reckin this ain't as friendly as our migo would like to believe," Shi drawled.

"They can't be in orbit yet," Hither piped in.

"No," Atom replied. "That had to be a distant message that they weren't coming for a routine checkup. Toks is on the warpath.

"Regardless." He waved a thanks to the native and turned on towards their destination. "We have enough time to get a meal, get hunkered, and slip out for some intel before Toks even pulls into orbit."

"What do you think we have to look forward to?" Lilly asked.

"From what we've seen, she's not afraid to come down hard." Atom led the way to the entrance to the inn and paused at the door. "My estimate is that she'll lock this rock down as best she can. She only has five ships and four of them are light. That probably means no more than a couple regiments of drop marines between them. They'll be heavy assault, trained to put down uprisings hard and heavy. They aren't typically trained for prolonged occupation."

"Could we just lie low and wait this out?"

Atom pressed the pram through the hatch into the low murmur of the inn's front lobby. A half-dozen low couches circled a simple fountain that burbled a calming song. Several groups of people sat or stood in nervous clumps about the room, but none of them bothered to register the entrance of Atom and the crew.

Having measured the room's occupants for danger, Atom lifted Margo from the pram before tousling her hair and turning her loose to wander over to the fountain.

"If only it could be that simple," Atom sighed. "Toks knows this system is our destination from Coffey's files, but that's all she knows."

"Then she won't be leaving anytime soon?" Lilly frowned.

Atom watched Margo wander around the edge of the fountain, trailing a hand on the ceramic tiles. The girl pranced without a care in the world, her eyes focused on the trickles of water dancing from a plain stone basin into the waiting pool below.

"Yeah," Atom mumbled. "We'll have to figure that one out. She's logged our ship. That means if we lift, she'll be able to ping us as long as she has line of sight."

"And that shouldn't be too hard, seeing as she has five ships at her disposal," Hither said.

"I don't reckin we're aimin' to figure this right now." Shi tapped a quick tattoo on her guns beneath her poncho. "What say you line us up some rooms, and we'll snatch a table in the cantina and save you a seat? I'll order y'all a hot bevie and some munchers."

Atom fixed her with a steely glare.

"Ah, Cap." She thrust out her chin and flashed her cocky, lopsided grin. "Y'all ain't serious about workin' the angles right this instant. We all know this is going to take some rollin' the pans to work out. Fact a the matter, we'll probably need Daisy's pan to work things fully.

"Plus, I do reckin Go could use some vits." Shi glanced around at the others. "An' no offense, but I could use some meself that ain't cooked by the lot a you."

"Fair," Atom grunted. "Grab me a red chi. I need something calming."

"Righto, Cap." Shi tapped a knuckle to her forehead. "And when you line a room for me, make sure it has a bath. I'd love a soak before we head out to die."

"We planning on dying on this one?" Atom asked.

"Hopefully not, but either way, I could use a soak." She grinned and followed her nose towards the inn's dining room. The others fell into step with her.

As they drew near the entry to the dining room, Shi stopped and chirped a low whistle that caught Margo's attention. The girl saw the crew and took a step in their direction before glancing to where Atom stood by the front door to the inn.

Atom nodded.

With a grin, Margo scampered off to join the crew, leaving Atom to push the empty pram through the common room in search of the proprietor.

*　　　*　　　*

Toks followed no ordinary protocol.

Atom jerked awake in his room to the chirping alarm piping through the com-set mounted on the wall beside the luxurious double-bed. With one hand, Atom slapped the noise to silence and with the other, he eased his finger off the trigger of the pistol tucked beneath his pillow.

Beside him, Margo slept on.

"Koze, what's happening?" Atom sat up, moving slow enough to leave Margo in her dreams.

"Searching the network," Kozue replied.

Atom shucked into his clothes and strapped on his gunbelt.

"Public reports are piecemeal, but it appears that Toks has landed a sizeable assault force to strategic points around the capital city and issued orders to local citizenry to lock-down. There are unofficial reports of scattered resistance and several sectors seem to be in open rebellion against this imperial attack."

"My guess is, they know she's exceeding her authority and aren't going to let her push them around." Atom kept his voice low.

"She is in violation of several mandates of imperial writ with her unprovoked incursion into sovereign han territory. The empire doesn't exist without the hans and the hans would destroy themselves without the empire. This won't end well for Toks."

"I imagine she's gambling on this and hoping to disappear to her own private planet during the firestorm she's likely to kick up."

"How does this affect your plans?'

"I'll have to talk to the others, but this might just give us the cover we need to keep our movements hidden from Toks. Ultimately, we need to figure out what this shepherd is we're looking for. That means we need information."

"Do you have a direction for that, or will you rely on Bextiple?"

"That's a good question, I'll reach out to Bex, but I'll see what we can scrounge up locally. What time is it?" Atom yawned as he wandered into the small washroom to splash water on his face.

"It's almost dawn," Kozue replied.

"If Daisy isn't awake, keep an eye on him for me. I don't want any imps sneaking onto the ship again. When you can, let him know what the situation is looking like. We're going to ground, and will likely skip around to stay ahead of whatever Toks has in store. This city is big enough to get lost in."

"It's good you didn't set down in the outer settlements," Kozue laughed.

"I'm glad one of us can keep a sense of humor." Atom slipped out the door and locked the room behind him. "I'm going to see what passes for bitter on this planet."

"I'll alert you as soon as Margo begins to stir."

"Fiver needs her sleep." Atom shook his head as he wandered down the deserted hallway towards the commons and the dining room beyond. "She's growing too fast."

"That she is, love," Kozue said with a wistful air.

For a moment, Atom let his mind dwell on his daughter, on their adventures, on their close calls, on the flight he called their life. Almost a third of her life had been spent on the *One Way Ticket* with her mother nothing more than a memory locked in a voice that spoke into his daughter's ear.

The thoughts weighed on Atom.

He longed for life to return to the past, to the peaceful times on Greenholm. He remembered the peaceful afternoons on his estates. He dredged up the scattered afternoons when he could sneak away from the court and spend time with his family. Despite the violence of his life, Atom managed to keep his family safe and sheltered.

Until the violence followed him home.

"Would I have been better off keeping you with me instead of tucking you and the family away on Greenholm?" Atom asked as he passed the fountain in the common area.

"No," Kozue replied without hesitation. "Statistically speaking, I would have compromised your ability to perform your duties as the Emperor's Fist. I could have helped you, but there would have been times you would have been forced to choose between love and duty.

"You know that," Kozue spoke with a smile in her voice. "And we know what path you would have chosen."

As he drew near the doorway to the cantina, Atom paused. Something tickled at the back of his mind, an instinct. He did not question what tiny detail had slipped past his eye or trickled into the background of his ear.

"Wake the others," he growled as he spun, dropped to a knee, and yanked his rail-pistol in one blurred motion.

Without waiting, Atom punched a line of holes through the stone walls flanking the front entrance, four uniformly spaced holes to each side of the door. Then he darted through the door into the dining room and vaulted over the bar. A terrified server crouched in the corner. Atom waved a calming hand at the young man, flashing a sad smile as he did so.

"Hither is on Go," Atom reloaded as he spoke, his fingers flying with practiced automation.

He pulled his second pistol and rose from behind the bar just as several armored troopers ducked through the front entrance. They moved with the practiced elegance of a long-standing assault squad.

Atom anticipated their cautious approach.

Ducking around the end of the bar, he darted across the dining room, firing as he shifted his position. His shots failed to take any of the assaulting troopers down, but the effect of the fire forced them to duck back into cover and drew more of the squad in from the tunnel outside the inn.

Atom skidded on his knees, knocking low stools out of his way with the move, and used his shoulder to flip a heavy, stone-topped table on its side. Leaning around the makeshift cover, he ripped off a few more shots.

From the common area, several troopers darted into the cantina.

Atom dropped one of them as the other two flipped tables to provide their own cover.

Leaning against the back of the table, Atom closed his eyes as a mixture of energy bolt and ballistic rounds gouged craters in the tabletop. He topped off both guns. Without looking, he squeezed off a couple rounds from opposite ends of the table in the enemy's direction.

Atom waited.

"Drop your weapons," one of the soldiers called out.

Atom listened to scuffing footsteps as more imps slunk into the room to try and flank his fortress of solitude.

He kept his eyes shut and took a steadying breath. Focusing on his hearing, he slipped a low shot around the side of the table. A cry rewarded his efforts. Sitting cross-legged with his back to the table, he rested his fists on his knees with his guns draped across his shins with a casual grace.

"Now why would I want to do that?" Atom asked.

"We have you surrounded. There's no way you shoot your way through all of us."

"You'll just kill me if I come out."

"We aren't looking to kill people. Our orders are to make sure people are staying locked down," the soldier spoke with a calm, measured air Atom recognized from numberless training sessions. "You lay down your weapons and come with us. The worst you have to look forward to is getting thrown in the brig."

"I'm fine right here, thank you." Atom grinned. He listened to the rustle of the enemy shifting their positions. "I've already killed a few of you. I'm not exactly prisoner material."

The soldier switched tacks. "You have any kids?" he asked. "I've a couple shin-kickers back home. If I were in your position, I'm pretty sure they'd want me to do everything I could to make it home to them."

"Then maybe you should leave while you still can."

The soldier paused, taken aback by Atom's brashness.

"Do I look like I have any kids?" Atom continued.

"You could have kids," the soldier continued, an edge creeping into his voice.

Atom's grin darkened.

"Yeah, that's me, full-time dad, heading for the bar before the sun is even up."

The soldier fell silent.

"It'd make my day if you just up and left me to my own worries," Atom said with an exaggerated sigh. "I could use a touch to take the edge off."

Atom heard the whispered murmurs of a conference taking place.

"Maybe it's time you walk away and save us all a verse of trouble." Atom thumbed the hammers back on his rail-pistol and then eased it back with a click of a spinning cylinder. Like a nervous tick he repeated the procedure several times. "Fact is, I'd like a drink more than a few more winks of sleep."

"No can do," the soldier called out.

"I'm sorry," Atom replied. His eyes drifted open and he lifted his pistols to his chest.

"What for?"

"That you had to die."

Atom sensed the hesitation in all the soldiers. According to his senses, six squad soldiers had fanned out through the room and another four had taken up reserve positions in the common room. Six members of the squad had fallen, four in the outer hallway and two in the cantina.

A nervous laugh broke out from the imps.

"You think you're going to take all of us out?"

"Nope, I don't have to." Atom fully cocked his pistols.

Atom heard a light skittering dance around the sound of laughter.

"Dada?" Margo's voice cut through the growing tension. "Where you, dada?"

Atom froze. He heard the sharp hiss of breath from his enemies. Arching his back, he peeked over the top of the table to see Margo wandering through the common room.

All attention flew to the girl.

"Dada?" she sang. "Where you, Dada?"

She stopped at the fountain, oblivious to the soldiers pressed to the wall across the room. She climbed up to lean on the edge with her bare feet kicking the empty space behind her. With a squirm, she worked one of her arms out far enough to splash her fingertips in the water. Margo hummed as her fingers danced through the fountain's ripples.

After a few moments, she hopped down and continued on her quest for her father. She wiped her wet hand on her coveralls.

The imperials remained frozen, their attention locked on Margo.

"Hi." She smiled at the soldiers crouched against the wall. "You see Dada?"

"Um, Sarge," one of the troopers whispered into her com. "What are we supposed to do with this? Do you think she's bound to the guy in there?"

The soldiers hesitated, caught between Atom's guns and Margo's innocence.

"Get her out of here," the commander hissed from the far corner of the dining room. "I don't want any dead kits on my watch."

Atom waited, neck craned, as he observed the drama unfold.

As she passed into the dining room, Margo waved at the troopers. Before she could make much headway, an older girl emerged from the hallway that led to the guest rooms.

Atom's breath hitched as he caught sight of his middle daughter dressed in one of his shirts that hung down to her knees. His eyes widened, caught somewhere between fear and amazement.

"There you are, Go." The girl stumbled to a halt when she caught sight of the armed soldiers and the playful smile fell from her face like a mask dropping to the floor. She stood like a prey animal, afraid any movement might trigger the hunter response of the carnivore staring her down.

A tremor ran through the girl's skinny arms as she stared at the four rifles not quite aimed at her, but close enough to preach harm.

"How old are you, girl?" the same soldier asked. "Is this your sister?"

The girl's mouth moved in silence as her eyes screamed.

"No harm, girl," the female soldier rose and slung her rifle.

Across the dining room, Atom watched in amazement. A few of the soldiers kept their rifles trained in his direction, but most attention gravitated to the pair of girls standing on opposite sides of the common room.

The woman held out her hand. "We need to get you clear of this situation," she said with a warm, disarming smile as she flipped up her visor. "What's your name?"

"Lilly," the girl squeaked. "I'm eight."

"Alright, Lilly." The woman shifted forward, careful to keep out of Atom's line of sight. "Let's you and I get your little sister out of here before someone gets hurt."

"Yeah, I think that would be a good idea." Lilly brushed her dark, shoulder length hair back from her eyes as she shuffled towards the soldier. "We were just looking for our da. He slipped out to find some breakfast and I thought we would catch up and eat with him."

As the soldier drew near, Lilly lifted her wide, chocolate brown eyes and smiled with nervous relief.

The woman glanced over her shoulder, making sure to keep clear of the doorway. As she turned back, Lilly's condensed mass focused into a lower leg kick that crumpled the soldier into a writhing heap.

The woman screamed. Her hands waffled between dragging herself away from Lilly and trying to protect her damaged leg.

Lilly, in her scrawny, eight-year-old form, pulled a blaster from behind her back and began to rain a deluge of fire on the unsuspecting soldiers. She darted to the side, making for the cover of the fountain, and crouched.

In the cantina, Atom rose like Triton from beneath the waves. His guns swept the room, searching for targets.

None of the imps moved.

Atom stood waiting.

An unearthly calm filled the room, only to be broken by Margo as she trotted toward her father with an amused expression. "There's Dada," she crowed, grinning as she reached out for him.

With guns trained, Atom waited for the soldiers to make a move.

No movement came.

In the other room, Lilly ventured a glance over the lip of the fountain and called out in her juvenile voice, "You ok in there?"

"Not yet." Atom slipped from behind his defensive table and positioned himself between Margo and his enemies. "How you look out there?" He drifted, one slow step at a time as he shifted to take a new angle for a shot.

"All down, one alive."

Atom crouched and snapped a shot that caught one of the imps in the side. The man flopped sideways in an unnatural slump. Guiding Margo with his bulk, Atom shifted his aim. He let his pistols drift back and forth between the hunkered enemies, but no return shots met his ears.

A movement caught his attention. Atom's rail-pistol leaped to track the motion.

"Easy," Kozue said before Atom could squeeze the trigger.

He looked closer and found Cody crawling from the shadowed corner of the ceiling.

"Should be clear, Atom," Hither called out from across the common room. "Byron let a couple of his pets off their leash."

Atom looked over the fresh corpses huddled behind their makeshift bulwarks and holstered his guns. Dropping his eyes, he scooped Margo into his arms and snuggled her close. With a contented sigh, she squeezed her arms around his neck and nuzzled with his shoulder.

"We need to move," he said before kissing the top of Margo's head, savoring the scent of innocence that clung to her downy hair. "We don't have much in the way of time."

Atom carried Margo over to the bar and leaned over to find the cowering tender.

"I know you probably get this from time to time," he said with a nod to the chaos of the dining room. He fished in the pocket of his coat to pull a chit and keyed in a couple hundred ko. "Hopefully, this will help with the cleanup, and feel free to keep some as hazard pay for being on the line."

Atom turned and left the speechless young man. The others stood around the fountain, looking with amusement at Lilly's current state.

"Reckin she could be yers?" Shi asked, tilting her head to study Lilly.

"She does look a lot like Clair," Hither chipped in. "If I didn't know better, I'd swear she was your daughter. Although, it's been several years since I laid eyes on your actual daughter."

"Enough," Atom snapped. "We don't have time for this."

"Sir," Byron snapped a smart salute. "Permission to date your daughter, sir."

Lilly punched Byron in the arm hard enough to leave the boy rubbing his shoulder. "Where's your accent, street-rat?" she demanded.

"Just tryin' ta be respectable," he grumbled in reply.

Atom locked the pair with a glare. He peeled Margo off his neck, depositing her in the pram, and took the controls from Hither. Without a backward glance, he moved.

"Koze, link me up with Bex." He exited the stone-clad inn and turned away from the *One Way Ticket*. Walking with unforced purpose, Atom led the crew in a subterranean path that carried them along the ridge.

A few minutes later, Bextiple responded through Kozue's com.

"Sorry for the wait, boss," he sounded harried. "Things've certainly gone sideways since you slipped in. I've a dozen ships on my slip and half of them are wanting me to do something special to hide them from the imps.

"On that flow, what can I do for you?" he asked with a weary sigh.

"Nothing too serious." Atom watched as frightened citizens scurried through the stone warrens like rabbits with a stoat in the tunnels. "I'm going to let the *Ticket* rest. There's nothing aboard that should cause alarm."

"Except that interceptor you've tucked away at the front of your hold."

"It's not mine. Paperwork shows I'm just transporting it for a client. I don't even have access to the interior."

The broker paused. "That checks with your manifest," he said after a distracted moment.

"The truth always does."

"What are you asking of me?"

"I need you to put me in touch with some information."

Atom led the group into a narrow side-tunnel and ducked into a small shop. The crew spread out, perusing the wares being offered. At the back of the long, thin cubby, a woman smoking a water-pipe glanced up at them and then returned her attention to the digital game holoed in the air above her counter.

"What sort of info are you in the market for?" Bextiple asked.

Atom hesitated. "Old references." He searched for the right words. "I came across a note on a scavers map that referenced a rich haul. I think it was talking about a mining vein, but I can't be sure.

"I figured an old timer might be able to point me in the right direction," Atom said as he rocked the pram back and forth by the front door.

"If you're looking for a mine, you're in the wrong place. Mines around here are all local source. Our main export is scrap from the new moon. That and ...." he coughed. "Discretion."

"Maybe it was referring to something else." Atom shrugged.

"I'll see what I can scrape. I'm a touch busy at the moment, but I can reach out to a few info-brokers and hope they can point you in the right direction. What's the info you're trying to track?" Bextiple asked.

"Nothing too specific. Just an old reference to Shepherd and a shelf," Atom ventured.

"Nothing hops out of my pan," Bextiple said after a thoughtful pause. "But I'll reach out to a couple associates. If they can't put you in touch with someone, there's no connection."

"Thanks," Atom said and cut coms.

*   *   *

The crew wandered for the better part of an hour, flowing with the natural traffic of fearful citizens, and dodging the scattered imperial patrols. Several times a patrol forced them to change directions, but in the end they found themselves moving through one of the main entrances at the base of the ridge.

"Wonder why they 'ave 'em tunnels if'n they don' really need 'em?" Byron asked as they passed through a heavy set of doors into the hot, humid air beyond.

"It's cooler," Hither said as her wavy auburn hair began to pull into ringlets in the humid air.

Atom hid a smile behind a cough. "Probably to tuck the contra." Atom slowed their steps as he caught sight of a patrol rounding up citizens at a bottleneck ahead. "I imagine it's easier to keep things tucked away out of sight inside the earth."

"They worry 'bout pryin' ocs out 'ere too?" Byron stared at the imps and started to unsling his pack.

"No soul likes a meddlin' gov." Shi sidled wide as they drifted towards the imperial patrol, caught in the slow tide of traffic.

Hither caught Byron by the shoulder and slowed them, allowing several people to fill the gap. In a matter of seconds, their group had dispersed, leaving Atom alone with his two daughters to wander into the enemy checkpoint.

Shots rang out.

Chaos broke the dam.

Atom triggered the cover on the pram and yanked Lilly to his side as he fought against the surging tide of humanity. With relative ease, he lifted Lilly and used the pram as an ice-breaker to forge his way to the side of the street. There he found refuge in a courtyard surrounded by a waist-high wall.

Crouching down, Atom deposited Lilly and watched as the street vacated like a part of a street-magician's act.

The smatter of shots died down.

The imperials turned away from the heap of bodies they left tangled against the wall. Without wasting any time admiring their bloody work, the soldiers fanned out into the now empty street.

"We have just received orders," the soldier's voice echoed through the still street, amplified by his light power-armor. "This city is in complete lockdown until further notice. You must stay wherever you are and are not permitted to return to your homes. We are looking for a specific fugitive. Our intel assures us that he has landed on this planet within the past cycle.

"His name is Atom Ulvan." The imp projected a holo-shot of Atom above the street. "He is a fugitive of the empire …."

"Well, seems you're getting a little big for your loons," Lilly said with a knowing chuckle. "Bet you wish you could change your face right about now. Although, I don't see how that would help lift the damper on the finding out info."

"These people have no love for the empire." Atom pulled his pistols.

Before he could take any action, a fusillade ripped from the rooftops on both sides, turning the roadway into a kill-box. Atom kept pressed to the stone block wall, and ventured a peek over. The fire cut down most of the imps with the first barrage, but a few managed to scurry for cover. Only the captain, in his power-armor, stood his ground in the middle of the road and returned fire.

Atom took aim as the man squeezed careful bursts at the rooftops.

A single shot blended into the cacophony of blaster and small-arms fire. The captain dropped, a single round punched through his faceplate.

"I see it now," Lilly said as the guns fell silent.

Atom holstered his pistols. "Now we just need to figure out how to stay out of sight until Bex finds us what we need."

"Think it will take long?"

"Longer with everything in lockdown. I assume they meant the planet was locked down as well. I can't imagine them letting ships move up and down the well."

"How will they enforce it with their limited troops?" Lilly rose and smoothed out the shirt she had converted into a dress for her miniscule frame. "Roaming squads with kill orders? Maybe a drone overwatch?"

Propping his arms across his knees, Atom leaned back against the wall and let his mind dash through possibilities and courses of action. As he proceeded, he tapped the pram open. Margo sat with a placid expression. She yawned. Then, with a smile, she clambered from the pram to stand in front of Lilly.

"Clair?" Margo held her hands up to Lilly. "There you be."

Atom pulled his mind back to watch the exchange.

"Be careful," he said after a momentary hesitation. "Please don't play with her mind like that."

The smile drifted from Lilly's face. "I understand." She hugged Margo and then nudged the toddler towards Atom. "I'll go change. It'll only take a minute or so. I'm sorry if I made things harder for her."

A tight smile pulled at Atom's lips as he wrapped Margo in his arms.

Lilly pulled a small bundle from beneath the pram and padded towards a narrow alley flanking their courtyard.

"Atom, what's our move?" Shi commed from across the street.

"Give me a span." Atom rose and dropped Margo back in the pram. "We need to keep moving and find some place to hunker."

"Let's hope we don't cross no more patrols."

"You don't think we could handle them?"

Shi laughed. "I ain't said that, but it'd give away our trail."

"I'm not sure how much of a problem that will be. Seems the locals don't like the imps any more than we do. We're just waiting on Lilly to slip back into her normal form before we head out. Any direction is as good as the other until we get a location from Bex."

A moment later, Lilly trotted around the corner, in her customary coveralls with Atom's shirt slung over her shoulder. She strapped her gunbelt about her waist as she joined him.

Just as she opened her mouth to speak, Kozue interjected.

"Atom," she said. "Bextiple has just contacted us."

"Patch him." Atom pushed the pram out into the center of the deserted street, just as the ambushers emerged from their rooftop positions.

"I've found an old-timer who might have a piece of that information you were looking for," the broker said without preamble. "I'm stretched a might thin trying to keep all my clients safe and satisfied at the moment."

"I understand," Atom replied.

"I'll send you his location, but I don't have the manpower to set you up with a guide."

"That won't be a problem."

"Even with the imps locking the city down?"

Atom grinned. "It'll just make things more fun for my crew."

"I wish I had your people on my roster."

"I'll let them know. Perhaps when this is over, they might care to work for you if you make the offer sweet enough."

"I'll keep that in mind," Bextiple said with a laugh. "Patching the info through now."

"Much appreciated." Atom waited for the rest of the crew to join him as he stood and watched the ad hoc militia strip the imperials with scavenger efficiency. Several of the locals glanced in the direction of Atom and the company, but seeing nothing beyond fellow outliers, they continued with their work and disappeared into the rich, red later morning sunlight.

"We should probably follow their lead." Hither glanced up to the sky. "I'm guessing we'll have company sooner than later."

"And we have a location," Atom said as he pushed the pram away.

*   *   *

Several hours, several detours, and more than a couple glancing firefights carried the group across the basin of the city proper. They snatched a late noodle meal on the fly. Most of the city maintained a semblance of operation, but the scattered people on the streets avoided the patrols like furtive rats.

"I en't seein' why we couldn't find proper transport," Byron griped as he hitched his pack up on his weary shoulders. "I'm just sayin' fings is runnin' in spite a this lockdown."

Atom brought the group to a halt outside a broad, stone structure. "Simple," he said. "Imps will have an easier time tracking a vehicle than they would a group like us. Plus, a transport makes it look like we have places to be instead of being a family that is just trying to get home. There are plenty of folks that got caught on the wrong side of town when this all went down."

"Too bad we couldn't help out more than we did," Shi chimed in.

"You hate the imps that much?" Lilly asked.

"Not so much." Shi grinned. "I just like a good scrap."

"Enough." Atom kicked up the pram to float up the wide stairs leading to the front entrance of the building. "The fighting has served its purpose. The imps are bogged down looking for us and the locals don't like being pushed around. As long as we keep our heads down, we should come out of this ahead."

"You have a plan for getting off this rock?" Lilly asked. "I don't see any ships going up or down at the moment."

"I have a couple ideas, but nothing solid yet," Atom replied as they reached the top of the steps. "None of them matter if we can't figure out where we're going first. If we can't find reasonable intel, then we might as well just sit this one out and wait for Toks to get a recall."

"Recall?"

Shi turned to look back down the steps, scanning the neighborhood for any sign of imperial troops. Seeing no sign of the enemy, she turned to Lilly and said, "Locals must've winged a com relay with an official complaint."

"Everyone knows Toks is out of line," Atom said. "Even though Stillwater is outside the normal travel lanes, they're still part of the empire. Toks can't come tear it up without cause.

"She's gambling," Atom continued, looking to Shi to ensure they hadn't been followed. She gave a clearing nod and he pushed the pram towards the front door. "She's hoping she can land this treasure we're all after before any sort of relief force can be deployed. Then she'll disappear and leave her troops standing here with their pants down."

"How do you know that?" Lilly asked.

Atom paused. "I don't. I'm just theorizing," he said with a shrug. "I can't see any other play making much sense at this moment."

"You don't think she'll take this force with her and disappear down the Fingers?" Hither asked. "They could always find the treasure and retreat to some low-planet to live out their days."

"It's possible, but what's the point of treasure if you have to hide the rest of your life?"

"You're alive," Hither said as she opened the door.

Atom maneuvered the pram through the wide double doors into the broad foyer beyond. He looked over the fine, yet simple, craftsmanship of the large room as he crossed the polished stone floor to where a young woman sat behind a heavy wooden counter.

She looked nervous.

"Afternoon, Miss." Atom smiled as he settled the pram beside the counter, allowing Margo to stand up and lean next to him. The others drifted to a waiting area beside the door and settled. "It's not looking too pleasant out there."

"Say that again," the woman said with a tentative smile. "We haven't received any official word about what's happening, but I've heard explosions and gunfire all afternoon. Imps say we're in lockdown, but I haven't heard anything from the local governor. Lucky for us, they haven't bothered storming our doors.

"I say, better off leaving us be." She rose from her seat and looked down at Atom. Slender of waist and thick through the shoulders, the woman caused Atom to subconsciously lean back. "Granted, we've just a bunch of old gaffers and gams sitting around here, living out their lives. There's not much reason for the imps to be bothering us in the first place.

"Hopefully, they'll just move along," she said with a weary smile. Speak of which." The smile faded, replaced by a suspicious look. "What brings you here?"

"I'm just tracking down a couple old stories," Atom said, once again leaning on the counter. "Just dropped the well last eve."

"You certainly picked a righteous time to drop in."

Atom shook his head in agreement. "That I did, but my broker, Bextiple, said there might be a couple old ones who might have some stories up their sleeves that relate to the information I'm in search of."

The woman narrowed her eyes and crossed her arms. "Bextiple?"

"That a problem, Miss?"

"Not necessarily. We just have a history and it's none too pleasant."

"Sorry to hear it."

"Not your concern," the woman snapped. "Who did he send you for?"

"Melvin Cheung."

"Cheung?"

"That's the name Bex gave me. Said he might still have enough faculties to remember the old days from before, and he might actually know what I'm looking for."

"And that would be?"

"Just tracking an old story. Something about a right vein near Shepherd. I'm guessing it's either a mountain or a ridge and Shepherd's just a nickname, because it sure doesn't show on any survey maps. If we could locate the spot, my crew and I had thoughts of buying a plot and staking a claim in the region."

"That a fact?" The woman glared at Atom, then she shifted her eyes to the company lounging behind him. "I don't like folks looking to bother my charges. Asking tales of the glory days likely gets them stirred, and then we have to spend the rest of the shift trying to settle them."

Before she could continue, the front doors slammed open. A soldier stepped through. He dropped. Shi sat unmoved in her chair, a smoking pistol in her hand.

She pulled back the hammer with a sharp clack.

Everyone else hesitated.

Atom broke first, diving headfirst over the heavy wooden counter, he left Kozue to button up the pram. As he dove, he caught the receptionist by surprise and tackled her to the floor.

They landed just in time for a squad of imperial troopers to kick open the double doors.

"Were you expecting company?" Atom asked as he pinned the woman to the floor amidst a hail of bullets and bolts that tore chunks from the wooden desk. "They weren't behind us a minute ago."

The woman stared up at him with wide-eyed terror.

Several more shots rang out from Shi's guns before Atom lifted his head from the woman's shoulder. Draped across her like a shielding blanket, he glanced up and waited for a lull in the firing.

"I don't know why they're here," the woman whispered as she clutched his coat with fear-strengthened hands.

Atom rose to crouch above the woman. He stalled as her hands and bulk held him down.

"I swear, sir." Her voice rose in a panic. "I'd nothing to do with them."

"I know, darl. Imps show up when you want them least, and are never to be found when you could really use some order," he soothed. "Now let me up, so I can see what this is all about."

Out in the wide foyer, more shots rang out. Atom held her clutching hands, pleading eyes locked into her fear. "Please, darl," he whispered.

With reluctance, her clamps released.

He gripped her hand as he frowned and turned his attention away. Rising to the level of the counter, he glanced over just in time to see Hither shepherding Byron and Lilly towards the broad stairs beyond the reception desk. She kept one hand on Byron's pack and fired on the run with the other.

Shi stood tall, her ladies singing as they ripped shot after shot through the front doors. A rhythmic cadence called her siren-song of death.

Atom pulled his own rail pistol as Hither ducked behind the desk. Lilly and Byron sprinted for the stairs as Hither darted around the desk and slipped to the pram, crouching as she scuttled. As Atom punched holes in the walls beside the door, she grabbed the pram and yanked it around behind the safety of the heavy wooden desk.

Glancing over his shoulder, Atom caught the flash of Byron disappearing around the corner of the stairs.

"Shi, fall," he commanded.

An imp poked his head around the corner only to be caught by a careful shot from Hither.

Without hesitation, Shi turned and sprinted for the desk. She dropped to her knees and slid across the marble floor, taking the impact on her shoulder as she spun towards the danger bottlenecked at the double doors.

Shi took a moment to run her guns through the auto-loader at her belt and then popped up to encore her song.

The imperials lulled.

Crouching down, Atom turned to the woman who had pulled herself up to huddle against the desk, holding her head in her hands. "Do you have a safe place you could get to?" he asked, making his voice as calm and reassuring as possible. "A back room or office, perhaps?"

She stared at him, drifting towards shock.

Atom snapped his fingers in her face. "Hey there, you hit?" he demanded.

The woman trembled like a startled fawn. "No," she croaked.

"Good." Atom gripped her shoulders and squeezed. "Is there some place safe you could get to from here?"

The imperials, spread across the front of the building, smashed open windows and resumed their fusillade. Bullets and bolts resumed their regimented pummeling of the wooden desk. Chunks and splinters began cartwheeling over Atom's head as the shots began taking their toll.

The woman nodded. Her nostrils flared wide as her breath came in ragged spurts.

"Breathe normal," Atom soothed as if talking to a scared child. "Slow, deep breaths. I'm going to lead them away from you." He glanced over his shoulder to where Hither hunkered with the pram. "When I do, I want you to wait for them to follow me and then get somewhere safe. I know you can't leave your people, but you need to stay safe as well. You can't help them if you don't survive.

"Don't put up any resistance." He gripped her chin and glared into her eyes. "Don't give them any reason to hurt anyone."

"I'll try," she gasped.

"Good. Where can I find Cheung?"

It took a moment for her head to grasp the question. Then she pointed off to the left. "Third floor. That wing. Stairs here or at the end of the hall."

Atom nodded a thanks and called to the others. "Shi, Hither, stick to Byron and Lilly." Without waiting for a response, he popped like a jackrabbit, bolting for the side door. He caught the pram as he sprinted by and ran before the imps could track his movement.

Halfway across the broad foyer, he swung the pram around and engaged the runners. Hopping aboard, he boosted the suspensors and covered the remainder of the floor on the fly.

The imperials hesitated, caught between two retreating groups.

As he sailed through the door, he tripped his com. "Kozue, tell them all to get to the third floor. Have Shi and Hither delay at each landing. Give the imps something to think about.

"Send Byron and Lilly ahead to find Cheung. I'll meet them there." He hit the far door like a floating torpedo, slamming it open, and screeching to a halt as he flew past the stairs, and had to brake hard to avoid flying out an exterior door.

Hopping off the pram, he backtracked and took the stairs three at a time.

In a matter of seconds he made the third floor. He paused at the landing, giving himself a moment to collect his breath and holster his rail-pistol. Straightening his coat, he pulled the door open and powered the pram through at a leisurely pace.

He stepped into the quiet of the dormitory-like building. Silence hung over the floor like an oppressive blanket of fear.

Atom strode down the hallway with purpose. Fading afternoon light spilled from the rooms on his right, battling with the harsh lights of the hallway. As he walked, Atom scanned the names printed beside each door.

Collins.

Lin.

Weir.

Yuen.

Cheung. Atom stopped outside the door.

At the far end of the hallway, Byron and Lilly reached the top of the central steps and caught sight of Atom. He nodded to the door. From below came the sounds of small-arms fire, shouts, and the occasional scream.

Atom looked through the door as Lilly and Byron trotted down the hall to join him. A low table occupied one side of the room, while bedding had been meticulously folded and set on a shelf in the corner. The only other furniture in the room was a bookshelf, set beneath the window, and overflowing with manuscripts in a dozen languages and piles of loose-leaf notes.

At the table, facing the wall, a wizened man sat, cross-legged with an unread book and neat stack of papers laid out before him. The man turned to stare at Atom, fear overflowing from him as the sounds of combat swirled into the room from down the hall.

"What's our timing, Koze?" Atom asked.

"If the imperials do not receive reinforcements and the girls are smart, you could have over ten minutes before they are forced to retreat to this level ... perhaps more."

"Three minutes," Atom said as he smiled at the old man and held out his hands in a peaceful manner. "We need to be gone by then."

"I'll keep the grains ticking."

Byron and Lilly joined Atom at the door.

"Who are you talking to?" the man asked as Atom stepped into his room and tucked the pram beside the door.

"My ship. Do you mind if I sit? I have some questions you might have the answers to."

"As long as you aren't planning on shooting me." The elder pointed to Atom's pistol.

Atom shook his head. "I've no quarrel with you," he said as he dropped to sit to the man's left. "My name is Atom Ulvan. As time is pressing, I'll come right to it. We are looking for Shepherd. The name was given to us in reference to something of value in this system. I'm sorry I can't be more specific, but that's all that was given on my friend's deathbed."

The man studied Atom. "I'm Cheung."

Wiping a hand across his bald pate, Cheung sat in silence. His thin frame, hunched over the table, told a tale of a hard life that carved people down to their sinews and left no luxurious excess to a body.

His eyes remained sharp.

"What do you want with Shepherd?" Cheung asked, his words clipped and cryptic.

Atom shrugged. "First off, I'd like to know what it is. Secondly, I'd like to know where I can find it."

"It? Ever stop to think it might be a person?" Cheung asked.

Atom exchanged a sharp glance with Lilly.

"I assumed it was a ship, or a town, or maybe even a landmark." Atom fixed Cheung with a curious look. "The story we are chasing is written deep enough in the annals that a name could be an entire han at this point. If Shepherd is relevant, then it must still exist, so a single person wouldn't make any sense."

"You don't have time for indecision," Cheung said, folding his hands on his book.

"Two minutes," Kozue whispered in Atom's ear.

"Would you be kind enough to tell me who, or what, Shepherd is?"

"Why?"

"Why what?" exasperation crept into Atom's voice.

"Why should I tell you? Why not wait for the imperials? If they are pursuing Shepherd as well, then I would assume they are doing so at the behest of the emperor himself."

Atom relaxed. "Have you looked outside?"

As if to make his point, a grenade detonated somewhere down the stairwell. Atom glanced to the door, half expecting troopers to pour through and gun them all down.

"If the imperials were following the will of the emperor, there would be no need for the bloodshed," Atom continued, centering his attention on the sallow man. "They aren't here in any official capacity. This isn't the first system Toks Marshall has walked over to get what she wants. And this is not the first blood she has shed looking for this information."

Cheung continued to study Atom and asked, "Then, do I truly have a choice?"

"There's always a choice. You could pass the information or not. You could choose who to give it to. You could choose to live or die. There are always choices.

"Although, I don't believe the imps have your name at the present time, so there's no reason to believe they are specifically coming here to ask you for anything. I'm guessing a patrol fell in on our trail and followed us to the building. They are most likely checking up on a group breaking the lock-down."

"One minute, Atom," Kozue counted down in his ear. "Hither and Shi have retreated to this floor."

"The time has come for you to make that decision," Atom pressed. "I want to leave before they realize I've been talking to you. I would like to not thrust you into my problems."

Cheung nodded. "Fair enough." He squeezed his hands together, trying to hide the tremor running along his gnarled fingers. "The only Shepherd that comes to mind is one my grampa spoke of. She was his captain. According to the old family stories, she saved his life when their ship went down."

"Captain Shepherd," Atom said to himself, leaning back from the table in realization. "I don't suppose she's still alive?"

With a shake of his head, Cheung frowned at Atom.

"Do you know what ship she captained?"

Cheung grew thoughtful as the seconds ticked by. "I don't recall. Strange, he told stories all the time about his days in the navy, but I don't remember him ever mentioning his ship. He must have, but I can't think of it."

"Kozue, can you access that information?" Atom looked away from Cheung.

"Negative, I don't have any record of a Captain Shepherd that could be tied to these quadrants." She paused. "Thirty seconds."

"What's the connection?" Atom thumped his fist on his leg and glanced at Lilly.

"Does she have a grave or a memorial anywhere around her?" the baug asked.

Cheung perked. "She is buried in the same wall as my grampa." The words gushed from the aged man as his energy escalated. "There might be something there. The burial walls aren't far from here. I could take you."

"That might be the safest course," Lilly said. "That way we don't run the risk of Toks getting her teeth on him. We'd probably be doing him a favor."

"I'll show you," Cheung said with a nervous gulp.

"Atom, you must go now," Kozue insisted. "They are pressing the stairs."

"It's time to go." Atom rose to his feet and pulled his rail-pistol. He extended his other hand to Cheung. "We'll do our best to keep you out of harm's way, but I can't predict what these imps are going to do."

Cheung half clambered to his feet before taking Atom's hand and grunting the rest of the way upright. "Can any of us know what the imps are thinking?" he asked.

"Not now," Atom replied with a grin. "They're off course with this."

The gunfire grew louder.

Stepping around Lilly and Byron, Atom moved to the door and cautioned a look out into the hallway. Behind him, the other three crowded after, moving with hesitancy, as if expecting the hallway to explode in a shower of destruction.

Atom held up a hand to halt them.

He waved them aside and retrieved the pram. Cracking open the cover, Atom smiled down at Margo as she lay curled in her blanket. The girl blinked herself awake and stretched.

Turning back to the hall, Atom watched as Hither and Shi appeared at the landing. As the Valkyrie pair backed up the steps, Hither reached over the balustrade to fire off several blind shots.

Shi drifted to the cover of the hallway corner. Atom could not see her target, but someone must have crossed into her field. Moving without hesitation, she snapped off a single shot. From the depths of the stairwell a cry and clatter of armor echoed. Shi's face remained passive as she slipped back into cover and checked the load on her pistols.

Across the stairwell, Hither caught sight of Atom and slipped away from the action enough to use her hands to indicate four soldiers remained on the stairwell.

The hall lights glared with antiseptic anger, driving back the fading dusk at Atom's feet. With the combination of imperial lockdown and the echoes of gunfire, the floor sat silent. Atom knew that life hid in each room, but no evidence came forth.

"What's the plan?" Lilly whispered in his ear.

Atom looked up and down the hallway. "I'm going to check in with Hither and Shi. I want you and Byron to head to the stairwell at the end of the hall. It's highly unlikely that they left that exit uncovered, but I don't want you to engage. Maybe send Cody down to scout how many are covering our retreat.

"And," he said to Cheung. "I want you to stay here. Stay covered. There's no need to expose yourself. If we don't come back, just hunker down in your room and pretend we just used your room for cover."

"I can do that," the old man said with a nervous gulp.

Atom nodded once and moved down the hall. He advanced with a steady step and cocked his rail-pistol as he approached Hither. Pushing the pram ahead of him, he struck an odd picture. Hither turned as he approached and waved at Margo who had awaked enough to sit with sleepy eyes and watch the world flow by.

Byron and Lilly crept to the far stairwell and as he halted behind Hither, Atom watched them slip through the door.

Atom left the pram beside Hither and stepped out to search the stairwell for movement.

"Have they been coming straight up?" he asked, after a moment observing the still stairs. "If they're following protocol they should be sweeping each floor to verify that we haven't diverted."

"We've been picking them off." Shi stood with her back pressed to the wall on the far side of the stairwell, her arms dangling loose at her sides. "If they was to follow proto, they'd have dropped to the ground by now to wait fer reinforcements."

Atom leaned out over the railing, searching the depths. "You sure there are only four?"

"Unless there are more waiting down in the lobby," Hither said

Atom pondered. He stepped back from the stairs and drifted over to the pram. "Could be a pinning force." He smiled down at Margo as he played with her hair. "We need to move before they can really pin us down. Whether that's straight down the gullet or slipping down the side, I'm not sure."

"Atom," Byron commed from the far end of the hall. "Sent Cody down an' we en't seein' nobody. En't sayin' nuffin' 'bout a body waitin' at ground, but we en't hearin' nuffin' 'ere."

"Hold there," Atom replied. "We're coming to you."

Atom motioned for Hither to follow. "Shi, twenty paces."

The gunslinger flashed a feral grin as she glanced down the stairs.

Atom and Hither moved. Pushing the pram before him he walked like a man on a Sunday stroll. As they approached Cheung's room, the bald man poked his head out the door.

"Care to go for a walk, grandpa?" Atom asked with a pleasant calm.

Cheung glanced behind them and then fell into step and asked, "Are you sure it's safe?'

"Is anything in the Black truly safe?"

"I guess not." Cheung frowned.

When they reached the far end of the hallway, Atom led them through the door. On the far side, Byron crouched in the corner, peering intently down through the metal railing. He started at the clank of the heavy door, but relaxed at the sight of his crewmates.

"Where's Lilly?" Atom asked.

"She's bleedin' nutso, Cap," Byron said as he stood and leaned over to stare down the stairs. "She said she don't full on trust Cod,y so she decided to poke ahead an' make sure the way's clear."

The others crowded onto the landing. As the door swung shut, Shi let out a barrage of pistol fire and sprinted to join them.

"Then we best go join her," Atom snapped.

The group descended the three flights, moving with a balance of caution and speed. At every switchback, Atom expected to find Lilly hunkered down, but the stairwell remained empty.

As they reached the ground floor and ventured outside, Atom began to worry.

"Cap, I took two more down up top," Shi said as she joined the others standing in a small group around a single trooper lying facedown on the pavement. "Jammed the lock mech on the door, but I reckin that'll only buy us a few seconds headstart."

"Looks like they might be spread a little too thin," Hither said as she nudged the solitary soldier with a toe.

Atom nodded. "Two left behind. Shi keep eyes up the stairs and let me know if they are following. Byron, where'd Cody get off to? I need to know where Lilly is headed," he grumbled and stared down the embankment to the street below.

In a buzz of wings, the mechanized dragon flitted from the stairwell and lifted straight up.

"Atom," Kozue said on the general com. "I checked up the stairs and it appears the last of your pursuers have fallen back. I am searching for Lilly as we speak, but am not seeing her."

Byron stood squinting into the evening sky, trying to locate his charge.

"Reckin we count our luck," Shi said as she joined the others on the paved walk.

"We can't wait," Atom snapped. "We need to be off the radar before reinforcements decide to show—"

"Afraid I've got some bad news," Daisy said, cutting across the coms "The *Hellkite* just overrode our controls and took to the sky. Nobody has entered the *Ticket*, so I'm assuming it was Ash who did the overriding. I don't know where she's headed or how she plans to avoid imp detection, but all of the sudden, I can't track her."

"I was afraid of that," Atom said as he looked to Cheung for direction, and then pushed down the grassy slope in the indicated direction. "Bring the *Ticket* online and be ready for anything."

"Firm," Daisy replied.

*　　*　　*

Cheung led them to the grave wall without incident.

Atom expected to find Lilly waiting for them, but when they reached their destination, the graveyard sat empty and silent. Built more like a labyrinth than a traditional burial ground, the dead rested in vertical tombs. Their grave markers lined the walls like flagstones with memorials carved in the surface.

Atom cast one glance around the twilit street before plunging into the regimented maze of fifteen-foot walls of the dead.

Once protected from outside observation by the walls, Cheung lit a lantern from an empty guard shack and took the lead. Holding the lantern high and trailing one hand along a wall, he shuffled along. He squinted at the names and guide signs posted at the silent intersections.

Behind Cheung, in a strung out line, the crew of the *One Way Ticket* wandered in silent reverence.

Atom followed.

As he drifted through the realm of death, he turned over the fleeting occurrences of the day: violence at dawn, a trek through the city, witnessing a firefight, tracked by an imperial squad to a twilight home as the sun began to set, and now a trip through a cemetery.

The day followed the course of a life in itself.

And where had Lilly gotten off to?

Had she been captured?

According to Byron, she had pressed ahead to make sure no imperials blocked their path. She had eliminated their only threat.

Except she had vanished.

Deep down, Atom knew Lilly. He knew she looked out for herself and nobody else. For too long, she had slipped through the travel lanes of the Black by herself. Tragedy followed in her wake, and even though he tried to see her with fresh eyes, Atom knew the course her wires followed that forced the entire galaxy into a box of irrelevancy at the expense of her survival.

They had struck a deal, but at the end of the journey, if she could skate ahead of the competition, Atom knew the chance of her sticking to their deal looked as solid as a ship adrift with a dead power-plant.

A tiny spark of fury glowed in his chest.

As quickly as the ember flared to life, Atom tempered it. He had learned long ago to never fully trust a spook. He had also learned early that decisions made on emotional grounds always ended badly.

"We are here," Cheung said, holding up the lantern before an old stone.

The group gathered around him as he halted before the rather simple memorial. Overhead, the last vestiges of the day slipped away, leaving them in a deep purple gloaming.

Soft lights flickered to life, spaced evenly atop the grave walls.

Atom dragged his attention to the monolith.

The memorial occupied one full vertical column. Where other graves stacked one atop the other, five high, this single grave spanned the entire space. In bas relief, a woman stood depicted as a regal warrior with her hand shading her eyes as she glared into the distance.

Beneath her feet the sculptor had carved an inscription.

The mother of Stillwater
Shepherd led us to our promised land
11,847 souls she saved that fateful day
Even though she lost her Tribune
We gained a home

"What is her Tribune?" Atom asked.

Cheung ran his hands over the words and said, "I think it was her ship."

Atom arched a brow as he knitted pieces of the puzzle in his mind. "Do you happen to know what it means exactly when it says she lost it?" he asked.

"Well," Cheung drew the word out. He scratched his bald pate in thought. "It's in our histories that there was a battle here around a hundred and fifty years ago. If I had to guess, the Tribune was one of the ships lost in the battle."

"That doesn't quite add up."

"How so?"

"If she lost her ship, how did she save all those souls?"

"I'm not sure," said Cheung as he studied the memorial. "My grampa just told stories about how he survived the battle and managed to start a new life here. He had lost more tales than he could remember, but he used to tell us kits snippets of the grand armada and how they were trying to escape something. According to him, they wanted to leave, and the imps wanted them back.

"I don't rightly know where we were planning on going." He shifted his gaze to the stars that had just begun to twinkle over their heads. "There's not much out beyond us. It's blacker than the black between the galaxies."

"Maybe they didn't want you back," Hither said softly. "Could be they aimed to destroy you?"

"I never heard much more than the great battle that covered the skies," Cheung said with a half shrug. "We're still here, so they couldn't have destroyed us too much. Now we're just a planet full of scrap from that battle, but we make most of our money from harboring smugglers, pirates, and scavs. It's easy to make a ship disappear out here among all the scap we pull off Squam."

"The artificial moon?" Atom lifted Margo from the pram and set her down on the ground.

"The same."

"Could the Tribune be there?"

"Not sure. This is a place people come to disappear. We don't keep too many records and our history has always been of the oral type.

"All I can tell, is that I've never come across a ship called Tribune in all my years as a scrapper. Granted, the majority of that moon is just fragments of old ships. The microgravity of all that mass has pulled it into a loose clump of shifting metal. To call it a moon is actually kind of misleading. It's about as stable up there as a sub-spring out on the plains."

"Sub-springs?" Atom rubbed his hands together in the evening chill as he worked over the puzzle.

"Out on the plains you can find watering holes, but more often you'll find a water source buried under the looser dirt. That's where you get the sucking sands. Good way to get yourself buried."

"Buried," Atom repeated, his mind wandering away from the conversation.

"Yeah, if you aren't careful, that waste will suck you down without so much as an 'excuse me'."

"What if the ship is buried?" Atom's eyes lit with the new line of thought.

Cheung frowned in thought. "I doubt even the biggest sub-spring could swallow a whole ship. Maybe a fighter or a small transport, if the sink is big enough, but I doubt there would be enough pull to get an entire ship sub-soil. Maybe down south, in the ocean—"

Atom cut him off. "Did any ships crash?" he asked along his fresh trail.

"During the battle?"

"More like right after."

"Sure," Cheung said as he stared at Atom. "Most of the wrecks that didn't get swallowed by Squam were pulled down the well. You can't walk a day through the plains without catching sight of some stripped out wreck."

"Have they all been scavenged?"

"I would imagine. They were the first wrecks stripped and scrapped. They would be a whole lot easier to get to and safer to handle than the shifting surface of Squam."

"What are you thinking, Atom?" Hither asked as she watched Margo wander about.

"I think we've been looking in the wrong place," Atom replied. "I think there's a good chance what we're looking for is here on the planet and not up in orbit like we assumed."

"So how do we find the Tribune?"

"Simplest solution is most likely." A smile drifted across Atom's face as he worked through ideas. "Melvin, where is the closest wreck site to Stillwater?"

"There are several within ten miles of the city limits, but they've been stripped down to little more than skeletons. They only left the framework because it's never been cost effective to get those massive girders up the well and we haven't run short of the small bits."

"This would probably be the biggest one."

Cheung played with his chin in thought. "I'd have to say the biggest one is west of the city. It punched a crater up atop the plateau where the ridge levels for a couple miles before it jumps up to run the plain all the way to Saffron Springs.

"It's a hike on foot, but if you could find transport it would take a couple hours."

*   *   *

Borrowing the land-speeder had proved nothing more than haggling once Cheung pointed them toward a semi-sympathetic mechanic. To Atom's annoyance, the shop owner would only sell the suspensor driven vehicle instead of just renting it out for a twenty-seven hour day.

"I actually feel bad about droppin' the lub all the way across town from the twilight home." Shi sat in the passenger seat of the speeder, holding Margo in her lap.

With their ranks thinned down, Hither and Byron sprawled in the cargo bed with the pram strapped down between them. They had bought dinner from the mechanic's wife and eaten with the family in the home above the shop. Then, as the planet's first moon rose they had set out, wandering the dimly lit city in a general westerly direction.

"I know," Atom replied. "I would rather have seen him to his room, but I'm guessing the imps will be all over that building looking for revenge. It's better for him to give things time to settle."

"Rekin they'll put him down?"

"It's possible." Atom's knuckles flexed on the yoke as he guided the junker through the narrow streets.

The speeder's power-plant belched and hiccupped, causing a power fluctuation in the suspensors. In the rear, Byron yelped as the suspensors dropped power and the vehicle almost bottomed out on the left side.

"When we get 'ome, I'm tearin' this 'ere kack apart an' buildin' us somefin' 'at won't blow us up," Byron called as he clutched at the sides of the bed. "Speakin' a which, you fink we've a chance a makin' it there in one piece? I mean, way this burper is fartin' us along, I'm 'alf tempted to sit in Go's pram an' race you bokes."

Instead of responding, Atom just laughed. For the first time in weeks, he unleashed his laughter.

At first, the others froze, the sound of Atom's mirth catching them by surprise. Then the land-speeder hiccupped again. This time Atom let out a raunchy raspberry. Margo joined in her father's merriment.

The mood exploded.

Using something so innocuous and juvenile, Atom broke the oppression that had crept over the crew. They all laughed. Each time the engine misfired, they joined in a group raspberry. The infectious laughter spurred a raucous round of side-splitting hilarity that bordered on manic.

"Thank you, By," Atom said when his laughter had subsided enough for him to come up for air. "I needed something to break my mind out of this rut."

Byron continued to giggle.

Shi wiped a tear from her eye. "Sometimes we all just need to cut loose. Hell, if we weren't slippin' imps, I'd let my ladies sing.

"I do miss Daisy a touch," she said, her voice sobering.

"He'll be fine," Hither said from the back. "He's recovering. Wake me up when we get there. Atom, I think your antics put everything in a perspective I haven't seen in a while. We get so wrapped in our business, we forget to laugh."

"That new perspective give you some insight on this gig?" Atom asked.

"Hush, love, I'm sleeping," she murmured. "We'll sort things in the morning."

*   *   *

Once beyond the city limits, Atom found a shallow hollow and settled the land-speeder for the remainder of the night. Wrapped in musty old blankets Byron had scavenged from a utility locker, they slept the sleep of the righteous.

Only when dawn's rosy fingers slipped over the horizon did Atom rise to wakefulness. Margo had nestled against his chest, cocooned in their shared blanket. Atom held her close, smiling at her tiny hand gripping the lapel of his brown coat while she sucked her other thumb.

For a while he sat, motionless, absorbing the image as the soft light of dawn caressed Margo's perfect features.

"Peaceful, ain't it," Shi's husky whisper infiltrated, but did not shatter the moment. "I've a feelin' this here's the calm before the storm. We'll see this little venture over 'fore the sun sets agin."

"You sure on that?"

Shi reached up and stretched. "With all three of us on this planet, someone's bound to figure the puzzle out, right quick."

"But we're the only ones who have a lead on Shepherd's ship."

"You bankin' that Lilly ain't figured it out yet?"

"I doubt she made it to the cemetery and found that marker before we got there." Atom shifted Margo and she murmured in her sleep. "We had the help of someone who knew where it was and it still took us a while to find it. She only had a few minute's head start. It wasn't enough to get what we found."

"Cap, don't you go underestimatin' that woman," Shi's lazy drawl gave Atom pause. "She's got strings to pull you ain't never considered."

Atom frowned.

"And Toks?" Hither asked as she rolled over in the back and propped herself on an elbow as she demurely covered a wide yawn. "What's your estimate on her?"

"She's been fishing."

"And she's got the benny of the high ground," Shi said before clambering from the passenger seat to stretch her legs. The prairie mist swirled about her like a waist deep lake. "If she got an inklin' of the trail we're on, she can scan from orbit and find what we're havin' to use our eyes to locate."

"Then we best get moving," Atom said. "Hither, can you tuck her in the pram?"

He shifted around to unwrap the blanket from his shoulders and warded Margo against the morning chill. Before he passed her back to Hither, he planted a delicate kiss atop her head. Hither slipped from her own blankets and shivered as she completed the transfer. Like a favored aunt, she smiled down at the slumbering child as she buttoned up the pram to keep Margo snuggled.

Atom waited until Hither had settled back into the bed of the transport before he kicked the engine to life. With a cough and cold whine, the suspensors sputtered awake and lifted the vehicle from the ground.

Puttering like an old man, the speeder nosed up out of the hollow, parting the long, tan grass of the broad plain surrounding Stillwater.

"Kozue, do you have an idea of where we are headed?" Atom asked as he picked up speed and began cruising in a westerly direction. "I know Cheung said it was only an hour or so by transport, but we could be headed on the wrong vector."

"Let me see what I can find," she replied and fell silent as the transport groaned onward.

In the distance a low ridge stretched across the horizon. It glowed with a purple sheen in the pale, dawn light. Like a rampart, the bluff dominated any western transport. Seeing no clear passes or indications of upwards paths to the ridge-top, Atom kept the transport in a low gear and glided over the plains, parting grass and mist as they puttered across a rustling sea of lush feedland.

Even over the chugging of the transport, Atom heard the bleating cacophony as a white creep appeared at the edge of his vision.

"That's a sight," Atom exclaimed as he slowed the transport.

"Ain't seen that many woolies since 'fore I left my homeworld," Shi replied.

Atom continued forward and the amorphous blob of sheep oozed towards them like an oil slick atop the sea of grass. Eventually, Atom brought the transport to a halt as the sheep enveloped them.

"Why'd you stop, Cap?" Shi asked.

"I don't want to crush any of them," he replied.

"They'll move."

"But what if they get under the skiff? The suspensors will crush them."

"Why you care so much?" Shi fixed Atom with a puzzled sidelong glance. "I've seen you put men down without a flinch. These beasties are nuthin' but a bunch a dumb woolies."

"Men inherently carry guilt." Atom glared at the sheep. "Sheep may be dumb, but they're just animals and don't warrant being put down, like most people I know." He powered down the transport and they settled to the ground, surrounded by an undulating tide of fluffy, bleating beasts.

Hither and Byron sat up in the back.

"Well, this is new," Hither exclaimed with a fast fading smile. "A new smell."

Byron stared at the sheep, his expression a mixture of interest and revulsion.

"Atom," Kozue sounded puzzled. "I'm not finding any records of a ship out in these parts, at least nothing as close as Cheung would have me believe. There is a record of a small building, a memorial chapel of some sort, in the records, but no ship."

"No ship?" Atom pressed his palms together and pressed his fingers to his lips.

"Perhaps it was dismantled before the latest survey scans were completed?"

"That wouldn't explain the lack of records," Hither said as she climbed to her feet and squinted at the distant shelf.

"Is there anything to indicate a wreck being there at any point?" Atom asked. "Perhaps what we're looking for is buried in the area. It would make sense that if there was a treasure to be had, they offloaded it and hid it in the area."

Kozue hesitated.

"You sain' we're gonna have to dig fer this treasure?" Shi asked.

"If I'd known we's diggin', I would've outfitted them rigs a might diffy." Byron leaned on the back of Atom's seat, thrusting his head up front. "Talkin' which, the rigs're outfitted all wrong. I've 'em upped for low-g."

"Still in the figuring phase, By," Atom replied.

"Byron, could you power Cody up for me?" Kozue asked.

"Firm." Byron dropped back and began rummaging in his pack. A moment later, he produced the little mech-dragon, curled into a loose ball, as if asleep. "What you want wiff 'im?"

"Wake him and toss him up in the air."

Byron looked at the little mech for a moment and then followed the instructions.

Cody woke, calibrated, and leaped into the air on a rush of fluttering wings. For a moment, he hovered over the land-skiff and surrounding sea of sheep before increasing thrust and floating higher into the sky.

Settling back into his seat, Atom closed his eyes. He pinched the bridge of his nose and blew out a deep breath of frustration. "Maybe we should just cut our losses," he said.

"Daisy's down. Lilly has jumped. We don't know where Toks is. And to cap it all, we don't even know if there is a treasure to find.

"Where I thought we would locate the treasure." His eyes drifted open, framed with heavy fatigue as he twisted to look at the other three. "There's not even a ship."

"Are you wanting to give up?" Hither asked, a simple question.

"I don't know." Atom shrugged. "I'm not one to go throwing in the towel, but I've always been able to balance losses against the outcome of any operation and this doesn't have a high probability of success.

"My estimates put our survival rates fairly low. Toks and Lilly are fanatic. That means they won't think twice about putting us down if they think we're between them and this treasure. Lilly hasn't turned on us hard because she didn't have all the information, but also because she knows she has a better chance of surviving Toks with us on her side. She might crawl back.

"Toks on the other hand is a K-bomb. She's already demonstrated her willingness to slag anyone who gets in her way.

"I just can't see any treasure being worth losing any of our lives." Atom fixed each of the others with a meaningful look. "Could you deal without any of the others?"

Shi glanced to Hither and ginned as she said, "I could deal without Daisy's feet."

"I heard that," the pilot growled through the com.

Hither smothered her own smile. "Personally, I don't like giving up before we really know what we risk losing if we don't pursue this," she said with slow thought. "I know you're thinking as the military commander, weighing our lives against the possible outcomes."

"If we knew for certain what we were chasing, would it change the numbers?" Atom asked.

"Statistics?" Shi scrunched her nose in distaste.

"Exactly," Atom said. "Do the numbers balance. Do they support our risk? Do they support our current vector? Because, if they don't there is no reason to press the present course, especially if that course threatens our lives or way of life."

The sheep continued to flow about the settled transport.

"Our way a' life?" Byron asked.

"Reckin we can't have a way of life if we ain't got a life to live." Shi frowned as she shifted in her seat and spun the cylinder on one of her pistols in absent thought.

"Atom," Kozue interjected. "It would appear that the imperials have discovered some sort of trail. They have consolidated their search efforts to an area ahead of us.

"While I am not seeing any evidence of a ship in that area, using Cody's vantage point, I can extrapolate that they are conducting a search in the center of an impact crater. They have established a rudimentary base and have deployed large excavation mechs."

"Crater? How recent?" Atom asked.

"Rough estimates based on spotty erosion and consistent vegetation growth, I would estimate 150 years, give or take a decade."

Atom glanced to the others.

Hither shrugged.

"Where is this crater in relation to the memorial you were telling us about?" he asked. "Are they in proximity?"

"The building is on the ridge overlooking the crater."

Wheels began turning in Atom's mind. "And is there any significance to the placement of the building in relation to the crater?"

"It is on a direct line from the epicenter of the crater."

"On the ridge?"

Kozue hesitated. "Shifting Cody to a higher altitude. By my estimation, the building is on the ridge, just barely. It is almost exactly on the seam where the soil from the impact joins the stone of the ridge.

"After further extrapolation, I believe we have found the landing spot of the Tribune or at least a ship that fits the description of an archaic heavy cruiser."

"And is the ridge you are seeing the same one we are looking at right now?" Atom pointed to the long, low ridge that covered most of the horizon in one continual elevated line without break or upheaval, with the exception of the lump ahead of them. "There isn't a second ridge beyond this that you're looking at?"

"There is only one ridge, Atom," Kozue said with exasperation.

"Does that look like a shelf to any of you?" Atom asked the others.

"You mean like the poem?" Hither asked.

"One and the same." Atom's eyes grew wide as he turned and grinned at her.

"You still spinnin' stats?" Byron stood in the back and squinted at the ridge as the morning light transitioned the cliffs from purple to crimson in subtle waves.

"Koze, how many imps are we looking at?" Atom held up a finger to Byron.

"I count three hundred and seventy-two, but they have erected several pre-fabs, so I would estimate over four hundred."

Atom fixed Byron with a knowing glance.

"And how big is the crater?"

"Touch over fourteen Imperial Units."

Byron flopped in the back, curling into a thoughtful pose as he tapped his fingers against his temples. Atom sat in silence for a moment, studying the lad. Then he turned his gaze to the two women with questions in his eyes.

"What's our path? Forward, back, or sideways?" he asked.

"If we had a K-bomb we could take them all out," Shi said, scowling at the unseen.

Atom settled back into his seat and crossed his arms as he stared out over the tide of sheep, fixating on the distant ridge. He glared in thought, but remained silent.

"It would remove the imp problem," Hither commented.

"Wishful thinking," Atom said without taking his eyes from the future.

"Infiltrate and remove Toks," Hither suggested. "Atom and I slip in and neutralize her threat while the two of you head for the chapel. Or we wait for Shi to lock down the ridge and provide cover fire."

"First off, I ain't brought the firepower to offer you any cover from range." Shi propped her heel on the seat and leaned her chin on her knee. "Second, I don't reckin they'd leave a firing position open with some sort of picket. Honest speakin', I'm surprised we ain't been picked by the imps already. If they's there in the force Koze is registerin', they should have remote scan and probably high-altitude survey to keep a secure perimeter."

Atom started laughing again.

The others looked to him in confusion.

He spread his arms wide. "Sheep," he said with a settled grin.

Shi looked over at him and then out to the flock. Understanding lit her features after a quiet moment.

"That's our in," she said as her smile mirrored Atom's

"So, what's our play?" Hither asked.

"We play the lowly shepherd, and the big eye in the sky will pass us by." Atom nodded to Shi and turned to the others in the back. "You two, head to the back of the flock and find the real shepherds. We need to turn the flow around and skirt the crater. I want to aim for the chapel without looking like we are avoiding the imps, so we can take a wandering route if that'll work."

"Why us, darl?" Byron demanded.

Atom shrugged. "You're non-threatening and she's pretty."

"And I'm probably the most likely to keep you alive in case there is some sort of real danger," Hither said. "Always play to your strengths and kill them when they least expect it."

Byron narrowed his eyes and stared over at Hither. "Yer tellin' me you's willin' to trudge a much, 'cause yer pretty?"

"Does it get us to the treasure ship?"

"Only if it's where we hope it is," said Atom.

"And we can't find that out if we don't get these sheep turned." Hither rose in the bed of the transport and looked over the undulating flock, searching for signs of humanity. "I'll do it because it gives us the best chance for success.

"And Cap's right, I am pretty. Have you looked at these two?" She gestured at Atom and Shi. "If a knuckler catches sight of them, he's either shooting or burning for town. Cap usually can't remember how to smile and I'm not sure Shi ever learned in the first place. Either way, they'd just as soon kill the flockers as get them to help us out."

"I take offense to that," Shi said, flashing her most ferocious smile. "I've been told I've a most beauteous smile."

"Did you have you ladies out when you asked?"

"Course," Shi chuckled.

"Case rests," Hither said with the barest hint of a sneer. "Byron, on me. We need to talk our way through this." Sitting on the edge of the bed, she swung her legs over, nudged some space between sheep and dropped to the ground. The sheep pressed about her in a bleating mass of wool, horns, and heat. "We'll be back as quick as we can get you some cover," she said and waved for Byron to join her.

*   *   *

With the late morning sun beaming down, Atom nursed the misfiring transport at the rear of the massive flock alongside another open-bed transport that ran as smooth as the day it had come off the production line.

A small flock of jet-bikes nipped around the periphery of the sheep, keeping them contained.

As they followed behind the sheep, the other suspensor craft edged closer.

"Why you want to get up to the old chapel?" the sun-crisped elder lounged behind the controls with a broad-brimmed hat pulled low over his roaming eyes. "Ain't nuthin' up that way but range for the flocks."

Atom eyed him, wary. "Meeting someone," he said and turned his eyes back to the flock and the golden sun beating down on the bleating backs. "Suppose to be a job, but I don't know much more than that. I don't like imp sticking their nose in my business any more than the next boke, so I'm trying to give them wide berth."

The man grunted in reply.

"Still not sure why they're even here," Atom said.

"I ain't never seen a shakedown like this," the man agreed. "From time to time, an imp ship'll drop in the system, but usually it's just a captain looking for a little ko to turn a blind eye to the usual goings on.

"Word spreads the system, but I ain't never seen a real imp in my lifetime. Their ships usually just hang in orbit for a day or two and then they head back to the finners."

A distant rumble drew the old man's attention.

"Fertile land, here abouts, but the weather can sure change on a whip," he said as he squinted at the horizon above the ridgeline.

Atom followed his gaze and found a dark line cresting the horizon. For a moment he stared at the line before registering a heavy cloud formation stretching across the edge of the western sky.

"How long do we have?" Atom asked.

"It'll beat us to the ridge, but not by much," the old shepherd grumbled. "We'll get wet, but we'll make it to the high ground before any of the beds cut us off."

"Beds?"

"Riverbeds. They run dry most of the time, but when a big storm rolls, they'll top off and cut off any overland travel until they drain off. It usually only takes a couple days, and if you've found some high ground you've nothing to worry about, but boredom."

"And if you don't find high ground?"

The shepherd shrugged. "They might find your body somewhere across the plain. Or maybe they don't. You know that shallow sea that rough follows the 'quator?" Atom nodded in reply to the old man's question. "The fish will probably nibble you down to nothin' in the shallows."

"Is that crater low ground?" Atom watched the clouds grow taller as they travelled toward the cumulonimbus wall.

"What do they teach you in school these days? Of course it's low ground, son."

"What happens to the crater? It doesn't seem like a riverbed."

"It ain't," the old man said with a sneer. "That ol' crater is where Stillwater gets its name. A bed comes pourin' off the ridge at the Weepin' Sister and it fills up like a cup. It'll start turnin' into a lake about thirty minutes after the rains start. Couple hours after that, the crater will look like a mirror, and that'll last for days after the rains as the waters drains down into the ground.

"It'll serve imps right fer what they done back in the city."

Atom puzzled as they followed the flock towards the rain. As they drew closer, he noticed the grey wall hanging below the clouds like a veil.

"Reckin we kin eliminate the actual impact point as our site?" Shi asked as Atom let the suspensor hauler drift away from the old shepherd's. "Any way 'bout it, we're headed fer the ridge. What are we doin' when we git there, ridin' out the storm or are you thinkin' we might actually be landin' atop what we're aimin' fer?"

"We head for the chapel. At least we'll be out of the wet."

Shi studied Atom for a moment. "What's up yer craw?"

"I don't like letting soldiers die."

"Even if they're tryin' to kill us?"

"It's Toks," Atom snapped. "If she were sitting in that crater by herself, I'd be the first to dump a bucket of water in, but she has the troops down there following her orders and she's probably sitting up on her ship waiting for word. I'll guarantee the soldiers don't know why they're here. She wouldn't be stupid enough to trust anyone else with her plans.

"I'm guessing she is using some sort of patrol protocol to hide what she's actually doing from her subordinates." He glared at the horizon, thumping the yoke with a fist in frustration. "And they're the ones who will pay."

"There ain't much we kin do 'bout that," Shi said in a level tone. "We alert them, we die. We don't, they die. Ain't nuthin' betwixt."

Thunder exploded in the distance. The clouds raced towards them.

"Dada," Margo cried out after the thunder.

Atom glanced over his shoulder to find his daughter staring at him with wild-eyes. Margo had opened the top of the pram from the inside and Atom could see the regret written all over her face.

Shi laughed like an amused parent. "She ain't never heard thunder before?"

Hither glared at the gunslinger as she reached over and pulled Margo from the pram.

"Poor bean," the ex-courtesan cooed as she curled the girl into her lap.

"You've an interesting kit." Shi shook her head and glanced up to the onrushing stormfront. "She can take a life without battin' an eye, but she goes half-wonked at the sound a rollin' thunder."

With blue skies behind them, the first fat raindrops splattered and steamed off the power-plant cowling. The sheep ahead bleated with nervous tension.

Margo fought Hither until she managed to squirm free. Just as the next peel of thunder shook them, the girl clambered into Atom's lap and pulled his coat over her head. Atom kept a hand on the yoke, but wrapped his other arm about his daughter.

He remained silent. Knitting his brow and bowing his head, he plunged them into the oncoming storm.

*   *   *

The outer rim of the crater provided the only natural ramps up the shelf within a dozen miles, and the shepherds deftly kept the sheep on the outer edge of that ramp as they climbed. They remained out of sight of the main imperial perimeter. At the base of the impact crater, an imperial patrol stopped to watch the roiling tide of sheep trudge up the mud-slick slope, but soon lost interest and returned to their sodden wanderings.

By the time the flock reached the top of the ridge, Atom knew some concern had seeped into the imperial base at the bottom of the crater

"Too late fer them poor bokes," the shepherd said as he pulled alongside and idled down to stare into the deep gouge. "They would've had to start pulling out before the rains hit to make the rim in time. There's a reason nobody ever did anything with the crater but scavving. It gives some nice shelter when the wind blows along the ridge, but it ain't no safety from the rains."

The two transports idled on the upper lip of the massive crater, miles from the epicenter. Below them, a rain shadowed patrol slipped and slid down the steep decline, making for their rude base.

Through the trailing curtains of rain, Atom could see wide pools starting to form in the basin.

"How far to that chapel?" Atom turned his back on the crater.

"Fifteen ticks, give or take." The shepherd throttled up his own suspensor truck and pulled in a slow arc, adjusting his wide-brimmed hat to keep the rain off his face. "We're taking the flock back to the ranch. You're welcome to join us until the rain passes. I'm not sure how much flying people will be doing in this weather, so you might have some clear skies on your hands if you head on up to the chapel."

"We'll take our shelter at the chapel," Atom replied as he wiped the rain from his eyes and scowled into the grey shrouded distance. "I wouldn't want to miss that contact, and with the imps so close, I don't want to miss that window."

"Suit yourself. If you change your mind, the ranch is about five miles west. Follow the shelf and you can't miss it."

Atom nodded a thanks and eased their hauler away into the darkness.

The rain-soaked mile to the small stone chapel only took a few minutes once they homed in on Cody's location. Despite the coming darkness, Kozue guided them by the most direct route.

As they approached the chapel, Atom slowed the open vehicle and circled around behind the edifice to power down out of sight of the crater.

"You know we don't have visual from the crater," Shi said as she clambered from the transport and shook her poncho to rid the pooling water. "According to Kozue, we don't even have to worry about an outpost anymore."

"Looks that way." Atom handed Margo off to Shi.

The gunslinger tucked Margo up under her poncho, shielding the girl from the worst of the rain. Propping her on a hip, Shi advanced on the stone structure.

"This place is bigger than it looks from the valley," Shi said. She squinted up into the rain, trying to pick out the top of the slate roofed building. Heavy stone blocks, hewn from the shelf on which it sat, gave the chapel more an air of a slit windowed fortress than any kind of memorial.

A single light flickered over the door.

"Too bad it en't big 'nough to hide what we're lookin' fer," Byron called out as he darted past them up the several, broad steps to a sheltered back door. Without waiting for the others, he pushed open the heavy metal door and disappeared into the unlit interior of the chapel.

"Hither, catch up with him," Atom commanded. "I'll be right behind with the pram."

As the women disappeared, Atom climbed to his feet and stepped over into the bed of the transport. He had long given up any semblance of being dry. He shook the water from his eyes as he kicked up the power on the pram. Glancing around the sodden landscape, he listened from anything beyond the hiss of rain on the long grass.

Fighting through the torrents, he followed the others into the chapel.

For all the diversions and byways, the hunt had driven them along, being this close to the goal seemed anticlimactic to Atom. Something seemed off. More than the sudden disappearance of Lilly, more than the flotilla orbiting above, something in the stillness of the downpour tripped a warning in the back of his mind.

As he powered the pram up the few steps, he paused.

Standing just out of the rain, he turned and surveyed the expanse of grassland. A primal part of his brain expected soldiers to rise from the grass and open fire.

All remained silent.

He opened the door and stepped into a different sort of silence.

The interior of the memorial centered on a wide, circular chamber lit from above by a faux-flame chandelier of a rough, frontier style. Set around the chamber, several steps inward from the walls, sat a series of free-standing bas relief sculptures depicting a space battle.

Atom stepped through one of the openings into the center, and found his crew standing together, arms crossed as they glared at Lilly. The baug grinned when she caught sight of Atom. Only Margo seemed impervious to the tense nature of the situation as she wandered around the room, trailing a small hand over the smooth carvings that summed the history of the planet.

"Nice to see you again," Atom said without smiling.

As he spoke, a shadow shifted on the far side of the stone circle.

Atom tracked the movement. "Afternoon, Ash," Atom called out. "It's a nice day to be inside."

The Golem hesitated and seemed to study Atom for a brief moment from above the carved stone. Atom watched the passive surveillance of the towering mech and knew that in a moment, his entire world could vanish in a vapor cloud.

"How's this play?" Atom kept his hand out and away from either of his pistols.

"Treasure for all," Lilly replied with a pleasant smile.

"Why the duck out?" Shi demanded.

"Can't knock a girl for trying?" Lilly shrugged. "A one-way split is a lot more profitable than the previous agreement. It's not like I tried to kill you.

"I mean." She sauntered over to Atom. "What I really did was closer to scouting things out than anything else. I managed to find this place without any help from you … and I got my ship out here without the imps spotting it."

"What you're telling me is that you're ready to run," Atom said as he watched her.

"Lifetime of self-preservation can be hard to overcome."

"You planning on running again?"

"Can't promise anything, but I'll do my best to stick it out."

Atom looked over to the group. Reading them as a whole, he registered their distrust.

Then, he looked to where Margo had stopped at the stone that hid Ash and peeked around the monument to look up at the Golem. She stood still, studying the hulking mech. Without a sense of danger, she stepped out around the stone and tilted her head back as she stared almost straight up at Ash.

"It's you," she declared.

Ash shifted out from behind the stone, his steps almost shy.

"Dada, it's a metal man," she said as she turned from Ash to grin at her father. "Him's huge."

"Trust is hard to earn," Atom said. "But you have my daughter's, so you have mine."

"And them?" Lilly looked to the crew.

"Don't give them a reason to not trust you. You're mighty thin with the running, but they'll probably give you some leeway until you give them a reason to put you down. You three aboard for the moment?"

They hesitated.

"S'pose," Shi grunted. "But I don't like gittin' crossed."

"Same," Hither said, her face unreadable.

Only Byron remained quiet, but he nodded after a moment.

Atom glanced back to Margo. She had turned her attention back to the armored giant and with a giddy grin, she reached up and touched the Golem's hand.

"She's fine," Atom sighed and turned his attention to their surroundings. "Have you made any progress on figuring this puzzle out? The clues all point to this location, but I'm not seeing anything that looks like a ship around here."

"Say that agin." Shi stepped to the middle of the room and spun in a slow circle to survey everything. "Pics of a battle, but nuthin' like what I seen."

"Yeah, it's just a memorial." Lilly crossed her arms in frustration as she stalked over to one of the carvings and pointed to the biggest ship. "Near as I can tell, this is the prelude to the battle. It looks like there was an armada surrounding this ship. There's nothing here that would indicate whose ship it was or why they were on their way out beyond the Black, but that's where they were headed.

"And here." She moved on to the next bas relief. "They made it to the system, but as they did so, this other group caught up with them.

"Battle." She turned, pointing from one carving to the next. "Death and destruction.

"And then," Lilly said as she came to a stop before the final pair, a hand pointing to each of them. "Battle's over. This ship picks up survivors and then crashes. I'm guessing they had crash-couches back whenever these were carved, because we have people emerging from the crater to discover a new land."

"Sounds like a more detailed version of what Cheung told us," Hither said from the far side of the circle.

"Yeah," Shi chimed in. "But it don't give us a step to take."

Atom stood next to her in the center of the circle, fingers tapping at his rail-pistol and a scowl on his face as he, too, rotated, taking in each panel. As he turned, he mumbled to himself.

"What are you yippin' about?" Shi asked.

"Just the poem. It's the only real clue we have in all this. The other three parts were coords."

"Reckin there's more?"

"That, or we missed something," Atom's eyes darted back and forth as they scanned the carvings. "Kozue, are you detecting anything that would stand out under scan?"

Cody poked his head up from Byron's satchel. The winged lizard took the serpentine route up to the boy's shoulder.

"I detect no anomalies within the sculptures," Kozue said as Cody pivoted his head with the grace of a snake. "Categorizing the images appears to depict exactly what Lilly described. However, I can find no correlating battle within the imperial records. My assumption is that whoever attacked this group was completely destroyed.

"I don't understand why there would be no record of a fleet this size in the annals—"

"Wait," Lilly interrupted, peering intently at the floor. "There's something under the floor."

"She is correct," Kozue sounded impressed. "There is a heavy metal layer beneath these stones. It is almost completely concealed by the composition of the stones themselves, but I can just detect the even atomic make-up of plasteel. It's an older alloy, but it is not a natural formation."

The dragon hopped into the air and glided up into the gloom. Taking a slow circle under Kozue's guidance, he examined the stone circle from inside and out. After a couple circuits, he landed atop the last tablet in the cycle.

"There appears to be a transmitter buried in this stone," Kozue said. "I can detect the EM pulses, but the creators have done a masterful job of spreading the current out through the whole stone. I believe whatever trigger of locking mechanism you are searching for lies within this stone, but I'm afraid I can't be of more help than that."

Everyone congregated on the single ten-foot section of the bas relief. They began running their hands over the protruding sculptures. Even Margo joined in, rubbing playful circles on the lower portion.

"Nuffin," Byron said in disgust several minutes later. "It's as smoove as the day is round."

"Truth, I ain't findin' nothin' either," Shi said as she stepped back with a glare.

Atom paused. He ran words in his head. "The only thing we haven't covered is the last two lines of the poem. 'The man takes solace turned into himself and Then buried her beside him, asleep on a shelf.' Do either of those lines match up with what we're looking at?"

The others stepped back and let their eyes do the searching.

"Maybe we need a key," Lilly said.

"There wasn't any reference to a key anywhere in anything we've been told," Atom replied without taking his eyes from the picture. "Did you come across something else?"

"Nope." Lilly blew out an exasperated sigh.

"Wait a second." Atom stepped close to the carving. "Solace turning."

"What?" Hither asked.

Without responding, Atom reached up and placed his hand on the sun that stood above the figures emerging from the crater. Even with his hand spread wide, the edges of the disc stood out by a full inch.

"Solace is one of the moons," Atom mumbled. "What if that isn't the sun, but the moon? Solace turning, but which way?"

Picking up on his train of thought, Lilly stepped to his side. "To himself." She pointed to the triumphant figure, rising messiah-like from the wreckage of the crater. "Or herself, as the case may be."

Atom strained against the stone and with the slowness of a heavy-laden pulley, it turned. With his hand above his head, Atom did his best to maintain forward pressure on the disc. After the stone sun completed a half turn, they all heard a loud click from below their feet.

The floor quivered.

"Careful," Atom commanded, stepping back from the carving.

The vibration shivered through the stones and into their feet. A crossing seam appeared and the floor drifted down several inches. Then with a low grinding, the floor pulled back into four quarters, revealing a plasteel floor beneath.

Moving with the shifting floor, Atom plucked Margo and dropped her into the pram. "I think we found what we're looking for, people," he said with a grin as they all stepped from the stone floor on the plasteel platform below. "I hope you are all up for a ride, because it looks like we're about to go somewhere."

"Ash, head back to the ship," Lilly commanded. "Lock her down and keep her safe. I'll alert you when we know what we're looking at."

The Golem stared, delaying for a moment, then turned and lumbered from the room.

"If I didn't know any better, I'd say he's worried about you," Atom said.

Before Lilly could reply, the floor began to descend. Above them, the stones slid back into place.

*   *   *

The bottom of the shaft opened onto another stone chamber. Harsh lights flickered to life as the platform touched down on a rough-hewn floor. Unlike the stone chapel above, this room had a wall that looked familiar to Atom.

"I think we found our ship," he said.

"That looks like a lock on one of the old training ships from my days as a rook," Shi said as she stepped from the lift and examined the lock. "They were obsolete then and we just used them to practice breaching."

"It is old imperial stock," Kozue chimed in.

"At the moment, I care less about where it came from and more about what to do about it." Atom followed Shi off the lift and crossed the room to the old lock. "All I care about is cracking this hatch and getting inside. Historical value aside, we came for a treasure and still have imps sitting on our heads. They haven't found this place yet, otherwise we'd have them holding the light for us, but that doesn't mean they won't stumble on us sooner than we'd like.

"By, can you get this open?" he asked, stopping at the lock to study the broad portal. "This isn't the main supply bay hatch, but it should do the trick."

"Give me a touch, darl." Byron slipped his satchel from his shoulder and laid a series of tools beside where he knelt. He then turned his attention to the locking mechanism. Frowning at the panel, he poked the main control and the door hissed open.

Behind him, Shi let out a low guffaw.

"Yuck yerself," Byron snapped.

"Always check the easiest solution first," Atom said as he pushed the pram past Byron. "It's good to know the ship is still powered after all these years. I was a little worried we'd be running on aux lights."

They cycled through the hatch and stepped into the interior of the ship. Stale air met them.

"Sniffs like 'ey need to change out the filters on the 'cyclers," Byron said as he wrinkled his nose and waved fluttering dust particles away from his face. "A few decades back."

"Still good enough to breathe," Atom replied.

Byron shrugged. "Guessin' they en't had much to tax 'em."

"What's the plan?" Hither asked.

"Judging by the size of the hatch, we're looking at a frigate." Atom hovered the pram to a halt at the crossroads beyond the hatch and looked at the options. "It's the smallest of the cap ships, but it still leaves us a lot of ground to cover. That means we need to frag to cover the whole ship as fast as possible.

"Byron, find engineering.

"Hither, bridge and get us the real story.

"Shi, we're going to need haulers, find the depot and see if you can round up some grav-sleds or something to carry whatever we find in here.

"Daisy, you up?" Atom asked over the coms.

"Better than yesterday," the pilot replied.

"Good, I want the ship prepped. Koze will give you our coords. I need you to find a way to get here when we need you without getting tagged on the way. I'm not sure how things are looking out there, but we're on our target here."

"Aye, the *Ticket* will be ready to fly on your word. If I keep low, I might be able to slip their eye in the sky. We'll just have to figure the next step once we get there."

"And you?" Hither asked, looking to Atom.

"I aim to find some treasure. Lilly, you're with me and Go."

*   *   *

A frigate, even one over a century old, had dozens of holds. In a universal principle of protecting the warship, the holds constituted the outer layers of the ship's skin. For a military ship, such as the one they explored, the inner holds would be the first place to look. Atom, however, took the time to examine any hold they passed as they moved towards the spine of the ship.

"Think they'll all be empty like these?" Lilly asked as they trudged through the dim light of their fourth empty hold.

"I hope not," Atom replied. "If they are, that means we wasted a trip out here."

"Not to mention being stuck with imps overhead."

"That, too."

Their footsteps echoed in the empty hold. Margo sat in the pram, her back stiff with nervous tension in the dim glow of the scattered overhead lights. Her tiny hands clutched the pram's edge, knuckles white.

The shadows hung heavy, slow with time.

Atom led them out of the hold and into a low, military-grade corridor. The stark utilitarian nature of the construction did little to help ease the claustrophobic oppression of the silent ship. The hatch hissed shut, leaving them in a flickering gloom as the hall lights sprang to life just far enough ahead to see the next twenty yards, but nothing more.

"They sure could have used a better decorator," Lilly said, trying to lighten the mood.

"Trust me, it hasn't gotten much better in the years since this ship last flew."

"I'm glad I got into my line of work, then."

"Which is worse?"

"We both deal in death, but my accommodations were up to my own choice. Outside assignments I was able to choose my own lifestyle and I don't have any complaints in that department."

"When I was in the service, I would have killed to have that opportunity."

"But things are different now, Atom. Now you have your own ship."

Another door appeared in the walking lights. "Should we check this one out?" Atom asked.

"I'd punch myself if we walked past the one hold that actually had something in it." Lilly walked ahead of Atom and triggered the hatch open. "So, are things actually better now that you're not in the service?"

"We're alive. That's what counts for the moment," Atom said as he stepped up beside Lilly and looked into the empty hold.

"Some days, that's all we can ask for."

Atom shrugged. "Most days," he said.

"Think we'll ever find anything? It looks like they picked this ship over whenever it landed."

"Honestly, I'm surprised there's even a power-plant here." Atom turned and wandered down the hall, moving towards the rear of the ship. "But the fact that there is power would lead me to believe there is something left on this ship somewhere. Otherwise, I would imagine they would have totally dismantled her and not taken the time to leave access."

"Then it's just a matter of where?"

Lilly trailed along behind Atom and Margo. She followed in silence with her eyes on the deck, letting Atom's footsteps guide her.

"Do you miss her?" she asked without lifting her head.

Atom slowed, but kept moving.

"Your wife, I mean." Lilly dragged her feet like a sullen school-child, uncertain of what lay ahead.

"I know what you mean," Atom's voice hung just above a whisper, forcing Lilly to edge closer. "Yes, I miss her more than breath itself. There are days where Go is the only thing that gets me out of bed.

"Could I ask you a favor?" He stopped and half turned without making eye contact. "Could you do that thing you did back in the prison?"

Lilly grinned mischievously. "Isn't this the wrong place to get frisky?"

"I don't want that," Atom whispered, lifting his eyes to Lilly. "I want Go to see her mother one more time, so she doesn't forget what Kozue looked like. And I miss hugging my wife."

Lilly cocked an eyebrow. "Just a hug? Seems strange."

"It's a comfort thing. I've dreamed of holding Kozue one last time, but never had the chance." He gave a half shrug. "And you could give me that peace of mind."

"Give me a minute, I need to change." She stepped closer to Atom with an understanding smile and laid a hand on his shoulder. 'This isn't the first time someone has asked me to grant them peace. It might be the first time I've done it for someone I would almost consider a friend, but I understand."

Atom stood in awkward silence as Lilly slipped back down the hallway and into the last hold they had cleared. He looked down to Margo and she back up at him.

"Dada," she said, clambering to her feet and reaching for him.

Atom took her in his arms and held her tight. His spirit roiled, caught between the past and the present, and a ghost that would walk with him as long as he would let her. Margo sensed the turmoil. In her childish mastery of the obvious, she snuggled into Atom's chest and wrapped an arm tight about his neck.

"I's ok," she cooed.

"I know, Fiver. We've got this covered. I think we're on the homestretch, but I just want a little insurance in case Lilly decides to disappear again."

"Lilly," Margo paused, searching for her words. "Funny. Not bad." Margo shook her head with exaggerated concern. "She's funny."

"She makes you laugh?"

"Nope." Margo tickled Atom's neck.

"Strange?"

"Yup, strange."

At that moment, Kozue appeared from the hold. She stopped in the middle of the low hallway and executed a slow pirouette. "Do I do her justice?" she asked as she came to a stop facing Atom with her arms spread wide.

Margo lifted her head from Atom's chest at the words. "Mama?" She looked at Lilly in confusion.

"No, dear," Lilly said with a sweet smile. "Just a ghost."

"Ghost?" Margo looked to Atom for answers.

"It's alright, Fiver." Atom set Margo back in her pram as he turned to Lilly, the baug dressed in Kozue's skin, slipped into his arms. She respected his words and melted against his chest with a simple longing for contact.

Atom tensed at the sudden invasion of his space, but then sighed and relaxed, folding himself into the embrace.

"Thank you," he whispered as he closed his eyes and leaned his cheek on the top of Lilly/Kozue's head. "This means more to me than you know. I never had a chance to say goodbye to Koze. Everything happened so fast. We were asleep, and then we weren't. I had a split second to decide whether to stay and die with her or save Go."

"Did you make the right choice?" Lilly asked, her voice muffled against his chest.

Atom shifted just enough to look down at Margo as she sat, watching the scene with puzzlement.

"Yeah," he said with soft remembrance. He opened up and nestled his ghost to his side, fitting her naturally into himself. "But that doesn't mean I don't have days where my soul crushes in on itself, like a black hole. There are days where hearing her voice in my ear is anguish, but I wouldn't trade it for anything."

"I understand."

"Do you?" Atom asked, unbelieving. His arm dropped down to curl about her waist and ended with his hand cupping her hip.

"I do," Lilly whispered up to him, her eyes imploring.

He reached up under her jacket and tapped the pistol strapped to the small of her back. "There's a difference," he said with a sad smile as he detached from the image of his love. "Kozue was a lefter and she always wore her pistol slung low on the hip. She was old fashioned that way."

Lilly smiled, the sadness drifting away. She leaned in and squeezed him around the middle, grinning up at him as she did so.

Atom blew out a sigh and returned the smile as he wiped his eyes dry.

"Little things," she said as she pulled back. "You give me time to fully absorb someone, and I'll know those kinds of things."

"And it ends," Atom closed his eyes and savored the moment.

"I've always worn my gun back there because I'd rather keep it out of sight. Unless I'm acting a part, there's no sense in seeming a threat," Lilly said, her voice drifting away from Kozue's and closer to her own. Atom opened his eyes with a new calm as she continued. "I like having a gun, but I don't necessarily want the entire Black to know it's there."

"I appreciate the effort," Atom said with a wry smile as he stepped over to stand beside Margo. "I know it wasn't much and it was probably outside of your wheelhouse, but it gave my mind a moment of settlement."

Lilly kept Atom's gaze for a moment before turning back the way she had come. "I'm going to change back. I don't imagine it'll do us any good holding onto this face. It's just a distraction for you at this point."

"We'll poke ahead. Maybe we'll even clear a couple holds before you get back."

"Don't make off with the treasure without me," Lilly said with a sincere smile as she ducked back into the empty hold.

Atom watched her go. "I don't know if I should have done that or not," he said to Margo as she fixed him with a quizzical look.

"Dada, go." She thumped down in the pram and sat cross-legged while gripping the sides. "Go fast."

"Not inside."

"Dada, go fast."

Atom ignored the command and fired up the suspensors. The pram hovered up from the floor to level out a few inches in the air and then glided forward at Atom's light touch. They pressed forward, clearing two more holds in rapid succession.

Then, as Lilly wandered back into the hall with a spent expression on her face, Atom opened the third door.

He froze.

The hallway hung in suspension. Lilly's boots echoed as she hurried to join him, underscored by the soft hiss of the pram's suspensors.

"You find something?" she asked with breathless eagerness.

He glanced back to her and then nodded to the open hatch.

Inside, sitting in a halo of light surrounded by darkness, four oversized packing crates sat in a square with a fifth crate centered on the four below. More than a dozen paces of darkness separated the doorway from the circle of light.

Lilly stopped beside Atom and looked out to the crates, sitting like an island in a sea of void.

"Think that's what we're looking for?" she asked.

"Only one way to find out." Atom left the pram idling in the hatch and stepped into the murk. With slow, measured strides he waded towards the pyramid. As he moved forward, he surveyed the room, both the golden island of light and the darkened veil beyond, as if expecting shades of ancient guardians to step through to contest his advance.

In his footsteps, Lilly drifted in ghostly silence.

"What sort of room is this?" Lilly asked, stopping just inside the ring of light and straining to see through the darkness. "The walls don't look smooth like the other holds."

Atom set a hand on one of the chests and looked around, waiting for something to happen. "It's too narrow to be a normal storage hold. Kozue, can you pull up any sort of schematics on this rig? I can't see what sort of room we are in. Experience says this should all be storage hold territory. I wouldn't imagine we would find anything small for at least another level."

"Just a moment," Kozue replied. "Hither is tapping into the schematics as we speak. The ship is both archaic and military hardwired, which means I cannot access anything remotely.

"Ah," the AI sounded perplexed. "According to Hither, it is a reserve stasis chamber."

Atom squinted into the darkness. "Why down here? On a warship, these decks are only visited to pull up supplies. They're a cushion to protect the heart of the ship. There's absolutely no reason for something like that on this level."

"What's she saying?" Lilly asked.

"This is a stasis chamber."

"Really?" she asked in surprise and walked into the darkness. "Yeah, there are pods out here. That's why the walls don't look smooth. I can't see if any of them are active without a light, but they are stacked as high as I can reach."

"Stasis pods," Atom said in thought. "Think they might be important?"

"More important than these?" Lilly asked with a grin as she strode back into the light and over to the storage chests. "These have to be what we're looking for."

"But it seems too easy."

"We've come halfway across the galaxy, dug up scattered clues, fought our way through ambushes, and even broken out of prison. If that's your definition of easy, I don't want to be around when you actually decide to tackle something hard.

"Regardless, let's crack these open and see what we're dealing with." She flipped the latches on the top chest and threw back the lid.

"Nothing?" she said in disbelief.

"Say again?" Atom stepped closer and looked down into the depths of the empty crate. He glanced up to Lilly and then back down in puzzlement. "This has to be the right place. There's nothing here except empty holds. This stasis chamber is the only anomaly on any of the lower levels.

"It just doesn't fit. Hither, Kozue, is there anything you can tell me about the layout of the ship that might shed some light?"

"Neg on my end," Hither replied. "I'm running through schematics and other than that stasis chamber, I'm not finding a single thing that would trip a query on any search. I've got nothing deeper in, but the guts of the ship."

"I find myself looping the same information," Kozue said.

"Think they could have taken it with them when they cleaned everything else out?" Lilly asked. "I mean, this was over a hundred years ago, if these people were sitting on a cache of any worth, wouldn't they have used it by now?"

Atom stepped back from the pile of crates. He looked back to where Margo sat in the pram, his mind turning.

"Is there a way to scan this room? Maybe there's another clue here we aren't seeing." He took a step towards Margo and froze. "Do you hear that?" he whispered without moving his mouth. "I don't think we're alone here anymore."

Lilly lifted her head just in time to find a blaster bolt winging past her cheek.

Dripping wet, Toks Marshall stepped through the door, past Margo and into the room. Margo drifted forward, but froze as Atom shook his head. She settled back to her idle position and Toks shifted the gun from the girl to her father.

"Good girl," Toks chided. "We don't want you or daddy to get hurt. Have you found it?"

Lilly tipped the crate forward to reveal the empty interior.

Toks studied her opponents, her face impassive, cold, threatening. "Where is it?" she demanded. "If I don't see treasure, I sure as hell don't see any reason to let the three of you keep on wasting air."

"That's what we were just talking about." Atom remained motionless, his hand held wide in a placating manner as he measured distance and probability. He wondered how Toks had managed to track their path. "There is the real possibility that there isn't a treasure. If people knew about it and it just sat here for all these years, why hasn't anyone come after it already. If it's been here under their noses, why didn't the people who buried it dig it up and use it to build their new world?"

Toks fixed Atom with a hard glare.

"If that's the case, there's no reason for you two to be here." She squared her blaster on Atom's chest.

His mind raced.

"I might see it fitting to save your life, Lilly." A predatory smile slipped over Toks' face. "If you happen to spin me a different tale."

Lilly gulped.

"Might be, you and I could even cut whatever it is we find," Toks said as the grin widened.

Lilly glanced at Atom and then gave Toks a slow nod. "I have the rest of the clues. There was a riddle one of the survivors passed on to the sheriff on that ice moon. I'll bet there's something in there about where the treasure's hid," Lilly's words fell from her mouth in a tumble, but her feet drifted her away from the empty chests and over to the far edge of the circle of light.

A seed sprouted in Atom's mind.

"I think I've got it," he said, his eyes wide as the information swirled.

"That a fact?" Toks' smile faded and her blaster drooped.

"Maybe," Atom said as he reached up and absently scratched his head. Toks brought her gun back to bear, but Atom failed to notice. "I just need to check something."

"Stay where I can see you. I don't want you trying to pull a fast one on me … either of you." Toks stepped to the side, trying to keep Atom and Lilly lined up.

"Kozue, is there a manifest for berth assignments for the stasis pods?"

"Stasis pods?" Toks asked.

"We're in an auxiliary stasis chamber," Atom replied, pointing out into the darkness. "If I had to guess, this room was stasis for non-military personnel. This ship was evidently more transport than warship." He turned his back to Toks and crossed his arms as he scowled into the darkness.

"And you're telling me, you think you might have the key?" Toks stepped forward with an interest that mimicked a thief's attention to an untended bag.

Atom cocked his head, listening to Kozue's reply before turning to squint into the darkness. He glanced back at Toks and held up his hands to demonstrate his peaceful intentions. Once she nodded at him, he wandered back to the door.

"Away from the pram," Toks growled. "I've seen a little of what it can do."

"Lights." Atom turned sideways and reached into the shadows beside the door. He fumbled in the dark and after a moment, tripped a switch.

Springing from the darkness, banks of stasis pods became more than just concepts in the darkness. The lights marched onward from what seemed to be the entire length of the ship, although Atom knew the room covered little more than half that distance.

Lilly gasped.

"There must be thousands of them," Toks said in flustered amazement. "Are you saying the treasure is in one of those pods?"

"That's my thinking." Atom returned to his triangled point of the circle of light.

"And you know where it is?"

Atom narrowed his eyes and nodded.

"Then tell me, or I shoot your partner." Toks flipped her blaster to cover Lilly, with casual grace.

Atom looked over to Lilly with a blank stare.

"Wait," Lilly stammered, stepping back defensively. "Weren't you just offering me a cut?"

"That was before he had all the information," Toks said with an offhanded shrug.

"Doesn't really matter either way. Lil was planning on shooting me anyway. I don't think the partnership was slated to pull through the long haul. Shoot her, or don't. It really doesn't change how things will play out."

"Well, then, give me the information, or I shoot your daughter." Toks' voice verged on hysteria as she half swung to cover Margo.

"And you die." Atom's eyes flashed with a new anger that gave Toks pause.

The imperial hesitated. Then with an uncanny grin, she holstered her blaster and tucked her thumbs in her gunbelt. "What'll it take for you and me to strike a deal?" she asked, glancing to Lilly with a flick of her eyebrow.

Studying Toks, Atom remained silent. He measured the ten paces to Toks. He slowed his breath and listened to the heartbeat, two parts, that would call time of death. He knew the half a beat to drop his hand and the second half to pull and fire.

Toks' hands hitched on her gunbelt, closer to her blaster.

He looked to Lilly. Her hands hung at her side. Her gun at the small of her back. She would turn to draw and fire.

Atom smiled like a lazy, sun-warmed dog.

Back to Toks. He ran possibilities.

Three guns.

Three triggers.

Three minds.

Atom took another breath.

He stood the highest chance of being Toks' primary target, but an outside chance hung in the balance that Toks would dodge and aim to remove the lesser target first.

And Lilly might have been swayed by Toks' offer.

"I have an idea," he said, his words causing Lilly to flinch. "I have something you both want. I want it too, but I also want my daughter's life. I'm sure some boke would work the math on this situation and run a proper threat analysis, but we don't have time for that."

"We all want the treasure, Atom," Toks snapped.

Lilly looked back and forth between the other two.

"I'm going to slowly pull a marker from my pocket." He pointed to his jacket with his left hand, making sure to keep his gun hand well away from the rail-pistol. "I'll put the location on the marker. Winner takes all."

"And your daughter?" Toks gestured with her head, without taking her eyes from the circle of battle. "I ain't planning on adopting a kit. I could either drop her at a home-planet or if you like, I could put her down merciful-like."

"I would prefer, whoever takes the pot sets her up. I have a friend who would take her on, but set aside a small percent to make sure she's comfortable."

Toks glared.

Lilly's eyes drifted to Margo.

The girl sat in her pram, her back rigid, and knuckles white on the edge as she looked on.

"What's your answer?" Atom asked.

"I'm game," Toks said, pushing her glasses up on her nose.

"Agreed," Lilly sounded nervous.

Atom nodded and reached into the pocket of his coat with exaggerated slowness as he kept his eyes drifting between the two women. He pulled the digital marker and entered some information, then tucked it in his left palm.

With flair, he flipped back his coat to free up his pistol. He studied the two women as he unsnapped his holster.

Toks angled herself to aid her pull.

Lilly's fingers tapped at her own belt. Atom knew the gun tucked in the small of her back would slow her down, but her augments remained a wild-card. He measured her.

The tension ratcheted.

Atom's breath slowed as he focused.

Lilly swallowed and he watched her throat pulse.

Standing square to the others, Atom noted a slight tremble to Toks' hand. She blinked.

He pulled and fired in one fluid motion.

The shot exploded in the confined space.

Almost before the eye could register that he had shot, Atom slipped his rail-pistol back into its holster.

Across the circle, Toks stood still, her eyes wide with shock. She tried to pull her own gun, but between shock and the catastrophic hole punched in her chest, her fingers could only fumble at the weapon.

A choking gasp escaped her lips.

On the far apex, Lilly had pulled her own gun. She had pulled on Toks, but nothing happened when she tried to fire. With an automaton's regularity, she continued to pull the trigger. It took a moment to register that her weapon made no sound. Then she turned on Atom, trying to fire at him with desperate urgency.

Her nostrils flared and her eyes fluttered.

Atom smiled, a sad smile, and nodded to Margo.

The girl triggered the pram and a long, blue electrical bolt flew out and struck Lilly square in the chest, driving the woman back into the open space between the stasis pods. The baug lay in a twitching heap, unconscious and incapacitated.

Atom turned his attention back to Toks. The woman had staggered back towards the door, as if trying to escape. Stalking behind her with his pistol held at his side, Atom watched her jerky movements with hawk-like intensity. She managed to make it to the door where she spun in a drunken circle and slipped down to sit between the door and the pram. Her glasses slipped sideways.

"I wouldn't have killed her," Toks managed to choke out. She tried to fix her glasses, but instead smeared blood across the lens.

"The alternative is worse." He stepped close to the warlord.

As he stood over her, his face smoothed and the look in his eyes drifted distant. He raised his pistol with measured smoothness and pointed it at her head.

Toks' feet scrabbled as the floor in uncontrolled panic.

"A clean death is always preferable to slavery," he intoned and pulled the trigger.

Turning away, he holstered his pistol and walked with a weary step back to the circle. He looked to Lilly. Her twitching had subsided, leaving her as still as a corpse. Only the sporadic gasp of breath kept the image of death at bay.

Atom knelt at her side and checked her thready pulse.

"She will survive," Kozue said. "Despite the unknowns of her baug system, I can say with some certainty that she will be out for several hours."

Lilly's eyes twitched.

Atom pulled her pistol from her hand and looked it over. With a half-smile and a shake of his head, he pulled a small disc from the underside of the cartridge. "There are two kinds of people in this galaxy, Koze: those with charged ammo cartridges, and those who sleep."

"Do you mean to tell me that whole embrace was a ruse to slip a null disc on her gun?" Kozue actually sounded put off.

"Not completely," Atom rose and tucked Lilly's blaster in his pocket.

He turned away and began pacing down the long room. "Hither, I need you to give me the number on a pod without a listed occupant," he said through the coms. He scanned the identical pods as he walked past, searching for anything that might give him a clue as to where the treasure had been hidden.

"Berth 281." Hither sounded uncertain.

Atom tracked numbers and made his way deeper into the chamber. Behind him ,the pram kicked into gear and drifted along in his wake.

Coming to a halt with hands on his hips, Atom grinned. "Found it," he said and swung the pod out from its rack. With a hydraulic hiss, it dropped down. A chuff of decompressing air puffed in his face as the pod swung open, revealing five chests packed snuggly inside.

Flipping the latch on one of the chests, Atom revealed neatly packed rows of silver bullion that glowed with an inner blue light.

"We just found our payday," Atom said, trying to hide the excitement in his voice. "I think we're looking at five crates of alloyed iridium."

"Too bad it's not six," Hither said with a laugh.

"Why six?"

"Easier to cut Lilly's split," Hither replied. "How did you know the treasure would be in one of the pods and not just stashed somewhere in one of the deeper holds?"

"Just a hunch. Everything else lined up with the poem perfectly. The last line talked about hiding her up on the shelf.

These lines of pods are the closest things to shelves that I've come across."

"But why call it she? I've never heard of treasure being referred to as a lady."

Atom snapped the chest shut and glanced to Margo with a thoughtful look. "Maybe you're right. What if this isn't the treasure?"

Stepping to the side, he wiped off the dust covered controls of the pod to the right and then repeated the procedure to the left. As he wiped off a thick layer of dust, he found the display blinking with dim readouts.

"Kack all," Atom said in amazement.

"Kack all," Margo repeated in a perfect mockery of Atom's expression. He shot her a disappointed look.

"Shi, how are we looking on those grav-sleds? I think we're going to need three," Atom said with a distracted air as he wiped off the stasis pod's window and tried to peer inside. "I think we found the real treasure, now the question is who are we looking at?"

"Who?" Shi countered.

"Someone is in stasis down here." Atom stepped back from the pod, his expression stuck somewhere between amazement and consternation. "We're taking this pod with us. We can figure out who it is out in the Black, where we don't have to worry about anyone dropping in on us.

"Everyone, on me, we need to load and burn yesterday. Daisy, you have fifteen minutes to find us."

*　　　*　　　*

"It is interesting to see you," Alderon Bronte said from the foot of the *One Way Ticket's* main loading ramp. "I was under the impression that you would simply send us confirmation of a completed job and we would never actually have to cross paths again.

"Not that I find your company something to complain about, but I am surprised that you found us again," the player followed up with unabashed superiority.

"Well, the way the job played out, I was given an unexpected opportunity." Atom stood with his thumbs tucked in his gunbelt and his feet spread wide in a relaxed, non-confrontational stance. "It's probably something more in line with Pips' paygrade. I won't burden you with the decision

400

making, but in the turmoil of the imperial confrontation out in the Nemo System, we actually managed to make a live capture of your bounty.

"I can't remember the last time I captured a bounty," Atom said with jovial amazement. "I usually prefer a quick, clean put-down."

"As do we," Bronte said with a sigh.

"I won't complain, as long as I get paid."

"I'm sure there won't be a reason to void the contract."

Atom laughed. "Then lead the way. The quicker we can get this settled up, the quicker can all be merry in the Black."

Bronte bowed his head without another word and turned to lead the way inward from the surface of the Tribe's asteroid. Atom waved to Shi, who pushed a grav-sled down the ramp. Lilly sprawled across the sled, an unconscious ragdoll, with her head lolled over the side.

"We've kept her sedated since we captured her." Atom fell into step with Bronte and they followed the same path from the previous visit.

They walked in silence for the rest of the short journey across rice-paddies and up the artificial mountain to the village. As they passed the cemetery, Atom once again marveled at both the scale of the deep space habitat and the longevity needed to actually populate a cemetery.

"Master Ulvan," Alderon Pips said with formal brusqueness from the top of the stairs at the village square. "What a ... surprise."

"I completed the bounty. Strange turn let me snatch her alive. I was just telling Bronte that it's not my usual procedure, but alive or dead, Lilly's in your hands. I just figured it would save the trouble of some docking hand-off if I brought our girl home." Atom came to a stop several steps below Pips. The Tribe leader blocked his path, his hands tucked into wide sleeves in a clear statement of unwelcome. Atom just continued, unfazed by the insult. "It's not often I make a live capture, but she just sort of fell into my lap. It usually doesn't suit my business. I mean I have to pay transport on them, and there's the off chance they break. But I figured you'd have a few questions for Lilly

"She was muttering something about a treasure," Atom prattled on, but took note as Pips stiffened almost imperceptibly at the information. He turned to where Shi guided the sled up behind them. "Thought it might be worth a drop-off instead of a confirmed kill."

Atom stepped down and bent over Lilly, checking her vitals as he did so and discretely slipping the old plasma punch into her hand. "She's still breathing, so hopefully she can give you something."

Lilly's eyes fluttered as Atom grabbed her by the shoulders of her jacket. Her eyes drifted open and she looked up to him with a dreamy smile. Then he dragged her from the sled and bounced her legs up the steps to dump her in an unceremonious heap at Pips' feet. The lord stepped back as if Atom had dumped a bucket of offal near him.

"Now, all we have left is to settle accounts," Atom said with a simple smile as he straightened up and cracked his back. "My fee, and I'll be on my way."

Pips stared Atom down for a brief moment and then nodded to a servant who stepped forward with a small metal box. "Fifty thousand ko as we agreed upon. It is a fair price for what you have brought us."

"My thanks." Atom affected a bow, and took the box from the servant. Without bothering to check it, he tossed the box on Shi's sled.

"One last thing," Atom said over his shoulder. "I didn't have any use for her ship and I don't want to go through the hassle of scrapping it. The blasted thing was twisted up tighter than a tweaked jub-rat jammed in its hole. I never bothered getting aboard, because it's too small for me to use, but you might have a purpose in your line of work.

"My crew should have it unloaded for you to do with as you please," he said with a bow. "Free of charge, of course."

He nodded to Shi and they started down the steps.

"Wait," Pips called after them, holding up a hand to halt them before they reached the first landing beside the cemetery. "You can't leave that ship here."

"Sorry," Atom called back as Shi pressed on. "I don't have room to haul it all over the verse. If you don't want it, just dump it out the lock."

"Do you have any idea what you've done?" Fear cracked Pips' voice.

"Just business," Atom said as he waved farewell, and turned to follow Shi. With his back turned to Pips, Bronte, and the rest of the contingent, Atom's evil, lopsided grin remained unseen.

As they reached the center of the bridge at the foot of the hill, Atom turned and looked back up the faux mountain. A distant shadow dropped from the ceiling to land where Atom knew the village lay, followed by a series of explosions that vibrated the wood beneath their feet. Sounds of violence wafted down through the woods and Atom noted the worried heads of field workers turning towards the exchange.

"Looks like we made our exit at just the right time," Shi drawled without looking back up the hill. "That Ash sure knows how to make an entrance. I'd hate to be up there right about now. But at least we got paid on top of getting paid."

"This one seems a little light in the pocket after that last one."

*   *   *

The crew gathered in the hold several hours out from the asteroid.

"I wish we ain't had to give her a whole chest," Shi grumbled.

"We voted," Atom replied. "We gave her cut to Ash and told him to wait long enough for it not to come back on us. Lilly got her cut, and we maintain our unblemished record. What happens to a client after we complete the job is no concern of ours."

"Fink they made it out?" Byron asked, his head hung in dejection.

"I have more faith in the two of them making it than anyone, but us," Atom said as Hither wrapped an arm around the boy's shoulder.

They all stood around the stasis pod without looking at each other. Only Margo seemed immune to the mystery of the box between them. She wandered around, following Mae as the cat wove around people's feet, trying for a scratch behind the ears.

"It was still a heavy payday," said Daisy as he shielded his tender stomach with an arm.

"So, you fink 'is box is the real treasure?" Byron stepped close and tried to see in the window for the umpteenth time. "Looks an old wendy to me. Why'd she be worf more 'an 'em boxes a bullion?"

"Let's find out," Atom said.

He stepped to the controls and worked through the interface to begin the stasis pod's waking cycle. The pod churned to life and Atom felt the ship's power plant surge to compensate for the draw.

The crew watched in nervous silence.

Finally, after a momentary eternity, the pod hissed and the lid rose in a puff of mist and condensed air. Margo jumped at the sound and ran to hold onto Atom's leg. He bent down and picked her up before edging closer to the pod to look down inside.

A handsome, middle-aged woman lay in peace, her breathing slow and steady.

The others joined Atom at the pod's edge.

The woman's eyes began to move as if in a dream state and then, with catatonic slowness, she fought to open them. Staring up with uncertainty, the woman blinked several times before focusing on Atom.

"Where am I?" she managed to rasp out.

"This is my ship, the *One Way Ticket*," Atom said as he studied the woman. Her dark hair, streaked with dignified grey, framed her narrow face. "Who are you?"

Before she could answer, Kozue whispered in their ears. "That is the queen mother, grandmother to the current emperor."

"I'm Martha," the woman said simply. "I could use a glass of water."

Made in United States
North Haven, CT
16 December 2021

12996065R00243